Praise for Mimi Yu's *The Girl King* Duology

'*The Girl King* is everything I want in a high fantasy. Yu draws fluently from history to create an exquisite world, brings it to life with gorgeous and atmospheric prose, and populates it with fascinating characters. I expect this to be one of the most talked-about books, and I can't wait to see what this very talented author does next'

Samantha Shannon, bestselling author of
The Priory of the Orange Tree

'An intricate, richly crafted, fantasy that will draw you in and keep you guessing to the last stunning battle'   Heidi Helig

'Fierce and unforgettable, *The Girl King* is an epic fantasy of tremendous lyrical power; that rare novel that leaves you breathless, as though your dreams and heart are bigger than your body. There's no greater pleasure than to find a novel that makes you feel more alive - Mimi Yu has that gift of magic'

Marjorie Liu, *New York Times* bestselling author

'An absolutely fantastic tale of legends, magic and destiny, Mimi Yu's *The Girl King* kept the pages turning. The myths are awesome, the heroes are unsinkable, and the antagonists are chock-full of twisted agendas. If you're down with dangerous magic, clans of shapeshifters, and worthy girls who somehow STILL need to prove their worth, then you will love this as much as I did'

Kendare Blake, #1 *New York Times* bestselling author of the
Three Dark Crowns series

'An epic tale of fate, desire, family and love, highly recommended'
School Library Journal (starred review)

'A beautifully written epic replete with magic, shapeshifting characters, complex political int⸺ ⸺⸺⸺ ⸺⸺ battles between good and evil . . . Strong fem⸺ ⸺⸺ ⸺ot make for a compelling ⸺⸺⸺ ⸺⸺⸺ ⸺⸺⸺ ⸺⸺ *uardian*

D0489755

90710 000 5⸺ ⸺⸺

By Mimi Yu from Gollancz

The Girl King
Empress of Flames

EMPRESS OF FLAMES

MIMI YU

This edition first published in Great Britain in 2022 by Gollancz

First published in Great Britain in 2021 by Gollancz
an imprint of The Orion Publishing Group Ltd
Carmelite House, 50 Victoria Embankment
London EC4Y ODZ

An Hachette UK Company

1 3 5 7 9 10 8 6 4 2

Copyright © Mimi Yu 2021

The moral right of Mimi Yu to be identified as
the author of this work has been asserted in accordance
with the Copyright, Designs and Patents Act of 1988.

All rights reserved. No part of this publication may be
reproduced, stored in a retrieval system, or transmitted
in any form or by any means, electronic, mechanical,
photocopying, recording, or otherwise, without the
prior permission of both the copyright owner and the
above publisher of this book.

All the characters in this book are fictitious,
and any resemblance to actual persons, living
or dead, is purely coincidental.

A CIP catalogue record for this book
is available from the British Library.

ISBN (Mass Market Paperback) 978 1 473 22315 8
ISBN (eBook) 978 1 473 22316 5

Typeset by Deltatype Ltd, Birkenhead, Merseyside

Printed in Great Britain by Clays Ltd, Elcograf S.p.A.

www.gollancz.co.uk

For my brother Joseph

LONDON BOROUGH OF RICHMOND UPON THAMES	
90710 000 506 059	
Askews & Holts	17-Mar-2022
JF TEENAGE 11-14	
RTTW	

Prologue

Dust

Adé lit the altar candles from right to left, like reading words on a page. The Mak family's shrine was modest: a red-lacquered cabinet as high as her knee, its doors propped open to reveal a wood statuette of the Mercy Goddess, her painted face smiling sweetly down at the incense and flowers Ori and Nobi had left at her feet. Normally her twin brothers would offer a bit of food as well – a bowl of rice, a peach, a pair of tangerines. But not with the shortages of late.

Adé shook out her pinewood match and bowed thrice. Beside the incense sat her late father's silver compass. She kissed the tips of her fingers and touched them reverently to its cold face. This part was her own private ritual, something she'd invented just for him.

Grant my mother peace, and my brothers joy, she prayed, her usual recitation. *And keep them safe from harm*, she added. Unrest had fallen upon the Outer Ring of Yulan City in the wake of the food shortages. Heated protests at the gates of the Inner Ring – and thieves borne of desperation padding across the rooftops. At night, her mother had taken to barricading their door and windows.

I

During the day, the whispers were all over the streets: granaries in the borderlands picked clean, fields that should have been forests of millet and sorghum this time of year blanched dry as old bone. Starving farmers selling their babies and eating the corpses of their neighbours. Oddly, despite these gruesome rumours, Adé had yet to hear anyone utter the word itself: *Famine*. As though to say the thing would draw it to the city.

One trouble at a time. There were other matters close at hand. She hesitated at the altar. She rarely asked anything for herself, but tonight ... *And please, don't let me make a complete fool of myself at dinner,* she prayed quickly.

'Adé, is that you? Shouldn't you be leaving soon?' Her mother emerged from the bedroom. She was smiling, until she saw Adé crouched on the floor before the altar. Lin's eyes darted to the compass and the candles. She didn't frown, exactly, but the muscles in her face twitched, working against the impulse.

Adé stood quickly. Their mother had stopped tending to the shrine after their father died, and while she'd never told the children to follow suit, Adé had taken to performing the daily ritual only when she wasn't looking, as though it were something shameful, or maybe just hurtful. Something Lin couldn't be allowed to see.

'You've already dressed,' her mama said. 'Well, I can plait your hair at least.' But all the merriment had slipped away. The hand she held out was limp, as though sagging with the spectre of grief.

Adé could have kicked herself. Nothing to do about it now; she followed her mother into their shared bedroom and positioned herself before the dented brass mirror – one of the few remnants of her mother's childhood home, her old life.

'The Ellandaise style suits you,' her mama said, looking her reflection up and down. Adé's dress had been a gift from Carmine, imported from his homeland. It was structured and stiff in the bodice, with a dense trail of golden buttons flowing from the low-cut neckline skimming her collarbones, down to a severely flared peplum. Below, the dress gave way to an absurd confection of tulle that served as a skirt. The colour was nice, though: a rich, deep burgundy that gave her skin a plummy glow.

'It's a pity the Ellandaise couldn't make your wedding dress this colour,' her mother commented, as though reading Adé's mind. 'White wedding gowns! The colour of ash and death. Barbaric. But I suppose we can't help that.'

Adé hid a smile. Nothing lifted her mother's spirits quite like cheerfully insulting others.

Lin loosed the silk scarf wrapped protectively around the tight, springy coils Adé had inherited from her father. Adé stared at their metallic, warped reflections as her mother set to work plaiting with strong, wiry hands. Adé's own hands fluttered open and closed as she gazed at the well-heeled stranger staring back at her. She reached for the pendant hanging around her neck: a dove carved from pure silver, the contours of each tiny feather painstakingly engraved. Its little jewelled eyes, lustrous blue-green, flashed as they caught the light.

Fluorite, Carmine had called the gems when he'd given Adé the necklace a week prior. How much rice could such a trinket fetch at market? How many tangerines or turnips was this hunk of silver worth? She swallowed the thought; her mother would never tolerate it. The *shame*. It seemed Carmine had a new gift for Adé every time she turned around, but they were never things a person could eat or *use*, only look at.

She tugged the dove charm absently back and forth along the chain. Back and forth, caught on its terse, tight, little track.

Her mother smacked her hand. 'Ouch!' Adé yelped.

'You're going to break it.'

Adé dropped the charm. It fell back inside her bodice, where it hung, cold and heavy against her chest.

'Make sure you eat a lot tonight,' her mother said. 'It will be the last full meal you'll see for heaven knows how long.'

Adé had to bite her lip to stop herself from asking again if her mother and the boys might join her at the Anglimns'. It would ensure they too ate something substantial this week. But she knew her mother would never accept it.

Lin had been born wealthy – the daughter of landed gentry, raised in a sky manse that been in the family for generations. But she'd lost it all – for love, Adé always reminded her, what better reason was there? – and being around Carmine's family would remind her of what had been, and by contrast, what she was now. Another harried mother in Scrap-Patch Row with coarse hands and broken teeth, eking out a meagre living cooking for labourers and darning aprons and socks for their neighbours.

There was nothing shameful in it. Never anything shameful in the ferocity of her survival, the brutality of life writ on her body, in the tired way she held herself.

Not in Adé's eyes. But Lin had been raised on different values from her daughter.

'You're beautiful,' her mother said, binding her plait and letting it fall against the back of Adé's neck. Then she rested her chin on Adé's shoulder, kissed her cheek and smiled at the both of them in the mirror.

'It's a pity you didn't get your father's height. But the dress makes you look taller, at least.'

Adé's eyes cut to her mother's reflected face, but there was nothing haunting the comment; Lin was only saying what she'd said. Adé let herself breathe. It felt wrong to find relief in her mother forgetting the pain of losing Adé's father, even if it was only for a moment. But that was life in Scrap-Patch Row; sometimes things were so dire you had to celebrate the less-bad option because there were no good ones.

'We should hire you a rickshaw to take you to Carmine's,' Lin said. 'I don't want to risk your getting caught up in the riots. Especially going into the foreign sector and dressed like that.'

They'd think I might be worth robbing, Adé thought ruefully.

'It doesn't feel right,' she said. 'To go to a fancy dinner when we – our neighbours – don't even have a speck of barley to their name.'

Lin sighed and tucked a stray curl back into the upsweep of Adé's braids.

'The shortages won't last forever. Empress Min's reign is young. Transitions of power beget precarity, even in the best of circumstances. Everything will sort itself out eventually.'

Adé watched her brow furrow in the mirror. 'Was it like this when Emperor Daagmun was enthroned?'

'Not quite like this,' her mother conceded. 'There was no drought. But there were similarities. Everyone questioned whether Daagmun would be strong enough to lead. He was the unfavoured youngest brother, and only ended up on his throne because Prince Hwangmun was killed in that terrible accident.'

A rockslide while riding in the borderlands. Adé knew that much.

'You know, I met Hwangmun, once. My father took me to court with him. I must have been Ori and Nobi's age. Gods, was the prince handsome. Like something from a fable. And such broad shoulders.'

Adé groaned. 'Mama!'

Lin gave a rare laugh. Then she went solemn again. 'Don't worry yourself about the current climate. Emperors – and Empresses – play their games, time moves forward, and the rest of us find a way to move along with it.'

Except for those that don't. The people as a whole might carry forth – but what of the bodies left in their wake?

'You carry such heavy burdens on your little shoulders,' her mother murmured, as though hearing her thoughts. 'Try to enjoy yourself tonight. A bit of indulgence would do you good.'

The silver chopsticks in Adé's hand beat a nervous staccato against her porcelain plate. Such a delicate, pretty sound. It matched the delicate and pretty everything-else of Carmine's parents' grand dining room: the brocade tablecloth with its bracken of prickly gold stitching, the stiff-backed wooden chairs and their tufted ivory cushions. The silk rug, and in the corner of the room, a gilded hutch larger than many of the shanties in Scrap-Patch Row. All of it capped with the coloured glass-plated dome that formed the ceiling above.

The Anglimns lived with the rest of the Ellandaise in the foreign sector of Yulan City. Located south of the Milk River, close to the harbour, it comprised a cluster of homes that had been inhabited by wealthy Hana a half-century prior, before shifting fortunes had changed the neighbourhood. While the area had fallen into disrepair during the intervening years, the properties maintained the haughty, elegant bones of their beginnings: sprawling estates of many buildings connected by wooden bridges arching over ornamental gardens.

The foreign sector was heavily defended by their own guards, as well as a combination of imperial soldiers and local mercenaries hired by the Eastern Flame Import Company. And if that weren't enough, each property on the street was shrouded behind high, gabled stone walls with elaborately painted – and securely locked – doors.

The Anglimns' home was easily among the largest. It was hard to take it all in without gawking. One didn't live in such splendour if they didn't wish for others to look, but Adé didn't wish to seem covetous in front of her soon-to-be in-laws.

In-laws. The thought made her tap her chopsticks harder, their rhythm quickening as though mimicking her pulse.

It occurred to her that chipping a dish might also leave an unfavourable impression, and she stilled her hand.

Grace renewed, she lifted a tiny bite of what Carmine had told her was venison to her lips.

'We pleased, so much, you are here,' Carmine's mother said to her in halting Yueh. The woman's name in her native Ellandaise tongue was something unpronounceable, but it translated in Yueh to Fuchsia, and that's what she had insisted Adé call her. It felt wrong, calling a parent by their given name, so Adé did her best to avoid calling her anything at all.

'Mother, you can speak in Saxil,' Carmine reminded her. 'Adé is nearly fluent, now. She has a talent for language.'

Adé flushed. 'Fluent' was an exaggeration, but not by much. She *had* been a quick study.

Missara Anglimn pouted, perhaps at the implication that she herself had not been such a quick study in Yueh. A small gesture, but one that reminded Adé that she was an interloper, not just in this family, but in this house. In this part of the city. No matter how proper her Saxil was.

The increased presence of household guards didn't help. Two at every entrance to the dining room, and more circumambulating the perimeter of the outside gate like nervous, oversized monks. They were all Ellandaise, garbed in stiff, high-collared wool uniforms, their eyes shadowed by helmets trimmed in fur.

The riots.

Violence hadn't yet reached the foreign sector, and given the wealth and steel protecting it, Adé had trouble believing it ever would. Elsewhere fear was an inevitability; here it felt like playacting. But the way Missar Anglimn kept making searching eye contact with the men, or ducking away to furtively speak with them, set her on edge.

There *was* a good deal of anti-foreigner sentiment among the rioters. The drought, the hunger, the unstable throne, and the Ellandaise with their money and their grasping – each had been a separate bit of kindling, but once set alight, they were indistinguishable in the flames.

'Adé?'

She blinked and looked around. They were all staring at her. She felt her cheeks burn, as though they could see the memories she was conjuring reflected in her eyes.

'I-I'm so sorry. I was just feeling a bit faint.'

'Oh, I hope it's not our food,' Missar Anglimn – Parthan – said. 'I know our cuisine must seem strange to you.'

'No! Of course not! The food is delightful. I especially like the . . .' Adé gazed down at her plate. Everything was mashed. Even the meat. 'Thank you for having me. It is a . . . a joy to be here.'

'The joy is all ours,' said Missar Anglimn. He folded his napkin and placed it on the table. 'Is everyone ready for the next course?' Without waiting for a response, he raised a little silver bell next to his plate and rang it. The double doors at the eastern end of the hall opened, and two Hana serving men entered to clear their dishes, then left as quickly as they had come. Immediately, the western doors opened and two different Hana men wheeled in a new cart of food on covered silver plates. Adé felt a pang of guilt when one of the men took her setting; *I'm no better than you,* she wanted to tell him. *I'm no different.*

'Adé, my dear, has Carmine discussed baptising you into the church?' Carmine's mother said as the men set a new array of porcelain plates in front of them. 'We must see you converted before the wedding, and the date swiftly approaches!'

'Mother,' Carmine chided, as though this were something they had talked about before.

Adé looked between them uncertainly. 'Conversion?' Carmine and his parents weekly attended their church, a rather pointy-looking building larger even than their home, but she hadn't considered that they would expect her to do the same. Though perhaps she should have. Their priests were a fanatical breed, ranting in the streets about idolatry and demanding passersby surrender to the will of their jealous god, until imperial troops or annoyed merchants chased them back into the foreign sector.

'The idea of baptism must be confusing to our Adé,' Missar Anglimn interjected with an air of mild academic interest. 'The Hanaman are not monotheists. Nor many of the Westermen. A very novel combination of blood, the Westermen and the Hanaman.'

Adé reached for her wine glass as Missara Anglimn eagerly nodded in agreement with her husband. 'I hardly think anyone back in Elland would believe such a ... a mixture!'

The wine caught in Adé's throat. Mercifully, a rap came at the dining room door just as she began sputtering. An Ellandaise guard detached himself from the wall and answered it. Another guard entered, strode over to Missar Anglimn, and leaned down to whisper in his ear.

Adé couldn't hear the words, but Missar Anglimn's brow furrowed, and a moment later he stood.

'I must beg your forgiveness,' he said, wiping immaculate

hands on his cloth napkin. 'Something unexpected has arisen and I must attend to it at once. Please, continue supper without me.'

'Business, Parthan?' scolded Missara Anglimn. 'At this hour?'

Her husband gave a tremulous, distracted smile. 'The flow of capital never rests. Neither can I.'

'I'm sorry we don't have anywhere to go,' Carmine said as they strode through the gardens after dinner, cutting through the wide, neatly clipped lawn. It seemed absurd to Adé, to have such an enormous garden and grow nothing in it but grass. If she had a yard, she would fill it with fruit trees and flowers. A bed of greens could be planted there, in the shade of the outer wall, and the heat-loving hot peppers Ori liked so much would thrive right in the centre. She'd spent most of her life in the city, but she knew a little about gardening from assisting Omair ...

Omair.

She'd been back just once to Omair's house since the incident three moons ago. The front door had been swinging open on the wind, all his tiny apothecarist's drawers yanked open, bereft of their contents. Nearby villagers had ransacked the abandoned property, most like. It had been eerie, a violation of her second home. But worst of all had been the blackish stains: one on the wall at the height of a man's head dragged down to a much wider patch on the floor. She'd told herself the first had been too high to be Omair or Nok. Still, more than one man might die in a room at a time, and there were

ways of killing that did not involve shedding a single drop
of blood—

Carmine squeezed her hand. 'Did you have a nice time
tonight?'

'Of course.' She groaned and rubbed her belly with
her free hand. 'So much food, though. Do you Ellandaise
always have three courses for dinner?'

'Only when we have important visitors.'

'I'm important?' she teased.

'Very.'

*Not important enough for your father to stay for the duration
of the meal.*

'Your family's house is as big as a sky manse,' she said
instead. 'Well, I'm guessing it is, at least. I've never actually been inside a sky manse.' Her mother's family had
owned one of the historic homes, embedded in the massive inner wall that circled the Immaculate City where the
emperor resided, but that had been before her mother's
disownment, and the subsequent collapse of the family's
fortunes.

'If I could, I'd buy it back for you.'

For a moment Adé did not understand. 'Buy it back
. . . you mean, my family's sky manse?' She couldn't help
it; she laughed. 'You can't *buy* a sky manse. Those plots
were gifts directly from the first Hana emperor to his most
trusted friends. They've been passed down by families for
centuries. Even when one falls vacant due to the absence
of an heir, the current emperor decrees a new holder. No
amount of money could—'

'I know, I know,' he interrupted. 'We learned all about
it in school: the properties are symbols of the emperor's

friends' commitment to protecting the capital and the integrity of the kingdom, each plot is like a brick in a wall, or a link in a chain, each deriving its strength from unity . . . and so on.'

Something about the way he recited it annoyed her. But he was being kind, so she allowed him to reclaim her arm in his own.

It took her some time to work up the courage to say it, but finally she could stand it no longer. 'Are you going to tell me, or do I have to ask?'

He looked genuinely baffled. 'Ask . . .? Ask what?'

'Carmine.' She put a hand to his chest, stopping him short. 'I'm the daughter of a dead foreigner. I come from Scrap-Patch Row. What could your family possibly gain from our union?'

'We're foreign, too,' he pointed out evasively.

'Yes, but you have a home you can go back to. A home where you would be just as rich as you are here. Richer, even, if half of what you tell me about Brekton is true.'

He cast his eyes around the empty garden before turning back to her, pale eyes full of something like guilt. 'You know I love you, right? Truly, I do. You're the most beautiful girl I've ever known . . . ever seen.'

'If you love me that much then be honest.'

'My father thinks it will suit the company's interests here if I marry a Hana,' Carmine conceded. 'He says the empire's rulers are so insular that the only way to gain true access to power here is to . . . you know, become part of the family, so to speak.'

A giggle escaped her. She couldn't help it. 'Are you serious? What connections does your father think I have?'

'It's less about connections at this point than appearances. He tried to arrange marriages for me before,' Carmine admitted slowly. 'Long, long before I met you. When we first arrived here from Elland.'

'First Ring girls?' she guessed.

He gave her a rueful look. 'Think higher.'

'A minister's daughter?'

'Higher still.'

She covered her mouth. 'No!' She looked furtively up and down the street before whispering, 'He thought the emperor would let you marry one of his daughters?'

'Not just one of the daughters.' Carmine grinned. '*The* daughter. The elder one. His best beloved.'

Adé giggled. She couldn't help it. The thought of a princess wedding a merchant's son . . .

'Well,' Carmine continued, 'his best beloved, before she killed him.'

The laughter caught in Adé's throat as she remembered a carnelian stone the size of a pigeon's egg, embedded in the pommel of a sword that was resting incongruous on Omair's cluttered kitchen table. Remembered turning to see the barbed end of a crossbow bolt aimed at her head. A tall girl dressed neck to toes in custom finery, glaring as Nok pushed her toward the door . . .

'My father didn't understand,' Carmine said. 'Here, everyone likes money, but not the dirty business of earning it. In Elland, there's no stigma against traders or merchants. In fact, wealth and honour often go hand-in-hand. We have a saying, "you cannot have a Capital without capital". Anyway, he assumed Emperor Daagmun would welcome the match if it meant an influx of Ellandaise silver, given all his debts.'

Adé forced out another laugh that sounded more like a cough. 'Well, obviously that plan fell through.'

He shuddered. 'Thank the gods someone explained why that would be a mistake before he could offer. Otherwise, I'm sure our family would be short a head or two.'

Carmine pulled his pipe out of his jacket, dusted tobacco into the bowl, and lit it. As they passed a pair of guards stationed along the wall, he spoke to them in the flat tones of Saxil around the stem of his pipe. 'Evening, men. Looks like everything is peaceful?'

'Let us hope it stays that way,' one of them said, glowering out into the darkness. The long rifle slung over his shoulder made Adé shiver. Suddenly, she was very glad the violence would not reach this part of the city – not out of fear for the Ellandaise, but for the rioters.

'Are you cold?' Carmine asked.

She pulled away so he couldn't feel her shiver again. 'No – I just had too much wine. I need to relieve myself.'

'I'll help you find the lavatory.'

'I'm sure it's in the same place it was last time,' she assured him. 'You stay out here with your pipe. I know your mother doesn't like seeing you smoke.'

The lavatory was not in the same place it had been last time. Or, Adé had to admit, perhaps she was simply lost. She found herself in a long hallway that was lined with heavy wooden doors on one side, glass-paned windows on the other, and empty save a Hana carpet and several quite detailed sculptures of women in scandalous states of undress. *Those* were definitely not Hana.

'But they had her buried!'

Adé jumped. Missar Anglimn's voice emanated from behind the nearest door.

'Did anyone see the body?' The voice belonged to a man and had a deeper, baritone quality. Blustery in contrast to Anglimn's reedy, academic tenor. Both men spoke in Saxil.

Praying they hadn't heard her, Adé made to leave, stepping as lightly as she could—

'She didn't lie in state, didn't have a funeral. Isn't that odd?' the blustery man continued.

'Not for a disgraced princess who killed her father, it isn't.' Missar Anglimn sounded unimpressed.

Princess? Adé paused. Once more, she saw a crossbow aimed at her face, glinting copper eyes. Nok, leaping between them—

'This isn't just one sighting from some drunken cadet,' said the other man. 'There have been multiple reports of a band of armed Yunians and slipskins, led by a girl with a sword bearing the imperial insignia. They ran into an imperial scouting party last week – killed all but one of their men. And, listen to this: they were headed south.'

'Hmm,' mused Anglimn. 'You said this information comes from the captain of the city guard?'

'It does. He says there'll be a curfew tonight, by the way. More riots expected.'

Adé leaned in. This was the first she'd heard of a curfew.

'This food shortage is becoming a true a hardship.' Anglimn sighed and wood creaked, as though he were leaning back in a chair. 'The crown declined my request to send more soldiers, so I had to hire mercenaries out of my own pocket – the passage here is not cheap when you have to pay it for thirty men. And that's on top of their fee. But what was I to do? Fuchsia can hardly sleep for worry. I had to get the best men available.'

'So sorry to hear,' the other man said, not sounding sorry at all. 'Anglimn, are you hearing what I'm saying? If the elder princess is alive, the throne is still in dispute. Empress Min's rule is even more precarious than we thought.'

'It's certainly not ideal. But I've been assured by Minister Cui that they have the leaders of the army and navy in their pockets. I don't foresee Princess Lu mounting a coup without either of those.'

'Still. Lu has the better claim, whether or not she murdered her father. And she has more charisma than the sister. Better-looking, too.'

'And harder to control.' Anglimn sounded irritated.

'What about the rumours of the younger one's ... dabbling in sorcery?'

'Contained. Cui assures me that wormy little priest with the shaved pate has her on a steady regimen of soporifics. We are well-situated. Cui even thinks we will be able to work out a trade deal for poppy tar within the year—'

'If her reign lasts that long.'

'It will last long enough for us to gain a foothold. And who knows? If we do it well, we may even be allowed to help select the next monarch.'

'You need to think bigger.' The man's voice came from closer to the door and Adé stumbled back, startled.

But then she heard the click of his boots – he was pacing. 'There's a chance for real power here. We need to make use of this instability.'

'Instability,' sniffed Anglimn, 'is bad for business.'

'Instability *is* business.' The man's tone was annoyed. 'Use your imagination! Even you must have had one at some point, to have built a company like yours.'

'I have a family to think of, now. I'm comfortable where I am.'

'A comfortable man is as good as dead,' drawled the other. He had an air of lazy superiority that suggested he was not subordinate to many, and certainly not to Anglimn. 'Think on it. If we reach out to Princess Lu—'

'You don't know where she is!'

'It won't be hard to find her once she returns to the city. Something tells me she won't stay away long.'

'Need I remind you, we have an audience with the Empress – Empress *Min* – tomorrow? Whatever creative notions you have, I would strongly suggest laying them to rest. We've worked hard to get this alliance. The Ambassadeur has his orders from King Ryvan—'

The other man made a dismissive sound. 'The Ambassadeur ... now *there* is a man without imagination.'

'Lamont,' Anglimn chided. 'What more could you want? Empress Min will do as she's told, and we will have her ear whenever we like.'

Lamont, Adé thought, turning the name over in her mind. She had heard Carmine mention the man before, though she could not recall the context.

'What good is an ear if someone else has the rest of her?' There was a long pause, and Adé leaned in, wondering if something was amiss. When he next spoke, his voice was pitched low and quiet, an excited orange ember of a thing. 'Think if we were the ones holding the puppet strings. No intermediary necessary. You've seen the wealth of this land. We could be as *kings*, Parthan.'

'I already have a king. And so do you, or have you forgotten?' Anglimn said primly.

'I'm not suggesting we break away from Elland – far from it. But imagine doing here what we've done in the South. That Governor-General of Banga, what's his name—'

'Visconte Elgyn,' Anglimn supplied.

'Right, Elgyn. He has all but free rein. If we were to take this place for Ryvan, he would happily allow us control, so long as we sent a steady stream of silver across the sea.'

'There's still the small matter of the imperial army and navy,' Anglimn reminded him.

'Their navy is weaker than ours,' Lamont dismissed. 'And as for the army, they're armed with what? Crossbows? A few rifles here and there? We have the superior weaponry. And need I remind you, we have ...' Lamont said a word Adé did not understand.

'The—?' Anglimn repeated sharply. Fearfully. 'That was ... Let it go, Lamont. If the stockpile Set spoke of ever existed, it is long gone, or—'

'We know it existed. I still have the samples the boy gave us, before we offended him – what a prissy idiot he was ... Heaven above, Anglimn, you look as though you've seen a ghost. You don't really believe that nonsense he fed us about magic and other worlds, do you?'

'Of course not,' snapped Anglimn. 'A thing doesn't have to be ... "magic" to be dangerous. And I thought you sent those samples to King Ryvan for examination?'

'Of course I did. I misspoke about the samples.'

'I should hope you did, Lamont.'

'I did,' came the blithe reply. 'You saw me, didn't you?'

There came the wooden creak of a body rising from a chair. 'I haven't given up hope on you yet, Anglimn. You're smart. You'll think on what I said. We have options. This is a wild frontier – we need only decide on a vision for it. Ryvan knows only what we tell him and will make his commands accordingly.'

'I will see you early tomorrow at court,' Anglimn said. 'And I suggest you let no one else know the thoughts you shared with me here tonight.'

The words broke Adé out of her reverie – as did their footsteps. They were coming her way.

Gods. Her eyes cut down the hallway, unforgivingly devoid of places to hide. At the last moment, she flung herself flat against the wall in the shadow of one of the scantily-clad statues. The door to the study swung open, and mercifully, the two men emerged and walked in the opposite direction. She kept her quivering breaths shallow until their footsteps died away.

Quickly, as silently as she could, she hurried down the other end of the hallway. Perhaps, if she took a left or right, there would be a door around the corner leading—

She screamed as she slammed into someone, then covered her mouth with both hands.

'Adé?'

20

'Carmine!' she squeaked, all but dissolving into his arms. 'I couldn't find the lavatory,' she blurted.

He looked incredulous, then laughed. She felt like crying, though she couldn't quite say why.

'Come on,' Carmine told her, 'I'll take you there. What were you doing this whole time?'

She shivered. 'Just ... lost.' And then, remembering: 'Carmine,' she asked slowly, trying to recall the texture, the contours of the unknown word Lamont had spoken earlier, the one that seemed to frighten Anglimn. 'What does this Saxil word mean?' She repeated it as best she could recall.

He frowned and shook his head. 'Where did you hear that? That's not a phrase I know.'

'Oh,' she said vaguely. 'I think I heard one of the staff say it earlier. Perhaps I misunderstood.'

He considered. 'Well, I don't know what it means, exactly. But I could give you a direct translation of the words.'

'Yes, please,' she said, perhaps a bit too eagerly.

'The first word is "speck", or "dust". Something tiny that accumulates into something bigger. Like a swarm, or a flurry.'

'"Dust,"' Adé mused. That didn't sound so bad.

Carmine continued, 'And the second is ... well, it's like "fire", only perhaps ... stronger. More specific. Poetic, even. I suppose the best interpretation—'

'Inferno,' Adé finished, almost to herself.

'Yes, that's good. Inferno,' he agreed. 'Or even, anni-hilation.'

'A dust,' she said slowly, 'that accumulates into an annihilation.'

Perhaps he saw the worry creasing her brow. 'Like I said, though, it doesn't mean anything.'

But Adé remembered the fear in his father's voice, and the avarice in Lamont's. And she knew it did.

Part One

Part One

I

A New Throne

Outside Min's window, rainclouds gathered over the empty courtyard. Last time she'd been here, she'd blown out the glass, showing her mother the terrible power she possessed and scaring her nunas, gathered below. Last time, she'd shown them all who she truly was: a creature wrought from a curse placed upon her in utero by a long-dead shamaness named Tsai.

Tsai was Lu's birth mother. Her true mother. Min's curse had been the shamaness's vengeance on the empress who had condemned her to death, and the emperor – Lu and Min's father – who had been too weak to stop it. Min herself was merely collateral damage.

But she'd become so much more since.

As for her own mother? Rinyi was locked away in her own apartments. She wrote Min letters most days, perhaps begging for clemency from her empress, or demanding remorse from her daughter. Min did not know; she had not read a single one.

Thunder purred slowly to life outside. She could feel the gathering power of the storm like heat under her skin. Fire in her bones.

Her magic felt different here. Up north, amid the barren mountains of Yunis, it had been cold and strong and certain − like a fierce wind, or the slap of choppy ocean waves. The change had begun with their journey back toward the capital, as the landscape shifted around them, from scrub trees and red dirt to pine copses to rice paddies. She felt it, like an urgent whisper just out of earshot. Then her carriage had passed through the outer walls of Yulan City into the Second Ring, and she'd been struck as though by a boulder to the skull.

It was the *people*. A hundred thousand minds seething with desire, their voices compounding and contradictory. Each one like a desperate hand raking its way down her body, clamouring for a fistful of her flesh. A city's worth of hunger, of want, channelled through her.

'You'll starve like this.'

She started. Behind her, Brother stood over a table spread with dishes. They'd been steaming when the servants had brought them in, but that had been hours ago.

Brother had been her cousin Set's man − part monk, part physician, part retainer, and the heavens knew what else before that. But Set was dead and Min was the one with power, and so, she supposed, Brother belonged to her now.

'The rain's rolling in,' he told her. As if she couldn't feel the power of the storm quivering through her. 'With any luck it'll be heavy enough to disperse the rioters.'

Min frowned. More riots. That made three days running. At first, the rioting had only been at night, but now they clogged the streets of the Outer Ring at all hours, set off like a cloud of flies smelling carrion. Didn't those people have trades to practice, children to raise?

'What do they want now?' There was a grain shortage, the result of last year's drought, and something to do with locusts the year before. But this monsoon season was already looking heavier than average. Surely that would set things right.

'They're gathered at the gateheads of the Second Ring. The city guard has them corralled, though. Court will carry on as planned. Nothing to worry about.' He lifted the lid from a silver tureen. 'Stewed duck. You haven't touched any of it.' He used the serving spoon to break up the oily skin congealing over its surface.

This had been the tedious pattern of Min's days since returning to the capital: Brother bringing her cups of hot broth, insisting she be dressed in linen one day, then silk the next, depending on the temperament of the sky. She suspected if propriety had allowed it, he would have taken to dressing her himself and sleeping in her room like a watchful handmaiden.

Not that hers slept here any longer.

They still fulfilled their duties: dressing her, plaiting her hair. But all with a rabbity anxiety and a silence that indicated they'd rather be anywhere else. That was fine by Min; it was best they kept their distance. Servants gossiped – none more so than nunas.

Ammas, she corrected herself. She was an empress now, and with her ascent they had also risen. Like parasites. Her sister Lu had treated her nunas like friends, but then, Lu had been born with charm enough to win the love of even her servants. Enough to buoy her through court and into their father's distracted, elusive heart, and to deflect their mother's barbed chiding. More than enough.

Until it wasn't.

Lu is dead, Min told herself.

It was what everyone said, and crucially, what had left her own path to the throne open. And they'd interred Lu – or at least something, someone – in a pared-down casket in an ignominious tomb reserved for lower-ranking family. But Min's heart, or whatever calcified, furious thing remained in its place, knew it all for a lie.

Perhaps it was denial. A failure of the imagination to believe in a world where someone like her sister, as vain and deathless as the sun, could die.

But the impossible could happen. Did happen. What was Min herself if not sea change wrapped in the body of a girl? A child prone to tears, now with the power of a shamaness, a phantom, coursing through her like blood. The unfavoured, second-born daughter, now about to ascend the throne as the first true empress of the Empire of the First Flame.

'Take this. It will calm your nerves for court.'

Brother proffered a glass vial of milky pink liquid. She recognised it: a dilution of the stuff he'd given her the evening of her return to the city. It had given her rest – oblivion – but also a chalky, bitter taste in her mouth all the next day. And it made the world dull and remote and big. Scary, in the way it had been before she had become what she was now.

'You'll need it. To control your . . . emotions,' he pressed.

He'd been told to keep her in line today – she could sense it. And judging from his nervous energy, by someone important. Perhaps a member of her Grand Secretariat, even. She scared those men, but clearly not enough.

'I'm in control,' she told him. 'I haven't had an accident since what I did to Yunis.'

Brother said nothing, perhaps thinking that it wouldn't be wise to point out the absurdity of calling pulling a city out of its immaterial world into this one an 'accident'.

'I need to keep a clear mind to review the notes from my advisers,' she told him, immediately wishing she hadn't sounded so defensive. She wasn't lying; her Grand Secretariat had given her a litany of information on the grain shortages, and the customs of the Ellandaise. They would be expanding trade with the foreigners, and she would announce it today in court, to hopefully set a friendly precedent for the public.

There was a knock at the door. Min suppressed the instinct to open it herself.

'That will be my ammas come to dress me. Let them in, then go,' she ordered. 'I'll see you at the ceremony.'

Brother frowned, still holding out the vial. She sighed and took it from him. Relief painted his face.

She dropped the vial to the floor and stomped it. Her feet were bare. She felt the sting of breaking glass, the cold of the liquid, the heat of her own blood.

Brother stared at her, mouth open.

'Get the door,' she told him.

In delicious silence, he did.

Behind the gliding pocket door, her handmaidens stood in two neat lines. Their hoods were raised and, as they curtsied, they had the appearance of flowers bent under a heavy rain.

'You're late,' Min said. They trembled, these girls who had once pitied her. Min found she preferred their fear, which had a shimmery, metallic edge. It tickled her tongue, like underripe persimmons.

Every eye fell on Min when she was announced.

Officials and onlookers packed the throne room so densely that the dark wood floors and silk carpeting beneath their feet were all but invisible. Overhead, the high walls and ceilings of Kangmun Hall teemed with delirious kaleidoscopic designs, the colours gleaming warm and sensuous in the flickering lamplight.

Brother, Butterfly, and a handful of new ammas whose names she had not learned, stood at her back. As she stood, the newly appointed captain of her guard fell into place behind them. An older man with a brow that was permanently creased, a hand that always seemed to be ready to reach for his sword. Yuri. She frowned slightly at him. He'd been her sister's beloved tutor once, until he'd forsaken Lu in exchange for a rise in rank. He'd been nothing but deferential on the few occasions Min had seen him since, but she sensed calculation and brooding beneath his stoic exterior. Could she really trust with her life a man who had already betrayed one princess?

Something to ponder later. Min lifted her chin and moved forward through the fray toward her throne atop its dais. Her audience watched, silent and rapt. They all wanted to be the first to see what she would do. They all wanted to eat her alive.

Let them try.

Thunder rumbled outside, distant and sluggish. Out the windows, towering clouds unfurled plush across the sky. The last storm had caused terrible flooding in the west, the Grand Secretariat had told her. Aid would need to be sent; taels and taels of it. She thought briefly of the rioters outside the gates of the Immaculate City, how drenched they must be. She felt a clench of pity in her chest and shook it off.

Rain will wash the filth away.

'When dams break, the old die and the young become bandits,' someone murmured. Min glanced back; Yuri. He nodded toward her but said nothing further. She frowned. Old men and their adages.

She ascended the dais, trailed by her retinue and the crisp scent of citrus blossom oil. The crowd breathed her in, exhaled admiration.

She had spent a lot of time looking in the mirror lately, learning to make herself pretty. Part of it was Butterfly's doing. Make-up could create its own light and shadow – its own reality. Under Butterfly's skilled hands, high cheekbones erupted under luminous moonlit skin and her mouth bloomed full and bitten-red.

The bigger secret was subtler, Min's discovery alone. Her face might be unremarkable, but she didn't have to wilt under it like a weight. This, she realised, had been the source of her sister's radiance all along: pride. Min was the one with the curse, but Lu had practiced her own sort of magic all along. Useful, but unsophisticated. Not difficult to learn.

Min ascended the dais, toward the throne. It was an intricate, heavy thing. Curved, muscular arms rose up to embrace its occupant, and ended in a pair of bristling paws, the claws clenched menacing around nothing. The back was a gold-inlaid tiger's face, teeth bared and eyes wild. Finials carved into conical flames as long as a man's arm jabbed up toward the ceiling. Together these symbols represented the original beast god of the Hu – the only remnant of their Gift, lost three generations ago when they came south – and the sacred flames of the Hana.

The Seat Of The Blazing Tiger. Min had never given it much thought before. As a child, she had known it only as intended for her sister, her cousin – always someone else.

But now ...

She sat. The wood of the throne was cold against the backs of her thighs, even through the layers of her robes.

'Let us begin.'

Her voice held a sharper edge than she'd intended, but it pleased her to see a few of the magistrates in the front flinch. Clearly, they'd heard rumours of the power she now wielded.

'The delegation from Elland,' announced the herald, and three foreigners spread in line before the dais, like gifts at her feet.

Min beckoned them forward, just as she had rehearsed with her advisers.

They came, bowing in their own strange style, stiff and from the waist. The first man resembled an anaemic reed, while the second, a much larger, older specimen, wore a bulky jacket spangled with metal buttons. The third had hair the brown of a mountain rabbit, and he was smiling at her.

It was the sort of smile Min recognised by now. Meant to make her flush and squirm, to cajole her into smiling back.

She did not smile back.

Min had met this Ellandaise delegation once before, when they'd sought an audience with her father. She'd barely noticed them. There had been so much else to worry about – her itchy undergarments, the hem of her robes falling under the heel of her pot-bottom shoes. She'd been such an idiotic thing.

That had been only moons ago; it felt like years. Her nunas had giggled over the foreigners' odd language, their hairiness, calling them 'pink men.' When Min repeated the phrase later, Lu had scolded her.

But now Lu was gone, and their emperor father, too. Min had watched him die – hadn't she? – and later, she had seen his body ferried off toward its eternal resting place in the Eastern Palace. Her duties to him in death were complete; she did not have to think about him. No more than he had thought about her in life.

Now Min stood alone, before the court – her court.

'We are most honoured to be in the presence of the young empress.' It was the anaemic foreigner. He dropped to the ground in a perfect imitation of the traditional Hu bow. Min was startled to find he had little of the Ellandaise accent, and his manners were so meticulously correct that it was nearly comical.

'Rise,' she said. He did. He had the round, sky-colored eyes not uncommon among the Ellandaise. The shock of hair that fell across his forehead was a limp white-yellow, the colour of weak tea. He'd removed his broad-brimmed sun hat when he entered the room, and now clutched it to his chest.

'Allow me to introduce myself,' he said. 'I am Parthan

Anglimn, founder and owner of the Eastern Flame Import Company.'

Brother leaned in from his place beside the throne, like a wraith loosing itself from the shadows. 'The largest trading company in the known world,' he explained in an undertone, but Min waved him away. Did he still think her stupid, after all this time? Hadn't she read her briefing notes from her Grand Secretariat twice last night, and again this morning, in front of him? And even an idiot like her handmaiden Snowdrop knew what the Eastern Flame Import Company was.

'We are honored to have you join us today, Missar Anglimn. Your company has brought great wealth to both our nations,' she said aloud.

This was not, strictly speaking, true, outside the brief few years when the Ellandaise had sold poppy tar to the empire. Otherwise, the foreigners had historically purchased much from them – tea, silks, cotton – while little silver flowed in the opposite direction. What could their tiny, grey-skied island provide that the Hu and the Hana didn't already have?

The purpose of their presence today was to find out. These men had come seeking favour from her; her duty was to take what she could and give as little as possible. The details would be worked out later, in private with her and the Grand Secretariat. But for now: this bit of theatre.

'Great wealth, yes. We thank the empress—'

'And perhaps greater wealth even is possible, in the futures. For both nations,' interjected a deep voice.

It was the smiling man. Something like annoyance

rippled across Anglimn's face – and that too of the Ambassadeur. Interesting. That could be of use in negotiations. Divide and conquer: a tactic she knew intimately. Hadn't her mother used it against her and Lu all their lives?

Min flicked her grey gaze back toward the foreign man and his familiar smile. He seemed oblivious to the discomfort he'd caused, or perhaps just unabashed. 'My name is Kommodeur Lamont,' he told her. 'I control flotte of ships, dispatched by Ellandaise crown to protect interests of Eastern Flame Import Company.'

His tongue, clearly accustomed to the thick, bland tones of Saxil, tripped over the words. A vulgar shock after Anglimn's meticulous display.

Perhaps mistaking Min's surprise for admiration, Lamont grinned. 'I practicing Yueh with Missar Anglimn daily,' he explained, clapping the smaller man on the back. 'The sounds are yet foreign to me. It is difficult toils.'

Weariness flickered across Missar Anglimn's face, suggesting it had indeed been 'difficult toils'.

Lamont was a tall, broad man nearing forty, perhaps a bit younger; it was hard to tell with these foreigners. His face was as sharp as a cleaver. The other men had beards, but Lamont was clean-shaven except for his upper lip, above which grew a thatch of moustache that matched the hair on his head. He was sweating quite profusely.

We live in the land of the First Flame, Min told herself. *A drop of the sun itself burns within our city walls. These men from their cold clime cannot tolerate its power.*

It seemed an auspicious thought.

'What brings you before me today?' she asked.

Ambassadeur Kartrum stepped forward, blustering in Saxil. The sound was heavy and coarse as unfinished timber. He had none of Anglimn's precision, nor Lamont's toothy eagerness, only an air of dull impatience endemic to old men used to getting their way.

Anglimn translated for him. 'You may not recall, but we met some moons ago with your late father – the heavens give him rest. At the time, he described his plans for further development of your Northern Territories. He told us that the existing colonies were flourishing, that soon they would become proper mining towns. He was especially excited about the prospect of new sources of iron, which would in turn increase your production – and potential export – of Hana sparkstone.'

'That excites all of us, to be sure,' Min said mildly. The Ellandaise had increased their purchase of sparkstone threefold in the past five years. They had developed their own modified versions back in Elland, as well as the guns to go along with them, though neither could match the strength of those created by the empire.

'Have you gentlemen seen a demonstration of the newest sparkstones yet?' she asked, reciting from memory the script her Grand Secretariat had provided. 'Recently, there have been exciting advancements from Bei Province – they are developing a new type called "Blue Flame" that they allege has the longest range of any powder to date.'

Missar Anglimn said, 'We have heard talk of "Blue Flame", but we import only the two varieties now – "Hu Steelfire" and the traditional sort, "Pride of Duhu".'

She awarded him with a smile. A small one. There was no need to be generous before she knew what they wanted. Or what she could take from them. 'So named for the late Hana emperor who sponsored its creation.' She waited for Missar Anglimn to finish translating this to his companions before continuing. 'We have come a long way since then, both in terms of firearms and their powder. It may soon become more efficient to arm our soldiers with rifles than with crossbows.'

'Marvellous,' said Missar Anglimn, though Min knew the Ellandaise must already have this information. This was part of *their* script.

'You must return to visit us at later date, when "Blue Flame" is perfected,' she said. 'We will give you a demonstration and, of course, a sample to show your King Ryvan.' On top of the potential for trade, the Ellandaise monarch was well known for his personal fondness of new styles of explosives.

Lamont cleared his throat as Missar Anglimn translated her words. Then he grinned and leaned in conspiratorially. 'Will you demonstrate yourself? I am curious if you are as deft with a weapon as your sister was.'

The room went still. Outside, thunder issued a low growl.

This was not part of the script. Min could tell in the way Missar Anglimn's neck flushed, in the way the Ambassadeur snapped brusquely at Anglimn, presumably demanding a translation in Saxil. He received it, then reddened and whipped his head toward Lamont.

Lamont just smiled again.

Min felt the impulse to smile demurely to hide her embarrassment, to save him from his own, but she choked it down. 'I think you will find I have many skills, though they do not extend into the realm of the martial arts. Perhaps in that regard I am a touch too traditional.'

Even with Lamont's weak grasp of Yueh, he should have heard the verge of warning in her words. But his smile did not diminish. Either he was stupid, or he did not care.

'You not look so traditional to me. You are a Girl King, you are not?'

Once, silence had made Min anxious. Every lapse in conversation was an absence, and her inability to fill it reproof of her character. But she had discovered this to be a weakness in most people. The trick was to wait them out, until they broke first.

'Elland, we lately are great success with colonies to your south. As you know, climate there is amenable for many desirable crops... like poppies. Perhaps we discuss possibility of import them, while we on subject of expand trade.'

The air in the room seemed to take on the weight of cold, deep water. Even Kommodeur Lamont seemed to register the misstep. Min resisted the terrible urge to turn in her seat and seek Brother's gaze. A cold prickle of sweat dragged its way down the back of her neck. She was alone in this; she had to be. But what to say?

Poppy cake was highly addictive. Her father had passed his ban on its import because the demand – the wild hunger – for it had grown alarmingly in just a few years' time. Small amounts were still grown domestically for use as a medical palliative, though, allowing the problem of its abuse to persist at a simmer in the population. Less potent – and therefore less expensive – varieties, including some mixed with tobacco, remained popular in parts of the North, and the grim, salt-lashed fishing villages along the Eastern shore. Min had learned too, that some purer forms were passed around among the wealthy – as tinctures, as paste for smoking, both for leisure, and for pain relief.

This latter route was how her late cousin, her late husband, Set – and possibly her father himself – had first fallen into its grasp. The Ellandaise would know the significance of what they were asking, and yet, they dared.

Her lips parted, but her throat clenched, cutting off the words she'd worked so hard to memorise. Not that they mattered anymore. They had destroyed the script.

Kartrum, sensing the change in atmosphere, barked in Saxil for a translation. As Missar Anglimn provided one, Kartrum's eyes widened and he whirled on Lamont in fury.

This was not part of the plan, Min thought with momentary relief. They would take it back. Apologise.

Missar Anglimn interpreted as Kartrum spoke: 'The poppy cake would be for medicinal use, of course.'

No apologies, no retraction. This might not have been the plan, but they were moving ahead with it anyway. This terrible breach of etiquette. This slight to her.

Anglimn went on, nerves evident beneath his sunny translator's lilt: 'The potency would be closely monitored. Our new refineries are quite sophisticated.'

Unable to catch herself, Min looked wildly toward the advisers lined up in the front row, the cluster of her Grand Secretariat. They looked back, some blankly, some puzzled. Who in their number was involved in this? She could not say. Only that some or all of them must have decided she was an easier mark than her father or her husband ... or her sister, and that they would use her to profit.

It was a familiar taste, this metallic tinge of terror on her tongue. The fear that came from watching the ground crumble out from beneath you, and realising you don't have wings. Once, it might have reduced her to tears in front of these men, these vultures.

But she knew what to do now. Turning fear to rage – this was what she was born for. She felt the alchemical boil in her belly.

Min sensed the next clap of thunder in her bones before it resounded over them, loud enough that the crowd started, and Missar Anglimn flinched.

'Go on, then,' Min said, softer and closer than even the thunder had been. 'Speak. Tell me more of your plans.'

Missar Anglimn's mouth flapped open, then shut. Min supposed a translator given no words had nothing to say.

The Kommodeur did, though. 'Closer distance make much drop in cost of shipping,' he rushed out. Min saw now he must have committed his earlier speech to memory; speaking spontaneously, his sentences barely held together. 'Th-things much different now from olden time—'

Another clap of thunder erupted, near enough now to rattle the Hall's windows in their frames. Someone shrieked at the sound, and all at once the hall filled with nervous laughter.

'Silence!' Min snarled.

The air in the Hall seemed to contract at the sudden still

that followed. She'd never dreamt so many people could obey her all at once, and so quickly. Min's whole life she had lamented that she wasn't born clever and charmed like Lu. But there were many ways to hold the world in your hand, and fear was the easiest of all.

'Continue.'

Kommodeur Lamont went on in frantic, sloppy Yueh: 'We know of poppy ban. But, we thinks: your sister an unconventional sorts. Perhaps, you as well? We wonder if you change the rules?'

He smiled at her again, but now it was solicitous.

Min answered with a smile of her own.

'So much talk of my family today,' she exclaimed, looking deliberately from one pink face to the next. 'First my late father and husband, and now my sister!'

'Yes ... Again, we were most aggrieved to hear of the passing of your father.' Missar Anglimn all but leapt forward, scrambling to salvage the fraying threads of the conversation. 'And your sister. And, of course, your late husband. He... held such promise.'

A smile rose on Min's lips like a shard of ice in water. 'Yes. My promising late husband. Full of vision. Wise beyond his years.' This time she felt no pain, no confusion in thinking of him. She paused, tilting her head as though suddenly recalling something. 'Didn't he pass a decree to banish you and your kind from our empire?'

Silence.

'And yet,' she continued, furrowing her brow like a consternated child, 'here you stand! In my courtroom, in my palace, in the heart of my kingdom, thinking to sell me poison in exchange for good silver. You must have paid handsomely for the opportunity – which of my spineless advisers did you bribe, I wonder?'

Min leaned forward as they drew back.

'What do you imagine I will do to them when I find out?' she continued. 'And what do you imagine I will do to you?'

The points of her fingernail guards – long, tapered golden caps like claws, inlaid with pearl and nephrite – bit into the carved paws of the throne's armrests, piercing the lacquer. Her great-great grandsire Kangmun had had the throne commissioned when he'd conquered the Hana – a careful symbol of the harmony between the Hu and their new subjects. The same intention with which Min was conceived.

How absurd. The combination wasn't harmony – it was coercion. One side triumphant, the other humiliated. That was ever the way of the world: someone won, and someone lost.

Perhaps in time she would commission a new throne. A new throne for a new winner.

'W-we certainly didn't pay – I don't know where you received this information, but clearly you're confused—' Missar Anglimn stammered.

Min's voice blew over his with the force of a hurricane snapping a sapling in two. 'You presume to tell me what I know?'

'No, of course—'

'It is time for you to go.'

She stood and Anglimn stepped back, as though when she moved, the whole world shifted to accommodate her.

She must have looked radiant; she felt unreal, just on the edge of drunkenness. Giddy with transcendence.

A hand grabbed her shoulder from behind. Brother. She did not even bother to shrug him off. It took a moment for the heat rolling from her body to penetrate the stiff layers of her robes, but at last he yelped and released her, shaking his hand as though he'd been burned.

'Empress—!'

Outside, the sky broke open. Rain lashed the windows, ringing sharp and deliberate and crystalline against the glass.

Inside, fire erupted from Min's fingertips.

A throne was only a chair, only wood. And what was wood but kindling?

Min rose from it as the flame-carved finials spat and roared to life, into the real thing. The hem of her robes caught and flared. She smelled burning hair and the air was electric with shrieks. She stepped to the edge of the dais, a column of heat surging up her spine.

The Ellandaise were already lurching their way backward, into the stampede of panicked magistrates. A sea of men scrabbling to put distance between themselves and her. She caught the Kommodeur's wild gaze in her own as he stomped his way over a magistrate in green robes.

'You have until nightfall to leave this city – my city,' she told them, and her voice roared louder than the fire, ricocheting from the painted walls. 'Get on your boats and sail back to where you came from, and pray my wrath does not burn its way across the oceans after you.'

She watched as they fled, along with as many officials as could bear themselves through the door. In their wake, they had left a dozen or so trampled bodies. Some moved. Most did not. Someone pushed closed the double doors of the Hall.

Min turned and saw Brother and a group of eunuchs stomping and beating out the smouldering pyre that had so briefly been her throne.

A new throne for a new winner, she thought, just before she collapsed.

2

Liberation

'We have to kill them all.'

Lu looked up from the manacles she was attempting to break open. Nasan gazed down, arms akimbo and jaw set hard like she was expecting a fight. Wanted one. Nothing new.

Apparently, even slashing their way into an imperial prison hadn't been enough for the Ashina girl. Perhaps it had been too easy. Lu could understand that. They'd crept in under the murky heather-grey of the predawn, slit the throats of the sleepy morning watch without a sound. Finding and overpowering the others in their beds had been quick work. Most were young – callow recruits from all over Bei Province, sent to sweep up the dirty, neglected corners of the empire. To press starvation-weakened prisoners into submission and labour. And now, here was Lu, just as ready to press them into service, helping her retake the capital.

No, she thought. That was just Nasan talking. Not the truth. Lu would give them a choice. Those who followed her would do so of their own volition. She'd freed them – they were prisoners no longer.

45

Lu returned her attention to the manacles. They were looped around the skinny ankles of a prisoner. The girl had been rigid with fear when they'd broken her cell doors open. Once she'd seen them binding the guards though, her tongue had loosened. She spoke almost no Yueh – a rare thing within the empire's borders. But some northern villages still persisted with their own way of life, disinterested in the business of their far-off rulers. Lu had eventually earned her name (Roensuk) and her age (16). She looked no older than twelve.

Lu filed away at the manacles. They were clenched like talons around Roensuk's skinny ankles, and rusted shut, their keyholes hidden beneath flaky orange layers. It made her wonder how long they'd been there.

It would be difficult to ask, Lu told herself. With the language barrier.

'Did you hear me?' Nasan demanded, still standing above her.

Lu set down her file and picked up a broken chunk of rock. 'Where's Jin?'

'He's with the guards. Who, incidentally, I'm trying to talk to you about—'

Lu brought the rock down hard on the left manacle. It sprang open in a shower of rust. Roensuk flinched.

'Are you listening to m—?'

Lu brought the rock down again, the clash drowning out the rest of Nasan's words. The remaining manacle fell open with a defeated creak. Roensuk didn't flinch this time.

Lu pulled her upright. The girl's atrophied legs buckled and trembled like a newborn calf's, but she did not fall.

She put a hand up to lean against the bars of her cell, then yanked it back, as though she couldn't bear the touch of the metal. Had she once clenched her fists around them, searching for a weak spot? How long until she'd given up?

Lu watched her totter toward a knot of women, newly freed and tending to one another. One of them placed a hand on her narrow back, drawing her into their fold.

'I hope you weren't expecting thanks,' Nasan said.

'I wasn't.' Lu bristled, but she couldn't fault her tone. Not so long ago, Lu had been the assumed heir to the throne of the empire. A reckless would-be warrior without a battlefield. A girl who had never shed blood, nor drawn it. That girl might have wanted gratitude. Love and glory. Now she wanted – what, exactly? She couldn't say. That was new. Her feelings had always shown themselves brightly, fireworks in a night sky. But then, her world used to be that way, too: one of stark, obvious contrasts.

'Princess.'

She no longer saw that world. It had died, along with—

'*Princess.*'

Lu turned and met Nasan's impatient gaze – only, for a moment, it was someone else's eyes she saw. Dark and furtive, yes, but flickering with a hidden undercurrent of gentleness. It was painful, how much Nasan could look like her brother. Then the light would shift, or she would tilt her head – as she did now – and the illusion broke, and she was nothing like him at all.

Lu shivered, feeling the phantom brush of fingertips against her own. There, and then not. Slipping away, as they did night after night in her dreams.

'All right,' she said, wiping her sweaty palms on her trousers harder than she needed to, as though to scrub away the memory. Nokhai sank back into the shadows of her mind. 'Take me to the guards.'

The dead were heaped in the corner of the prison's mess hall. Jin stood over them, a hand resting on the hilt of his sword, as though they might still pose some lingering danger. He had been the Silver Star of Yunis, its protector, the leader of their paltry army. Yunis was no more, but he was still a soldier, alert and ready to serve. *Her* soldier, now, Lu supposed.

She forced herself to look at the bodies: a sodden pile of blood-blackened cloth and pallid flesh. It was scarcely past dawn but already hot, and flies gathered in glittering fistfuls. She swallowed bile. *Traitors*, she reminded herself. These men were Northerners born and bred. They wore imperial uniforms, but they'd served under her cousin Set when he was assigned governance over these territories, and that loyalty ran deep in their bloodline. They never would have come over to her side. They had to die.

Just one more life. Those were the words that had come to her each time she'd slashed her blade. That was the cost of victory. And each time she found she could pay it.

Jin strode over. His hand went to her shoulder as he neared. She jerked away.

'Not now,' she said, far harsher than she'd intended. It sounded like *not ever*. 'I – I'm sorry,' she breathed. She had to remember they were betrothed – or, were they? The terms they had agreed upon had changed drastically. He no longer had an army, a kingdom, to offer her.

She looked up. Jin's eyes brimmed with hurt she had caused, and she forced herself to witness it. There was a kind of terror there as well – the abject, sterling loneliness of being too far from home. That was also her fault. His proposal had been part of a bargain between the Triarch and herself.

She'd come to Yunis an exile begging for an army. In exchange, once her throne was won, she would grant them self-determination, a chance to come out of hiding. Marrying Jin would be a gesture of good faith that she would keep her pledge for a free Yunis.

Just a dream she'd had no business offering. One that had left Jin's people decimated, Yunis dragged from its otherworldly cloister and ravaged, by her sister, of all people—

No. She could not allow herself to think of Min. Not now.

'I'm sorry,' Lu told Jin again. 'I didn't mean ... I can't—'

I can't look weak.

Jin nodded, and she thought she saw understanding in his eyes before he lowered them.

'Come away from here. It does no good to dwell on them,' he said gently, gesturing at the dead.

He was right. Besides, she still had to think of the living: survivors of their ambush on the prison. There were dozens of them, their hands and feet bound together, bellies pressed to the floor – and faces as well. The better to avoid looking them in the eye, Lu thought. A few wore sleep clothes, but most were in uniform – a motley sea of dark green and blue. Were it not for their rabbit-quick breathing, they could've just been sacks of grain, heaps of cloth.

Just one more life.

Nasan's people stalked between the men, weapons in hand, faces hard and wary. Nasan herself entered the hall, striding toward Jin and Lu. Her people crowded in around immediately. Lu frowned. She did not expect them to love her the way they did Nasan, but if they were going to fight with her – under her – they ought to take notice when *she* entered a room. In the end, she would be the one with the power.

'What's the plan?' asked Ony.

One of the displaced Gifted Kith who had banded together under Nasan, Ony struck Lu as something between Nasan's second in command, and her closest confidante. And now, as always, she addressed Nasan.

Lu replied, pointedly. '*I* will address the freed prisoners and tell them we intend to march on Yulan City. Ask them to join my – our army.'

Ony flicked her a look, equal parts disdain and trepidation. 'All right,' she said, still to Nasan. 'I don't know how well that'll go over. They don't trust imperials, so they're wary of the Girl King.'

The Girl King. How many people had called her that in the same derisive tone? 'I'll talk to them—'

Nasan's nostrils flared. 'You need to do more than *talk*. You need to give them something.'

'Such as?' Lu demanded. But she already knew.

'I told you. I've been telling you since before we arrived. We had an agreement.'

'The agreement was that we wouldn't let a single guard escape. And we didn't.'

Nasan pointed at the bound guards. 'What's the difference between escaping, and leaving here alive, exactly?'

'I came here to free prisoners, not commit a massacre.'

'A massacre?' Nasan retorted. 'Look around at this place. Look at what they've been doing to these people. It would be justice!'

'It would be a bloodbath—'

'So, you're the only one who gets to kill out of vengeance?'

Lu heard the hideous crunch of cartilage, felt the vibration radiating through the handle of her dagger. So much blood, hot and sticky on her hands. Set's blood.

Why did the gods make you like this? Just to torment me?

No, not for him. But he may not have been wrong to blame the gods. Perhaps a violent heart wasn't about circumstance. Perhaps it was something innate that made someone a monster.

'Other people deserve what you allowed yourself.'

She looked up sharply at Nasan. *Allowed.* As though killing her cousin had been an indulgence. The prize in a game.

But hadn't that been the way of it with Lu and Set? Since they were children, neither would let the other get the last word, the final punch. No matter how bloodied they became, each would sooner tear themselves apart than surrender. Each would sooner die than lose.

And then Set *had* died. Under the bite of her sword and dagger. The game was over.

'That wasn't vengeance,' Lu said, but the words caught in her throat. 'That was – it was him, or me.'

'And this is them, or us.'

The released prisoners had begun to close in around them as they spoke. One of them, an older woman with a rough, sullen face, stepped forward. She had the jerking gait of a body broken and broken again, then poorly healed. But Lu could sense the tautly wound malevolence in all that stiff, starved muscle. Jin moved in, his hand reflexively migrating toward his sword belt. Lu gave him a quick shake of her head. No reason to escalate things.

The woman could have been thirty, or perhaps fifty. Her hair was stark white. It was hard to know what was the natural wear of ageing and what had been accelerated by imprisonment. She looked Lu up and down. 'You're her, then? The Girl King?'

'I am Emperor Lu, daughter of Daagmun, great-granddaughter of Kangmun, the first of the Hu Emperors,' she told the woman. 'How may I be of service to you?'

'Service? That's a good question!' The woman barked out what might have been a laugh. 'We hear you're looking for recruits for your little upstart army,' she continued, gesturing to the wary-eyed men and women gathered behind her. 'Do we have a choice in the matter?'

'Of course you have a choice,' Lu said, opening her words to the others, taking care to meet the most receptive eyes she could find. 'You all have a choice.'

A murmur rippled through them. It sounded more doubtful than pleased.

'What's your name?' Lu asked the woman.

'Sinda. Or, it was, once. I've been in here six years.

They locked me up because they said I killed my baby girl. I didn't – she got the shaking sickness,' the woman said, loud enough that her coarse rasp echoed through the room. 'The first few months I was here, I prayed to the gods to stop the beatings, to relieve my hunger. Hunger so bad it burned. Bruises so bad I couldn't sleep.'

What was Lu to say to that? To any of it? Words could not fill this woman's belly, could do nothing for her daughter, long since dead and relinquished to the ground, no matter how she had died.

Sinda's voice scraped on: 'The worse things got, the harder I prayed. But no god ever answered. Because there are no gods.'

As she spoke, she moved almost imperceptibly forward. Now she was so close Lu could smell her – the musty reek of unwashed hair, sour breath and, faintly, urine. 'Tell me this,' she said, her crooked mouth taking on something like a sneer. 'If I don't believe in the gods, why should I believe in a king, man or girl? Why should I believe in *you*?' She punctuated her final word by stabbing a finger toward Lu, not quite touching her, but coming close enough for it to feel like a threat.

Lu didn't allow herself to flinch. 'Unlike your gods, I am very real. And you need to step back.'

She didn't, but neither did she move forward. And then, swift as a gasp, a shank appeared in the woman's hard fist. A high murmur rippled through the crowd around them.

Lu's fear was quickly overtaken by rage, white-hot and cleansing. Who did this peasant think she was threatening?

Nasan stepped between them. 'I know you're angry,' she told Sinda. 'But Emperor Lu isn't the one you're mad at.'

'What would you know of my anger, child?' the woman demanded.

'I was a prisoner, too,' Nasan snapped. 'In a place like this one.'

'There are no places like this one.'

'Oh, there's a few, actually. Why do you think they're numbered?' Her tone was all disarming nonchalance, but Lu saw Ony shouldering her way closer through the crowd, fists clenched tightly around her staff.

Sinda didn't respond, but Lu thought she saw an ember of curiosity ignite somewhere in the far reaches of her eyes.

'I may not know what you've been through, but I can bet I've seen things just as bad,' Nasan continued. 'It's not Lu. It's the guards – they're the ones that beat you. The ones who pretended to hand you a ladle of filthy water, only to splash it into your face. Who killed your friends. Maybe someone you loved. *They* deserve your rage.'

The woman shook her head, and a young man behind her shouted: 'The Girl King is just as bad as they are, she's just been far enough away not to know it. She's got blood on her hands, even if she can't see it.'

'You're right,' Lu interrupted, stepping forward into the crowd. 'I didn't know. But I'm here now.'

'She's here,' Nasan said. 'And she's giving you a gift.'

'What? A chance to be in her little army? To die for her?' Sinda said, but there was curiosity in her voice now.

'Not die,' Lu heard herself say. 'Kill.'

Jin looked at her with warm, puzzled eyes. He did not yet understand. How could he, when he still had a heart?

You can still take it back, she told herself. But she couldn't. Or wouldn't. It was the same either way.

Cowardice filled her mouth like wool, chased by the metallic tang of shame. She'd known what she would do, what she would allow, before Nasan had ever suggested it. She knew what to give them because it was what *she* would've wanted.

'Kill,' Lu repeated the word, firmer and with more fire. But that wasn't enough; that wasn't what they needed to hear. 'Take your justice.'

The crowd followed the direction of her gaze across the hall, toward the guards tied up and trembling on the floor. Lu felt more than heard Jin's intake of breath beside her.

'Lu,' he whispered urgently.

She did not turn to face him. 'You should wait in the main hall. Take the children with you, and anyone else who does not wish to stay.'

'Lu, this is not how ... this is a ...'

A crime. Against men and gods and any creature that has ever had a heart.

But Lu was none of those things.

And Jin – he was a soldier. He was duty and obedience. She looked at him then, and he saw the inevitability of what lay before him. He nodded, and something in his eyes dimmed, retreated. But he turned, gesturing toward the nearest child, a boy of no more than twelve. The boy fell in step behind him, followed by another child, and another. A few adults followed them, closing the door at their backs.

Lu searched Sinda's face to see the flickering of realisation ignite her dark eyes like an oil fire. It roared to life – but then the flames were buffeted with uncertainty.

'Do we have a deal?' Lu asked. 'You grant me your loyalty. I grant you compensation once we've taken back Yulan City. And in the meantime, you may have your justice.'

'They're bound,' Sinda said, the blade of her shank dipping just slightly. There was an edge of trepidation in her voice. After all this woman had been through, it had not made her as bloodthirsty as Lu.

'She's right, they are bound,' said a voice behind Sinda. Bodies parted, disclosing Roensuk. So, Lu thought. She did speak Yueh after all. The girl dragged one of her feet, but she was upright. She was such a small thing, but the way she held her chin, the steely defiance in her eyes made her look more wiry now than starved. Pared down to the ancient, charred iron core of a thing from which all the excess had burned. She met Lu's eyes with her own. 'Not very sporting if your prey can't run, is it?'

Lu swallowed. She lifted her chin coolly. 'Depends on the sport.'

Roensuk took the shank from Sinda's hand. She stepped toward the closest of the guards. She raised her weapon, face pensive and nearly reverent. Then she bent and sliced the ropes from the man's wrists. The movement was slow, almost gentle, but the man yelped, and when Roensuk stood, Lu could see blood where she'd cut him. Perhaps it had been an accident. It wouldn't matter, in any case. Not for long.

Nasan raised an eyebrow. Lu was surprised to see apprehension twisting her face. She turned away. So that would be the way of things; she was alone in her duty.

Lu leapt up onto the closest table, drawing the attention

of the room. 'Anyone else who wants to leave, go now in peace, with our every blessing.' She paused, letting the unspoken 'or' hang in the air. 'Anyone who wants to join me – we will head South. It will not be easy, and it will not be pleasant, but if you help me reclaim my throne I will reward you beyond your every dream. We will end my sister's corrupted reign and take back the capital, the empire, for its people! For you.'

'Why should we trust you?' a voice demanded from the crowd. It sounded interested, though.

'Ask the Gifted I travel with if I keep my word,' Lu told them. Then she licked her lips. Her mouth had grown so dry. 'And in the meantime, I give you this gift: make sure not one guard leaves these walls again.'

She leapt down from the table and strode from the hall, slow and deliberate. Perhaps no one would notice the shame hounding her if she did not run from it.

'Princess Lu!'

She jerked, startled to hear the respect inflected in her name. This was the voice of someone who had been instructed on the matter of honorifics like a second language, and who believed in them like a religion. She hadn't heard that particular sound since she'd left Yulan City.

She turned. A man, kneeling on the floor, wearing a green uniform marking him as a guard. The chest of his tunic bore at its centre a badge embroidered with the likeness of a mountain lynx. Not just a guard, but one of rank, then.

'Princess Lu,' he repeated, and there again was that respect. Respect – and only the barest edge of desperation. His hands were bound behind his back, but he inclined his neck to suggest a bow. He was older than her, but not old, perhaps in his thirties. He had a black moustache, neatly trimmed, and keen, alert eyes.

'Do I know you?' She had a good eye for faces but she did not recognise his.

'No,' he admitted. 'But I wish to surrender. Take me with you. I served under Lord Set – I am a strong fighter, and I know my way around the North. I know many things. You're heading back to the capital, are you not? You will need a guide. I can be that guide.'

'What else do you know?' she asked, intrigued.

The guard's voice rose, his tone urgent, but clinging still to dignity. 'Down in Yulan City, in the court, they all say you're dead, but only half of them believe it. The court's gone mad, divided between you and Princess M – Empress Minyi. Hana against Hu. Pro-Ellandaise and pro-trade supporters against the isolationists. They say it's like a war without weapons.'

Lu's brow creased. 'Tell me more.'

'Don't listen to him,' Nasan hissed. 'He's just trying to distract you—'

But Lu raised a hand to quiet her. This was valuable information. Nasan couldn't see it, because she hadn't grown up watching this game play out.

'It isn't just the court. The city folk are unhappy with their new empress.'

'And why would that be?'

'In my experience, people get angry when you do not let them eat,' he said mildly.

'A food shortage?' Lu asked. 'Stemming from what, exactly?' The past summer had been hot and dry, and there had been the issue of locusts the year before, but two years' troubles could hardly deplete the empire's granaries.

'That I don't know,' the guard admitted.

Could this really be Min's doing, and so fast? Or, perhaps more accurately, the doing of whoever had their claws in her sister. Their mother, or Set's moth-coloured monk, who she'd seen clinging to Min's robes in Yunis. It was hard to believe they could devastate the well-bolstered systems of the empire in a few short moons, though.

A flash of black eyes, gnashing teeth, thrown lightning speared through her mind's eye and she resisted the urge to flinch. Her sister might be capable of doing quite a lot on her own terms, Lu reminded herself.

'Tell me what else you've heard,' Lu pressed. 'What about the army? My sister clearly still has its service in name, but does she—'

A hand clamped down hard on her right arm. The one she'd injured in Yunis. One of their healers had mended it before she'd left, but under Nasan's fingers it still felt oddly tender, like a newborn thing. 'Enough,' the Ashina girl hissed. 'You can't. Not even one.'

Lu shook her off with more force than was necessary, but she kept the growl of irritation from rising to her mouth. 'I wasn't—'

'You were,' the other girl snapped.

It's just one man, she thought. But the words died before they made it to her lips. Not a man. A guard, wearing a uniform, armed by the empire with the power and the tools to kill.

Just one more life. And one more, and one more after that. If that was the trade Lu had to make, she'd make it a thousand times and never blink. She was an emperor, a king. She knew what was right, and what had to be done, and when those things were not the same. And she knew which she would choose, every time.

She looked down at this man and his shackled wrists, his tidy moustache and clever face. And beneath it all, she knew he was no doubt frantic and dumbfounded by the circumstances that had brought him here, a hand's width from death.

Circumstances? Most likely, it had been his decision to become a guard. To beat and terrorise women like Sinda and Roensuk, forcing them to work until their hands bled. Even if it was devoid of passion – it was still a choice. And in a way, wasn't that worse? To let yourself do the unspeakable, not out of malice, but by rote.

How dare he ask her for this? This thing he must have known she could not give.

'You say your life is mine. Your loyalty,' she said.

'Yes.' His voice was almost vicious with conviction.

She stooped down beside him, studying him. Seeking out the burgeoning shine of hope in his dark eyes.

Until she asked, 'Did you say the same thing to my cousin?'

'I . . . excuse me?' Hope dimmed under the fog of confusion.

She stood, brushing dust from her trousers. She arranged the front of her tunic and adjusted her belt. 'Men like you are loyal only to your own flesh,' she told him. She raised her voice, loud enough that the bound guards near him would hear. Loud enough that the freed prisoners would, too.

'You did not ask to be here. Neither did I. Neither did Nasan, or Roensuk.' She met the freed girl's eyes. Had he ever struck her? Thrown her food to the floor? If he had, would he even remember? Or would those have only been the events of an ordinary day, indistinguishable from any other?

'No one brought you to this moment but yourself.'

She walked away from him, her steps slow and even.

Just one more life.

The knives began to fall before she was gone. She heard the wet thunk and tearing slide of them, the disbelieving gasps of the newly dying, the soon-dead. Screams filled the air, chased by the acrid bite of iron. She closed the doors behind her and did not look back.

Night was falling by the time the freed prisoners had finished their bloody work. Lu and Nasan stood at the front gate of the prison and watched them depart, in large surges at first, then a trickle here and there. Not one of them stopped. Not one of them looked back.

By the time Roensuk limped through the gate, supported by two older women, Lu knew better than to hope. But she could not resist meeting the girl's gaze as they passed. It yawned back at her, blank and dark and so far away from Lu that it scarcely seemed plausible they shared the same planet.

'Well. What now?' Nasan asked.

'Yulan City.'

'Correct me if I'm wrong, but wasn't the plan to build an army with the people here, then win your city back?

Well, I don't know where you've been – but your army
just left.'

I hope you weren't expecting thanks.

Lu shook her head. 'We'll do it backwards then. We
need people. The city is where the people are. City first.
Then we'll get my army.'

3
Pull

'We call upon the Amma and the Anno to remove this one's suffering.'

As the words left Nok's lips, Shamaness Jiwa gave an encouraging nod.

The elderly goatherd lay between them, supine on the examining table, one pant leg rolled up to expose a swollen, purpled knee.

Nok wiped away the sweat brimming on his lip with the back of his wrist.

Focus.

Jiwa proffered a hanging bowl of flame – pulled from the temple's eternal pyre – so Nok could light his bundle of mugwort. He shook it out to smouldering, then held it over the goatherd's knee.

'In the name of the Ana and the Aba, *release.*'

At first, nothing happened. Then, slowly, a wisp of malignant energy like black-grey smoke seeped from the woman's knee.

Nok could have cried with relief, but there was no time. He worked his wrist in slow, methodical circles, like Jiwa had shown him. The tendril of energy rose tentatively, enticed by the mugwort.

When the two clouds – one of smoke, one of energy – met, he gave a sharp yank with his hand, like a bird pulling a stubborn worm from the earth. The ribbon of black-grey energy went taut. The goatherd let out a gasp as her knee jerked up with it.

Nok worked his wrist faster. A drop of sweat fell from his forehead and hit the lit end of the mugwort. It sputtered, and for a moment – just a moment – his eyes flicked toward it, distracted.

Long enough.

His concentration broke, and along with it, the binding between the herb-smoke and the malignancy. The goatherd cried out in pain as the black-grey tendril of energy retracted back into her knee quick as a snapped string—

'*Stay.*'

Shamaness Jiwa reached out with an open palm across the table, then clinched it into a fist. The tendril froze in the air, then swayed gently, as though in a trance.

'Give me the mugwort,' she directed, voice strained. But she gave Nok a quick smile as he placed the bundle in her free hand.

The shamaness worked her wrist. The tendril snaked back upward toward the bundle of herbs. Another moment and it was done, the black-grey energy shrouded and subsumed by the herb-smoke. The shamaness dropped the bundle of mugwort into a bowl of water. The smoulder went out of it with a truncated *hiss*.

'Be gone,' Jiwa intoned. She cut through the lingering

cloud of smoke and illness with one hand. It dissipated as though it had never been.

The goatherd sat up on the table and prodded her knee. Already, the swelling was fading. The old woman murmured a reflexive prayer, touching three triangulated fingertips to her forehead in a sign of thanks before taking Jiwa's hands gratefully in her own.

'Sorry,' Nok mumbled after the old woman had left.

'What for?' Jiwa asked.

'I messed up.'

The shamaness dipped her hands in a basin of water, then used a clean cloth to slowly blot them dry. 'You're learning, Nokhai. Learning demands failure. Do you think I did this correctly the first time I tried?'

'Well ... yes?' She was so consummately competent that it was difficult to imagine otherwise.

'Well,' she said, mimicking his tone. 'I didn't.' She gentled the teasing with a warm smile. It felt uncomfortably like charity. 'You will get there. I know this.'

But how can you? The words stuck in his throat. He swallowed them; if there was anything he had a talent for, it was not asking questions.

'Is there anything else I can do while I'm here?' he offered instead.

'Yes,' Jiwa said, pulling the cloth from the table where the goatherd had sat. 'You can share lunch with me.'

'I'm not hungry.'

If Nasan had been here, she'd tease him for pouting. The thought sent a pang through him; he'd spent years without his sister, believing she was dead. A few weeks of having her back and he'd already grown accustomed to her company.

He would see her soon enough. Once he was done here.

'Stop brooding and sit,' Jiwa said, punctuating her words by slapping a spoon into his hand. 'Energy pullings take a lot out of a person.' She slid two wooden bowls onto the table.

'Good thing I didn't do one, then,' he said, more petulant than he'd intended. But he picked up one of the bowls, prodding at the congealed porridge with his spoon.

Jiwa sat across from him and dug into her own bowl. Her movements in all things, this included, had a spare, economical elegance that somehow made him think of home. His first home. His real home, he supposed. Jiwa even reminded him a bit of his cousin Idri. Perhaps it was only because they were of age with another – or, at least, the age Idri had been when she'd died.

'I don't know what you want from me,' he blurted.

The shamaness did not seem surprised by the outburst. 'What I want is for you to return tomorrow. The steppe is full of goatherds with bad knees, or backs, or burns, or strange rashes, and tomorrow will bring more of them to us for healing.'

'All right,' he said. But the sense he'd lingered too long itched like fresh skin over a wound. 'Has there been any news of when your head shamaness will arrive?'

He had thought himself a full Pactmaker, able to caul – shift his body – into any of the animals who had made ancient agreements with the Gifted, whose beast gods had appeared to him on the shores of Yunis. He would still have his original wolf's caul, but also that of all the other Kiths. Too, as a Pactmaker, he would have the ability to grant the gift of cauling to others.

So, in the barren steppe, amid the rubble of Yunis, he'd first drawn upon the golden eagle, hoping to fly from there, find his sister. Find Lu. But though he'd begged and prayed, first in Yueh, then his Kith's dialect of B'shon, and finally without words at all, nothing came. No surge of strength from the core of his belly, no rush of heat in his veins, no comforting velvet strength in his muscles. Nothing to alleviate the silence around and within him, nor the pain in his leg that, as the rush of survival wore off, he was quickly beginning to register as a sprain.

Finally, he'd been forced to assume his wolf's caul and limp off through the barren steppe. Fleet, but not airborne, and in desperate need of help.

'Are you so impatient to meet her, the Our Mother?' Jiwa asked.

'That's why I'm still here, isn't it? Your head shamaness is supposed to teach me how to access all my cauls at will. If she ever gets here.'

He didn't mean to be short. These women had healed his wounds and fed him. They'd sent a message to their Our Mother. There was little they could do but wait.

But the call to the Our Mother had gone out nearly two weeks ago. Word travelled slowly across these dry lands, if at all. One could shout into the steppe all they liked, but there was no guarantee anyone would hear it.

Everyone I love in this world thinks I'm dead. Nasan has had to lose me twice.

'She will come,' Jiwa said, as though hearing his doubts.

'How do you know?' he said aloud. 'We haven't heard anything—'

'The Our Mother will come.'

Jiwa's words held a knife's edge of devotion. Nok studied her. She was all solemn dark eyes fringed with thick lashes. Deadly serious. Not just an adherent – a believer. It made him think of Lu when she spoke of her birthright, or Nasan when she argued for her people. *Their* people, as she was always pointing out. It was funny; these memories were of both girls at their most maddening – irritating, even – but they only made him miss them more.

Jiwa's zeal made him think of his father, too, something he mostly tried to avoid. But he'd seen the same light in his father's eyes when he'd insisted the Kith keep the path, defend their home and fight. When he'd rushed off into battle, hungry for glory, leaving his wife and children to die alone.

Was there anything Nok believed in that strongly? Only, perhaps, the vastness of his own uncertainty.

'You really trust in her,' he said. 'Your head shamaness.'

'I do.'

'Why?'

'The Our Mother sees things others don't.'

'So do mad people and little children.' He said it with a carelessness he didn't feel and was instantly sorry.

But Jiwa spoke before he could apologise. 'The Our Mother sees *truths*.'

'Like what?' He sat forward to show his earnest interest.

Jiwa looked away for a moment. 'When I was born,' she said finally, 'everyone thought I was a boy. They were wrong, of course. I knew the truth in my heart. But it's hard to live the truth when everyone around you sees its opposite. It makes you feel ever a bit unreal. Alone. People aren't meant to be alone.'

She sighed, stirring the contents of her bowl. 'But I was. And then the Our Mother came to my village. She was making the yearly rounds – seeking gifted girls from the area to come and serve the Order. I wasn't one of the ones presented to her, of course. I had some aptitude – mostly with herbology – but I was a boy. Or so everyone thought. But she saw me. And she knew. I left with her the next day.'

Nok met her dark eyes. There was no mistaking Jiwa now for anyone other than who she was. She wore the dull green-grey robes of her station. Her lank black hair was separated into three loose plaits spangled with beads that draped over her shoulders. Three golden-yellow dots were painted across the crest of each of her high cheekbones. She would earn more markings as her training continued; some of the older shamanesses Nok had seen scarcely had any unpainted skin left, their sun-hardened faces a matrix of fading yellow lines and swirls.

'I learned there were others like me. Some of them were here, some were not. Some of the girls here were not like me. But the Our Mother gave us all a home, a community,' Jiwa said. 'Is there anything more meaningful to human life than having a place where one belongs in this world?'

I'll let you know once I find mine.

The door slammed behind them. Nok jumped, nearly upsetting his bowl of porridge. A neophyte stood in the doorway. He recognised her, though not by name.

'Charsi, welcome,' Jiwa said. If she was startled by the girl's sudden entrance, it did not show.

'Did I scare you?' the neophyte asked Nok as he stood.

'You did.' He grimaced.

'I was skilled as a hunter back in my home village before I was chosen to serve the Order, but even I should not be able to surprise a wolf,' Charsi said, though not unkindly. Most of the neophyte girls spoke this way to him: in frank, unflinching observation, rather than judgement. Like Nasan, but without the sly malice.

'I always thought a Pactmaker would be more naturally gifted.'

Her words piqued Nok's existing uneasiness. Had his contract with the beast gods really happened? If so, why couldn't he unlock his power? But then, nothing had ever come easily to him. Not his gifting dream, not friends, not being a son, a brother, an Ashina.

Jiwa cleared her throat. 'Charsi, is there a reason you're gracing us with your company?'

'Oh, yes.' The girl nodded. 'The Our Mother has arrived.'

Nok was on his feet before he'd even thought to stand. *Lu.*

'They told me to bring Nok to her,' Charsi continued. 'Can I take him now?'

Nasan, Nok amended. If all went well here, he would see his sister again soon.

'I'm ready,' he said aloud, before Jiwa could speak for him. 'Let's go.'

★

The Our Mother had a kind face, worn and weathered and brown as the shell of a nut. She sat on a stack of carpets at the far end of the temple building, tended by shamanesses encouraging her to take a sip of water, to rest, to drape another blanket over her lap. She was stout, yet haunted by the spectre of frailness that follows very old age. She was smaller than he'd expected. He hadn't realised it until that moment, but he'd been imagining an older version of Vrea, the oracle of Yunis, stately and towering. This woman looked like any of the aunties he'd known growing up. Yet, like those aunties, there was a canniness in her eyes that told him she was not to be underestimated.

'Ten thousand years ago, this earth crashed into a star,' she said. Her voice was like burlap stretched tight, scratchy and thin and coarse. The hall had been alive with murmurs, but they evaporated now.

'The collision was so hard, so fast, the two fused together,' the Our Mother continued. Her eyes were closed. 'The star was populated by spirit peoples – ethereals. The survivors of the collision established a new city, what we today call Yunis. That is why the earth holds different properties, different powers, in the North.

'Where the earth and the star met, that seam, is called the Inbetween. The people who live there are halfway between this world and the next – halfway between flesh and spirit. Planet and star. Earth and light. Their magic is denser, more tied to the here. They learned to communicate with the lower animal gods, to change skins.'

A smile emerged on her face like ripples on the surface of a pond. She opened her eyes. Age clouded them with a drifting, pearlescent white. And yet, when she looked at him, she *saw*. He could feel it.

'All that had to elapse between the end of nothing and this moment to bring us together, Nokhai of the Ashina. And I am so happy it did.'

'I ...' He hesitated. Someone gave him a shove from behind. He stumbled. Looking back, he found Charsi staring at him with bland innocence. He made the rest of the walk forward on his own.

'Closer, darling,' the Our Mother said, her smile slight and maternal. 'The light is dim in here and I'd like to see you better.'

He wanted to tell her that was the consequence of building a temple underground. Instead, he stepped into the pale, flickering glow of one of the lamps lining the walls. He had the feeling somehow, that she did not need the light.

'My daughters here tell me you are a Pactmaker,' she said warmly. 'That you have the caul of each beast god at your disposal – and that you may Gift them to others if you so wish.'

'That's what I was told.'

'You do not know yourself?'

'Well, I have my caul. The caul of an Ashina. But that's all. I can't do the others. So ...' He could hear the hopeful ring in his voice, false and childish, but he said it anyway: 'Maybe they were wrong? Maybe that's not me after all.'

The Our Mother was nodding slightly as he spoke, not unlike someone's doddering grandmother drifting off to sleep on a hot afternoon. When he finished though, she smiled, and Nok suddenly had the unpleasant sensation he was being read like words on a page.

'You want them to be wrong.'

'No!' he said quickly. 'Well, I'm ... I know the world needs a Pactmaker. But I just, it can't be me, because I can't ... I can't even do an energy pulling. I've never been especially strong or brave, or all that smart. It just doesn't make sense. How am I supposed to be a conduit for the gods into this world? I-I don't even know how to *be* in this world.'

'Oh, sweet child.' The Our Mother's cloudy eyes gleamed in the scant light. 'You're doing a fine job right now, standing before me. You look entirely solid. Quite alive.'

In spite of himself, Nok felt his throat constrict. 'Maybe so. But it's really hard.'

'To just be this,' she said.

'Yes.'

She nodded, and he was shocked to see a narrow tear work its way down her lined face. Then, abruptly, she laughed. Had she been anyone else he might have flinched, but the sound she made was kind. Rueful and knowing. 'Just wait until you are as old as me,' she said.

I won't live to be as old as you, he thought, and realised he believed it. He'd never even expected to live this long. And yet he had outlived so many others who hadn't deserved to die.

'It is difficult to be what we are,' the Our Mother mused. 'We are a contradiction. On the outside, only meat. On the inside, though ...' She looked to him like she expected him to complete the sentence.

More meat, he thought.

No, said another voice. One he felt – understood, viscerally – rather than heard.

On the inside we are eternal and expansive; smoke and ether and swirling cosmic waters.

He looked up sharply. The Our Mother just smiled again.

'I know what my daughters called me here for. What you told them. But now that I am here, what is it you need from me, child?'

'Will it always be like this?' The question tumbled out of him, like water flowing over the lip of a cup filled too high. 'Will it always be this hard?'

'Come here, child.'

He stepped closer.

She raised a hand. His own followed as though compelled by some magic. But before she pressed her fingertips to his wrist, she asked, 'May I?' and waited for him to nod. Then she did it once again before pressing a thumb to his forehead, between the eyes, at the spot where his eyebrows itched to knit together in concern.

Energy emanated in the wake of her touch. Like cool water seeping under his skin.

He recoiled at the shock of it.

'Stay still now,' she chided. 'I'm mapping your meridians.'

She hummed, nodding to herself. 'Yes. There's a blockage. More like a chain of them – like an archipelago.'

'What ... what are they?'

'Scar tissue and calcium, tartar ... and rot,' she murmured. 'This is an old wound, never fully healed.' She released him. 'I cannot heal you. But perhaps we can find a way for you to heal yourself.'

'I can't ...' He saw the dark slip of malignant energy falling away, back into the goatherd's knee. 'I can't even do an energy pulling. I don't know—'

'You do. I can see it in you. We are going to take a small journey to find it.'

'Our Mother, you must not do this!'

Nok started at the sound of Jiwa's voice. The shamaness emerged from the shadows at the entrance of the temple. She must have come in while they were talking.

'You are too old to expend your energy,' Jiwa protested. 'Use mine instead. I am young, and I mean little. I beg you.'

'Your offer is beautiful, our daughter Jiwa. But this will not require my life energy, nor yours. This a journey that Nokhai of the Ashina must take on his own, within himself. He already has all that he needs.'

The Our Mother placed her fingers on his forehead again, and this time she *pushed*. She didn't move, but Nok had the sudden sensation of falling—

When he opens his eyes, a banquet is ready. He smells it before he sees it, and just by smelling it, he remembers everything:

The Kith has spent the morning rolling out dough for dumplings, chopping greens, borrowing spices from this neighbour or that one, while aunties argue over how to perfect their family sauces. All to honour an emperor they have never seen. A man who lives leagues away, and who they only know by the barest, furthest ripples of his power.

But no matter; for the Ashina, a guest is a guest. And now, the pheasant dumplings, piles of skewered grilled vegetables and dried honeyed fruits sit stacked in steaming, glorious pyramids. Now vats of hot milk tea big enough to bathe in rest over spicy-smelling wood fires. Only one task remains.

He looks to his left and sees the goats, just as he knows he will. Young and spirited, the little beasts kick at the ends of their rope leads, nipping at one another's floppy brown ears.

'No,' he whispers – but to no one. The room where he'd been with the Our Mother is gone. He is alone, here in the past. He can hear the childish panic in his voice. He knows this particular bitter memory; he already lived it some five years ago. He knows what is coming but there's nothing, no one to stop it.

I've already done this.

The men step forward and take their positions, each beside one of the goats.

Don't make me do it again.

They joke and laugh and move in easy motions that feel big and impossible to his eyes. He's supposed to grow into that – a man, a warrior, someone who slips into his place like it's a well-worn pair of boots. He doesn't understand how. The other boys seem to know already, somehow. But it is as though Nok was born with a crucial organ missing.

He watches them, and although he stands there like a spectre, a ghost, a thing out of time, he feels his own knees fold beneath him. He feels the hard-packed earth. There's a small rock biting into his right kneecap. He knows he can't do anything about it without looking like a fidgety child. Without angering his father.

His father ...

Nok looks to his side and there he is, shadowy and large and sure. The goat in his father's grasp blinks back at him, golden eyes hooded under long lashes. His father has a practiced hand; his goat will die well.

Nok's own hands shake.

'Go!' comes the shout. The men's knives descend, quick and clean. Eight goats pitch forward, skipping and flailing as though in a rollicking collective dance. One by one, they come down hard onto the packed earth, spurts of blood measuring the rhythm of their hearts' swansong. Nok makes himself watch. Around him, everyone cheers: his Kith, and the visitors, too. The emperor, his retinue, and his pretty, eldest daughter, who is only a child, but whose angled, coppery eyes Nok would recognise anywhere. In any time.

In his hands, his goat is still alive. It smells blood and though it is only a kid, it recognises in some primal way its own death.

His knife goes in. Too high. He can feel the error as it happens, and yet he cannot stop himself. And now the goat is screaming, flopping and streaking blood in wild, wide spurts. And now his father is wrestling it to the ground. And now his father raises his own knife, and he has ended it.

Nok already knows the look of disbelief on his father's blood-streaked face as he gazes up at his son over the goat's body.

He is a coward; he looks away. Down at his own

shaking hands, down at the red-brown earth, pooling with black blood.

The blood reminds him of another time – only a spare few moons later than this banquet. He sees it, just for a moment, like a flash of lightning in the dark: His father, Delgar, lying prone, gazing up at the sky with a vacancy he'd never displayed in life. There is blood seeping from the edges of those eyes, red and radial as the petals of a flower that does not grow here in the desert.

Nok blinks, and Delgar's body is gone, leaving only black lifeblood pooling on the dry earth. The goat's, or his father's?

'Nokhai.'

Nok looks up. His father's disappointment-ravaged gaze, the one from his memory, is gone. The man looking at him now is present. He sees.

'So then,' his father says. 'You've returned.'

4

Ashes

'They'll tear her to pieces.'

The voice drifting down was low and terse. Min's eyes fluttered. Colours smeared together incoherently above her.

'We have to get her out of here.'

She blinked and the hazy colours became the painted ceiling of Kangmun Hall. A searing, acrid stench assailed her. Tears rose in her eyes against the sting of smoke. She blinked hard and a stern, haggard face materialised, gazing down.

'My head hurts,' she told the face. Her mouth seemed to move too slowly. 'My skin hurts.'

'You're lucky to be alive,' Yuri said harshly. Unsurprising. The man had been Lu's sword instructor since they were little girls; a man prone to any softness, any yielding, would not have survived the position.

'Luck had nothing to do with it,' Brother countered. He bent and took her hands up in his own, caressing them as though they were sacred objects. 'Not a single burn. Not even a singe.'

'Her hair is a different story.'

Min raised a hand to the side of her head and felt ash fall away under her fingertips. She shuddered, belatedly registering several of her nail guards were missing.

'Eight dead,' Yuri grumbled, shaking his head.

'Who's dead?' Min croaked.

He looked down again. 'Not you, apparently.'

'And thank the heavens for that.' Brother fluttered beside her, soft as a moth. How could such a dry stick of a creature be filled with such ambition, such envy, such lust?

'Who's dead?' Min repeated.

The men exchanged dark looks.

'No one of great consequence,' Brother told her, just as Yuri said, 'A few magistrates were trampled trying to flee the Hall.' Both men went silent, looking at one another. Yuri spoke again, louder, as though to pre-emptively drown out the monk: 'One server. A boy of nine.'

Nine. Min imagined herself at that age. A shrinking, silly child with a whole unlived life ahead of her.

Footsteps approached at a quick clip, chasing the thought from her mind. A eunuch pushed his way through the hall doors.

'Rioters are blocking the main entrance to the Ring. We will need to open one of the service gates so those who were at court might return home. They're growing anxious.' He kept his voice low, but the hall was empty and silent but for the occasional popping ember, and Min could not help but overhear his words.

Brother cursed. 'How on earth did they make it into the First Ring? I thought we'd doubled the guards on the walls.'

'Rioters?' Min demanded. At least, she'd meant to demand it. Her voice was smoke-hoarse, barely above a whisper. She cleared her throat, ignoring the raw red pain, and tried again. 'Rioters have breached the First Ring?'

The eunuch's eyes flicked over to Brother, as though seeking his permission to speak to her. She itched to command he address her directly, but her burning throat won out. Brother dismissed the man with a wave of a hand, then turned to give her a slim, tight smile. He was as skilled in comfort as cold tea was warming. 'A few must have slipped in. Nothing to be concerned about, certainly. Just some angry peasants,' he told her.

'And w – what have they to be so angry about?' she demanded around a hacking cough.

'Nothing at all,' the monk said. At the same time, Yuri scoffed, 'Everything. They're poor.'

The looks they exchanged were positively venomous.

Min had supposed Yuri loyal to her sister, but Brother told her the man had provided great assistance in Set's coup. He was a man loyal to his own advancement, like all the rest. She supposed Yuri must be of some vital use to them yet; Brother clearly did not keep him around out of fondness.

Whatever ire they bore for each other could not rival the fury broiling in Min's chest, though.

'Explain. I won't have secrets kept from me,' she said with deliberate calm, as though she were speaking to a pair of errant boys. 'I am not my father.' She didn't quite know what that meant, only that it felt good, and a bit vengeful, and that the hidden vein of truth it cut into made her feel wise and grown.

When the men did not respond, she pressed on. 'Well? I've never been poor, have I? Explain it to me.'

'Just a temporary disruption in the food supply chain,' Brother told her. 'Our grain stores were low due to last summer's drought, and we've been having ah, some ... complications getting grain into the city.'

'Can't they grow their own?' Peasants were farmers, if they weren't tinkerers or blacksmiths, surely.

'Grow ... grow their own? In the city?' Brother repeated. This time the looks he exchanged with Yuri were confused – until they weren't. Brother hesitated; Yuri looked away in disgust.

Min's face went hot with understanding. Then the panic set in. She'd said something very stupid.

It's not my fault! I wasn't taught the things Lu was ...

But that didn't matter. These men did not care; no one did. Nothing mattered to them but what Min could give them. A thing to be used up and stripped for its component parts.

If she let them.

Or, she could kill the useless voice within her. Only then could she find a way to turn the game around on them, these smug and knowing men. Only then would she find a way to survive.

'Come on. Up with you,' Yuri snapped, pulling her by the elbow. But his gnarled hands were surprisingly gentle. She yanked her arm away and rose on her own, brushing ash from her robes, as though that would make any difference.

'I'll take her to her chambers,' Brother said, interjecting

his spindly hands between them, coaxing her arm into their grasp.

Yuri shook his head. 'Those magistrates and secretaries were running scared from the fire, but if they see her now? Like this? A little girl with burnt hair? They're liable to kill her. You heard what they were calling her. Even before this.'

Witch. Did they think she didn't know? *Just say the word. I'm not afraid.*

'Of course I have heard,' Brother said loftily. 'Men of my power and interests know all about such persecutions. Who better to protect her than me?'

Yuri's hand went to the hilt of his sword, slung in its usual place at his waist. 'Someone who can wield a weapon, perhaps?'

Brother's lip raised in the barest suggestion of a sneer, but Min did not miss the shine of fear in his eyes, the softly-slippered half-step backward that he took. Still, he did not release her hand from his own.

'Empress Minyi already has all the weapons she needs.'

'Certainly,' Yuri said. He gestured at the ruins about them. 'But can she control them?'

Min looked around for the first time — truly looked. The muralled walls of Kangmun Hall were scorched in high, wild black arcs. Upon the dais sat a charred, gnarled stump of timber blanketed with soot. The remains of the throne Kangmun had commissioned, and from which generations of monarchs before her had built their empire.

The windows were unmarred, though their glass was fogged with heat. Outside them, the rain fell, steady. Trees bowed under its stern weight. The thunder, it seemed, had rolled on past.

'She is still learning,' Brother said, his cool hands still grasping her own. Min pulled away from him.

'No,' she said. And hearing the tremor in her voice, she repeated the word louder: '*No*.'

'Empress—' Brother began, and with every syllable she felt that possessive *want* emanating from him, like noxious gouts of yellow-green smoke.

She was too tired to scream. Too tired to lash out and strike him, rake her fingernails down his pallid cheeks.

She looked instead to Shin Yuri.

Could he be trusted? He wasn't one for lying, perhaps, but that alone didn't make a person honourable. Then again, what use was a man of honour in this world? What, even, was honour in a soldier, but gilt laid over a blade? Pretty to look at, but in a battle he would use the sword to cut your head off all the same.

'Shin Yuri is correct,' she said. 'I'll be safer in his care. He will escort me back to my apartments. You should go and speak with what amenable magistrates and officials you can find. Rally them around me until this has ... settled.'

She saw the protest in his eyes and so she used what little energy she had remaining to put hardness into her own. Seeing that edge and flash, he bowed low.

'As you wish, Your Highness.'

'And find Butterfly, and the other girls. Send them to my apartments.' The fools had fled in the chaos.

'Of course, Your Highness.'

'If they expect to serve me, they will need to build up stronger constitutions.'

'I will tell them as much, Your Highness.'

He swept from the room, light as dust.

'You can't trust him,' Yuri said, barely audible under the echo of the closing doors.

'But I suppose I should trust you?'

He went silent. She turned to study him. He gazed back gravely, as though she were a thing that might break – or perhaps explode – at any moment.

'You were Lu's shin,' she said slowly, watching for his reaction to her sister's name. A tremor; did she imagine it? She probed on, fingers tracing over armour, searching for flesh. 'But you were more than that to her, weren't you?'

'You need to rest,' he said. 'Let us go to your apartments.'

'You cared about her – you care about Lu,' she pressed.

He hesitated, but his eyes did not leave her face.

'Yes,' he said at last. 'As though she were my own child.' The words were sacred, like a blood oath.

And what was an oath but a promise? A liability. She had found it. Even in this gnarled, strong man, there it was. The thinnest skin, tender and untouched by light or hands, like the sac around a human heart.

'Lu would want you to help me,' Min said.

And she could feel them realise at the same moment that it was true, like feeling the wind change direction. It was barely even trickery. 'Lu' – she weighted her sister's name with all the worry and pain she imagined he might feel – 'would want you to keep me safe.'

Yuri did not speak, but nor did he look away.

'Tell me how to survive,' Min pressed. 'Tell me what I need to do to stay alive here.'

He shook his head, breaking eye contact. 'I can't help you.'

Irritation flared in the cauldron of her gut. Her own fault. She had let herself grow too gentle with him. Who did he think he was, that he would have a choice in this? That he could allow himself these split loyalties? He lived or died at her pleasure. Irritation leapt inside her, a flame that unfurled into anger.

She saw a flash of scarlet before her eyes and something thrummed in her veins. Something familiar, and all at once not her own.

'*Even after all these years, you're still letting me down.*'

The voice that passed through her cracked lips belonged to another. She recognised it nevertheless – and so did Yuri. His head snapped up.

Tsai. The name rose in her throat like bile. Her curse, her gift. The thing she needed, and the thing she reviled. She felt a rush of power surge through her, and had to clench her hands to tamp it down. She'd thought the creature gone, but in truth it had only sunk deeper into her – etched its name on her bones, knitted itself into the marrow—

'Tsai?'

The word had not come from her – neither part of her. It came from Yuri. And the way he said it, it wasn't a curse at all, but something holy and precious and so long ago lost.

No one had ever said her name that way, and perhaps that was how Min recognised it for what it was: *love*.

The creature abated, descended. And in its wake, Min saw her opportunity.

'She's in me,' she whispered. 'I have her spirit – and her power. She may have given birth to Lu, but *I* am her daughter.'

'How … ?' He was staring at her in wonder, as though searching for traces of her in Min's grey eyes, in the set of her mouth. But she was hidden away, in a place only Min could access.

A new weakness. She would not let this one slip through her fingers.

Yuri reached for her, too quickly. He only meant to take her arm, to lend her his stability. But she flinched, holding her open hands before her instinctively. She felt the burning, roiling itch of her magic gather in her palms like a living thing before she could help it. Yuri stopped, but did not retreat. Tiny tongues of crackling light licked out from her skin, twining about her fingers. She curled them into a slow fist, cradling the heat, willing it down.

'S-sorry,' she murmured. 'It takes a while for it—' She stopped. She didn't owe him an apology.

But he did not seem to expect one anyway. 'Come with me,' he said gruffly, taking her deliberately but slower now by the elbow.

'Where are we going?' she asked warily. 'My apartments?'

'No,' he said, his grip tightening on her. 'To the dungeons.'

Min recognised the man crouching on the floor right away.

The heavy door to the cell slammed behind her, solid wood on wood. She turned in alarm. Yuri had closed the three of them in together. For privacy.

And if not ... magic itched in her palm, begging for release. She clenched a fist around it.

Control.

The upper floor of the prison building was filled with open-air cages, the prisoners held behind walls of crisscrossed solid wood beams. Down here in the lower level, the rooms were stone. Built to contain the most dangerous of criminals.

The man before her did not look dangerous. But then, she'd seen before that he had two faces: the weakling who wet himself at her cousin's feet, and the cunning creature behind the mask. The face that looked up at her now was blank and expectant in the dim light of Yuri's lantern.

She stepped closer. And felt ... a visceral sense of recognition. No – not recognition. That was what she, Min, felt. The thing inside her pulsed with *familiarity*. A near-physical feeling weighted with memories she could not recall.

'You shouldn't be here,' the prisoner said, but the words were directed past her. 'You never did have any judgement.'

'You're one to talk. Can you not see what I've brought?' Yuri raised his oil lamp higher, illuminating her in full, from the limp, ruined fall of what remained of her hair to the charred ends of her robes. The flame flared and danced as he moved, and Min winced, dizzy with how the shadows in the cell deepened and shivered in response.

'Yes, I noticed her,' the prisoner said dryly. 'The cell *is* rather small—'

'You don't know who she is. *What* she is.'

'The small princess?' the prisoner asked, his brow creasing.

The small princess. The younger one, the weak one. The one who was not Lu. She was sick to death of being a thing only in relation to others. Sick to death of men talking around her, about her, through her, as though she could not hear them – as though it did not matter one way or the other.

The frizzled burn of energy prickled under Min's palms. Again, she made to clench her fist around it, but this time, narrow tendrils broke free. The force of it splayed her fingers, and the energy snaked up her arms, a dozen glittering bracelets of sparks.

'My name is Minyi,' she snarled.

She stepped closer to him, and there it came again – the distinct sensation of familiarity.

This time though, she leaned into it, pressed forward another step. The man watched her approach warily – and then those dark cunning eyes went wide. He felt it, too. That keen familiarity between them. It burned brighter, louder even than her fury, until all she could think was to seek it, to understand it.

Before she could think better of it – of the grime on his hands, the filth caking the rushes on the floor of his cell – she knelt and reached out a hand toward him.

He took it, and the world fell away.

When her sight returns, she is standing in daylight, impossibly bright. She winces, blinks, and all at once realises the body she is in is not her own. It is heavier, broader – and then, too, her mind is not her own.

'Ohn?'

She looks up. An instinctive response to his own name. 'What?'

'I asked what you thought.' Yuri leans forward, the smooth, youthful planes of his face creasing in annoyance.

'Thought about what?'

'This.' Yuri gestures around them. They stand at the edge of a courtyard. It is empty, save for a cluster of girls at the far end.

'Remarkable,' Ohn says. 'Such beautiful paving stones, the likes of which I've never seen before.'

'Don't be daft. I brought you here for the girls.'

Ohn raises an eyebrow. 'What use do I have for girls? I'm a monk.' But he turns toward them nevertheless, hands on his hips. 'All right, tell me what I'm meant to see.'

'Don't look,' Yuri hisses. He paces the edge of the yard in a tight track. If this is his attempt at appearing casual, it fails. 'Do you see?'

'How can I? You told me not to look!'

'Well, look a *little*.'

Ohn does. Four girls, sweeping the courtyard with straw brooms. The brooms are short, forcing them to hunch. They look like morose old women. Each wears a telltale white robe. The Yunian hostages. 'Shamanesses,' he says.

'No: *a* shamaness,' Yuri corrects. He draws his sword and levels it in their direction. 'That one.'

A fifth girl. Ohn hadn't noticed her. She squats in the dirt, apart from the others. Her broom lays across her lap. She stares down at it accusingly, as though it has insulted her. Black hair hangs down around her shoulders. Back in Yunis, her Order would have shorn it, but Yunis has disappeared and with it, Ohn supposes, its rules.

'Very well, I'll bite,' he sighs. 'What's special about her?'

'Nothing.' Yuri lets his sword drop.

'Nothing,' Ohn repeats. 'You brought me here to show me a not-special girl. Wonderful.'

'Perfect, even,' Yuri says cheerily. 'She's neither pretty, nor ugly. She's never left an offering or burned a single stick of incense for an ancestor. She doesn't have friends, or really any enemies. I've never seen her talk to anyone. The other girls forget she's there half the time.'

'What's her name?'

Yuri considers. 'I think it started with an 's' sound. Or was it an 'm?''

'You want to coerce her into committing treason, but didn't ask for her name?'

'Keep your voice down. And I didn't talk to her directly.'

'Then how'd you learn all this about her?'

'Another shamaness. Dok.' Yuri's face lights up when he says her name, just the way it's supposed to.

'Mhmm,' Ohn says wryly – just as he's supposed to. It's easy, falling into the familiar rhythm of their patter. Yuri's ogling, his own exaggerated exasperation. 'And this Dok, she just ... told you all this? Out of the goodness of her heart?'

'I asked nicely.' Yuri considers for a moment, then grins. '*Very* nicely.'

And if he catches the spasm of unpleasantness gripping Ohn's face, what does it matter?

Ohn recovers quickly, at any rate. He rolls his eyes, manufactures a grin. A practiced approximation of the real thing. 'You know shamanesses are supposed to be celibate, right?'

'Tell *her* that.' Yuri frowns, thumbing nervously at the hilt of his sword. 'Anyway, compared with what we're planning, that's hardly anything at all, is it?'

'Are you having second thoughts?'

Yuri looks up, his jaw set firmly. He shakes his head. 'I can't go to war, Ohn. You know I can't. My mother – she's been so weak as it is. It would kill her.'

'There's no certainty you'd ... You were the best swordsman in your class.'

'That's like saying I'm the best swordsman in a sty of piglets with armour strapped on,' Yuri snorts. 'Nobody dies in a practice ring.'

'Not everybody dies in a war.'

'Let's switch places, then, if you like the odds so much.'

Once, Ohn would have reached out and taken his friend's hand. Back when they were boys newly enrolled in the imperial academy. But in the past few years, while they weren't looking, something has changed. He can't pinpoint when it happened, but the knowledge that they aren't to touch anymore has crept in and established itself.

'Let's talk to her,' Yuri says.

'Wait.' Ohn grabs his arm. 'What's in it for her?'

Yuri stares dumbly back at him. 'For her?'

'We're asking her to help us conspire to' – Ohn lowers his voice – 'you know. You don't think that maybe we need to offer some sort of incentive?'

That gets Yuri's attention. He sits back down. 'So, what do we do?'

'No family, no friends, no name,' Ohn murmurs. 'What does someone like that want, more than anything in the world?'

'She has a *name*, I just can't remember it.'

Ohn ignores him. 'My question wasn't rhetorical, you know. I'm open to suggestions.'

'How would I know what she wants?'

'You could've asked your ... sweetheart.'

'Dok's not my anything. And it's not like the girl talks to her. Or anyone, for that matter,' Yuri says. 'Like I told you, she doesn't have friends.'

'Lucky her,' Ohn sighs. 'Where is she from?'

Yuri perks up. '*That* I know. Dok told me she was born in a brothel down at the base of the mountain, near their temple.'

A common enough tale. Because they are already considered unclean, shamanesses can and did come from any and all walks of life, including country brothels.

Not that such low origins are limited to shamanesses. No one has told Ohn – and he has the good sense not to ask – but he is fairly certain his mother was one of the underfed girls skulking around the docks along the Milk River, or leaning against the doorframe of this or that known house in Scrap-Patch Row.

He used to wonder if he had ever walked right by her. He was sure that he would somehow know her if he saw her – it would simply be too cruel, too chaotic for the gods to allow otherwise. But that is stupid. He knows now that this world is a cup spilling over with cruelty

93

and chaos. And he hasn't thought about her in years. A mother. What was the point?

'Money?' Yuri muses, bringing him back.

'Have a lot of that handy, do you?' Ohn says, not missing a beat. Yuri's family might be wealthy, but this mainly manifests as gifts sent from the Yang home – brocade tunics, silver-toed boots, sweets wrapped in silk and foil. When it comes to actual coin, Yuri relies on his meagre stipend, just like anyone else.

'Let's just go and talk to her,' Ohn sighs.

The girl has shifted positions while they talked. Now she holds the broom in one hand, pointed at the ground, using the tip to scrawl something in the dirt. Ohn recognises it right away: an obscene line of verse from one of the bawdier poets popular among men of the court.

He looks sharply at Yuri. But Yuri isn't looking at him. He's looking at the girl.

Ohn looks, too. Up close, she looks bony as a street cat, and just as mean. As though sensing this appraisal, she meets his eyes with her own. Fierce and black.

And in that moment, Min knows her. Knows herself. The young versions of Ohn and Yuri disappear, along with the courtyard, and the daylight. Dark creeps in at the edges of the world like a drawstring pulling shut – closing out everything but the girl.

Tsai.

The shamaness's mouth falls open. The voice that emanates from within is a wordless shriek. Sound so big, it is like the oncoming rush of an ocean swell, pummelling Min in the chest, filling her vision with blood – and within that field of red, she sees someone else. With them, comes a chill, a sense of dread.

Death.

Their face comes into view, pale and cold as the moon, and Min knows her.

It is her mother, Rinvi.

Min fell back, clutching herself, fingers clawing at her robes, as though she meant to tear it out – only what was there to remove? How could she extract something that was a part of herself?

'What did you do?' a voice was demanding.

'I didn't – gods, what ... what *is* she? Yuri, she has – did you—'

Strong hands grasped Min's wrists, pulling her hands away from her body. She opened her eyes, still flailing, still wild, teeth bared.

Yuri stood above her – the Yuri of now, old enough for his hair to be streaked through with silver. She blinked, and his face shifted, smooth and youthful and unconcerned – perhaps a trick of the dim and flickering light—

Betrayal.

The thought came to her not as a word, but sensation. Just as before, when she'd recognised the prisoner – Ohn? Omair? – and felt the vast depth of a history she could not recall.

She jerked out of Yuri's grip.

'What did you all do to her?' she demanded.

The men exchanged a look. Watching them, she felt the sensation hit her over and over, an echo ricocheting between the narrow, dank walls of the cell. Her vision swam drunkenly, like her head were the clapper of a bell striking over and over—

Betrayal. Betrayal. Betrayal.

'We needed her help,' Ohn began. 'Your grandfather was about to start a war. I had a premonition of Yuri, and many men besides, dying in battle. The war would be a terrible mistake. I had the idea that we could perform a spell, to change your grandfather's mind. But I wasn't strong enough to perform it myself. We enlisted Tsai's help—'

'You used her,' Min corrected with a viciousness she felt but did not understand.

'We did.'

She looked up sharply at Yuri.

'We used her for her magic,' Yuri said. 'And when she needed us, we abandoned her.'

'It was more complicated than that,' Ohn protested.

'Was it?' Yuri demanded, his voice heavy with scorn. No, not scorn. Shame.

'We tried to help her. You did. I watched you. She wanted nothing to do with us. She didn't even want Daagmun's help—'

And my mother? Min wanted to ask, but not here – not them. 'I'm going back to my apartments,' she said, clutching her head.

'Empress ...' Yuri raised both hands toward her, showing her his scarred palms, as though mollifying a wild animal. 'You're not well. You need help to control this thing in you—'

Min laughed, a hollow, bitter sound she barely

understood. 'Control it? What, so you can use me, like you used her?'

'That's not what I—'

'Is this the bargain you made with Tsai? Did you tell her you could help her?' She scraped herself up off the filthy floor and drew herself up to her full height.

'Empress.' This time it was Ohn who spoke. She fixed him with a withering glare, but he did not seem to feel the heat of it. He watched her with sad eyes. 'Yuri is correct. The energy I sense in you is corrosive. It began as a curse, did it not?'

She hesitated, then nodded.

'It was never meant to last this long. The thing in you – it was only a part of Tsai, a manifestation of her fury, her scorn. It should have burned itself out long ago. It must be keeping itself alive by feeding off your own vital energy. It could kill you.'

He seemed to speak in earnest, but then, the best liars did. His words did not concern her either way. Death did not concern her. She still had time left. She turned toward the door.

'Empress,' Yuri said. 'You're not wrong about us – about me. But you can't trust the others, either. Brother? He thinks because he has access to your power, he can use you as leverage over the magistrates. But these men, they've been at this game far longer than he has. They have their clutches deep in the veins of this city, this kingdom. In ways he can't even imagine. He dreams of power like a child dreams; they were born into it. And they won't let him – or you – change that.'

Min turned to face him, feeling the itch in her palms,

heat like want, spreading to the tips of her fingers. 'And I suppose you think I should look to you for guidance, then. The lesser of two evils.'

He looked very tired. 'I like to think I've never been particularly evil. But I suppose I've never been quite good, either.'

Her fingers twitched. If she wanted, she could send a tongue of flame across the room now, slap that self-indulgent shame out of his mouth.

She clenched her hand into a fist. Better to save her energy. She felt him release a breath as she resumed her steps toward the door. This time, neither of them tried to stop her.

She could not win love the way Lu could. All she had was their fear. Enough of that, and she would not need anyone's love for anything at all. But in burning them, how could she avoid burning herself?

Tsai, I need you, she thought. But no, she was the source of the problem.

Perhaps, she realised with no small degree of dread, it was time to turn to a different sort of mother.

5

Memory

'A-are you really here?' Nok breathes. 'Or are you just my idea of who you are – who you were?'

The look of disdain on his father's face is painfully familiar. 'Would you know the difference?'

Nok tries to parse whether that is a thing he or his father is more likely to say, and finds he really doesn't know. Maybe the two of them aren't as different as they'd thought.

Where are they? He looks around for something to ground him in time and place, but there is nothing to see. Not the nothing of a barren landscape, but true, stark nothing.

A dream.

But then, why does he feel so awake?

Something brushes his leg. He recognises it, even by that barest touch: his wolf.

His father looks as well, but does not speak. Does not acknowledge what it took for the animal to be there.

Nok reaches down, feels coarse fur beneath his fingertips.

Shapes begin to materialise before him, like mirages

made substance. The longer he stares, the more tangible they become. As though his attention makes the world. The details fill in around them, the air growing dry and hot and unbearable, like a fever itching under the skin. Then come the smells. The heavy musk of goats. Sour tanned leather and burnt prayer offerings and that dusty, unmistakable non-odor of the sandy soil spreading endlessly toward the horizon. They are back home.

There is no banquet this time, no emperor. No Lu. Just a day that could have been any of a thousand of the ordinary, numbered days of Nok's childhood.

'Is this truly how you remember our home?' Delgar's voice is torn between disgust and disbelief.

'Yes ... what's wrong with it?' Nok asks. He's not the boy he once was, and he means for the words to be a challenge. But they sound plaintive and small. After all these years, he still fears his father's criticisms.

What's wrong with it? He had asked. But what he meant, just as he always had, was *what's wrong with me?*

His father does not respond to either question. Instead, he raises a hand, as though gesturing to some unseen thing in the distance.

Nothing changes at first. Then it is everything, and all at once. Above them, the sky stretches, deliriously blue and terrifyingly immense. Suddenly, here is the nutty aroma of boiling milk fat masking the musk of goats. Here are happy children toddling after one another, round-cheeked and screeching. And here is laughter – everywhere. So warm it's like sunlight dappling Nok's eyelids.

This world of his father's is lush, saturated. Alive. This is a place that was loved.

It may as well be somewhere Nok has never been.

His father lowers his hand. The chatter and light and colours die away like sundown. They are back in Nok's memory of home now – his world. Barren and still by contrast.

It is easy, he thinks, to love what already loves you.

His father strides forward and Nok follows. Their footsteps are soft and pillowed against the sand. Absently, he reaches out a hand and the wolf bumps up against him, reassuring and warm.

'That creature isn't a pet,' his father says. 'The wolf comes easy to us because of the Pact. It is drawn inexorably toward our people – it can scarcely help but come to us. But that doesn't mean you should indulge in it.'

'Mine didn't come easy,' Nok replies.

'Yes, well, you did little to make yourself a suitable master, did you.' He does not frame it as a question.

Nok holds out his hand again, seeking the comfort of fur beneath his fingers, but this time there is nothing. He looks down and sees a void. Only his father remains. Nok can smell him, the fermented milk on his breath, greasy leather, the oil he runs through his hair to keep it flat and sleek. Nok's guts twist like wringing out a wet rag. The world shivers and shines before him, precarious.

'You give too much of yourself when you caul, and you ask too much in return,' his father continues. 'You cannot ask the Wolf, the Eagle, the Asp, to affirm your existence when they answer your call. How can you receive them when you are not whole yourself? A cracked pot cannot hold water.'

Nok blinks, and tears brim in his eyes, then fall.

There are hands on his wrists.

The Our Mother. The thought ignites like cheer in his chest. Like finding the stub of a candle, a flint, in the growing darkness.

But, no. It is his father's hands, gripping his wrists like he might break them. Hope ghosts out before it can truly begin.

'Mother?' his father repeats aloud, and his voice is heavy with scorn. 'Your mother is dead.'

'And so are you.'

The words have left his lips before he realises: this is true. A weight lifts. His father has released him.

Nok lowers his hands from the pose of supplication they'd been forced into. 'I want to see her,' he blurts.

'What?' For the first time, there is an edge of uncertainty to his father's voice. It is such a foreign, impossible thing that he's unsure if it's real. So he speaks again:

'You're dead, and I see you. Let me see *her*, then.'

His father hesitates, and Nok knows then that he has understood correctly.

'You're here because I think it has to be you,' he says slowly. 'I've always thought it had to be you. Because that made things harder. But it doesn't have to be like that, does it?' Nok sets his jaw in triumph. 'I want to see Ma.' He is no longer speaking to his father, though. This is his journey, a world – whether a dream or not – of his own making. And he will see it through on his own terms.

She is touch before she is sight. He feels the warmth of her first, like he's an infant learning the world all over again from the beginning. And there she is: a figure before him, whole and lovely.

His father is still there, a silent figure of mute foreboding, but Nok raises a hand and he retreats. Just a few steps.

It is enough.

He realises suddenly that his mother is smaller than him. She's young. His father, too. Of course, he's grown, and they have stayed the same. They will never be older.

'Nokhai,' his mother murmurs, and her hand goes to his face, pats it softly. She does not seem to mind his tears beneath her warm fingertips.

'You were here all along,' he blurts. 'I didn't think to – I didn't know.' Hadn't thought to ask, to demand, to see her, because what he wanted always seemed so far outside his control.

'I'm your mother. Do you think I could ever leave you?'

She smiles. He sees now that he has her mouth, her eyes.

You look just like your mother.

One of the Kith's chattier aunties had told him that once, when he was small, long before the empire had set its soldiers upon his people and the world ended. That night, he'd stolen the little bronze mirror Idri kept among her things and searched for the evidence. He hadn't seen it at the time, had been so unfamiliar with his own reflection that he didn't yet understand how to break a face into its component parts. How to search for his mother amid the fragments.

Perhaps he hadn't wanted it to be true. Hadn't wanted to accept what it implied: that he was more his gentle mother than his harsh father. But he sees her now, sees that it is true. Save for the taut, dark scar streaking his cheek, his face is all hers. And for the first time, he is glad for it.

Her hand slips into his and it has the sensation of something lost returning, something long left ajar pushed back into place.

His father approaches on Nok's other side, looking somehow smaller than he did before. He gazes out before them, and when Nok follows his eyes, the landscape dissolves. It reminds him of when Yunis fell from the Inbetween: the solidity of a world falling away into a void. Colours and sound, but no earth, no horizon, no sky. Nothing to stand upon, just a hazy, suggestible possibility, like heat off sand on a summer day.

It calls to him, this vagueness. But when he steps forward, he feels his mother's hand slip out of his own and he looks back to her, questioning.

'We've reached our end. We can go no further,' she says regretfully.

He looks between them, his parents, and the beckoning void. 'What is that?' he asks.

Annoyance flits across his father's stern features. 'What are you talking about?' he says. Again, there is that edge of uncertainty. An almost childlike anxiety.

And Nok realises then that his father cannot see it. There is nothing in his eyes but a dull wet sheen; nothing reflected, nothing taken in. And he thinks he understands.

We've reached our end, his mother had said.

Nok looks into the beckoning tumult that lies ahead of him. Into the future.

When he glances back at his mother, she looks oddly

faint, like pigment splashed through with too much water. Like she is disappearing into the vague grey of the sky.

Was she always so quiet in life? Retiring and solemn? He realises, then, that he can't say. That the fear of his father had crowded out all else, shrank his world down to a colourless binary of fear, and relief of its absence. When he'd been with Ma, he'd been safe, and he'd been tired. Too tired, perhaps, to think of anyone else. He might have loved her best, but he had scarcely known her at all. And now he never will.

We can go no further.

'And what of me?' he wonders aloud. 'Should I go?'

He doesn't mean for his father to answer, but he does. Perhaps he always will, regardless, and that is something Nokhai will have to accept. 'That is up to you,' he says. 'You're a man now.'

Am I? Uncertainty flutters in Nok's chest. He looks back at them, and they are suddenly so, so far away. For a moment, he thinks they look hollow-eyed and gaunt. For a moment, he sees the careless hack that laid open his mother's throat, red and hot. The pulpy ruin of his father's skull, riddled with gleaming bits of white bone like seeds in old fruit. The remains of his face, contorted in rage and anguish.

Then Nok blinks and they are whole again. Young and lovely and troubled. They did their best, he thinks. This is how he will remember them.

He moves forward, into the void. Into this place where his mother and father cannot follow.

It is like vertigo, like falling without falling. He closes his eyes to steady himself, and when he opens them again, there is nothing but flame. A wall of fire before him. His gaze follows it upward, to where its peaks grasp and scrabble at a night sky, brown and choked with smoke.

He flinches and stumbles back – and then he hears it. Nasan. His sister's unmistakable shriek. Instinct jerks him forward, toward the sound, into the fire.

He sees them: Lu and Nasan, scrambling over rooftops, Jin at their heels. Loosened tiles cascade in their wake, their ceramic shiver and clink swallowed up by the fire's roar.

They're moving parallel to the walls of the Immaculate City, toward the Milk River. Lu must be taking them to shelter by the water. He feels a spike of relief in his chest; no one survives better than Nasan, and no one protects better than Lu. They will be safe. He will reach them and they will be—

The scene before him falls silent. Sudden, like a blow.

And in that silence, something moves in from the west.

Nok thinks it is water at first: wavelike, tumbling and fleet, filling the fetid ditches lining the streets, overspilling the gutters, dripping from the flared eaves of houses. But the movement is all wrong, and as it moves, he sees a residue in its wake. The colour too, is wrong. An uncanny, hypnotic blue that nature never made.

Smoke. But one without fire. It carries with it a strange sweetness, cloying as temple incense, but with a metallic undertone that is somehow alarming, that bespeaks poison and—

'*Run!*'

He jerks his head back toward Nasan's scream. The group have left the rooftops. They skitter through the streets, straight for the strange blue smoke. But they don't seem to see it.

No, he thinks without meaning to, without quite understanding why. They struggle toward it, and his heart seizes at the notion that the smoke may touch them. *Turn back*, he wants to say. But to where?

Nok lunges forward, into the flames, because that is his instinct. He will not watch his friends, his sister die. He will not lose Nasan again.

He closes his eyes against the glare of it, but it is too late. The fire has eaten through to the core of him. He is screaming, but the fire consumes the sound, just as it consumes everything else.

He tumbled forward and met the earth, dry and solid beneath his splayed palms. The impact kicked the air from his lungs, and when he drew a pained breath the air was cool. No smoke, no flames. He rolled onto his back. The Our Mother's face stared back down at him, luminous and intent.

'You have seen something,' she observed, her eyes never leaving his. 'And you have learned something.'

'I have to go,' he blurted up at her. He pushed himself upright. 'My sister—'

Pain flared in his side, where she had touched him earlier, just below the ribs. He curled in on himself without meaning to, pitching back toward the packed earth floor.

There, her voice chanted in his ear. *There*, his mother echoed. And he felt her fingertips press down against his flesh.

His mouth flooded sour. He hunched over and

retched. First, nothing. Then thin, yellow bile. His body seized again, this time with such violence his head hit the ground. He barely felt it; he was already retching a third time. The sound that came with it emerged from somewhere deep, as though his body were trying to purge itself of its very organs.

Something flew from his mouth and rolled shortly, coming to a rest an arm's reach from where he collapsed on the floor in a puddle of bile, smelling of wet rot and cold metal. A dingy, green-grey knot of tissue laced through with clots of tarry black.

The sour taste in his mouth remained, but he felt his heart resume its normal rhythm.

'Easy, easy.' There was a warm arm at his back, helping him to his feet.

Ma?

But, no. Not his mother; not ever again. Instead, Jiwa's concerned face came into view and he remembered where he was. 'Easy,' she told him.

The Our Mother stepped forward and very slowly, very unsteadily, bent to the ground. She picked up the ball of tissue he'd expelled and examined it closely.

'What is it?' he demanded, his voice hoarse and foreign to his own ears.

'Waste,' she told him. When he did not respond, she continued. 'Our bodies cannot always expel that which ails us. Sometimes they settle for merely holding our afflictions at bay. Growing over them, keeping them bound up. Over time though, we no longer have the space for them. Perhaps they are blocking the path of something else that needs to take its place.'

She stepped back toward her seat in the front of the temple space, then tossed the knot of tissue – this rot that had come from within him – into a brazier as she passed.

Nok felt it burn, like a phantom pain in his side. It was a good pain, like bearing down on tight scar tissue. He felt emptied. He closed his eyes and saw once more the barren expanse of the steppe, the faces of his parents. Then he allowed them to dissolve, like sand slipping from his grasp.

Jiwa still held him, protective and watchful. As close to anything maternal he'd known in years. He pulled away. 'The visions. Were they real?' he asked. 'The things my ... my sister and friends were in peril. Was any of it real?' He did not ask about his parents; he did not need her word on that.

'If you were an ordinary person, I would say the things you saw, the people you spoke with, were likely generated from your mind alone. Manifestations of your desires, spectres of your fears.'

'I am an ordinary person,' he said stubbornly.

'Are you?' Sparse grey brows raised high over her milky gaze. 'Very well. I suppose the things you saw were not real, then.'

But they had been. He saw the truth of it now, so stark in contrast to the lie.

'No, that's—' He felt his mouth collapse into a firm line when he realised what she had done.

'You are extraordinary,' she told him gently. 'That is not flattery, child – only fact. You have been Gifted. And you have a responsibility to learn to use that Gift. Stay here. I see such possibility in you. You are crackling with it! Imagine what you could learn from another week. Another moon.'

'I can't. Not when my sister and my friends are in danger.' His voice rasped as though the fire had been real, as though his throat had been scorched. 'I — I'll try to return.' But his words sounded flat even to his own ears; he had never been a very good liar.

'You may not be able to find your way back,' Jiwa told him solemnly.

He turned to her. She had been kind to him, patiently teaching him skills he had no affinity for. She did not deserve his lies. 'I know.'

'You cannot be sure that what you saw will come to pass,' said another shamaness from the fringes of the room. More murmured and droned their agreement.

'Stay,' said another.

'Yes, stay!' Charsi was at his side now, stern eyes looking accusingly at him.

The Our Mother stood and they fell silent. She moved with great authority, but little grace. She looked not unlike the aunties of his Kith, hunched and lumbering and pragmatic.

'How many twists of fortune do you think it took to bring you before me? What is the likelihood that you and I would both be here, now, standing face-to-face? You think this is an accident?' the old woman said, and there was a light now in her milky eyes as she stopped before him, nose-to-nose. 'You have been granted an enormous power – and it comes with immutable purpose. What you possess does not just belong to you, but to all of your kind. Your people. Do you know who you are, Nokhai, Pactmaker of the Kithless? *What* you are?'

He met her gaze. 'I don't. Not yet,' he admitted, feeling a bitter smile trembling its way across his mouth. 'But I know I'm not someone who leaves his friends to die.'

He ascended the earthen steps out of the dug-out temple alone. The shamanesses followed at a distance that told him they did not intend to stop him. Only to see what he would do, what he would choose.

The land was flat. Not even a scrub tree in sight to use for height. He didn't think it would matter, though. He'd seen the Iarudi, the Kith of the Golden Eagle, don their cauls, back when he was a boy. They did not need a drop to gain air or speed.

But more than that, he felt the collective memory of his ancestors – all those who had come before him. Not just the Ashina, united under the banner of a single beast, a single god, but all who had walked this land, tended its creatures, drunk its waters. They were all with him now, and he could not be what he was – neither boy nor Pactmaker – without all of them. Every life exquisite and essential.

Ten thousand years of knowing itched deep in the marrow of his bones, and he was ready to receive it. Ready at last to try.

He looked back. Jiwa and Charsi stood at the front of the crowd. When he waved, Jiwa waved back. Charsi did not, even when Jiwa prodded her with an elbow.

'Thank you,' he called to them. 'You've been good to me.'

He ran. It was all instinct, no finesse, but it did not

matter; he could already feel the pin-line itch of feathers in his bones. The eagle's caul dropped down over him and he rushed up to meet it, arms outstretched. He thrust them out to his sides, threw them back like bursting from deep water, like throwing off fetters. Like flying.

And then he *was* flying. He and the eagle beat its wings, the sound big as typhoon winds, enough to fell trees, but with the control, the surety of a drum beat. He was flesh and feather, bone and spirit, god and boy, all of it lighter than air. They rose higher and higher. It was too late to look back for a final farewell, but that didn't matter anymore. They were bound south, for Yulan City.

6

Ambush

Night hung around them like a cloak as they trekked through the northern country leading toward Yulan City's massive walls. By the time they reached Ansana, though, all that remained was a threadbare cover of grey predawn fog. Lu took the lead, and for once Nasan and Ony did not chafe at that – she was the only one who had been there before.

The silvery branches of the ancient, stout-bodied trees – into which the locals had, for centuries, carved their homes – stretched into the sky, visible from miles off. Lu felt her heart clench at the sight. They walked on, and slowly the rest of the village spread out before them: a patchwork of fields, most freshly harrowed from a recent harvest. Rough-hewn stables and sheds housed ploughs and mule and oxen. All of it was still and silent in the spare, cold first light of morning.

They came to a stop in front of Ohn's – Omair's – tree. Its lush canopy had looked nearly impenetrable when Lu had last been here, at the height of summer. Now though, it had begun to wane with the autumn, and red bled into the edges of its leaves.

Lu started at a sudden creak of wood from behind her, but it was only the open door to the stable buffeted by the light wind. The stable was empty; the apothecarist's old mule had escaped then, or had perhaps been taken by a neighbour. Speaking of—

'Let's get inside,' Lu told the others. 'The villagers will be waking soon. We shouldn't be seen.'

From the outside, the house had appeared unchanged from the first time Lu had sought refuge there. She made to push through the heavy wooden door and jumped back when it creaked and slouched inward. One of the hinges was broken. Had that happened during the raid that had sent her and Nokhai on their path north?

Jin helped her push it open.

It was dark inside. Her foot connected with something that skittered across the floor. She squinted and recognised a palm-sized wooden drawer. There had been dozens of them fitted into the wall closest to the door, filled with herbs and tinctures, bandages and powders, each neatly labelled. Someone had yanked most of them free and left them scattered around the room, leaving a wall of gaping sockets. The soldiers who had flooded the house after Nokhai and Lu's escape. Or perhaps the looters that inevitably followed.

'It's abandoned,' Ony said flatly.

Nasan grunted in agreement. 'No apothecarist, then.' It sounded like an accusation.

Astute as ever. 'I didn't say he *would* be here – only that he could be,' Lu replied.

In truth, she hadn't expected to see the apothecarist – indeed, she hardly expected he was still alive. But they needed hope. An answer for dealing with Minyi and her powers once they were in the city, in the palace. Something beyond simply capturing Brother and forcing him to assist them. Plus, Lu had thought Yuri might have come by. That perhaps he'd have left her a note, a sign – *something*.

'At any rate, it's good to have a place to wait out the daylight,' Jin interjected, ever helpful. 'We wouldn't want to be seen on the open road this close to the capital gates.'

Nasan stood in the centre of the room, a fist on her hip. She spun on the heel of her boot, surveying the overturned stools, the unswept hearth littered with the ashes of its final fire, a blackened pot half-filled with rot still suspended from one hook. The mournful grey veil of dust that had settled over it all.

'So,' Nasan murmured. 'This is where my brother was living all that time.'

'It was quite nice, before,' Lu said, feeling oddly defensive. It hadn't been *her* home. 'Nokhai was – we were ambushed by soldiers. My cousin Set's men. There was a fight. They left a mess.'

Nasan toed the large black tarry spot on the floor with her boot and made a face. 'I can see that.'

Lu followed her gaze, remembering when that dried stain had been wet and red, spilt by a soldier with one arrow sprouting from his throat, and another from the centre of his forehead.

'That bit was me,' she admitted.

'Of course it was,' Nasan said. 'Can't take you anywhere without someone dying.'

There was no malice in it. Perhaps just a hint. Lu wasn't

really listening. She could see the glint of her arrow point, still embedded in the wall, the broken shaft protruding just higher than her waist. The ragged path it had drawn through the wall above.

What had the man's name been? She'd heard him say it, or perhaps it was the other soldier he'd been with. Either way, she'd known it once. Now she couldn't remember. She'd killed and forgotten him entirely.

No worse than he deserved, she told herself, remembering his big hands, the way they'd gripped Nokhai, slammed him up against the wall—

And in the end, what had it been for? Nokhai had still died, after all that. She'd as good as killed him, too. She closed her eyes. She'd been on her feet too long. Her head ached—

The sudden scrape of wood on wood. Her eyes flew open. Jin was pulling a fallen stool upright, setting it back at Ohn's massive slab of a kitchen table.

'Don't touch that!'

He looked up in surprise, the stool still clutched in his sturdy, constant hands. She looked back in equal surprise; she hadn't meant to speak so harshly. She hadn't meant to speak at all. It had just been too much, to see the desecration of this place where Nokhai had lived his life, and that he would never see again. To see someone try so fruitlessly to put it back together. For what? For whom?

'Just – just leave it.'

Jin set the stool down back down on its side and cleared his throat, perhaps to apologise.

'I'll be back,' Lu told the group, cutting him short.

'You all wait here. Get some rest. And don't go outside – Ohn mentioned his neighbours were the suspicious sort.'

Jin's brow creased in concern. 'You don't suppose any of them saw us, do you? The sun was nearly up when we arrived.'

'And farmers wake early,' Nasan added. It sounded like an admonishment, as though *someone* should've thought ahead and better timed the dawn.

It sheared Lu's already-thin temper down to a thread. 'Yes, thank you for enlightening us, Nasan,' she snapped. And then, her eyes falling on the narrow series of hand-holes carved into the tree's walls: 'If you need something to do, that ladder will take you to a covered platform in the branches. There should still be enough cover from the leaves. You can keep an eye out for your early-rising farmers.'

Jin made for the handholes, ever eager for a task, or perhaps just curious to see more of this novel living house. Ony lingered though, seeing Nasan had not moved.

Nasan was still regarding Lu, now with narrowed eyes. 'And what will you do?'

'I need to look for something,' Lu said in a tone that she had intended to be firm, leaving no room for argu-ment. The words came out ragged though, edged with exhaustion, a kind of pleading. But perhaps in the end that was what softened Nasan's curiosity, her insistence that she have the final say in all things. Something in her face shifted and she shrugged.

'Makes no difference to me,' she said, heading toward the ladder.

★

Nokhai's bedroom looked mercifully intact, more or less. Someone – either soldiers, or looters – had shaken out his bedding, but that was all. Looking for what? Hidden riches, or some clue of where he might have taken her? Evidence of who he might be?

They'd have had better luck finding riches. Nokhai's bedroom had the fastidious, severe tidiness Lu usually associated with soldiers' barracks. The first time she'd seen it, it had looked so impersonal she'd only realised it belonged to him at all when, after spending the night in it, she had emerged in the morning and nearly tripped over his sleeping form prone on the floor by the kitchen hearth.

She hadn't known if it had been the Ashina boy or the apothecarist's decision to let her sleep there, but she'd felt a bit guilty about it regardless. The empire had invaded and destroyed his first home, killed his family, and there she was, its living embodiment, invading every corner of his current home. Sleeping in his bed, wearing his tunics and trousers. She should've realised it sooner – the blankets, the clothes. She had smelled him in all of it.

Now, she knelt beside his bedroll – she hadn't had time to put it away that final morning – and folded the blanket atop it, paying it the sort of reverence she'd seen mourners lavish at the viewing of a casket. Nokhai had left no body that they could bury, but she had this, at least, the place where he'd laid his head for years in relative safety and comfort.

His pillow had been tossed to the far end of the room; she rose and fetched it. It was covered in two layers of thick fabric, block-shaped, and filled with some kind of grain. Whatever it was absorbed the sound well enough when she pressed her face to it and screamed. She held it there until all the breath had left her body – breath, and whatever it was she poured into it. Rage. Fear.

As she pulled the pillow away, she realised something was missing. She could smell the earthy, woody scent of its filling, the lingering must of months in the dark, disused, and ... nothing else. Nokhai's smell was gone.

The pillow fell to the floor. Why had she come here?

She thought then, perhaps, that tears would come, but they still did not. Just as well. There was no time for any of this.

Something on the floor caught her eye. It poked out from under the outer casing of the pillow. A little doll made of sticks and old bits of cloth. She recognised it at once. She reached for it.

'Don't touch that!'

She'd whirled around, startled, wincing as her wounded arm bumped the floor. 'I wasn't going to hurt it.'

But Nokhai was already leaning over her to snatch it away from where she'd found it, propped on the floor between his bedroom and the wall.

'Is it a charm?' Lu had asked. He clearly hadn't wanted to talk to her, but gods, lying there all day had been maddening. If she wasn't thinking of all the terrible ways her father might have died, she was thinking of killing her cousin, and if she wasn't thinking of death, well, she was bored.

'Did you make it?' she had pressed. The boy had been frowned suspiciously. 'My friend,' he said shortly. 'She made it.'

She. Lu blinked in surprise. A girl.

'What's her name?'

He'd scowled. *'I'm not telling you.'*

'Why not?' she had demanded, surprised to find she had the capacity to feel offended by such a slight at a time like this. It had felt oddly comforting.

'Because you'll just get her into trouble, or hurt her, somehow.'

She'd scoffed. *'I only asked for her name, not where she sleeps and her weaknesses.'*

'Everyone you know, everyone you touch, gets hurt,' he had countered, the words bursting from him as though he could not contain them if he tried. *'You hurt them.'*

She'd sat up, wincing as pain shot through her arm. *'How many times do I have to tell you, I wasn't the one who hurt your family.'*

'Killed my family,' he had corrected. *'You killed them. You don't get to forget that.'*

'That wasn't me,' she'd said. But she'd known what he had meant. And she had had to admit that she was beginning to see his point.

'You would've, had you been there. Had you been of age. If you were Emperor. I saw how you were yesterday – how you killed those boys. And they were your own people!'

Wailun.

The name rose up in her periphery and barrelled into her, knocking her clear out of the memory. The soldier she had killed in Ohn's kitchen had been named Wailun. She hadn't even known the boy's name – the one Nokhai had mentioned all those months ago. The one who had been with Hyacinth's brother, Wonin, when she had killed them both.

She grabbed the doll, wrenching it with more force than was perhaps necessary from the sleeve of Nokhai's pillow. A small, folded piece of paper fell loose along with it.

She stared at it, her heart fluttering as though — what, exactly? Nokhai was dead. This note, if it was a note, couldn't have been left by him. But perhaps it had been something he'd written before, something she'd never seen. Having that new bit of knowledge would almost feel like seeing him again, wouldn't it?

Lu pulled the paper apart. The handwriting was neat and small, with a subtle flourish to the letters. It was addressed to Nokhai. So, not his hand, then. She swallowed her disappointment and forced herself to read:

Dear N.,
You have not come to see me as you promised when last we spoke.
    If you should receive this, please find me at the usual place.
    Or, if I'm not there, you can seek me out at the Anglimn residence in the foreign sector. Ask around for 'The Trader' — that is how most people know Carmine's father. Their house is quite large, and easy to find.
    Ever yours,
    A.

A date was scrawled below. Just over a week after Lu's father had been killed. Just over a week after Nokhai and Lu had been forced to flee north, setting in motion the unretractable events that would ultimately lead to Nokhai—

A.

Adé. The name came to her with a memory in hand: a slight girl with dark skin and tight coils of black hair. Lu had mistaken her for a foreign-born Westerman at the time, but when the girl spoke, it was clear she was all Yulan City. She'd come bearing cake and wondering why Nokhai had missed her engagement party. Wide eyes, filled with recognition and fear as Lu had pointed a nocked arrow in her face, until Nokhai had leapt between them. Not a threat – his friend, he had protested.

A clever friend. Adé hadn't been there to witness what had befallen Nokhai and Lu, but she'd seen the soldiers arrive at Ohn's door beforehand – and apparently had returned sometime after to witness the aftermath of over-turned furniture and blood stains. She'd seen enough to think to protect herself, and Nokhai. The cadence of the letter had stuck Lu as halting while she read it; now she saw it for what it was: restrained. Careful to avoid disclosing anything that suggested distress or incrimination, or even a clear identity of either party.

All except for the Ellandaise names. Anglimn. That was a name Lu remembered without difficulty. Amusing that a man as wealthy and powerful as the founder of the Eastern Flame Import Company could be reduced to so pedestrian a title as 'The Trader.' Likely in committing his name to writing, Adé had assumed – fairly – that these important foreigners were beyond the touch of the politics and law of the empire. Perhaps she had even speculated they might be able to extend that protection to Nokhai.

Too late for that. Lu crushed the note in her hand. Then she jumped, seeing the figure darkening the doorway to the bedroom.

'Nasan!' she said, sharper than was necessary. 'I told you I'd be—'

'Soldiers,' the Ashina girl interrupted breathlessly. 'Maybe a dozen of them. Nearby. Come see.'

The note was still in Lu's hand, the paper hot and itchy against her palm. She'd have to think on its contents later. She pushed it into the pocket of her trousers and followed Nasan up into the canopy.

Ony and Jin were lying on their bellies when Lu emerged. She and Nasan slithered up beside them and she saw Jin was peering out toward the road with a brass spyglass. Imperial issue – something they must have lifted from one of the guards at Prison Camp 4.

Nasan reached for the spyglass but Lu batted her hand out of the way and yanked it from Jin's grip.

Nasan hadn't exaggerated. Lu counted a unit of fifty, mostly infantry on foot, but flanked by neat rows of Hana officers on horseback, and a few higher-ranking Hu astride traditional war elk.

'Do you think it has to do with our raid on Prison Camp 4?' Jin asked.

Lu shook her head slowly. 'Unlikely. If so, why come this way? They'd be sending men north as reinforcements to guard the other camps, not toward the capital.'

'Unless they were tailing us,' Ony pointed out.

Nasan snorted without humour. 'If *that* were the case, they should know it wouldn't require half a hundred trained soldiers to snuff us out.'

'Look,' Jin pointed. 'They're stopping at that farm.'

Lu brought the spyglass back to her eye. The building

stood off to the side of the road. Not a traditional Ansana tree homestead, but a low, wood-panelled structure with a roof of black clay shingles. An orange flag bearing the roaring tiger of the Hu snapped in the wind atop a tall pole out front.

'That's not a farm. It's a local police precinct,' Lu told him. As she watched, a man emerged from the building. The spyglass granted her a clear enough view of his nervous face, the crumbs of a hastily eaten breakfast still caught in his stringy moustache; he hadn't been expecting anyone. His orange tunic was in want of a wash, as was his hair, but the golden tassel and milky quartz rooster pendant he wore around his neck distinguished him as the precinct captain. Four men, also in orange tunics of varying degrees of shabbiness, bumbled into a line behind him. The smallest of them nearly tripped in his eagerness.

The closest Hana officer trotted his stallion forward, not bothering to dismount. The exchange that followed was brief, with seemingly a good dose of haughtiness from the officer, and repressed dismay on the part of the precinct captain. The officer gestured south down the road, toward the capital, and the captain proffered a weak protest, jerking a somewhat derisive thumb at the young men lined up behind him.

The officer shrugged, apparently agreeing with, but unmoved by, the captain's assessment. He pointed, not without disdain, toward a wagon parked at the far end of the precinct building, and then toward a stable beyond it, where a large grey-brown mule hung its heavy head out the door.

And then the imperials were rolling on, continuing their march toward the capital.

'Well?' Nasan demanded.

Lu lowered the spyglass slowly. 'They're sending everyone toward Yulan City.'

Jin understood. 'For the peasant riots. Like the guards up north said.'

Lu nodded slowly. 'They must be desperate if they're pressing country police into imperial business.'

'Wonderful,' Nasan muttered. 'So, the city will be crawling with police *and* soldiers.'

'Parts of it,' Lu mused. She thought of Adé's note crammed in her pocket. The frayed ends of a few hopeless ideas were knitting together in her mind.

She raised the spyglass again. The police captain and his men had disappeared inside. A moment later though, they emerged from with a paltry cache of weapons – spears, a few crossbows, probably all a county precinct like this was equipped with – and one by one loaded them into the wagon parked outside. They hadn't wasted any time responding to the military officer's instructions. Did this reflect discipline on their part, or just the urgency of the orders? Once more eyeing the precinct captain's stained tunic, Lu thought she could guess which it was.

'Not that we have a way into the city, anyway,' Ony was saying. 'Unless those prison guards up north were lying about the lockdowns, we'll have no way of getting through the gates.'

'We don't,' Lu agreed. 'But they do.' She lowered the spyglass and offered it to Nasan.

The other girl looked surprised, but she took it and trained it toward the precinct building. 'Four against five? I think we can manage that.' She lowered the glass with a slight frown. 'But what about afterward, once we're in the city?'

Ask around for 'The Trader'; that is how most people know Carmine's father. Their house is quite large, and easy to find.

Lu allowed herself the smallest smile. 'You know, I think it's time we made some new friends.'

A thousand years ago, Lu had left Yulan City in ceremonial finery, astride a war elk worth double its weight in silver, a retinue of highborn sycophants flanking her. She returned now flat on her back, in the rear of a farmer's stolen wagon, hidden from sight by a scratchy wool blanket that stank of old mineral oil and mule. Parts of it were threadbare enough that if Lu shifted it around, she could make out the hazy blue of the early afternoon sky, the dark arching shapes of passing trees overhead – and Ony's sour expression as she reached down to tug the blanket back into place.

'Stop that,' she hissed. 'Someone's going to see you moving.'

Beneath the sharpness of her irritation, Lu heard fear. Fair, given the circumstances they were riding into. But there was something else – she could see it in the way the girl's eyes darted around the changing landscape around them.

'Different from the North, isn't it?' Lu said.

She didn't say *better*, but perhaps it was implied by her tone; Ony grunted noncommittally.

Then Nasan's voice floated up from behind her, where the Ashina girl and Jin were driving the mule pulling them down Kangmun Boulevard.

'Both of you, stop *talking*. We're getting close to the

outer gate. The road's getting crowded. Ony, you're supposed to be a grown man, remember? And Lu, *you're* supposed to be a pile of spears.'

How could she forget, when the poles of those spears hadn't stopped rolling around beneath her since they'd left Ansana? It had been Nasan's idea – of course it had – for the three of them to disguise themselves as officers in the stolen uniforms while Lu hid, lest she be recognised by someone in the city.

Ony shifted back into her seat, adopting a bored slouch – apparently her approximation of a rural county police officer. Not bad, though the orange tunic she wore did most of the work. It fit her well. The man they'd stolen it from had been slight, barely more than a boy.

'You're her, aren't you?' he'd blurted as Jin tugged the uniform free over his head and set to binding his hands. 'The Girl King. I know all about you.'

'Everyone knows about me,' Lu had said, ignoring Nasan's snort.

It had been almost too easy to overcome the precinct. Ony and Nasan had limped in through the front door, begging for help from the men within – a terrible accident, her leg was ruined, until it wasn't – while Jin and Lu had rounded up the two loading the cart outside. They'd surrendered their uniforms without complaint and allowed themselves to be bound and gagged and pushed into a small storage room where, hopefully, they would not be found until Lu was long gone. Neat and quick. Until that last one – the boy.

'Is it true, what they say? That you're taking back the throne from your sister?' he'd pressed on.

'Shouldn't that be "Empress Minyi" to you?' she asked lightly.

'That witch is no empress of mine,' he spat back.

Lu felt the unexpected twinge of hope ... chased by the urge to strike the contempt off his undeserving face.

'Witch?' she repeated. 'I don't know how things are done in your family, but I prefer not to hear my sister maligned in front of me. It's true, we're not currently on good terms, but I still take it personally.'

He licked his lips as she pressed the point of the knife down harder against his skin. 'M-my apologies, Princess. I was only repeating what others have called her.'

Lu had recalled the pools of black engulfing the whites of Min's eyes. The crackling fistfuls of light she'd thrown. But how had this country boy heard about that? Had the tales spread?

'Why would they call her that?'

'You haven't heard?' he asked, incredulous. 'She set the throne on fire. With her eyes!'

'Her eyes?'

'Or – or her hands. Or her mind. It depends on who you hear it from—'

Nasan shoved her way in front of Lu and slammed the boy up against the wall.

'We're hearing it from you,' she gritted out. 'So make it easier to understand.'

He swallowed hard, the tendons in his narrow throat straining. The tips of his boots scrabbled against the stone floor.

'I'm just telling you what everyone's saying!' he insisted. 'I – I wasn't there. But Empress Minyi nearly burned down Kangmun Hall. They say you can still see the scorch marks on the walls, the broken windows. The Heart reeked of smoke for a week.'

Nasan loosened her hold on the boy; he slumped forward in relief as his feet hit the ground.

'This might be easier than we thought. Sounds like your sister's lost control of her strongest weapon.' She smiled, big and wolfish.

Lu could not return it. Was that true? Min losing control of her power did not necessarily make it less dangerous. You could just as easily drown in the waters of a broken dam. And this was Lu's sister they were discussing. There again was that dual, conflicting twinge of hope and – not quite anger this time.

Fear.

But was it for Min, or of her?

There had been a time, not so long ago at all, when Lu could not have imagined asking that question without laughing. Perhaps that had been part of the problem.

Nasan had taken over binding the boy's wrists. When he flinched, she tugged harder, causing his arms to jerk.

'Be careful, Nasan. He's a person, not a doll,' Lu had said absently. She'd taken the precinct captain's identification tassel from her pocket: the one with the rooster pendant that he'd worn around his neck. She tossed it toward Jin. 'Here,' she said as he caught it. 'You'll be our captain.'

It happened quickly. One moment, she was watching the grin play across Jin's lips, unsure of what to make of the small jolt of pleasure it gave her. And then there was the slightest sound outside: a muffled thump that might have been a knock at the door. Later, they'd find it was only the mule, butting up against the building as he grazed. What the young officer heard though, was a chance.

He took it.

'Help!' he shouted, bursting free from Nasan's grasp and lurching for the door. 'Help me—'

Nasan leapt for him. She couldn't keep her hold on him, but his feet were bound and she managed to knock him into a *forward stumble. Ony rushed over, but Lu was closer. She cut between him and the door, and as he fell forward onto her, her dagger slid between two of his ribs.*

That had been how it happened, hadn't it? An accident. But how had the dagger got into her hand?

His mouth opened, and a deflated huff escaped. Lu felt it against her neck.

She tried to pull her dagger free, but the blade caught on bone with a wet grate. The hilt slipped from her hand as she stepped back. He fell to the floor, taking it with him.

He wasn't dead. His arms were wrapped tightly around his belly where her knife had sunk in, but his legs kicked wild, like a goat's. His mouth gaped, and a moan like nothing human lowed from deep within him.

Behind her, the floor creaked. Lu whirled — and came face-to-face with Jin. His eyes widened, taking in the blood streaking her face and hands, the dying man on the floor behind her. Absurdly, for the briefest moment, she felt compelled to hide what she'd done. As though Jin hadn't already seen it, hadn't watched her do it. In his eyes, she saw confusion, chased by disgust — at her? Or was it just the blood?

The boy on the floor moaned again.

'Shut him up!' Nasan hissed.. Ony fell upon him, fumbling her hands over his mouth. He shrieked, his body rolling so hard he managed to throw her.

'Oh, for heaven's—' Nasan pulled a handkerchief from the waistband of her tunic, balled it up and shoved it between his gnashing teeth. 'This is a damned mess.'

Lu knelt beside her and moved her hands toward Nasan's, as though to help clamp his mouth shut. Then, almost without her intending it, they moved lower, floating pale and mothlike over him. When they settled beneath the high collar of his tunic though, they became iron.

'What are you—' Nasan began, but her voice fell away.

'Princess ...' It was Jin. Lu did not look up. Was he going to offer to kill the guard for her? Share the burden of blood so she could pretend she wasn't responsible? But it was too late for that.

It had taken a long time for him to die. Even a slight boy like that found his mettle when faced with death; he writhed like a serpent beneath her. Nasan and Ony and Jin remained mercifully silent.

Lu's hands had still been wet when she stood. The blood was bright red – new. She searched her hands and found the cut on her left palm. It must have happened when she stabbed him. She hadn't even felt it.

Nasan had stared down at the body. She hadn't looked at Lu. 'Good thing we already got his uniform, I suppose.' Was that a tremor in her voice?

Lu wiped her hands on her tunic. Just another layer of filth. The cut would stop bleeding on its own, eventually.

'Do you want your dagger back?' Jin had asked hesitantly. He and Ony were standing over the body. Ony bent down and gave the handle an experimental wiggle. 'It's stuck.'

Lu had looked down at her dagger, rising out of the man's gut. She'd loved that knife. It had been a gift from Yuri for her eleventh birthday: a steel blade as long as her forearm, marked by segmented fullers and engraved with her name in classical Yueh script. The handle was elegant and tapered, wrapped in creamy white rayskin. Impossibly soft in her palm.

'This is a real weapon, Princess,' her shin had said. 'Should you brandish it, be prepared to draw blood. I had to get special

permission from your father to give it to you, so if you stick your cousin with it, it's my hide he'll be wanting.'

She'd let out an exaggerated sigh. 'Yes, Shin.'

'Good girl.'

She could almost feel his coarse fingers patting the side of her face, just once, a bit too hard to be sweet. She didn't mind. Yuri wasn't demonstrative, but when he did deign to show affection it was with a stilted awkwardness that she always thought of as particular to a man who had never been a father. Although, she wasn't sure where she'd got that idea from; her own father had two daughters and was little better.

'Princess?' Jin had said, his voice soft. 'Are you all right? Your dagger...'

Lu had refocused on the white rayskin handle, streaked with dark red blood, clots of viscera. Someone would find this guard, eventually. They would remove the blade from his body. They would notice the inscription on the handle, and recognise it as hers.

'Leave it,' she'd said. 'We have what we came for.'

She would be announcing herself soon enough anyway.

The spears beneath her suddenly jostled toward the rear of the wagon, jerking her back to the present. The wagon slowed and tilted; they were climbing an incline. Lu shifted the blanket covering her again and saw the sky had darkened. The autumn days were drawing short, and evening was falling fast. They must be close.

The wagon levelled out as they crested the hill. Above her, Ony took in a sharp breath. 'That's the city wall? It's massive.'

It took everything in Lu not to tear the blanket off and look for herself. Her home. She was nearly *home*.

Nasan grunted in agreement with Ony. 'I didn't expect it to be quite this large,' she admitted. But then, in a very different tone, 'But, over there – look. Is that *fire*?'

This time nothing and no one could have stopped Lu from leaping out from under her cover. None of the others protested. The cart stalled and stopped as Jin drew in the reins. Lu squinted; the sky was dimming into evening, but it was still brighter than beneath the blanket and it took her eyes a moment to adjust. She smelled it first, the barest acrid bite on the cooling air.

They couldn't have been more than half a league from Yulan City. At this distance, the yellow-hued outer wall looked not unlike the face of a mountain, eternal and implacable. Unchanged from Lu's memories. All but for the plume of black smoke rising up from behind it, like a question.

'*Go*,' Lu commanded.

She spent the remainder of their journey uncovered, only ducking back beneath the blanket when they slowed to approach the Northgate. It was closed. She felt, rather than saw, their arrival below the looming wall: a cold, swallowing shadow. From above, a posted guard called down for them to state their business.

'Ay!' she heard Jin call back. 'Reinforcements and weapons from Ansana!' He did his best to conceal his accent. Not perfect, but then, there was no shortage of regional accents swirling around the empire. It wouldn't be unusual for a guard in the capital to be unfamiliar with one of them.

'What sort of weaponry? Let's see it.'

Lu resisted the urge to shrink away as Ony pulled up

a corner of the blanket to show their cargo, stopping just short of exposing Lu's legs.

The guard's tone was scornful. 'Dull spears, and crossbows older than my grandmother. Well, they need as many bodies as they can get at the Southern Gatehead to the Inner Ring. Take the western route. Someone set a fire in Scrap-Patch Row, and it's spreading fast. East side's all blocked up. There's a curfew in place, so you shouldn't have too much trouble from civilians, but maybe get a few of those crossbows ready.'

Scrap-Patch Row. Lu sucked in a breath. The place was all tinder. A fire would eat it up in no time at all—

The iron screech of the opening gates drowned out the thought. And a moment after that, they were passing under the shadow of the wall, into Yulan City.

The streets were eerily quiet along the west side. The curfew meant no night markets, no merchants' carts creaking past. Lu's stomach churned with the wrongness of it – the tension that underscored the apparent peace. The bite of far-off smoke in the air.

All at once, at a distance, there came angry, panicked shouts – and then, the sluggish pops of discharging sparkstone.

Guns? How on earth would regular city folk get their hands on such weaponry? Who *were* these rioters? Who was supplying them?

Ony gave Lu a kick with the toe of her stolen boot. 'We're coming up on something – looks like a mob surrounding a check point. What do we do?'

Lu took a risk and craned her neck out to look, the blanket still draped over her like a hood. The light was fading swiftly around them, turning everything the same indistinguishable gloomy blue-grey, the deep shadows distorting what little signage she could see. Up ahead, she could make out a crowd. Thirty, fifty people, perhaps. A barricade of appropriated wood and parked wagons. Torches flaring bright in the gloaming.

Where were they? Yulan City was Lu's home, but the Outer Ring was not. Who they really needed was Nokhai – and how many times had she already had to quell that wish?

'Take the next left,' she hissed. 'The Ellandaise sector is near the harbour. Find the smell of salt water, and we won't be far off.' Jin gave a spare nod of his head and did as he was instructed, taking them down a narrow road lined with low row houses. Every single window they passed was closed; a few were boarded up. No light nor sound escaped from behind any of them.

The only noise she could hear was someone's ragged breathing, much too fast – her own? – and the clatter of the wagon wheels on uneven paving stones. Beneath that, footsteps? But were they headed toward them?

Overhead, gas streetlamps suddenly appeared. Delicate blown-glass globes hung like pearl earrings from swirling cast iron posts tall as trees. Foreign design.

'We're close. We're here—' she started to say.

Light and sound erupted overhead, like a dozen fire-works ignited at once, shredding the quiet. Something immense slammed into a nearby building, collapsing it like sand. Disintegrated brick plumed up in its wake, enveloping them.

The wagon overturned. The mule screeched. Spears scattered.

In the instant it took to happen, she had two thoughts. The first was confusion, and the second was *Yunis*. It was happening again—

Lu threw out her hands and felt the street rise up to meet them. Stone. Solid enough to tear open her palms. The ground was not falling away beneath her this time.

Lu shook her head, cast about for the others. All she could make out were orange-grey silhouettes, dark against the billowing white dust. Was that Nasan's rangy form, pulling someone else up from the street? She made to call out to them – to anyone – and fell into a fit of coughing. She tried to brush the dust from her face. Futile; the air was thick with it. She could feel it clinging to her eyelashes, turning her spit thick as paste.

This is no peasant uprising—

Another blast of light and terror. Again, she fell.

When she stood, the dust was clearing. At the end of the street, illuminated by the light of the gas lamps, a man appeared.

It was too hazy for Lu to make out the colour of his tunic, the shape of his jaw, even his build. What she did see was that he was standing in an open doorway, and that it led to a building that still had its roof.

'That way!' she screamed, looking wildly about for the others. She felt someone fall into step behind her, and a hand landed on her shoulder.

'Are you all right?' Jin choked out. She nodded, breathless.

Another figure appeared in the haze. Nasan, followed by Ony. 'That way!' Lu told them. 'Do you see that man?'

'Who is it?' Nasan shouted.

'Does it matter?' Lu yelled back. 'We're going to die if we stay out here!'

They'd only run a few paces though, before Lu stopped short, Nasan hurtling into her back.

'What are you—'

'It's him,' Lu murmured, almost to herself.

'The Trader?' Ony demanded. 'The one from your letter?'

No. He'd been with Anglimn, though. Someone important. She'd only met him once, moons ago – Gods, it felt so much longer. His name escaped her, but she remembered the harsh, blunt tones of his title.

The Kommodeur met her eyes. His narrowed, and he reached for something at his waist – then stopped. She saw recognition and disbelief battling on his face.

Lu flinched, raising her hands to show him she meant no harm. 'We come as friends! I have an offer for you—'

Another blast struck a nearby roof, raining soot and debris down around them.

'Don't just stand there, then! Comes on!' the foreigner shouted in broken Yueh. His face was red and streaked with sweat and grime. 'Gets inside!'

'Do we trust him?' Nasan's eyes were wild with terror. *I don't even know him.*

'Lu!' Nasan insisted.

'Do we have a choice?' she hollered back.

It was all she needed to say. They ran forward. But even as they drew closer, Lu's stomach clenched. This was what she'd come here for, she reminded herself. This was what she *needed*. Behind them, there was only the chaos of the street. She kept moving.

Lu was near enough to see see the whites of the man's eyes, shot through with dragged pinprick lines of red, when the street exploded. She felt Nasan slam into her side before they both went sideways, down against shattered flagstones and rubble. Lu rolled onto her back. All around, the air was choked with smoke and screaming, and above it all, the dark, spangled sky sprawled uncaring and infinite.

7

Witch

There was a knock at Min's doors. Dread followed, grey and unfurling like smoke. The explosions had stopped shortly before dawn, but perhaps things had taken a turn. Was it Brother come to announce her own guards had turned on her? That the city's poor had stormed the palace gates?

'Come in,' she said.

'Prin – Empress?'

The doors parted, just enough to reveal a sliver of wan skin, a single shining eye. It was Butterfly, returned from the errand Min had sent her on. The amma pushed her way into the room. Min did not miss the tremble in her long, thin hands. Weariness or wariness? Her mouth was a grim line, like a crack running through porcelain.

The crack widened and Butterfly's voice drifted from it. 'It's noon.' Your – she's here. The guards brought her. As you requested.' This last part sounded like palms raised up against an impending blow.

As though Min could have forgotten. 'Send her in.' Then, 'No, wait—'

She went to the hammered mirror over her vanity. It

was a new acquisition – polished to a higher degree of refinement than the one that had previously hung in its place. The better to check for red in her eyes, to spot any blemishes that might emerge beneath the skin.

The face that gazed back at her now was free of either. The black starburst of veins that had appeared days earlier, after her first audience at court, had faded to a sunset violet, dull enough to hide beneath a slathering of paste and powder. Her skin was opaque as a mask, stretched over newly prominent cheekbones. A faint, acrid reek of burning still clung to what remained of her hair, defiant to repeated washings and the perfumes her ammas combed through it daily. They'd trimmed the frizzled ends and filled in its missing length with false attachments woven with her own before pinning it in her customary Empress's upsweep. No one would be any the wiser – if they hadn't already heard what had happened during her enthronement.

She looked like her mother. Her red lips twisted ruefully. How long had she wished for that to be true?

She straightened, made to smooth her hands down her jade-green robes. An old nervous habit – one she could no longer perform. The pointed nail guards she wore over her fingers snagged on the fabric. They had never found the ones she lost in the fire. These were newly crafted: ivory, and inlaid with shards of onyx and carnelian. She straightened the one that had caught on her robes.

'Send her in,' she told Butterfly. 'Have her guards wait outside. We shouldn't be long.'

The amma slid the doors open wider, and Min's mother glided into the room.

Her movements were elegant as dropped silk. Her lips

were painted their customary garnet red, fuller and darker than Min's. But there were poorly stitched tears in the hem of her cream and lavender robes, and Min noted the absence of jewellery around her neck and her fingers. Her long black hair was clean and brushed, but hung in a flat sheet down her back. Was there no one left to comb and plait and pin it into its usual high upsweep?

Min had said her mother could retain her ammas, but perhaps they'd fled, either when word of Set's death had reached the capital – or when Min herself had. They wouldn't have been alone. More than a few servants, and even some magistrates, had left the palace under cover of darkness, rumours from the North echoing in their ears, the word *witch* upon their tongues.

'You look pretty,' her mother said finally. 'A bit thin, though.'

Min flinched; it had been so long since she had heard that voice. She'd imagined it in her dreams, and in her waking thoughts as she had rehearsed how this encounter might unfold. All that preparation felt silly now. A paltry approximation of the real thing, which set her heart to racing. She started to lick her lips, then stopped. She would only smear her lipstick. She had planned to let her mother speak first – it was weakness to speak first, wasn't it? And yet, this way felt no better: now Min had to respond, and she found she did not know how.

'I had hoped you would come and see me sooner than this,' her mother continued, her melodious voice containing a gentle indictment, a hint of chiding.

You came to me! Min thought, but the distinction sounded petty and plaintive, even in her mind. She swallowed the words down before she could choke on them. She had to remember why she'd called her mother here. She needed answers, not these stupid games. She would waste no more time like this.

Her mother drifted from her place by the door without invitation, without needing one. A long, pale hand extended out from the embroidered sweep of her sleeve and floated over the divan, not quite coming to a rest, but nevertheless giving the impression of having touched it. 'I don't remember seeing this before,' she said, somehow conveying a mild, offhand disapproval.

Much of Min's furniture was new. She hadn't been able to stomach moving into her father's apartments — just the thought sent her reeling back to the fever dream of his death. Her staff had settled for replacing many of her things with new ones. Min hadn't paid much mind to the style of it, though she suspected these new things were meant to be nicer. What she did appreciate was how devoid of memory they were. None of them had been touched before — by Lu, by her mother, by the idiot girl she'd been. None of them carried the stink of history.

She stared at her mother's hand, floating ghostlike over the curved back of the divan now. The hand lifted, turned over, reached for her.

'Come here.' And the way she said it was so easy, like an old habit, that Min almost went.

No.

She had come alive, the last time they'd seen each other. For the first time, she'd been her own creature. A thing apart from her mother — more than what anyone could ever have imagined her to be. It hadn't just been the fear. It had been the surprise. Awash in her mother's realisation that Min did not begin and end with what she perceived, what she wanted.

'I should have been there for you when Set died,' her mother said, as though it weren't Min herself who had prevented her from doing so.

Set. Min tried not to think of him. It hurt, the way she supposed grief was meant to, but worse, it was confusing. Imagining his face – and already it had become as vague and shifting as sand in her mind's eye – always led to a single question: had he loved her? Had he ever even said as much? It was strange she couldn't remember. He had always seemed to be either looking beyond her, or behind himself, as though to make certain the thing of his past wasn't dogging him.

Had she loved him? If she hadn't, it was as close to love as she'd ever felt for anyone. After all, he had been her husband, however briefly.

'You should not have had to mourn him alone, young as you are,' her mother sighed.

A devastatingly fine imitation of care. The words almost felt true; Min felt the phantom pain of wanting them to be so. But she didn't need any of that. Not anymore.

Her mother should be congratulating her – even thanking her for taking the throne away from Lu. Which, in the end, was all her mother had truly wanted. Wasn't it?

How much else did her mother know, and who had told her about Set? How much detail had they shared? Min hadn't given very explicit instructions for her mother's imprisonment – only that she be unharmed, kept in her apartments and given every luxury she requested, save her freedom.

Let her see how it feels, she had thought at the time. It was wrong to want to teach a parent a lesson, but sometimes there were things parents needed to learn.

Had it changed anything, though? Her mother looked shabbier at the edges, perhaps, but no less her mother.

'I'm sending you away,' Min said abruptly, her voice overly loud in the still of the room. 'To your family's home, up north.'

Something in her mother's face hardened. A moment, and it passed. Her expression went placid again, with just an edge of disapproval at the corners of her mouth.

'I don't think that is a good idea, do you?' she asked, as though Min hadn't been the one to just suggest it. 'Now, more than ever, you need your mother close by.' Rinyi floated from behind the new, untouched divan, over to Min's new mirror. She studied her reflection, smoothing the already sleek fall of her hair.

Min balled her fists in her skirts, the ivory tips of her nail guards biting the silk.

Her mother left the vanity and approached. The closer she drew, the bigger she became, until she eclipsed Min's field of vision. 'You don't know it yet, but these magistrates – they want to take you apart,' she said. 'Cut you into little morsels they can portion out among themselves. Even the ones who support your rule. Perhaps them most of all—'

'Did you kill Lu's mother?'

Silence. The look that clouded Rinyi's face was difficult

to parse. Behind it, Min sensed a kind of paralysis, like a cornered rabbit, outwardly frozen, and all its inside parts quivering.

'How did ... what do you mean "Lu's mother"?' Rinyi caught herself, but it was too late. *How did you know?* she had begun to ask.

Betrayal.

'What I don't understand,' Min said, and now it was she who was circling the perimeter of the room, dragging the tips of her nail guards across the mahogany lines of her chairs, 'is why you wouldn't just make it known? You only ever wanted to put Lu in her place. So, why not reveal what she was? You had the opportunity.'

Min stopped, facing Rinyi. If they both held out their arms, their fingertips might have brushed. She couldn't quite bring herself to meet her mother's eyes, though. Instead, she stared at the phoenix embroidered across Rinyi's chest and stomach.

'This isn't proper to speak of,' her mother said. But the words were like wet paper, and Min slashed through them with a wave of her hand.

'Was what Set said true?' Min mused, stepping closer. 'Could it really just be pride? That seems a silly trade for a grown woman to make: risking the fate of her empire, her family, for ... what? Escaping a bit of embarrassment?'

What little colour her mother's powdered face had left drained away. She always went bloodless when she was at her angriest. Perhaps she would strike Min. A part of Min hoped she would. She wanted to feel the spark of violence. 'Or maybe you were afraid the truth would come out. That you killed a girl—'

'She wasn't a girl.' Rinyi's voice was vicious. 'She was a shamaness. A lowly, dirty thing. A *witch*.'

The molten thing lingering like illness in Min's bones flared. For a moment, she wasn't sure who her mother's words were meant for. For a moment, she wasn't certain who she was – the empress, or the dead girl – and in that moment, she did not know if it mattered.

Min's voice quavered as she asked, 'If she was a witch, what does that make me?'

'You?' her mother repeated. 'You're not … you're mine. You're my—'

'I'm cursed!' The words were an animal snarl. Her mother flinched. 'You've seen what I can do. *I'm* the lowly, dirty thing you hated. She's inside me, and it's all your fault.'

Rinyi's eyes were wide, wild, as though she were watching something precious slip away before her. 'How can you—'

'At least she sees me,' Min surged on, and now there was a ragged edge of laughter to her words. 'In a way, she's more my mother than you'll ever—'

Her mother's voice was ragged with fury. 'Don't you dare say that. Don't you dare. I carried you inside me. I made you from my body, rebuilt my entire life around you. Who was she? A peasant, a prisoner. Nothing!'

'So why bother to kill her, then?' Min demanded, leaning forward.

'I didn't kill her!' Rinyi barked. '*Lu* killed her. Cut her up from the inside coming out, until she bled to death. Murdered her own mother. She came into this world a wicked child.'

'And so did I.'

Her mother froze, as though she could not quite believe what she'd just heard. To do so would mean she had lost control of the daughter she'd birthed. The perfectly docile, stupid daughter she'd dreamt up so she wouldn't have to acknowledge the unknown child standing before her.

Silence hung between them like a frail pane of glass; Rinyi broke it.

'I think I'd like to go north soon,' she said softly. 'It's been some time since I have seen my sister.'

And her mother turned and swept from the room, leaving Min standing alone, facing her reflection in the mirror. An underfed girl in far too much make-up, made somehow smaller by the opulence of her robes, the towering height of her headdress.

Min watched as the girl screamed, pulling the ivory nail guards from her fingertips and flinging them at the brushed surface of the mirror. They glanced off with a cheap, glinting sound, like chips of ice filling a bowl. Furious at her own impotence, the girl seized the thick wooden headpiece from her own head, tearing away hanks of real hair, raining hairpins across the carpet beneath her feet. She flung the heavy thing at the mirror. It hit with a bellow like a gong. The mirror shook, tumbled from the wall, falling forward onto the surface of the vanity and smashing glass bottles of oils and perfumes, sending jewellery cascading to the floor.

'E-Empress?' Butterfly appeared in the doorway. 'Oh, Empress!'

Duty, and perhaps what history they had together,

overrode fear. Butterfly was at her side at once, checking her for damage, for pain, smoothing back the swinging, ragged hanks of her hair. Min could no longer see herself, but she saw well enough what was reflected in Butterfly's eyes: a sweating, sobbing fool, no different from the useless girl she and the other nunas had grown up pitying. A girl who would never be more than that.

Her hands reached for the amma's throat before she could stop them. She felt the searing heat in them a heartbeat before Butterfly's startled scream filled the room. The sound was enough to startle Min and she released her.

Butterfly went to the ground, a perfect red outline of Min's hands stark against her long, pale throat.

Then Brother was there, flanked by a dozen guards.

'Get her out of here!' barked the monk, gesturing to Butterfly. One of the men grabbed her roughly, and for an absurd moment Min nearly chided him. That was her handmaiden. A highborn girl.

'Empress.' Brother's voice was urgent at her back. She watched him draw a glass vial from his pocket. 'Empress, you're not well. Your nerves.'

She took the vial from him willingly, not failing to notice how he recoiled as their fingers touched. Hers were still hot, though no longer lethal. She made to tip the vial down her throat, grateful – how long had it been since she'd slept? – but he stopped her.

'Not the full vial, just a drop or two,' he cautioned. She wanted to shake him. The other day he'd wanted her to take the draught, to make her pliable. Now that she sought oblivion on her own terms, he was the picture of caution.

But she tilted the vial less steeply and one, two, three drops fell on her tongue, bitter and oddly cold. *Poppy tears*. She allowed herself to acknowledge what they were. And then she let him take the vial away.

He guided her over to the divan her mother had touched earlier.

No, she thought, *not that one – my bed*. But she was already so weak. Speaking felt like an insurmountable struggle. She settled back against the cushions instead.

'You must be careful with medicines. Too much of anything is poison,' Brother chided lightly as her eyelids fluttered. 'You wouldn't want to sleep forever, would you?'

You have no idea what I want, she thought. Then the darkness unfolded over her, and gratefully, she knew nothing at all.

8

Sanctuary

Their house is quite large, and easy to find.

Adé's letter hadn't lied about the scale of the Anglimns' residence, a two-storey stone manse dating back over a century, retrofitted with foreign-style domes and windows. Even now, under the dusting of soot and the dying flames, Lu could see its elegant bones. Perhaps a day ago, she might have paused in the vestibule to marvel at what a career in import and export could earn the right sort of man. But that had been before Missar Anglimn had learned the indelible lesson that while money could buy comfort and beauty, nothing in this world could grant freedom from grief. Before explosions set off by rioters – or meant to look as though they had been – had blown down his gate, his doors, shattered those fine imported-glass windows, and killed his only son.

As though to punctuate Lu's thoughts, a throaty wail rose up behind her, from the corner of the room where they'd laid the dead boy out across a divan. The ivory upholstery was soaked through with black-red blood. The boy's mother was the one making the noise: a small woman with limp, dun-coloured hair pulled into a chignon. Missar Anglimn stood beside her with a stillness that rivalled that of his son. Lu had remembered him as a sallow, fragile-looking man. She would not have supposed his face could grow any paler, but it had, blanching to the faint non-colour of unglazed porcelain.

'Are you all right?'

The voice was too close. She whirled.

'It's only me!' Jin said, holding up his hands in defence. For a moment, she did not understand – until she did. She'd reached for the knife at her hip. The knife that was longer there, because she had left it behind in the belly of a young man who would never go home again.

She dropped her hand.

'Sorry,' she muttered, her neck going hot with horror – and an odd kind of embarrassment. She was not accustomed to her body acting against her will. Once more, the officer in Ansana flashed before her eyes, and she could not help but wonder if Jin, too, was thinking back to what she had done. If he had thought, even for a moment, that she might do the same to him.

'Where's Nasan?' she asked quickly.

Jin gestured toward the distant end of the room where the Ashina girl sat, as far from the mourners as she could possibly get, with her back toward them; Ony sat cross-legged on the floor beside her. Nasan appeared to be doing an inventory of her weapons and taking long, throaty pulls of water from a crystalline pitcher that had certainly been crafted to hold something finer. She was, Lu thought, quite studiously oblivious to the adjacent mourning spectacle. But her shoulders clenched tighter with every wail they issued, like a crossbow cranked to breaking.

'Are you all right?' Jin repeated. 'Perhaps you should sit.'

'I—' Her throat tightened, and she could not finish. Dizzy, she looked down, and saw red. Blood. Spreading on the floor. And white: the creamy rayskin handle of her dagger was emerging from the young man's belly—

'Princess?'

She blinked. The blood disappeared. The dagger was gone.

Jin remained. She met his eyes. Warm and brown, usually boyish and dreamy, then by turns, abruptly focused, steely. Right now though, they were hesitant – but wanting. Wanting her. Or, what he thought she was: someone needing comfort. Someone who deserved it.

He doesn't know. Even after what she'd done to that guard. He'd seen, and yet he still didn't see her. The thought left her hollow.

Nokhai had known. He'd seen what she was from the beginning, well before she'd seen it herself: a killer. Ruthless, when she had to be. The realisation filled her with a kind of fluttering terror – and something oddly like hope. The soaring, boundless sensation of being known by someone whom she could trust with that knowing. Until, like a stone to the wing, she remembered. In the end, he hadn't been able to trust her in kind.

It would be so easy. To take what Jin was offering—

A loud pop resounded behind them and they both jumped. It was only Kommodeur Lamont, though, breaking the seal on a small cask of wine. Lu glanced at the Anglimns to see if they had noticed, but they were still cocooned in mourning, oblivious to the world. Lamont didn't seem to have given them any consideration. He sloshed the wine across two Ellandaise-style teacups, heedless of the runoff filling their saucers, then held one out in her direction.

Lu looked to Jin. The hesitation, the want was gone from his eyes, replaced with a soldier's cool appraising stare.

'Diplomacy calls,' she told him.

'I should join you,' he suggested. 'It will make your coalition look stronger.'

Or it will look like I need a man as a chaperone.

'Go and wait with Nasan,' she told him. 'I'll be back.'

He was clearly displeased. But he was a soldier at heart, and he obeyed.

Alone, she walked to where Lamont stood, still holding out the wine for her. His hand trembled and the cup rattled in its saucer, the porcelain so delicate it seemed obscene it should be unbroken amid all this ruin. She took it but did not drink.

'Sit.' He gestured to a velvet settee before pulling up a mahogany side chair for himself, brushing fistfuls of ash and crumbled stone from the seat.

Lu found a clear patch on the settee for herself, glancing over at the Anglimns. Now was clearly not the time to announce herself. But perhaps she didn't need to; she had the ear of the Kommodeur, now. He wouldn't have Anglimn's riches, and he didn't have the Ambassadeur's political clout, but he clearly was a man of some influence and power. She would just have to see how much.

Missar Anglimn broke away from the circle of grief, moaning in Saxil to himself. He'd been a very different man when last she'd seen him, presented before her father in court. Small beside his countrymen, but impressive in his own right. Years of living in the Empire of the First Flame were reflected not just in his fluency with Yueh, but also in his manners.

Lu supposed she'd looked somewhat better then, too. She was barely recognisable now: dirty, ash-caked, and wearing a peasant's tunic, greasy hair cut short like a young boy's. The only indicator of her former self – her true self – was the sword strapped to her back. And even that was masked with ash and grime.

The Kommodeur cleared his throat, drawing her attention back his way. He slouched in his chair, right arm propped by the elbow upon his armrest, chin atop his fist, one long leg tossed carelessly over the other. The toe of his boot gave an intermittent twitch, like the tail of a cat.

'I would asks Anglimn join us,' Lamont said, and Lu followed his gaze over to where the other man was still bent at the waist, hovering over his own sick. 'But he is preoccupied.'

She looked sharply at him. The gaze he returned was placid. Was this the Ellandaise sense of humour, she wondered, or did he really feel so little for the dead boy?

Lu attempted a belated, polite smile. It felt like her face were splitting in two. His eyes never left her. Without meaning to, she sat up straighter. Her face might be streaked with blood and soot, and she might be wearing the threadbare tunic taken off the back of some poor dead Yunian, but she was still a princess. An emperor. Or she would be, if she played this game correctly.

'I apologise for my appearance,' she told him with

forced grace. 'Had I known I would be meeting with someone so distinguished I would have presented myself accordingly.'

The Kommodeur continued to stare and Lu wondered briefly how well he could understand her. Perhaps she'd spoken too quickly. But then he broke into a wide, white smile. 'You ares truly something, are you not?' he said. There was curiosity in his faint, glass-coloured eyes, and something else, too. Amusement, perhaps.

'I'm impressed you recognised me,' she told him.

'I see you fight, once,' he said, as though that should explain it. 'You strike your instructor's blade so hard it breaks in half. I was very long aways, but I will never forget way you looks.'

'That was the day of my betrothal ceremony.' She'd nearly forgotten about that. A thousand years may as well have passed.

'When I saw that, I thoughts for certain: you will succeed the father. But I suppose much happens since.'

'It certainly has.'

Lamont's gaze went canny. 'You are clevers,' he said. 'But are you also wise?'

Bold words to toss so casually at royalty. This man was a fool, or he had more power than she'd anticipated. He was arrogant enough for either to be true.

'I've never heard otherwise,' she said coolly, taking a sip of her wine. It was pomegranate. Good quality. 'Why do you ask?'

He reached for his cup, his sip a suspiciously prim mirror of her own – was he mocking her? Then he leaned forward. 'You returns to the capitals, despite price on your head. Smart girl like you? Not do so without plan. You have friends' – he nodded across the room where Jin and Nasan were watching them warily – 'Though, it seem to me, not enough. Perhaps I helps in this regard?'

'One can never have too many friends.' She allowed a neutral smile to rise to her lips, careful not to display any eagerness. He recognised her situation; she did not know what the Ellandaise wanted. What game they were playing at. What they would want in return. Sheltering her at all posed a risk; she was a fugitive. It discomfited her to think how much she already owed them.

Lamont stood, holding up a finger. 'I have a gift for you, our new friend. Wait here.'

A gift? 'There's no need—'

'I insists.' Seeing the suspicious frown unmoved from her lips, he grinned, wide enough for the two of them. 'What can I say? I have weakness for beautiful woman in distress.'

And horrifyingly, he winked.

Before she could respond, he disappeared into the next room.

Lu cast about the room anxiously, but the other Ellandaise were too distracted to take notice of her. She wondered if, like Kommodeur Lamont, they would recognise her if they did.

A line of Ellandaise men in matching dusty uniforms hugged the adjacent wall – Anglimn's private guard. Some still stood at attention, but others were slumped in shabby defeat, ash-streaked faces staring off into nothing. A few of the men shouldered Ellandaise-style muskets. The weapons looked impressive: black metal barrels, and dark wood handles inlaid with mother-of-pearl. But they were relatively primitive, from what Lu understood. They'd failed to protect Anglimn's son, at any rate.

One of the men moved aside, and then Lu saw her: a slight, dark-skinned girl in pale peach robes, hunched and shivering over the divan bearing Anglimn's son. Last time they'd met, her black hair had been pinned back. Now it fell loose, a soft cloud dusted with white ash, framing her stricken, heart-shaped face.

Lu had mistaken her for a foreign-born Westerman at the time, but as soon as she'd heard her speak, it had been clear the girl was all Yulan City. Not even the likes of Missar Anglimn could have mimicked an accent that authentically. So, then, what was she doing here with the Ellandaise?

As though sensing her stare, Adé looked back. For a moment Lu thought she would not know her, but then her dark eyes widened in recognition.

Before Lu could react, a tremendous groan filled the room, drowning out even the Anglimns' weeping. The broken remnant of the door that had been propped up to cover the blown-out entrance fell to the floor. Lu was on her feet before it hit the ground.

The crash sent up a plume of dust. As it cleared, Ambassadeur Kartrum pushed his way into the room, flanked by half a dozen Ellandaise soldiers. Each bore a musket, and unlike Anglimn's defeated-looking private guard, these men still looked eager to use them.

Anglimn was already striding over to the Ambassadeur. The two men commenced rapid discussion in Saxil.

'The Ambassadeur is asking Missar Anglimn if the

rioters have specifically been targeting the Ellandaise.'
The voice was soft and low in Lu's ear. She jumped. It
was Adé.

'You speak Saxil?' Lu asked.

Adé nodded across the room to the blood-soaked divan.
'I learned from Carmine – Missar Anglimn's son – he is
… he was my fiancé.'

Of course. Her engagement party. At the time, it had
surprised Lu. She would have guessed from the way Adé
had looked at Nokhai – well, it made no difference now.
'I'm so sorry,' Lu murmured.

'Thank you. Do you—' The other girl hesitated, her
red-rimmed eyes already primed with tears. Lu knew
what she was going to ask. 'Nok. Is he – is he still with
you?'

'I'm sorry,' Lu repeated, hating the feel of the words in
her mouth. Useless, for all that she meant them.

Adé looked up toward the ceiling, as though to keep
her tears from spilling. They fell anyway, cutting fresh
tracks through the dust on her face. She wiped them away
with shaking fingers, then nodded over to Nasan. 'When
she first came in, I thought …' Her voice tightened and
choked to nothing, as though she couldn't bear to remember the hope she had felt in that moment.

Lu nodded. 'His sister.'

'She looks just …' She could not finish the thought. Lu
understood, though. 'And Omair? Is he …?'

'I don't know,' Lu replied. 'Last we saw him, he was
alive. He wasn't at his home, though. Likely he's been
arrested.' Gods, could she share nothing but sorrow with
this girl?

'How did you come to be here?' Adé asked. 'I left a note for Nok, but I didn't dare hope—'

'I found it,' Lu admitted, feeling a bit guilty about it now.

Adé did not seem bothered, though. 'I had thought perhaps the Anglimns could extend some protection to Nok, if he sought them out. That was before Empress Minyi called for the expulsion of all foreign—'

Shouts erupted across the room from the Ellandaise. The Ambassadeur looked distressed, meaty hands fisted at his hips.

Adé rushed to translate. 'The Ambassadeur wants to take Anglimn's private guard and head down to the harbour, take refuge in their ships. Anglimn says it's too risky, they'll be torn apart if they're caught by the mob.'

The words tickled Lu's memory. 'You said before that the Ambassadeur thought the rioters might be targeting them specifically – why would that be? I thought the riots were over a food shortage.'

Adé shook her head. 'They are. But there's been unrest against foreigners for some time now. Their wealth, the way they're taking over a larger and larger part of the city. And after the empress's display in the throne room, well, hostility's never been higher.'

But hostility between who? Again, Lu could not shake the feeling there were more players in the game than were immediately apparent.

Hana against Hu. Pro-Ellandaise and pro-trade support-ers against the isolationists. They say it's like a war without weapons.

Well, someone had escalated to using weapons ...

A rattle of exploding sparkstone rang out somewhere close by, as though to punctuate her point. 'Let's move away from the window,' Lu said.

'These explosives,' Adé mused as they moved toward the centre of the room. 'Where could they have come from?'

Lu nodded grimly. 'I had the same thought. If this is a peasant revolt ...'

'Your average family in Scrap-Patch Row barely has the clothes on their backs,' Adé filled in. 'They don't have guns lying about, let alone the sort of sparkstone necessary to cause this sort of damage.'

They stared at one another. This close together, Lu saw what distance had previously masked: Adé's face and neck were freckled with a rain of dried blood, culminating in a large, much deeper patch of black-red marring the front of her pale peach robes. Lu saw no injuries on her own person, though. She must have been nearby when someone else was grievously injured and held them in her lap as they bled. Most probably Carmine, to whom she had been betrothed, whom she must have loved.

'Listen, I need to get to the palace,' Lu told her. 'I came back here seeking the assistance of the Ellandaise. If this revolt is the scheme of someone with access to these sorts of weapons—'

'Princess Lu!'

The Kommodeur had returned and now strode over to her. He held a curved, foreign-style pistol in his cupped hands, as gently as a different man might hold some delicate living thing.

Lu looked at it quizzically. A snubbed silver barrel and a dark wooden handle. Unremarkable. 'I'm afraid my martial skills begin and end with a blade,' she told him.

Before he could respond, the Ambassadeur barked Lamont's name from across the room. She and the Kommodeur both looked up – and at that moment, recognition dawned in the Ambassadeur's eyes. He barked out an exclamation she did not understand, but there was no need for Adé to translate. He knew her – and he was not pleased.

In an instant, Jin and Nasan were at her side. Lu was glad to have them there, even as the Kommodeur stepped in front of her, blocking her from the Ambassadeur. The men began a rapid-fire exchange. Lu looked quickly to Adé who shook her head in frustration.

'They're speaking too fast,' the other girl said. 'The Ambassadeur – he's berating Lamont for squandering all the work he's been doing to appease someone – I didn't catch the names.'

Lu thought she understood well enough. The Ambassadeur had his hooks in someone – likely several influential someones – in court. Her presence in the Anglimns' house threatened that.

She backed up, as did Jin and Nasan. Nasan grabbed Adé by the arm to pull her with them as the older Ellandaise man strode over, yelling, until he was face-to-face with the Kommodeur.

'The Ambassadeur says the Kommodeur is committing treason,' Adé whispered breathlessly. 'He says he doesn't know what bargains the Kommodeur is striking – whether it is for wealth, or power, but the Ellandaise ruler, King Ryvan, will hear about them.'

Silence overtook the room, interrupted only by shouts

coming from somewhere far off in the city. The riot was moving away from them – but a new danger now seemed to loom.

The Kommodeur's back was rigid in his wool jacket. Lu watched a single thread of sweat drip from beneath his straw-coloured hair, down the back of his neck.

Then, he laughed. A quick, careless shout. Across the room, Missar Anglimn crossed, and then uncrossed his arms uneasily.

'You're right, my old friend,' the Kommodeur said, clapping the Ambassadeur on the back.

It took Lu a moment to realise she'd understood him. The befuddled expression on the Ambassadeur's face indicated he had not. The Kommodeur was speaking in Yueh. But why?

Lamont turned and met her eyes. His gaze was taut and nervy. Someone on the verge of taking a tremendous risk.

'Ambassadeur Kartrum,' he said, loud enough for the whole room to hear, though his gaze never left her. 'You always beens loyal subject to the Ellandaise crown. I admire it. Such blind, uncompromising faith – certainly I can never manage it. But then, I was born with imagin-ation.'

At last, he tore his gaze from Lu. 'King Ryvan,' he said, 'will surely be strickens to lose such a steadfast servant. We will be sure to tells him how bravely you fight, before you are tragically killed in the riots this night.'

And then abruptly the gun was in his grasp. Jin grabbed Lu's arm, but she pushed him away and drew her sword in the same motion.

Anglimn gave a wordless shout of warning. Too late.

A shot rang out and a hole appeared between the Ambassadeur's eyebrows, black and smoking, slightly right of centre.

For a moment, the Ambassadeur remained standing, his mouth forming a circle to mimic the one in his forehead. Thick, dark blood began to weep from the hole, impossibly slow and gentle. Someone yelled. The sword trembled in Lu's hands, futile, without a clear enemy to strike at.

The Kommodeur, though, just leaned forward with a terrible lust like hunger contorting his face, looking for – what, exactly?

The Ambassadeur swayed forward, his knees gone soft. But before he could fall, the hole in his forehead let out a glut of strange grey smoke – more like fog than smoke at all. And then, the edges of the torn flesh began to glow, like paper put to a burning candle.

The Ambassadeur lit up just as quickly. One moment, he was there, a swaying corpse in free-fall. The next, he was a column of melting flesh and fierce, blue flame.

This time, the screaming was louder, and Lu heard her own voice in it. Missar Anglimn stood rooted to the spot, his face a rictus of horror, but his wife fled from the room, hands clutching her face. Lu felt Jin grab her again, but this time it was not protective; it was terrified. She seized his hand, stumbled back as the fire that had been the Ambassadeur consumed itself and collapsed into black ash. Beside her, Adé and Nasan were grasping each other, silent with terror.

One of the Ellandaise soldiers who had arrived with

Kartrum stepped forward, raising his musket to his shoulder and taking aim at Lamont. The Kommodeur did not hesitate; he discharged two bullets into the man. One missed and hit the floor, incinerating immediately and dropping through the hole it had burned in the wooden planks. The other tore through the wool of the soldier's jacket and buried itself in his gut.

He caught fire as quickly as Kartrum had, but did not have the mercy of already being dead. A stomach wound did not kill the way a shot to the head did. He burned, and burned, and screamed the whole while of it.

At her side, Adé breathed something to herself. It might have been a prayer, but none that Lu recognised: 'Dust. Dust ... of annihilation.'

The room fell into silence once more. Lamont broke it, announcing something loudly in Saxil.

Lu looked instinctively at Adé. The girl's voice shook as she translated his words: 'Is anyone else feeling incurably loyal to King Ryvan and his bloody crown?

Lamont turned jauntily on his heel, swivelling between the other Ellandaise soldiers and Anglimn's private guard. His face was red and wet with the heat of the flames and his own excitement, a drunkard's smile swaying on his lips. He resumed speaking in Yueh, but Lu had the feeling the men understood him well enough.

'No one?' he asked, twirling the gun around his finger again. 'What about you, Anglimn?'

The merchant shook his head. He uttered something that scarcely resembled words.

'Speak up, Parthan,' drawled Lamont.

The merchant looked nearly bloodless. 'Lamont,' he murmured. 'What have you done? King Ryvan will ... How far do you think you can possibly take this?'

If his words were meant to temper the Kommodeur's feral joy, they missed their mark. If anything, Lamont's grin intensified. 'Quite far indeed.'

The buckles of his boots rattled as he strode over to Lu, each step deliberate and resounding in the silence. She tensed, fingers clenching around the hilt of her sword. It would do little good against Lamont's demonic pistol – but even a demonic pistol required an arm to fire it. She knew how to remove one of those.

But Lamont stopped well outside the range of her blade. He cocked his head, considering her with a grin. Then he knelt, offering his hands up toward her. In them, lay the gun. The room seemed to draw in a sharp breath around them. Lu wanted nothing less than to touch the thing, but what choice did she have? She sheathed her sword and took up the pistol. It was heavy and clammy in her grasp, like some half-living thing.

'Princess – Empress Lu,' Kommodeur Lamont said, still on his knees. 'I offer you my service, and that of the men in my flotte. All soldiers of the Ellandaise Royal Army. And I'm certain Anglimn will volunteers his household guard. They are... what is the word? Mercenaries? But train well enoughs.'

Lu took a deep, controlled breath. This was it. The leverage she would have with this weapon – over Brother, certainly. Perhaps even over her sister. Not that she would think to use it on Minyi, of course. But the sheer display of power ... Her sister would have to see reason.

She hadn't even had to ask – this man was giving her everything she had come here seeking. But she had to be careful. She did not yet know all that he expected in return.

She looked from the gun to the Kommodeur's pale eyes. 'A dozen or so men is not an army.'

Instinct packed her words with bravado. Better to project strength, even at a disadvantage. She looked to Jin, stalwart and competent at her right. On her left, Nasan stood tall, an arm still protectively thrust in front of Adé, who held up her chin, despite looking as though she wished she were anywhere but there.

'A dozen men to make an army? No, of course not,' Lamont said. 'It is good thing, then, we have more than a hundred.'

A *hundred* foreign soldiers in Yulan City? That sounded more like an invasion than a household guard, or military escort. How could her father have permitted that? Or, perhaps, had they taken advantage of his death and the disarray that followed and snuck them in under her sister's nose?

'And what,' Lu said, 'would you hope to gain in return?'

'Your cousin gives me the sparkstone that is gun you hold.'

'*Set*? Why would he have done that? He distrusted foreigners.'

The Kommodeur smiled wryly. 'We met with him shortly after he was named your father's successor. In private. He was a... haughty boy. But the wealth of Elland is no secret, and even he saw the wisdom in expanding trade with our little nation. He gave us a sample of this sparkstone. He tell us he forms it from minerals he collect from the shores of Yunis—'

'He took stone from Yunian soil?' Jin stepped forward in alarm. Lu rested a hand on his arm.

'Yes. And he say there is more where it comes from. He tells us, if we are able to reach an agreement some – much – can be ours. We don't know where is the rest – but someone in your palace, they do. Your sister, she will not reason with us; or rather, the men who control her won't ...'

'But I'm not in a position to be choosy about such things, am I?' Lu concluded for him.

'This sparkstone – your cousin, he names it Dust of Annihilation – it is power,' Lamont said. 'If you control its source, you control the empire. Beyond.'

It seemed unlikely her cousin could have kept such a cache of powder like this hidden. But if what Lamont was saying was true...

'And what of you?' she demanded. 'What would you be, with such power in your hands?'

'A free man,' he told her. 'No longer beholden to my rank, my king.'

She frowned. Was he mad, or simply stupid? She had no interest in entangling herself with a rogue agent acting against his own king, nor the internal squabbling of his foreign backwater. But by the time he could cause her any real trouble, she might well be back in her rightful place, and easily rid of him.

Something else was still bothering her, though. 'My cousin wanted your people gone. It was to be his first official decree. Why would he even have agreed to meet with you?'

The Kommodeur gave a weary sigh. 'Ah, yes. Well, as I say, initially our discourse seems promising. Then the subject of poppies arises.'

Understanding dawned. And for the first time since she had killed him, Lu thought of Set – really thought of him. Remembered his face, his voice. Oddly, the memory that came to her was that of her cousin when he first arrived in court as a boy. He'd been so full of arrogance even then – but so, she supposed, had she. Perhaps, given the right circumstances, he might have outgrown it.

Instead, she'd knocked loose half his teeth and sent him home in disgrace. His household physicians had given him poppy tears for the pain in his jaw, but it had lingered – and so, too, had the tinctures, growing stronger with every dose, until they were replaced by cakes of tar and a pipe. He'd spent the remainder of his childhood in a haze of bitter indolence, dogged by a ravenous hunger, and the fear of losing his oblivion.

'You see,' Lamont told her. 'The mens of our southern colonies have develop new procedure for refine and package poppy cake. Of course, the cheap labour, too. All of it amounts to significant drop in cost. I am sure you would be most delighted to hear more about this proposition once your throne, it is secured.'

'Once my throne is secured,' she repeated sardonically, understanding the bargain he was floating.

Lamont grinned. 'It is good, yes? Having allies?

'She already has allies.' A hard voice emerged from behind her.

'Nasan, not now,' Lu snapped.

'I'm not getting pushed aside just because some new, shiny—'

'Not *now*.'

'Princess Lu seems a magnanimous person. Capable of having more than one friend, I thinks,' Lamont interjected.

'You clearly don't know her yet,' Nasan said flatly. But mercifully, she left it at that.

'Lu,' Jin murmured. 'Perhaps we should all discuss this first—'

'There is nothing to discuss,' she said, cutting him off with more force than she'd intended.

Lu looked at Lamont. This was not a good man. She had felt it the moment he laid eyes on her, out in the tempest of the street. She had known it when he'd pulled the trigger and turned his countryman into kindling. But what he was offering ...

She shifted the enormous weight of the small gun in her hands. She had fired a musket before, but never a pistol. It looked perversely easy. She pocketed the weapon, feeling its hot, sullen weight against her thigh. She was sick of fighting, sick to death of uncertainty. She was a king; she would do what was necessary.

'How soon can you gather your men?' she asked Lamont, meeting his pale, watery eyes with her own.

'How soon do you needs them?'

'Now. The city guard are distracted with the riots. The palace will have sent out their guards as reinforcements. We won't see another opportunity like this.'

The Kommodeur dipped his head so low his

bark-coloured hair brushed the rubble-choked floor. 'As you wish, Emperor Lu.'

And she told herself those words she'd been longing, killing, to hear, only meant so little because they had come from him.

9

Reunion

Up this high, the air was so hot and dry it felt solid. It reminded Nok of the earth on his skin when he was a boy, using sand to scrub his hands before supper. Steady, seething heat against his flesh, scouring him clean, making him new.

The eagle had flown this way before. It knew this land, the ruddy sands giving way to staggering brush and then to the clay banks of streams, the hot upsurges of wind buffeting its body upward, reliable and ever. It would be here again, perhaps with Nok, and certainly long after he and anyone who had ever spoken his name were dead and dust.

The hot upsurge of air they'd coasted on ended, and for a harrowing moment they were in free-fall. Then the eagle flapped its mammoth wings, once, twice, and found loft again. Nok had the strange, phantom sensation of his stomach lurching, though of course, that was the boy's stomach – and it was not there now to lurch. Still, he felt it, like a phantom riding tandem. It summoned a memory: sitting astride Lu's war elk, bounding from tenuous foothold to foothold.

Below them, the landscape was changing. Gone were the vast, unmarred swaths of sand, the sporadic scatters of gnarled thorny brush; those wide, hot plains with nothing to do but reflect the unbroken light of the sun back up as heat. He saw now, too, the marks of humans: the green spread of fields, clustered houses nestled in valleys, growing denser as they sailed on.

Something unclean came in on the wind. The eagle sensed it first, and it took him a moment to understand it, to interpret what the creature felt.

Smoke.

He cast his eagle's eyes toward the horizon and saw it there. Like a lost thundercloud rising from below. The whole of the city felt rank and heavy.

Perhaps sensing his dread, the eagle banked hard, sending them circling around the perimeter of the city walls. It seemed to Nok to be a question.

Stay? Or go?

He let the eagle cast another wide, lazy loop through the sky before responding.

Stay, he said, finally.

They plummeted together toward the ground.

A city in flames. Just as Nok had seen in his vision.

The eagle touched down on a rooftop and its caul slipped off him. The absence left him breathtakingly heavy. The soles of the boy's boots slipped on the same ceramic tiles his talons had readily gripped only a moment earlier. He scrabbled for purchase with thick, clumsy fingers, righting himself before he slid to the ground. It took him a moment to adjust to the premature darkness brought on by the smoke as it blotted out the sun. He squinted, struggling to make sense of the landscape before him with the boy's weak, smoke-stung eyes.

He recognised the high rise of the First Ring wall, could even make out the frantic shapes of guards atop the watchtower of the Southern Gatehead. They were sounding the city alarms. He'd never heard them before; their clangs were deafening.

He was west of the garment district. Where, though, to find his sister and Lu? His vision had granted him the omniscience of dreams: to look one way was to know all that was relevant in that direction, to see what he needed. Here and now, he faced the constraints of his human body, his weak human eyes.

Or perhaps not.

Nok sank into an instinctive crouch, even before the blue-grey fur emerged and enveloped him.

In two bounds, they were down on the street. The wolf gave an exploratory huff, seeking the scent of the girls, then snorted and whined, pawing at its snout in irritation. The smoke had choked all the information out of the air.

'Kangmun Boulevard is cut off north of the smithing district! We can't get back to the First Ring that way.'

The wolf froze. Men. The clatter of boots.

Soldiers.

'Let's head down to the harbour,' said a second man. 'The air will be clearer there.'

'We need to get back to the palace,' snapped the first man. 'Everyone went to help when Scrap-Patch Row went up in flames. There's hardly anyone left to guard the empress.'

The palace.

The wolf leapt atop an abandoned cart, half-burnt but still erect, and used it as leverage to gain access to the rooftops once more. There was less rubble up there, making their passage more fleet.

'That witch doesn't need protection.' The second man shuddered. Nok could see him now, dimly through the haze. He was tall and slender, where his cohort was slightly shorter and stout. When the taller man turned, Nok saw he had a crossbow in hand, and very prominent sideburns. 'Have you seen what she did to the throne room?' he demanded.

'No,' said the stout man. 'Have you?'

'Well, I didn't *see* it, but I heard—'

The wolf was nearly upon them. Reflexively, it stopped. They felt it at the same time, boy and wolf, like voices echoing in a canyon: a ceramic shingle worked its way loose from beneath their back foot and slid down to the alley below. The street was packed dirt, but hard enough. The shingle shattered on impact.

Both soldiers whirled. Boy and wolf froze. Which form would be safer if they were spotted? Wolves were known to come down from the mountains during droughts and plagues, picking off the weak, the elderly, unwatched children. They were seen as ill omens during catastrophe, and this certainly qualified. They'd shoot him on sight.

And a boy? Well, that depended on what sort of men these were. Experience had taught him not to anticipate goodness—

'Who's there?' the stout soldier called out. 'Do you need assistance? We can escort you to safety.'

'Come on,' the tall soldier with the sideburns said uneasily, hefting his crossbow with greater purpose now. 'If someone's hiding from us, let them. Might be a rioter.'

They were too close. If Nok ran, he'd surely knock free more shingles. Even then, he might escape them, but he might not.

The soldier was moving down the alley, until he came to the shingle Nok had loosed.

Close. Too close.

The man toed the shingle with his boot, scooting it through the layer of white-grey ash dusting the street. Then, he looked up at the roof . . .

Nok gazed back at him through the dim, glassy eyes of a Ruvaiian pit adder. Or, at least, he assumed the vaguely man-shaped hazy blur of heat he was looking down at was the soldier. Snakes, he was learning, could not see very well.

He had wondered before, idly, if it was possible for him to move from one caul into another without first changing back into his human form. It seemed that he could. His new body – no longer than a man's leg – draped over the far side of the roof, its dappled clay and sand-coloured scales melding with the colour of the shingles. The soldier stared in his direction a moment longer, squinting fruitlessly up through the haze, seeing nothing.

'This neighbourhood is barely a rung above Scrap-Patch Row,' complained the other soldier, not lowering his crossbow. Their voices came to Nok as vibrations, and he had to strain to interpret them. 'Anyone left isn't worth the trouble.'

'No one's here anyway,' the stout man grumbled. 'Let's go.'

They departed, and silently – gliding over the rooftops, down gutter-spouts, wending his way over rain barrels and window ledges – Nok and the pit adder followed the lure of their heat, all the way up to the Southern Gatehead.

'Ay!' the stouter soldier called up to the gate watchtower. 'Infantrymen Ryu and Eng reporting! Open the gate.'

Nok raised the snake's head and made out a new, third blur of heat emerging from high up.

'We're under strict orders not to let anyone in or out. First Ring's on lockdown, haven't you heard? Who's your commanding officer?'

'Captain Lum. We got separated from him and the others while tamping down fires in the cobblers' district. Had orders to meet back at the palace.'

The warm blur of the soldier in the watchtower disappeared back into the window. Ryu and Eng waited for the response from the watchtower, stationary and distracted. It was as good a chance as Nok might get. Nok urged the snake forward, fighting its instincts. It slithered past Soldier Ryu's boot, and coiled itself within a broken pile of brick.

The soldier from the window reemerged at the base of the watchtower. 'I'll unlock the service door for you. But if this bites you in the ass, don't bring my name into it.'

Ryu and Eng followed him to the service door. And as they passed through into the First Ring, Nok's adder followed swiftly on their heels.

★

The streets here were broader than any in the Second Ring, clear not just of rubble and soot, but of deep gouges left by wagon wheels in the mud, sleeping bodies huddled on corners. Here, the world was neatly laid slate, and flower boxes lining closed-up gates and doors, protecting the wealthy denizens sheltering inside against nothing.

The snake's senses allowed Nok to keep pace with Eng and Ryu – two oversized red-orange plumes of warmth, like distant hearths.

New figures appeared on his horizon, deep red, searingly warm with exertion. He counted four – no, six. Flicking out his black tongue, he tasted them. Smelled them. To the adder, the two senses were, if not indistinct, at least muddled. It flicked its tongue out again, and this time Nok paid closer mind to the information it received. Not food; big creatures. Predators.

Humans, Nok corrected. But the snake's mind did not seem interested. Nok swore he felt it give him the equivalent of a shrug.

'Westgate's been compromised!' one of the newcomers shouted as they approached. The snake flicked out its tongue, tasted the tang of sweat, old leather and fear. Nok felt the rattle of boot buckles shiver through him. More soldiers, then.

Soldier Ryu stepped forward to meet them. 'The rioters broke through?'

'Not the rioters,' corrected another of the new men. 'We had orders from Magistrate Ok to funnel them back down along the harbour.'

'Since when does the city guard take its orders from Magistrate Ok?' demanded Ryu.

Nok picked up an uneasy, unspoken tension then. Duplicity. A uniquely human flavour.

'Never mind that,' snapped Soldier Eng. 'Who's taken Westgate?'

And then, from the near distance, came a new sound. Popping. Like firecrackers lit on the streets to celebrate the New Year.

'Foreigners,' said one of the newcomers. 'The pink men. Must be three-, four-dozen strong. They have muskets with them.'

'Well, we have crossbows,' countered Soldier Ryu, though his voice sounded somewhat less bold than his words.

The snake slunk further into the shadows, hugging a nearby building as the men turned toward the direction of the gunfire. It flicked out its tongue – and tasted something familiar.

Nok should not have been able to recognise the scent. There were too many bodies, all clustered close together, for one. The snake had no previous knowledge of her, had never met her. And the boy should not have been able to interpret the abstract sense information he was given. Yet, all at once, the snake tasted – and Nok knew.

He needed better eyes. He focused. One moment he was the snake, and then, like a warm wind prickling over his skin, he was washed over in grey-blue fur.

The wolf sniffed the air and knew her immediately, just as Nok had. It registered others in her company – including its packmate. His sister.

The first of the figures to appear at the end of the street was no one he knew, however. A foreign soldier in moss-green attire. He dropped to one knee, raised a long musket to his shoulder, aimed—

'Muskets! Get down!' barked one of the city guard.

'Wait!'

And then, there she was. Behind her stood Nasan and Jin and Ony, and incredibly, rows and rows of armed foreign soldiers. She was clad in a man's tunic, streaked with soot, and brandishing her familiar sword.

'Stand down,' she told the imperial soldiers. 'I am Princess Lu, daughter of the late Emperor Daagmun, and I am taking control of the city. Pledge to join me, and no one will be harmed.'

The soldiers Eng and Ryu exchanged uncertain glances. The city guard looked to their commanding officer. The officer lifted his crossbow to his shoulder.

Nok was upon him with a single leap, the wolf's jaws locked around his arm. The man howled, the heavy weapon dropping from his hands as he went down to his knees. Around him, his men panicked, some lifting their own crossbows, and at least two drawing their swords.

'Don't shoot, you idiots!' shouted Soldier Ryu. 'You'll hit him!'

'Or me!' interjected a man adjacent to the soldiers bearing crossbows.

'Is that a wolf?' another yelped.

And over the din, the shouts of men, Nok heard a single, quavering voice ring out above them all.

'*Nok?*'

He released the soldier's arm from his jaws. The man curled in on himself, whimpering.

The wolf took one step forward, its form already shifting, lengthening. The boy took the next step – and was nearly bowled over by Nasan, who caught him around the chest and held on as though she meant to crush the breath from him. She released him, but he scarcely had the chance to recover before she lunged forward and punched him hard in the shoulder.

'Ouch!' he yelped.

'I thought you were dead.'

If they'd been a different sort of family, he might have laughed at that. But he just touched her arm, in the same place she'd hit him, and hoped she understood.

And then, he couldn't help himself. He cast about – and found Lu's gaze upon him. She was perhaps a handful of strides away. Too far to reach out and touch, but near enough that he could see the surging fire in her dark, coppery eyes. The way they burned when they met his—

All at once, Ony screamed behind them.

'Look out!' someone, perhaps Jin, yelled.

Nok pushed Nasan down as one of the city guard ran at them and swung his sword wildly at their heads. His sister hit the slate street hard, but rolled to the side, out of the man's reach.

Nok leaned back as the man swung again, all instinct.

'Slipskin!' The soldier seethed the slur like an accusation.

'True,' Nok agreed. The boy leapt backward and landed again as the wolf. The soldier advanced, sword raised. Dimly, Nok registered that the alley had suddenly grown quite a bit more crowded as new Ellandaise soldiers filed in, squaring off against the city guard. The city guard had disposed of their crossbows – no use for ranged weapons in a fight this close – and taken up their swords.

A shot rang out like a firecracker. Nok's eyes went to the Ellandaise – had one of them fired a pistol?

But, no. It was Lu.

She had climbed atop a toppled wagon and held a small, ornate gun in one hand. As they all watched, she fired it again, this time at a large urn painted with soft ivory-peach peonies and containing a small, ornamental mandarin tree. The ceramic shattered upon impact, but as the bullet buried itself into the soil, it erupted into flames. The mandarin tree lit up like a burning matchstick.

What in all the hells was that?

'Do I have your attention now?' the princess demanded. She seemed to take the ensuing silence for assent. 'Good.'

She hopped down from the wagon. Jin made to help her, but she waved him away.

'In case you were curious, this sparkstone works just as well on flesh as it does on wood,' she said, still holding the small gun aloft. 'Now, I am making my way to the Immaculate City. If you are in any way displeased with my sister's rulership, follow me and prepare to take orders. If not, I highly suggest you stay out of the way.'

The city guard parted like grass for a strong wind. Lu walked through, chin held high, followed by Jin, Nasan, Ony, and the girls Nok didn't recognise. After them came dozens and dozens of foreign men touting muskets. The wolf loped forward and fell into step beside Nasan. Then, seeing the stares from some of the Ellandaise – some merely uneasy, some oddly repulsed, bordering on mutinous – he dropped his caul and shifted back into his boy's body.

He felt Lu's eyes on him immediately, as though her gaze had a weight, a gravity that pulled him toward her, pressed him down.

'Personally, I think it's rude you haven't said hello to her yet,' Nasan commented airily.

He looked sharply toward his sister, but she was already cutting through the crowd to talk to Ony.

Lu was immersed in conversation with Jin when Nok reached her side, but she turned immediately upon his approach. He had the distinct impression she was fighting the urge to stop and seize him by the shoulders, to prove he was solid.

'Tell me,' she said, turning to face ahead again. A muscle in her jaw twitched. 'Tell me this is real.'

'It's real,' he said. He hazarded another glance at her, but never broke his stride, matching her brisk step for step. They were close enough, he thought, that if they weren't careful, their hands might brush by mistake.

'This is real,' she repeated throatily. 'You lived, and you're real, and you're here now.' It was almost a command, the way she said it. An imperative.

'By the grace of the Ana and Aba,' murmured Jin from her other side. He touched three fingers to his forehead, between the eyes. 'A miracle.'

'Perhaps,' Nok allowed. He thought of the Black flame and the Violet one, the forms taken by the Yunian gods, how they'd spoken to him in the hidden depths of their temple. He had his own gods, but they'd been hospitable to him.

Jin was still looking at him, and something gleamed in the depths of his chestnut eyes. 'Nokhai,' he said thoughtfully. 'You are something new, now.' It was not a question.

Lu looked up at that. 'What do you mean, he's something new?' The tone of her voice suggested she didn't like the idea.

'He has a power he did not before,' Jin said. His brow furrowed very slightly. 'There is something familiar in your energy that ... it reminds me of my sister – the Oracle, Vrea.' He looked back to Lu. 'I wonder if he might possess the solution to our problem.'

'What problem?' Nok asked.

Lu frowned. 'We were talking about how we might handle Min. From the intelligence we've gathered, it seems like the palace guard is stretched thin. We should be able to fight our way inside, but, well, you've seen what Min is capable of.'

Nok shook his head, remembering the splitting Heart of the Grey City, chunks of paving stone the size of men crumbling away beneath their feet to reveal the blue terror of open sky ... he shut his eyes, shut out the image. Shut out the sensation of falling.

'I don't have power that looks anything like hers,' he said. 'If Minyi does the equivalent here of what she did up there, breaks open the earth or something—'

'I don't believe she will have the same sort of strength down here,' Jin interrupted. 'Yunis is – was – a rare site of power. Millions of years of raw, feral magic entrenched in the stone, floating amid the fog, pulsing in the trees. And for thousands of years, our people enriched it, helped it to thrive. Add to that the way it was cloaked in the Inbetween … we are lucky she was not a more experienced practitioner. She might have done much worse.'

'And what do you think she's capable of doing down here?' Nok asked doubtfully, licking his lips.

'There are rumours,' Lu interjected. 'She apparently set the throne room on fire.' She frowned. '*My* throne room.'

'I'm assuming you don't mean with a flint and kindling?' Nok asked.

'Her mind. Or her eyes,' Lu replied ruefully. 'Depending on who you ask. Reports are … muddy.'

'Princess,' Jin murmured. 'Tell me again what it was your sister told you about her power back in Yunis.'

'Something about my … a shamaness. Min said the woman gave her something – only the shamaness was dead well before Min was even born,' Lu said, tossing her head in frustration. Her once-sleek hair was greasy, streaked in soot and debris. Her overgrown fringe hung in her eyes. Nevertheless, she made the gesture look elegant. 'There was something else. Strange, the way she stated it. She said what she had wasn't from the heavens.'

'A curse?' Jin blurted, and this time he froze mid-stride, causing Lu to follow suit. Ony nearly crashed into them, followed by Nasan. Nok paused alongside them, as did the Ellandaise men behind them.

'What are we stopping for?' demanded his sister.

'If the source of her power is a curse, it may be able to be removed,' Jin said excitedly, oblivious to Nasan's annoyance. 'A curse – it's like a malady. Something foreign to the body. There are spells that can be done. I watched

Vrea extract them at least half a dozen times when I was a child.'

'Do you think you could replicate what she did?' Lu asked doubtfully.

'Not me,' Jin said.

And then he turned to look at Nok.

10

Seedpearl

When Min awoke, Brother was hovering over her vanity, both hands sunk in an open drawer, grasping at its contents. She stared, uncomprehending for a long moment. His sleeves were rolled up nearly to the elbows, as though this were a task that might dirty his robes.

She sat up. A sharp, searing ache in her head cut through the fog of her thoughts, and with it, clarity. She winced and closed her eyes, taking in the throbbing pain, the bitter, chalky residue of the sleeping draught on her tongue.

He started, seeing her staring back at him. It was almost funny, she thought. He was someone who traded on his ability to affect an eerie calm to unsettle others, but in the end, he was only a man, and his serenity only a mask.

'How long have I been asleep?'

She tried to stand; her feet felt oddly thick and clumsy. But when she looked down, there was nothing strange about them. She slid them crookedly into her slippers and stood – only for her legs to give out.

Brother was at her side in an instant, guiding her back to her feet. When she looked up, the drawers to her vanity were closed, not a spangle of jewellery in sight. The sleeves of his robes were still rolled up, revealing skinny arms. His skin was pale and thin, but freckled, as though at some point, much earlier in his life, they had been accustomed to sun. Not the cloistered life of a monk, nor the adviser to royalty.

She slipped his grasp. 'Water,' she ordered through parched lips. 'Bring me water.'

He left her, and she pushed herself upright at the edge of the bed. Her legs trembled as life ached its way back into them.

'How long have I been sleeping?' she repeated.

'Not too long,' Brother assured her. 'A few hours—'

'And the city gates?'

He hesitated over a tea service someone had left on the lacquered table by the door. So, her ammas had come and gone, then. Had he sent them away?

'Unclear. They're saying the First Ring has been compromised.' He poured a cup of tea from the gaiwan and handed it to her as he spoke. It was oversteeped, but the bitter liquid felt like salvation on her dry tongue and she drained the cup.

'Tell me what else you've heard,' she directed.

He hesitated. 'Thus far, only rumours, I'm afraid. We cannot confirm—'

'Then tell me the rumours, if that is all we have,' she snapped.

He cleared his throat. 'Of course. The military appears to have taken control of Kangmun Boulevard back from the rioters. They sent out a contingent of men from the palace, including your personal guard, to help. The peasants fled into Scrap-Patch Row – no surprise there – where a small fire broke out, but it's been mostly contained ...'

That, to her ears, all sounded promising. And yet, she could hear the dread in his voice. 'What else.'

'Ah,' he sighed. 'Well, again, none of these reports have been substantiated—'

Min's eyelids went heavy as her head began once more to throb. 'Just tell me,' she interrupted hoarsely, struggling to stay upright, 'or I will tear out your tongue.'

As though hearing her, the pink tip of it darted out and nervously ran over his dusty lips. 'There have been reports of armed foreigners in the Second Ring.'

'Foreigners?'

'Ellandaise,' he clarified. 'But possibly others, travelling together. Some claim to have spotted Westermen and slipskins among their number.'

Westermen? An improbable alliance, given what little she knew about the history of the two nations. *Rumours,* she reminded herself.

'You said they're armed,' Min said. 'Armed with what? In what capacity?'

'Soldiers. With swords and firearms.'

Foreign soldiers marching through their city streets. An invasion sanctioned by the Ambassadeur and his King Ryvan, then? Was this their response to her banishment of their lot?

Min crossed her arms and looked away, toward the far wall of her bedroom. The Ellandaise were known to be fond of guns, though Min had always heard their sparkstone did not compare favourably to that produced in the empire – it had been her ancestors who invented the stuff, after all. Still, depending on the situation, guns might prove advantageous. The empire's own soldiers had access to firearms, but in what numbers? Certainly, the majority were not well-trained in their use...

When she turned back to him, Brother's face was clouded. He was still withholding something.

'W-what is it?' The words felt oddly thick in her mouth.

Ambivalence flickered over his features and she had the brief notion of slapping him clean of it. She thought to tell him as much, but he spoke before she could push her tongue into the shape of the words: 'Your sister,' he said.

Lu?

'Some of our men insist the Girl King is with the pink men.'

Absurdly, her sister's words came back to her – *not the pink men,* she thought. *It's not proper to call them that. It doesn't do for someone of your station ...*

'If Lu is in the city, she'll be headed here,' Min said. The thought made her oddly dizzy. Was that fear? She supposed she ought to be afraid. Her sister was frightening.

We need to call back my guard, make sure we have our best men securing the gate of the Immaculate City ...

She'd meant to say that aloud. Min stood – and swayed. Her legs were water beneath the weight of her body. She could not understand it, only had the time to perceive the wrongness of how she felt before she stumbled back down onto the bed behind her. She tried to sit, but the best she could do was slump onto her side.

She should have grown stronger, more clear-eyed since waking, but instead her head felt... what was the word?

'Something,' she worked immensely to push out the contours of the word. 'Some ... thing is wrong.' The sounds that came out sounded distant, impossible to parse over the high ringing in her ears.

But Brother wasn't listening; instead, he bent over the teacup on her bedside table, swirling its contents.

'You didn't drink very much,' he observed. He set the cup back down and sighed. 'Well, at any rate, that was last of my poppy tears.'

Her brow creased, as heavy as if weighted with stones. She was struck with the strange fear it might not regain its shape again. She blinked, or tried to. Once she closed her eyes, she found it very difficult to open them again. When she finally did, Brother was standing once more at her vanity. This time she saw he was holding a bag, already sagging with the weight of precious things. They clinked delicately as he plucked a fallen ring from the floor and tossed it in.

It was clear what he was doing, and yet there was something so absurdly base, so ordinary about his actions that she could not quite believe what she was seeing.

'It has been many years since I've had to stoop quite so low as common thievery,' he murmured, both to her and not quite. He moved on to her dresser, lifting a jade trinket dish to the light, as though examining it for worth. Then he stopped and chuckled. 'Force of habit. Forgive me; the places where I learned to loot were not exactly the apartments of an empress. I had to be discerning – to pick and choose with care.' He tossed the dish into his sack. 'What a luxury this place would have been for that young man – to know everything he touched had value.' He sighed. 'Young men are such fools. They misunderstand value, every time. Has anyone taught you that yet? I suppose your mother might have.'

My mother, she thought, and for a brief, animal moment she felt a surge of instinctive hope. But she had sent Rinyi away hours ago, and besides, what reason for hope had her mother ever given her?

'I suppose I can find it in me to be grateful for this bounty, even now,' Brother murmured. 'We will find buyers for these trinkets no matter how far we travel.'

We?

'Where are we going?' she managed to slur out.

'Still awake, then?' he sighed, cinching the drawstring of his sack closed with a quick, terse jerk. 'I've confused you. I'm afraid *you* are not going anywhere. The "we" I spoke of is me, and your creature – your gift – which will soon be mine.'

She lurched as the elbow she'd been propping herself up with slipped, sliding up the sheets until she was laid flat on her side. Her eyes were unfocused, but she refused to let them shut. She kept them locked on the monk with the last, desperate surge of energy left to her, like wringing out the dregs at the bottom of an empty gaiwan.

The blurred, shaky outline of his body came into focus as he knelt by her side with a truncated, utilitarian grace. For a time, he held her gaze, dark eyes locked on her greys. Too long; she had to blink. Her eyes rolled back in her head as she did so, kidnapped by exhaustion, the longing to surrender. She felt his cold, powder-dry hand on her forehead, a grotesque mimicry of care. She did not have the strength left to even recoil. To try to scream.

Who would hear her, anyway? Too late, she remembered his words. *I took the liberty of sending out a contingent of men from the palace, including your personal guard ...*

'I had hoped you'd be asleep for this.' His voice shuddered softly in her ear. 'It has been many years since I made a similar attempt, and those children ... well, they suffered. I wouldn't want you to suffer that way. Oh, I won't patronise you and tell you how much you mean to me – little more than I mean to you, I would imagine. But suffering of this sort ... well, it's very untidy.'

He shifted, and Min heard the whisper of cloth, the tinkle of small metallic things. She strained to open her eyes, forced them to focus. He was still kneeling on the carpet, but now he unfurled a rolled cloth, revealing an array of knives. She had seen one of them before – a glass blade. As though in recognition, the seam of scar tissue on her neck throbbed. It all came back then: her cousin pressing the knife to her throat, her mother's screams, of shattering windows – so long ago, and for nothing.

'Untidy, and, as it turned out, quite unnecessary. All that blood spilled, and I still wasn't able to get what I wanted from them. A young man's mistake – thinking more was better. But I've learned since then,' Brother murmured, fluttering his pale, dry hands over the collection of weapons before him. He touched a probing finger to each, one after the other, like a doting father greeting each of his children: a short, slim knife of onyx; a dull arc of steel that ended in a cruel, forked curve; a flat pearlescent blade nearly the length of Min's forearm.

The one he selected was unremarkable. A crude stone blade that looked like dark slate, winnowed to a sharp edge on either side. Its handle was discordantly fine: ivory, with a lambskin grip.

'It doesn't look like much, does it? Perhaps not. But then, neither do I.' He turned it in his hand, smiling slightly. 'Does it look familiar to you? I suppose it wouldn't – how could it? Nevertheless, you were there when I found the blade. I took it as we fled Yunis. As the temple began to separate from the mountain's face, there was a terrible rain of debris. And stone.'

The knife disappeared as he leaned in close, filling the entirety of Min's field of vision. She flinched as he reached for her, but could not resist as he lifted a hank of fallen hair from her neck and dropped it over her shoulder. A rough fingertip traced the puckered, purpled scar across her throat – the only gift beside her title that her late husband had left her.

'The boy should have taken more care,' Brother tutted. 'Any deeper and this could have caused real damage. I told him to be careful – I told him what he had, but I suppose he never quite believed it.' The way he said it, he may as well have been speaking of a lacquered porcelain vase, a broodmare, a favoured set of robes.

But he would not have done what he did next to any of those things. The knife reappeared in his hand, and with the economical precision of a calligrapher, he used its tip to draw a line along the pulse point below her ear.

Min felt the heat of beading blood before she felt pain – though that came soon enough. In close pursuit, her shuddering fear. Something was wrong. It hurt, but in a blossoming, urgent way that was new, and terrible, and not just physical. It was like the cut in her neck was the epicentre of a rift in the world. She heard a terse, taut animal low coming from somewhere inside her.

'The Ruvai mountains possess enormous power, even on this side of the Gates, even among we who have forgotten the old knowledge,' Brother said, holding her firmly by the jaw as she bled and felt her body fracture like shattered glass. His voice rose, dry and fervent above her cries. 'Just imagine the strength of that same stone, that same ancient earth, in the Inbetween. A single step away from the gods.'

Min did not have to imagine; she could *feel* it burning through her flesh.

Then he had both hands on her, seizing her by the crooks of her elbows to bring her toward him for a kiss. No, not a kiss. His lips met the screaming flesh of the open cut on her throat, and latched there, sucking, searching. She could feel *something* else emerge from within him and into her. Diffuse and wandering.

Min was wood. She was lead. Impossibly heavy, and yet not there at all. How else to explain that she'd forgotten how to use her arms? How else to explain why she did not shove him away?

She surrendered. It was too much; the poppy tears he had put in the tea had weakened her beyond the point of fighting. She would have fallen but for the surprisingly strong clench of his hands, still at her elbows, pinning her in place. She could feel the warmth of his palms through her sleeves.

He was the splaying of a hundred thousand tendrils,

a million knifepoints, prodding and picking over every slick surface of her insides, searching for the source of her curse – her gift. The thing that made her magic.

A wave of revulsion rose in her, green-black, the colour of deep water and fever dreams, and she saw that when it crested and fell, it would crush her.

He would find it, her gift, like a seed pearl sewn at the base of her heart, and—

He pulled away from her with a wet sucking sound, his eyes slick and dark with zeal. 'Exquisite,' he seethed hungrily. 'What you possess – you have no idea how immense, how powerful it truly is.'

Of course I do, she thought faintly. *How could I not? It's* mine.

But he had taken her strength, her ability to speak, so she merely stared at his lips, painted wild red with her blood. He pulled a handkerchief from his robes and dabbed them primly, leaving just a rusty ring of silt around his mouth. He looked disapprovingly at the bloodied handkerchief, as though it had insulted him. 'Magic can be so backward. One wonders what progress our civilised society might have made with it by now had we not lost the knowledge so long ago. But here we are, forced to rely on primitive practices left behind by the people of old.'

He sighed, refolding the handkerchief and tucking it into his robes. 'Still, I suppose there's a kind of base poetry to it. Here, for example: all the elements have come together. The water of the blood, the fire of your curse, the earth in my knife – only one element left.'

Before she could begin to parse what he meant, his knife sank into her side, just above the waist. It must have been quite sharp; the dense weave of her robes yielded neatly to its point.

He was chanting now, a low mantra in a language she did not recognise. She could not open her mouth, but words could do nothing for her now anyway. The knife was in, no protest would unstick it; even if she screamed, there was no one left to care about her pain.

And then, something did emerge from her mouth. Not voice – though it was a kind of air.

One element left.

She felt it passing over her tongue, tasting of sulfur. She felt it emanating from the cut in her neck. Her head lolled as she strained to look at the wound he'd opened in her side, and at last she saw it: smoke, black as rot.

I'm sorry. The monk's mouth was still chanting in the unknown tongue, but she heard him say the words as though from within her, a jarring and uninvited echo filling the spaces from where Tsai used to speak to her. The spaces from which the black smoke now poured like lifeblood.

It is the only way, he continued. *I had hoped I would have more time to refine this procedure, but I must take what I can while I can. You are of no use to anyone now, but what you have… that is not something you leave behind.*

Brother lowered his face back to hers, this time in a surgical kiss, covering her mouth with his own and *pulling*. Sucking the curse, and its power, from her marrow. Parting spirit from bone.

The pain was earth-shattering; the kiss oddly banal, repugnant. She wanted to scream her disgust, her fury. But she was too weak. Blood and smoke seeped from her in equal measure. Soon she would be emptied out, just a husk of the imagined thing she'd tried so hard to become. Less than the nothing she'd begun as.

A sound emerged over the roar of revulsion and pain. Distantly, as though travelling across open water. Only – not so far. The anteroom. Just beyond the pocket doors of her bedroom.

Mother? she thought incoherently, and with the word she pictured not her own mother, but the shamaness, the girl from her visions, that catlike face, those dark eyes burning with untold fury.

Brother's mouth tore away from her own as he turned to face the sound, and the absence of him, and the pain, was as sterling and exquisite as the ringing of crystal. Then she saw his face, and horror replaced her relief.

His eyes were flooded black, the papery skin around them cracked and split with spidery veins. His carefully placid face was transformed into an animal snarl, and from between those clenched, newly sun-white teeth, black smoke curled and seeped, like blood oozing from a predator's jaws.

More sounds from outside. The monk half-rose to meet it, but he kept one hand on her, pressing her down against the bed. Min's mouth opened again and a squeak of pained protest emerged as her ribs compressed. She could scarcely breathe. The strength in his narrow, brittle arm was unnatural – like that of several men his size.

From outside, they could hear voices – men's voices – now, layered over the footsteps.

Not her mother – not either mother. Hers, nor Tsai,

who had, in the end, been a sort of mother to her, hadn't she? Birthing the most valuable part of Min.

They were right outside. There came a crash, fore-grounded and clear where the previous sounds had been muffled. The sounds of violence.

Rioters, she thought. Or the Ellandaise. Someone come to claim what little was left of her blood.

A pause, and then a hole splintered into one of the pocket doors. An arm reached through and unhooked the lock. The doors slid open at their centre, revealing a tall young man Min thought she recognised. He was clad in a grey-green tunic spattered black with drying blood, and he hefted a long spear in both hands.

Before Min could gauge whether or not he meant to use it against her, her sister slid past him and into the room. Behind her, a trio of girls filed in, flanked by the enormous wolf Min had seen in Yunis. The slipskin boy.

She told herself it was the haze of the draught that left her heart suspended between relief and apprehension.

Lu held one hand out in front of her. Something small and metallic was grasped in it, and for a moment Min mistook it for a knife. No. Not a knife. An Ellandaise gun, pointed directly at her.

Fear dragged itself down Min's spine.

'Get away from my sister,' Lu snarled.

Min realised then the weapon was not pointed at her, but at Brother.

The monk stood, hands raised tremulously, his back to Lu, blackened eyes still locked on Min. There was noth-ing human left in them, but hunger was not exclusive to humans, and Min could see it still etched on his face.

She had to warn her sister—

Brother whirled, flinging his arms out toward Lu. A surge of wind emanated from them. The young man with the spear leapt in front of her, taking the brunt of the invisible blow, but the force of Brother's push was enough to toss them all back. One of the girls hit the doors hard with her back, further splintering the existing hole, landing half inside the room and half out. Lu was trapped beneath the young man with the spear, but she righted herself quick enough, pushing him off her and searching the floor frantically. Her hands were empty.

Min spotted the gun, well out of arm's reach, where it had skittered under her vanity. She opened her mouth to alert her sister, but all that came out was black smoke, denser now, and alarmingly hot on her tongue.

When that happened, what would be left?

Brother was walking toward her sister, hands outstretched. Min could see the exertion shaking his body. The magic was an uneasy fit inside him – this was not his curse to bear, not his power to possess.

Lu saw his approach and abandoned her search for the gun, drawing her sword instead.

Brother swiped a hand and a thin whip of air cracked her sister across the head with a smart, snapping sound. Lu went down hard on one knee, shaking her head clear, sword still in hand.

Again, the monk shook his hands, clearly frustrated.

'Lightning!' he snarled. 'Not wind, damn you. Lightning. *Fire!*'

The fire doesn't belong to you, Min thought, and suddenly, she was all instinct and embers kindling back to life. The rage flared in her again, finally. Roaring and bone-deep; her marrow was oil, her blood bright red flame.

And it was true, she realised. Her power was given to her by the curse. But the shape, the form, the strength and expression of it – that was hers alone. It could not reside in him, and it would not last. It could not regenerate like blood in his bones, the way it did in hers. He was merely a cracked vessel holding water; she was the sea.

The monk was stalking toward her sister. Lu made to rise, but he drew back his right hand and brought it arcing down in a vicious slash. Wind swiped her shoulder, striking her back to the ground. Another slash with his left hand sent her sprawling. He raised his right hand again—

Min pushed herself upright. The wound in her side released another gout of dark blood, but she couldn't think about that now. She forced herself to stand.

She saw now what she could do with what time she had left – however long that might be. It took tremendous effort to speak, but when she did, the words were all instinct.

'Leave my sister alone,' she hissed.

Her voice was charred, guttural. He heard her, though. They all did. The monk turned.

The black was ebbing away at the edges of his eyes; they were ringed thinly white, giving him an absurd, startled look. He'd taken some of her power; he should have taken it all. Instead, what he had left behind rushed up to the surface, just under her skin, like blood welling up to clot a wound.

A final surge of strength. Fine. She would not waste it.

She staggered forth, reaching him in three, four lurching steps. She seized his raised hands in her own.

'You want fire?' she demanded. Smoke poured out from between her clenched teeth. '*Take it, then.*'

The flames that surged from her palms were the brilliant blue of thick ice, of blameless summer skies, of dew-kissed hydrangeas freshly plucked. They tore from her, bone-deep and screaming. *She* was screaming, and it was both ecstasy and annihilation.

The moment she took his hands, Brother was still there, still a man with a face, a form. And then, a heartbeat later, he was a column of fire, burning fast and fleet. It lasted as long as he did – not very long at all. He'd been a slight man.

Dry as kindling, Min thought, remembering his cold, papery hands. And then, staring at the charred, greasy ring in her carpet where he'd been a moment earlier, she fell down to join it.

Footsteps pattered hard all around her. Someone crouched over her body, touching her side gingerly. Such a gentle hand. It felt ... not entirely foreign, only long-ago. Nearly forgotten. Something she'd forfeited in exchange for ... what, exactly?

'Lu,' a terse voice said above her.

I'm not Lu, I'm Min. Her eyes fluttered open and she saw a boy. The wolf. 'I'm going to staunch the bleeding,' he was saying. 'She's badly hurt...'

I'm dying, she corrected, feeling a little sorry for the boy. Her sister wouldn't want to hear that. Lu didn't like problems without solutions.

'Adé, come help me hold this over her neck – yes, like

that.' And then there was a gentle hand on her face, her neck.

As he tied a cloth tight around her waist, the boy brushed her upturned palm and he hissed. 'Careful,' he said. 'Her hands are still hot.'

'Nokhai.' Lu's voice. She was close. 'Is she ... is she going to ...?'

'I've seen worse,' he said grimly. 'But I've seen much better.'

Min opened her eyes. She was already gone, but she wanted one last look at her sister. Just for something familiar.

And there she was. Hair chopped short and strange, and a long cut streaking down one side of her vulpine face. She looked, Min realised suddenly, so much like her mother. Not Rinyi – like *Tsai*.

'Nokhai,' Lu was saying, her voice terse. 'Can you still do what we discussed?'

He's doing his best, Min thought, feeling sorry once more for the boy. He would not save her.

'Lu, I don't think now is—'

'If there's a chance she's going to live, we have to do it. You saw ...' Lu shuddered, and though it wasn't the first time she'd witnessed it, Min still had trouble believing her sister could be afraid. 'You saw what she just did. It's worse than before. You have to do it now.'

'I don't even know if I can. A Pactmaker *gives*, they don't—'

They both fell silent looking down at Min's fluttering eyelids.

'She's waking up,' Lu told him. 'You have to do it. Now.'

Do what?

The boy looked down at her, and his face held far more pity and regret in it now than it had a moment ago, when she'd been certain she was going to die. And then, he held a hand over her, and she felt him *pull*.

Her whole body went rigid. Then, all at once, it jerked upward. The sensation was different from when Brother had cleaved her with the knife. That had been the searing pain of a cut, the seeping of a slow bleed. This was like having her bones pulled apart.

She shrieked.

Above her, the boy's face was a rictus of terror. His hand shook, faltered—

Lu grabbed his wrist and steadied it.

'Keep going,' she ground out through clenched teeth.

Smoke poured from Min's mouth, her nose, wept out from the corners of her eyes in lieu of the tears she could no longer shed.

He was not the cracked vessel Brother had been. The curse went to him willingly. It snaked up around his shaking hand, up his arms, and sunk in through his parted lips, his nostrils.

Min watched it for as long as she could – all that streaming smoke. Her rage, her worth. And when it ran dry, the world went white, and she fell into a dreamless sleep that may as well have been death.

I I

Rubble

Nok caught himself just before he fell forward onto the girl, bracing himself hard on shaking arms. He looked down at her face, a breath away from his. He knew what a corpse looked like, and this was not it. But she was still enough that he reached a shaking hand down to feel for a pulse. There; faint, and rabbit-quick, but she was alive. He breathed a sigh of relief, and hot smoke huffed out between his lips, the rims of his nostrils, clinging to his skin. It was an odd thing – not really smoke at all. It felt almost heavy, dense. Wet. Like blood.

'That was all of it?'

Lu crouched beside him, her tawny face turned the washed-out grey of old porridge. But her jaw was set; she'd made her choice, given the order, and there was no undoing it. He looked at her and thought how little this girl and the one lying before them resembled one another, for sisters. Even half-sisters.

'I think so.' His voice shook. The smoke that seeped from him grew thinner now, as though the girl's magic were settling in his body. It had scalded his throat on the way down. Perhaps it was less a matter of settling than invading.

He coughed and a thick plume of smoke puffed out. Lu leaned forward, raising a hand toward his mouth, as though to wipe it away. Their eyes met, and he saw the alarm blossom in hers as she remembered herself. She quickly lowered her hand.

'Your sister needs a physician. A real one,' Nok said, turning back toward Min. Movement in his periphery. Adé scooted along the carpet from where she'd been flung back by Min's thrashing.

'She'll need to be sewn up,' she corroborated. 'Her side, her neck ...'

Lu nodded. 'Of course. Right away.' She stood and turned in Jin's direction. He was already moving toward her. As though anticipating her need of him. Nok looked away.

'I have to get a physician for my sister – they'll be hunkered down in their quarters, the gods willing,' Lu said to Jin. 'Once I get back, we will need to secure the palace. We'll have minutes, not hours. I need you to find Lamont and his men. We left them in the—'

'Eastern corridor,' the Yunian supplied. 'I'll bring them back here.'

Nasan slid in beside him. 'And what about me?'

'You stay here,' Lu told her. And when she saw the objection rising to Nasan's lips, she added, 'I need you with Min.'

'Oh, you need me to watch an unconscious person. A fine use of my talents.'

'I need you to keep her alive. She's my sister, Nasan.'

Nasan's eyes flicked over to meet Nok's. She nodded.

'Nok,' Adé whispered at his side. 'What *was* all that?'

He shook his head. 'It's ...'

'Forget it,' Adé said. Her hand slid into his, their skin tacky to the touch with Min's drying blood. 'Tell me later. We'll have time.'

He nodded gratefully. 'Later.'

'It's good to see you.' She grinned ruefully. 'Been a while. What've you been up to?'

'Oh, you know. I died. Just for a bit,' he said, trying to match her playful tone. He failed – he always failed – but she didn't seem to mind.

Lu was pushing past Nasan, toward the doors. 'I don't have time to argue. They may try to take Min captive, use her as a puppet—'

'*Who* would?' Nasan demanded. 'I don't know if you noticed, but your palace is all but abandoned. It wasn't our numbers or skill that got you this far – it was the other side's negligence and the fact that *no one stopped us.*'

'Yes,' Lu conceded. 'And what happens when all those missing guards finish putting out fires in Scrap-Patch Row and come flooding back into the Immaculate City? Who will they follow then?'

'I imagine they'll fall in line behind their rightful empress.'

The answer came from behind the broken pocket doors. Nasan and Jin hefted their weapons and angled themselves defensively toward it.

But the voice was viscerally familiar to Nok. It wasn't raised, but it carried nevertheless. It belonged to someone used to issuing commands and having them heard.

Lu was already striding toward the doors as they rolled open.

Stranger, saviour – the man that stepped through had been many things to Nok.

'*Yuri*.' Lu's throat was tight around the syllables of his name. She stepped toward him, and it seemed only natural they would embrace. But she stopped before him, and Nok watched her body change from that of a girl happy to see a friend, to a political entity, performing for her subjects. Slowly, deliberately, she bowed.

'*Shin* Yuri,' she corrected herself as she rose. And then the old man lowered himself to the floor, touching his forehead to the carpet.

'My empress,' he said.

She seemed unable to speak for a moment. 'Rise,' she said finally.

'Your sister—' Yuri began, looking over to Min's still form laid out on the floor.

'She needs medical help. Is the court physician still in the Immaculate City?'

He nodded. 'You stay with her. I'll fetch him.' He paused, considering. 'And someone else.' His eyes rose to meet Nok's then, and he gave the slightest nod of his head in acknowledgement. 'He's only a country apothecarist, but I suspect he may be able to help.'

'You should remove her clothing in order to perform a full examination,' Omair reprimanded as the physician struggled to work in the tiny window he'd rent in Min's blood-soaked robes. 'How can you expect to work like this? You can scarcely see the wound site.'

The physician shot a scandalised glance over his shoulder. He'd been obviously discomfited by Omair's ragged presence to begin with; this suggestion seemed to confirm all his suspicions about the apothecarist, and perhaps apothecarists in general. 'This is a *lady* of the royal family. An emp ... former ... A princess,' he stammered. 'Perhaps *your* patients do not value their modesty, but mine certainly do.'

'Mine value living,' Omair countered. 'Do yours?'

The old man looked thin and pale, but he was as clever and focused – and tart – as ever. Nok could've kissed him. He nearly had, when Yuri returned with the apothecarist. Perhaps he would have, if he'd been a different person. Things being what they were, Omair had embraced him, and Nok had closed his eyes to hold back the possibility of tears.

'Enough,' Lu snapped, stepping between the squabbling men. 'Can you heal my sister's wounds or not?'

Omair grunted. 'We'll see if his stitches are as refined as his manners. And I'd like access to his supplies – there's a herbal poultice I can make to reduce the chance of infection.'

'Fine,' Lu said. 'Once you've finished, I'll have her nunas bathe and clean her. Yuri should be back by then with a full report of which staff are still on the grounds.'

Nok heard the subtext: *And which have fled.*

Lu flinched as the physician pierced Min's belly with his needle, then turned away. Nok went to Lu by instinct, though he did not move to touch her, to rest a hand on her shoulder. It wasn't in his nature anyway, to comfort another person like that.

She glanced up at his approach, her face pained. She did not reach for him either, but he could feel plainly *her* instinct to do so. She did not look back at her sister. Odd; she had seen so much worse – done much worse. But then, the precise brutality of the medical arts made some people uneasy in a way spontaneous violence did not.

He watched Min for her. Wisps of grey-black smoke clung around the edges of the girl's wounds – the last of the curse still clinging on. A few tendrils snaked up toward Nok, as though sensing his presence. The physician, to his credit, merely shuddered and kept at his work.

'What in the God's name is that?'

Nok jumped as Kommodeur Lamont peered over his shoulder. The Ellandaise man's lip curled in disgust at the sight of the smoke.

'It's part of her ... affliction,' Lu told him.

'It's only energy,' Nok supplied, cutting a hand through the smoke to disperse it. 'Residue. It won't hurt you.'

Lamont tore his eyes from Min's prone form toward Nok now. His sneer deepened. '*Witchery.*' There was a new kind of bristling hostility to his voice.

Nok had only just met the man, but it seemed at odds with his carelessly arrogant demeanour.

'You are not there when she sets her throne room on fire with just her hands,' he went on. 'Back in Elland, we do not allows this ... unnaturalness. Girls like that? Lose heads.'

And what of boys who change their skins for fur and feathers? But Nok thought he already knew the answer.

'Let's give the physicians some space to complete their work,' Lu suggested, moving between the two of them.

'They can haves all the space they likes,' Lamont said haughtily. 'I wait out in corridor.'

Nok moved over to the divan, where Omair had retreated.

The apothecarist gazed at him with shining eyes. 'You look well,' he said.

'I didn't know if I'd ever see you again,' Nok blurted.

Omair's hand was coarse and warm against his face. 'I know,' he said. 'When I heard the news from Yunis, I confess I feared the worst.'

And Nok saw there was something more Omair wanted to give – an apology, an explanation, perhaps. Nok hoped he wouldn't. Sometimes when there was so much to say, it was easier to say nothing at all.

It was Adé who rescued them, striding over to embrace Omair.

'Sweet girl,' the old man murmured, patting her shoulder. 'Where will you two go now?' he asked.

Nok shook his head. So much had elapsed, there had been no time to think about any of it.

'I need to go and see my family, make sure they're all right,' Adé said.

Lu pulled her gaze away from her sister. 'Be careful. Scrap-Patch Row is still smouldering, and there may still be rioters in the streets.'

'I'll go with you,' Nok said immediately.

'Me, too,' Nasan said, hopping over the side of the divan to sit on Adé's other side; Adé jumped.

Nok shot his sister a look of surprise. She would go with them instead of keeping tabs on Lu and the important players of her alliance as they determined the fate of the empire? 'Why?' he asked incredulously.

'I just got my brother back, I'm not about to lose him again.'

She stretched across Adé and gave his cheek a playful pinch. A rather painful pinch.

'*Ouch.*'

Nasan ignored him, instead slapping both palms on her knees and rising from the divan. 'Let's get going, then!' She offered Adé a hand up with exaggerated courtesy. Adé regarded her with a quizzical smile.

'You should go in your caul,' Lu told him. 'It'll be good for them to have the wolf's protection.'

Nok nodded, following Adé and his sister toward the door. He closed his eyes and beckoned the wolf, waiting for its familiar warmth to draw up over him... But it never came. He tried again.

'Nok? Are you coming?' Nasan called from the doorway where she and Adé stood waiting for him.

He tried once more, but even as he did, he knew it was pointless. It shouldn't have been a matter of trying at all. How could this be? Something the Our Mother had done to him? The apparition of his father? But, no, he'd been able to caul after that. And then he knew.

His head whipped toward Min's unconscious form.

'Nok, what's wrong?' Lu was still hovering over her, but at the sight of him she stood, her face moving from one kind of concern to another. She must have seen the wildness in his eyes, the fear. She stood slowly. 'Why... why are you looking at her like that?'

Why indeed. As though there might be something of his caul remaining there, something tangible that could be seen. But of course, he saw nothing. His caul was gone.

12

Remains

'Who's going to guard her?' Lu asked, resisting the urge to reach out and touch Min, to check that her skin was still warm, to feel for a pulse. Her sister looked distressingly pale, but her chest rose and fell in slow, even intervals. A chambermaid someone found cowering in the kitchens had been conscripted into redressing her sister. The poor girl had done her best, but she was no trained handmaiden; the ribbons that secured Min's robes had been tied as if for a sack of laundry, rather than in the traditional knot. But she looked comfortable.

Some small, sleepy part of Lu felt compelled to climb into bed beside her sister, the way they would as children, when one of them was ill. Nestling in close so the fever one bore heated the other, until it was no longer clear which one was ill and which was well.

'I'll watch her myself.' Yuri said.

'After all she's done, I don't know who, but someone's bound to come after her,' she said. Likely more than one someone. The Mul monks, perhaps. They were always going on about the dangers of sorcery – and the sorcery of women, well, that was the worst kind. And then there were her sister's political foes. Those who supported Lu's claim and feared leaving alive a rival for the throne. Those who supported neither and would have them both slain in favour of some hidden male heir they could dig up afterward. Lu could control those loyal to her, but that was a distinction that would be difficult to parse even under less contentious circumstances ...

'I'll protect her with my life,' Yuri said, breaking through the cascade of her worries.

Lu finally tore away from Min to meet his eyes. They were as sharp as ever, solemn with the weight of his pledge. Her shin had always been a stoic man, but she rarely saw him look quite so grave. Perhaps only the last time she'd seen him, in the forest, when he'd told her to flee, and – though she hadn't understood it at the time – that the world she'd known was ending.

Lu stepped away from the bed. 'I'm going to my father's ... *my* apartments to clean up and dress. I'll need you in the throne room with me afterward, though.' Yuri had clout among the paper-pushers and the soldiers alike. His support would be crucial in securing the Immaculate City. 'Who will watch Min then?'

'I will.' Jin stepped forward from his station by the broken doors, now barricaded haphazardly by Min's up-ended vanity.

Lu frowned. 'No, I'll want you in the throne room as well. I should announce our bargain—'

'Our engagement, you mean?' he asked. But his eyes were earnest as ever – he hadn't meant anything by it. Why would he?

'Right. Our engagement,' she repeated. 'The people need to grow accustomed to seeing you at my side.'

'I'll watch the girl,' Omair said from his seat across the room.

Lu fixed her eyes on Omair. She knew there was more to the apothecarist than met the eye – she'd seen what he was capable of – but even so, he looked weak, his ageing body embrittled by weeks spent underfed in a sunless dungeon.

Yuri seemed to sense her thoughts. 'I have men I trust. Soldiers. Real fighters. I'll send for a few of them, have them posted at Min's doors leading outside.'

Lu resisted the urge to ask how Yuri knew they couldn't be bought. She had precious few people behind her as it was. She needed to trust their judgement, not just their loyalty.

Still, she couldn't help but think it would be safer to move Min to another location – preferably one that wasn't the first place one would think to look for her. But moving her now, with her stitches so fresh, also seemed unwise. Too many factors to consider.

Lu suddenly and keenly regretted Nok's absence. She was surrounded by allies, but some childish part of her needed a friend.

'Has there been any word about my nunas?' she asked Yuri.

He hesitated. 'Not yet. I have men still checking the dungeons ...'

The idea of Hyacinth and the others locked away was not an image Lu wanted to entertain; she pushed it away. 'Fine. I'm going to dress now. If they turn up, send them to me. And see that we have Kangmun Hall full in an hour.'

'There's been word some of the magistrates have fled the Immaculate City,' Yuri cautioned her. 'Those loyal to Min, and some just fearful of a regime collapse. I don't know how many, exactly.'

Lu had expected as much. 'No matter. They will face the consequences of their choices another day. For now, round up anyone left in the city who matters. It's time they met their true emperor.'

Her father's apartments had the stillness of a mausoleum. The lavishly appointed sitting room – the mahogany chairs, ornate silk carpets, and gilt-laced tapestries – still retained a sense of otherworldly leisure.

But there was nothing more earthbound than the fine layer of dust blanketing everything. Lu ran a finger down the spine of a gilded lion-dog statuette, cutting a golden trail through the fuzzy grey. No one had been here in months. It surprised her that Set hadn't moved in immediately, but then, perhaps her cousin had not had the time before he'd ridden out to Yunis – and his death.

Min had been sleeping in her own chambers – that much had been apparent when they'd broken down her doors – but she hadn't so much as set foot in here, even for appearances, it would seem.

Min. Lu recalled her newly pared-down form, the grey pallor in her slackened face. A far cry from the vicious conduit of power Lu had encountered in Yunis. The enemy she'd kept in mind on her journey back to Yulan City.

Once, Lu had believed she knew her sister down to the bones, but perhaps what she'd known was the habit of her presence. While she'd looked and seen only her Min, had this other girl been there the whole time, unseen? Who was this other girl, this sister she did not know at all? And what would she think when she awoke and learned what Lu had done – had ordered done – to her?

Someone had left several sets of Lu's robes draped over a divan. Seeing them, her heart leapt, until she realised it couldn't have been her nunas. Hyacinth would have used the empty dress form at the far end of the room. She would've begun dusting, and opened the windows to refresh the stale air. She would've been here, waiting.

Lu selected a crimson outer layer embroidered along the edges with a cascade of golden waves and pale blue rosettes, and a complementary sky-blue dress for underneath. Bold, but not overly showy. Red to symbolise the power of the Hu.

The first woman emperor. She had said the words so many times as a child. More than a dream – a manifesto, usually declared to no one but her own reflection in the mirror. Or Hyacinth. Hyacinth, she thought, should be there. Perhaps that was why this moment felt so unremarkable. Perhaps the dream needed its other dreamer to cohere.

She's fine, Lu told herself. A girl from a prominent family in good standing, an imperial handmaiden, would have been protected, could not have been left to languish in a dungeon cell. *She's fine, and they will find her, and soon she'll be here at my side again.*

Tossing the robes over her father's dress form, she stripped down to her underthings, letting her clothes fall to the floor. They had been mostly cast-offs from Yunis: a grown man's coarse wool shirt and tunic, cinched over her own finely tailored trousers. Not that there was much to distinguish the difference anymore: all had been reduced to a heap of rags, saturated with sweat and reeking of smoke and blood and things still fouler. Her underclothes looked no better, she realised with distaste. Yellow rings had formed under her arms, her breasts, seeping outward until their edges met.

She finished undressing and found herself staring in the mirror at a body changed. She'd always looked the same before: whole and strong, and tall. This new body was tired and rangy. All over, bones jabbed up from under skin that was chafed and flaking. Blisters had beaded along the soft flesh of her palms, between her thumbs and forefingers, burst, and left behind callouses. She bent and scratched at her leg, loosing a flurry of dead skin and dirt.

The servants had left a basin, towel, and a jug of water on the stand by the mirror; it had gone tepid. No matter. She splashed as much grime off her face as she could. There was no one to plait her greasy hair. Any attempt she made would have been laughable – as Hyacinth liked to tease her – so she just slicked it back as best she could with water, then pulled on the robes, the slippery weave of the silk a strange, out-of-place memory against her filthy skin.

She considered herself in the mirror once she'd finished, then grimaced. What she really needed was a bath. But that would have to be later, once her nunas – ammas now – had been located.

She turned and faced the bed. The place where her father had lain down and drawn breath for the last time.

Someone had drawn up the blankets after they'd removed the body. Likely, the bedding had been changed as well. Lu traced the silk pillowcase with her fingertips. What did she expect? An indentation left by his skull, the weight of his shoulders creased into the sheets, the lingering hint of his smell? A sign that her father had once inhabited a body and walked this earth.

Her throat went tight with longing, the sadness seizing her body with such force that her knees buckled. As she lurched, she slammed up against the bedside table, knocking open one of its cabinet doors, the mother-of-pearl inlay catching the dim light as it swung loose.

Dammit.

Lu bent to close the door – and stopped, not understanding what she saw. Inside, a panel had fallen askew, revealing a hidden chamber in the rear of the cabinet. She jiggled the panel until it came loose, then tossed it aside, exposing a small stack of ledgers. But Lu's eye was drawn to what was beside them: a lacquered tray bearing a small lamp, its glass globe stained brown-black with use, and a long, thin metal flute.

No, not a flute.

Impossible. *My father wasn't... he wouldn't.*

Her fingers shaking, Lu reached it and withdrew the pipe.

But it's illegal, she thought absurdly.

As though any emperor or king had ever been beholden to the laws of mere men. As though the cold metallic proof weren't right there, in her shaking hands. Thin and silvery, ending in a jade bowl. The telltale sickly-sweet smell of poppy tar still clung to its insides.

Strange, that she could have no thoughts – a vacant expanse of mind, as white and unmoored in time and space as if she were lost in a snowstorm.

Her cousin's face surfaced amid the murk of her mind, sudden and loathsome.

It's not the same, she told herself. Her father was old. In constant pain. Perhaps it could only be silenced in a cloud of sickly-sweet smoke. And he'd never had Set's laziness, his easy arrogance and need to have everything come easy.

She set the pipe in her lap and turned her attention to the ledgers. They were small books, each labelled only with a year on its plain cover. She thought perhaps they were her father's journals and the idea filled her at once with curiosity and dread. What else didn't she know about this man who had been her father, her emperor? What else did she not wish to know?

But flipping through the pages she saw only annotated tables and tidy commentary on the grain stores and pricing in Kun, Xiawei, Fuyan Provinces. All agriculturally significant, but not highly populated. Names were written in the margins – she recognised a few. Governors, mostly. The names had numbers beside them, but nothing to explain what they meant. All in all, dry reading. She could not help but feel relieved. Still, she thought, there must be some reason they'd been hidden—

A sound in the hall, followed by the doors sliding on their tracks. Someone was here.

She stood in alarm and the pipe fell from her lap. She gasped as though it were some scaly thing come alive, then gave it a kick. It rolled under the bed, out of sight.

She crammed the ledgers back into the cabinet and shut
it.

'Princess?'

If she died a dozen times and woke up in an entirely
new life, she would still recognise that voice.

'*Hyacinth*.'

She crossed the room at a run, throwing her arms
around the other girl — and scarcely stopped herself from
recoiling in shock at the unfamiliar frailty of the body
beneath the familiar orange nuna's robes.

As they pulled apart, their eyes met. So habitual a thing.
Or, it had been. Then, all at once, those dark, familiar
eyes no longer belonged to her friend but to Hyacinth's
brother, and Lu was flung back into the forest, watching
Wonin slip from his saddle. Watching the light leave his
eyes. Soaking the earth with his lifeblood.

This time there was no hiding her flinch, the way her
body shrank into itself. Nonetheless, she had the presence
of mind to notice the strangest flicker of something like
guilt cross Hyacinth's features. It was fleet as a flat stone
skimming the surface of a lake; there one moment, then
swallowed up by dark, placid waters. For what reason
could her friend feel guilty? It was Lu who — no. She
closed her eyes, as though to shut out the memory, as
though it wasn't already inside her, like a stuck bit of glass
that her skin had grown over.

She forced a grin. 'Did you miss me?'

'Oh, were you gone?' Hyacinth grinned back. She
reached out and flicked at the streaks of dirt on Lu's neck.
'I don't have to ask if you missed me. You can't even bathe
on your own, it seems. And gods, did you cut your *hair*?'

'A friend did that,' Lu said, smiling faintly at the memory.

'A *friend*?' Hyacinth was watching her face with a shrewdness that was so familiar Lu could almost forget everything else. 'Must be some friend to make you smile like that.'

'You can meet him soon. If you promise to behave.'

'*Him*?' Hyacinth repeated. And then, delightedly, 'Are you blushing?' She grabbed Lu by the shoulders, as though to inspect her cheeks and neck for red.

Lu rolled her eyes and pushed her away. 'I was so worried when they couldn't find you,' she said, eager to change the subject. 'Where were you?'

Hyacinth's face darkened with shocking alacrity. 'Oh,' she said in a would-be light tone. 'We were locked up together. Me and the other girls.'

'In the dungeons?' Lu demanded.

'No! No... they let us stay in unused apartments. Here and there. They moved us all around, it's hard to remember.'

'They didn't send you home to your parents?' Lu demanded.

Again, that strange grimace from Hyacinth. 'No,' she said. 'I haven't seen them... not for some time—'

A knock came at the door.

'That'll be the others,' Hyacinth said, and Lu might have been offended by how relieved she sounded if it wasn't so puzzling. 'Yuri told us you were going to need a bath. I had the girls bring up water—'

She opened the door, disclosing Lu's other hand-maidens. Syringa came first, carrying a tray of oils, followed by Oleander and Sweet Olive. Last came Lotus and Plum Blossom toting heavy, steaming buckets of hot water. At the sight of Lu, the girls immediately set down their burdens in order to bow.

'Empress Lu,' they murmured in unison.

It robbed her of her breath, merely seeing them here after all these weeks apart. Like Hyacinth, they were clad in their customary robes of warm, sunset orange. Like Hyacinth, they looked haggard and drawn. Where had they been? Wherever it was, Yuri had seen fit to send them straight to their duties. But they looked nearly as in need of a hot bath and long rest as Lu.

'Through here.' Hyacinth directed the others. Or, the others that were there. Where was Plumeria? And Azalea? Had they fled the city? Perhaps returned to their family homes? But if Hyacinth hadn't been allowed to return, then—

'Wait.' Lu grabbed her friend by the shoulder as she made to follow the others into the back room.

'Hyacinth, what's happened to you? And the other girls, the ones that aren't here? Are they safe? Where *are* they?'

'Plumeria went home to her family,' Hyacinth said. 'They were supporting Min, so she was allowed to leave. We don't know about Torch Ginger or Azalea or Jasmine. Or anyone else. One morning we woke up and they were gone.'

Lu could hear murmurs from the other room, the churning of buckets filling the wooden tub. It should have felt familiar, comforting.

'What about you?' Lu asked.

'What about me?' But she was looking off to the side

at nothing, as though desperate for a way out of this conversation.

'Your family – Yuri told me they were part of the coalition supporting Min. Why didn't you go back to them?'

Hyacinth's eyes met her own, suddenly, almost viciously defiant. 'And, what? Abandon you? Assume you'd take me back regardless when you returned?'

'I would have,' Lu said immediately, without thought.

'And how would that look to the court?' Hyacinth demanded. 'Making a traitor your head amma? Do you really think Yuri – any of your advisers – would have allowed that? No, you would have executed me along with my family. What's left of it—'

'*Executed*?' Everything in her rose up to deny it, this hideous future being proposed—

And then, looking at her friend's face, she saw Hyacinth's brother once more. Wonin, whose youth she had struck from the world of the living.

That was his fault, she told herself, though she knew it wouldn't make a difference. Wonin had died because he tried to kill her. Wonin had died because she put an arrow between his eyes. Both these things were true, and one did not alter the other.

She looked up at the girl standing before her, met those canny, dark eyes she knew better than her own. Her true sister, as she had always thought of her – partly out of disappointment in Min, perhaps, but also on the merit of their love alone.

'Hyacinth,' she began. 'Something happened—'

'Don't.' Her friend's voice was quiet, but Lu flinched at the lash in it, like a leather strap to the face.

'Don't ...?'

'Or do,' Hyacinth said, her tone turning aggressive. 'Tell me about Wonin. That's what you were going to do, wasn't it?'

Lu found herself at a rare loss for words.

Her friend did not. 'Before you do, though, is whatever you tell me going to bring him back? Will it change a single gods-damned thing?' Hyacinth looked up then, and her eyes had become like those of a stranger. She nodded when no answer came. 'So, don't talk,' she whispered. 'I don't have a mother or a father anymore. I won't, at least, when you – well, they made their choice. And I don't have a brother. I suppose he made his choice, too. I can't lose this, too. You're the only family I have left. Do you understand? Don't turn my choice to stay here, with you, into a mistake.'

'I understand,' Lu said at last. Then, as an afterthought, 'You couldn't have known I'd come back.'

And at that, Hyacinth laughed. A dry, empty sound, like autumn wind skittering through dead leaves. 'That,' she said, 'was the only thing I was sure of.'

13
Hope

They sit facing one another and Tsai, forming a triangle within the circle she has drawn in the the dirt. To her right is the boy who thinks he loves her; on her left, a boy who thinks he hates her. He is probably correct, the latter of the two. The neophyte. The heart breaks easy in the fist of jealousy, almost like it longs for that particular ruin. And hate grows so readily, like a weed, in those fertile remains.

Love, though? If such a creature even exists, Tsai's either never seen it, or she mistook it for something else. And if that were possible, then what even was the point?

It is a fancy, a distraction for girls who weren't born and abandoned within a day in the slums under the long shadow of the Grey City's morose, looming walls – a place where flowers could not grow but misery readily blossomed.

'Are we ready to begin?' The neophyte's voice is terse, the fear rolling off him like fog off a mountain. A nervous boy. She can smell the reek of poverty on him: like recognising like. Not entirely alike, though. He still labours under the delusion that this world will allow him to have anything for himself. Anything he could even own enough to lose. It makes him scrabble; it makes him afraid.

Tsai stopped being afraid years ago. She has nothing and, therefore, she has nothing to lose.

'Everything is prepared,' she tells him. This much is true. The air smells spicy, earthy. The supplies for the spell are arrayed before them: dried herbs in metal dishes, rushes strewn in precise configurations across straw mats. An unlikely epicentre for the fall of an empire.

She glances briefly at the two boys flanking her. They see only what they asked her for: a spell to soften the heart of their emperor, to avoid the coming war with Yunis, in which they believe Yuri will die.

These boys only care about the immediate. They care about their own skins, the sorrow of Yuri's mother. They think only of Yuri, and perhaps the other young men like him. Eager, foolish soldiers. Not the women and children and frail elders besides, those who cannot even lift a sword to defend themselves. Those who fall easiest under blade and foot. Just as they have in every war that has preceded it, and just as they will in every war that comes after.

If these boys paused to think on that, perhaps they would see her betrayal laid out before them, looking as innocent as the coarse wares of some country apothecarist.

But they do not live their lives under the imperative of revenge.

The neophyte should recognise the potential function of most of the ingredients – studies at the academy aren't completely useless – but he's deferred to her throughout much of this enterprise, finding ingredients for her, but never asking questions. Perhaps, as she suspects, he has felt that if he doesn't have a hand in the planning of things, that will make his treason less. If he'd been paying closer attention, he might have noticed the discrepancies between the spell she claimed to be building, and the ingredients he was fetching.

As for the rich, handsome one, Yuri? Well, he wouldn't know mugwort from hog shit.

She meets his eyes as she thinks this, and he smiles at her. It makes her belly flutter, and that makes her angry. She ought to hate him, she thinks for the hundredth time, the thousandth time. And for the hundredth, the thousandth time, it annoys her that she doesn't.

She's not a fool; this is not love. It is not even infatuation, which would require a degree of naivety she has never experienced, even when she was a little child. It is far worse than either of those things.

Tsai has never had a friend, has never wanted one. It seemed a vulnerability. Almost as bad as having a family.

She could end it, she knows. All she has to do is tell him about the boy – the unfavoured prince, that simpleton with his sweet, accidental smiles and instinctive strength, steady hands. *He* had not been a liability. Discovered and spent and discarded in an afternoon.

Better yet, it had been revenge. On the treacherous, idiot creature of her own heart, still bending toward fondness. Even after all the hard lessons it ought to have learned. And on the boy to her right, who bears the blame for her weakness.

She looks to him; Yuri smiles back.

The heart breaks easy in the fist of jealousy, almost like it longs for that particular ruin.

She should tell him about Daagmun.

But that would cause a scene. And that in turn, she reminds herself, looking at the innocuous-seeming ingredients of the catastrophe laid before, would spoil this betrayal. The important one.

Ohn will be angry when he realises, but he will not be surprised. Not in the way Yuri will be. Not in the way that will fundamentally alter his understanding of who she is. The way that will rend the soul, rewrite its ability to trust, to love again in the future.

Ohn will think he should have suspected. Because he is not her friend. He is more than that: Ohn sees who she is with the clarity of reluctant familiarity, the intimacy of loathing. They are, in a way, kin.

Tsai holds her hands out to these two unwitting boys. They are the final ingredients for her spell.

'Wait!'

Ohn pulls his hands away back. She could scream with frustration.

'What?' she snaps instead.

'We should pray. For the spell to work.'

'You know what will make the spell work?' she asks sweetly, as though to a child. '*Performing it.*'

Yuri snickers to her right. He always laughs at her jokes, no matter how mean-spirited they are. She almost doesn't hear it anymore, the way a person stops hearing the omnipresent roar of cicadas in late summer. But Ohn hears it; he looks at Yuri with that combination of annoyance and disbelieving hurt that makes Tsai want to shake him because how, *how* on earth has he not been disabused of that vulnerability yet?

Ohn turns back to her, and she struggles to train the contempt out of her face as he says, 'According to Mul ritual practice, prayer is an important precursor to spell-casting. It places the practitioner at the feet of the gods, reminding him of his place as a conduit for the will of the heavens, rather than as master or—'

Tsai is very close to forfeiting everything and strangling him, her plans be damned. 'Why do this at all if we can just *hope* Emperor Hwangmun's heart toward peace?'

If prayers and wishes did anything, the world would belong to the wretched. She wouldn't be here; neither would Ohn. They would be home – whatever home might look like in such a world.

Ohn's dark eyes waver, flicking from hers toward the ingredients of the spell arrayed before them. 'The point of prayer is to sanctify your spell. Not to make things bend to your will.'

Then it's more useless than I thought.

Mul practitioners were tedious. Perhaps once they'd possessed true knowledge, but time, and the corrupting lure of what comforts the empire's favour could offer, had neutered them. Now they were all piety and book-keeping. No wonder they feared her kind so much – they had been complicit in the indenturing of her Order after the war, turning them into little more than washerwomen and temple groundskeepers.

Even Ohn, with his would-be rebellion, dabbling in so-called feral magic, would not know what to do if he saw the extent of her power. He still needed her, after all. He'd sought her out. She would pay money to see his reaction to it – though, of course, she doesn't have to. She'll see it soon enough.

She allows him to say his little prayer. There is no need to fight him anymore; she has already won.

When he finishes, she reaches for the boys' hands again, and they offer them willingly, then clasp on to one another. When the triangle closes, there is an ice-cold charge. Enough to widen even *her* eyes in surprise, steal the steady rhythm from her breath, punch a soft '*oh*' of wonder from her throat.

Their combined energies produce a rare alchemy. One, she must admit, that might not exist without the way Ohn feels for Yuri, or the way Yuri feels for her. It was the boys who sought her out, but she wonders now if perhaps destiny hadn't chosen *them* for *her*.

The boys feel it, too, their shared power. Ohn's hand trembles in hers.

'Steady,' she warns. 'Don't let go.'

'I won't,' Yuri says, his eyes never leaving her.

Tsai closes her own eyes, closes him out. And in the dead tongue of the first Yunians – a language older than the Triarch, older than the first shamaness – she begins to chant.

She casts a spell; she tells a story. It is one of blood and terror, of the strong and their rapacious hunger for the weak. A tale the boys whose hands she holds cannot understand. Not just for lack of language, but because they think to ask for peace, when what they truly want is to be unchanged at the cost of a million unseen, fragile lives. To enjoy the agreeable illusion of change without losing a thing. Never realising the empire will inevitably consume, subsume, use them to extract more pain, more blood. Because that is all an empire is: a beast that must kill to stay alive, in numbers that render death easy, cheap.

Her voice swells in undulating song, guttural and not quite her own anymore. The heat between their joined hands grows in response, and all at once it flares to searing.

Ohn yelps and Yuri winces. Tsai's eyes are closed, but she can see them nevertheless – more keenly, perhaps. It is as though she is within them, feeling what they feel, seeing what they see.

'Tsai! What is this—?'

She senses Ohn beginning to pull away and her hand tightens. Something audibly pops under her fingers.

Ohn cries out, and her eyes fly open. But she keeps chanting, as though the cadence of the spell has developed a will all its own.

'Yuri!' Ohn yells, his voice nearly drowned out under the thunderous swell of her own. 'Let go of her hand! This isn't right, this isn't the spell we wanted—'

It's too late, she thinks rapturously. The voice that is no longer quite her voice is still chanting, still rising, and all the while the voice that belongs only to her, only to the girl Tsai, laughs in delight. *You're too late.*

Yuri's eyes are open, but they do not see. He stares up at nothing, his strong jaw gone slack. Energy moves through him, but he is a passive conduit, an empty channel into which the waters of her spell pour. She can see it, like liquid starlight, spreading through his meridians, glowing through skin gone translucent as rice paper.

She watches it flow into her own hand, up her arm,

veins of energy intertwining at the ball of her shoulder, then emptying like a waterfall into her—

'What is *that*?' Ohn demands, and she looks up at him. He's no longer trying to free his hand from hers. Instead, he is staring at her belly.

She follows his gaze back down, and there it is. Another girl might not have understood. Someone who had not grown up marked unclean, in a shamaness's temple, washing bodies, performing the last rites of the dead – including those for children who had died before they could be born. But Tsai *had* been marked unclean, and she had done all those things. And she knows what a foetus looks like.

No, she thinks. The guileless, handsome, wretched face of the Third Prince flashes in her mind. And the spell on her lips falters, like a guttering candle.

'You're pregnant,' Ohn says dully. She looks up and sees the calculation in his dark eyes, watches the unspoken dread become fear, become hatred. His hand feels suddenly cold and heavy as lead in hers.

Ohn's words seem to wake Yuri from his stupor.

'Pregnant?' he repeats, head snapping toward Tsai.

Concentrate, she thinks, willing herself not to meet his eyes. Her lips fumble around the chant, reviving it, her voice low and terse.

'You're going to be a father,' Ohn says. However he means it, it comes out a sneer.

'*Me?*' Yuri says, still staring at Tsai. 'But we've never ...'

She stutters, and a shock roils through their joined hands. The boys flinch, but she will not relinquish them.

'Whose is it?' Yuri says, his voice rising. 'Tsai? Stop — just, stop. Talk to me!' And he has the audacity, the gall to look at her with those wet, hurt eyes. As though she ever promised him anything. As though he had any right to dream he might mean something to her—

Her chanting wavers wildly. The energy that once flowed between them like water now spits and sputters like a dying fire.

'What do you care? What does it matter?' Ohn demands on her other side. There's a wild relief on his face, but a viciousness, too. He's never been a handsome boy, but she's never seen him ugly like this, either: wretched and pained and cruel. 'It's not yours!'

'And *I'm* not *yours*,' Yuri snarls back.

Ohn recoils, like he has been smacked. His hands stay bound with theirs, though, locked tight by the unseen force of their bond.

Tsai repeats the words in her mind — and then aloud.

'*And I'm not* yours.'

It leaves her lips in the same guttural moan of her chant. The final syllable clings to her tongue, wavers, pitches, rises, until it is like a gale. An animal shriek.

The boys turn to face her, eyes wide in terror, as though her wordless cry was comprehensible. A message conveyed in a language they did not realise they knew all along.

There is a moment of stillness. Then the herbs and rushes laid in the centre of the circle burst into flames.

Tsai sees the fire, and then she *feels* it, curling, burning energy welling in her chest. Her body goes rigid as it explodes outward, rushing through her arms, her fingers, and sends both boys sailing backwards as though they are no more than straw dolls in a storm.

Her first thought as she pitches backward into oblivion is: *I had the faith of the heavens, and I failed.*

The second is of her child.

She is having a daughter.

When Min's eyes opened, it was morning, and she was brand new. Like the unnerving white-pink flesh beneath a picked scab: shiny, and taut, and ripe for pain. This was the first thing she recognised.

The second was that she was alone. Profoundly, in a way she never had been before. All the fire, all the heat and fury and poison in her had been emptied out.

Someone cleared their throat.

So, perhaps not entirely alone, then.

She made to roll over but was immediately wracked with pain. It returned to her then, all of it: Brother's rolled bag of knives. His stone blade cutting into her. The heavy smell of iron filling the room as her blood rushed out of her.

She settled for turning her head; the thick bandage around her neck forced her to do so slowly.

Yuri sat in a chair pulled up beside her bed. This Yuri was the one she knew, had always known. Her sister's cantankerous shin, ever carrying himself with a soldier's rigidity. A far cry from the handsome, insouciant boy in gilt-tipped boots who had once helped cast a spell to commit treason and escape a war—

She frowned. Where had that image come from? She

could not recall, though a moment before it had been so vivid.

And then she saw there was a sword laid across Yuri's lap. It was sheathed.

'Is that to protect me, or protect yourself?' Min blurted, surprised by her own boldness.

He raised an eyebrow and looked down at it, then back at her.

'That depends,' he said.

'On what?'

'On you.'

She turned her head back slowly, gazing up at a foreign ceiling. This was not her bedroom. This room had the stark impersonality of a servant's quarters. Nice ones, though, with high ceilings and painted scrolls on the walls. No chambermaids' dormitory with dirty bedrolls stacked a dozen deep. It was for the best; her own apartments likely still stank of charred flesh. It made her feel lonely all the same. She had become a girl without purpose, and now she didn't even have a bed of her own.

'I don't think you have to worry about me anymore,' she told him.

'Your sister is worried about you,' Yuri said. 'And so, now it is my duty to worry as well.'

Min closed her eyes. *Lu.* They'd become enemies in Yunis, but standing there at the threshold of Min's apartments, her weapon directed at Brother, Lu had been on her side. Her sister, beneath it all.

Then she'd told that boy to take everything Min had that was worth anything at all. And that, too, was her sister. Incapable of letting Min escape the long, cold cast of her shadow. Always certain that she, the older, smarter sister, knew what was best. What should be done.

Anger flashed through Min. It was chased by pain. Her side and neck throbbed hotly. Sweat beaded her hairline and she gasped, clenching the clean bedding beneath her with clawlike hands.

Yuri shifted in his seat. 'The physician will be here soon. He has you on a schedule of poppy tears.' He did not look directly at her.

She almost laughed. His discomfort at her pain was palpable. It reminded her of Lu, how she could not bear to see others cry. What was it about warriors that they could not stand to see suffering, when their entire purpose was to create it?

She heard a door slide open and a man in fresh linen robes entered, carrying a tray of steaming bowls. Ohn – Omair.

'Is that my physician?' she asked.

'No,' Yuri said, his eyes tracking the other man as he made his way across the room. 'But I suppose he'll do for now.'

'I've brought lunch,' Ohn said. 'I'm afraid it'll just be broth for you, Princess. I did not know you would be awake. I can fetch something else if you'd like—'

'What she needs are poppy tears,' Yuri told him.

'No,' she said abruptly, thinking of Brother and his draughts. 'I'll take some later. How long have I been asleep?'

'Several days,' Ohn told her, pulling another chair up beside Yuri's. 'You awoke here and there, but the physicians and I felt we should keep you sedated, to let your body heal.'

'Has my sister come to see me?' she asked.

The two men exchanged glances.

'She has been very preoccupied,' Ohn said. 'They're planning to lift the curfew and reopen the city walls—'

'She'll be here when she can,' Yuri interrupted, cutting Ohn off. Perhaps he did not want Min to know the details – as though she still presented a threat to Lu's claim. Laughable. She could scarcely turn her head without bleeding to death. 'She has an empire to salvage.'

That is all an empire is: a beast that must kill to stay alive, in numbers that render death easy, cheap.

The words came to her like an echo across time. All at once she remembered where she had heard them. *A dream*, she told herself. But she knew now – she had seen enough, been shown enough, to recognise the difference between dreams and these memories belonging to others, being shared with her. Something like hope dared to prick at her throat – and then faltered.

Her power rushing out of her body in gouts of grey smoke, seeping into that slipskin boy. That had not been a dream either.

'Am I a prisoner?' she asked aloud.

'There are quite a few in court who would like you to be,' Yuri responded. 'Your sister is trying to keep that from happening.'

His tone irritated her. It implied she ought to be grateful. Her sister, the saviour. What had it cost her the last time she'd allowed herself to believe that?

'She loved her,' she murmured.

'What's that?' Yuri asked.

'Tsai,' Min said, looking up to meet the shin's eyes.

He flinched at the name, as she'd known he would. 'She hated everything in this world. But even she loved Lu.'

'She was her mother,' Yuri said shortly, as though that explained anything. Perhaps to him it did.

She was mine, too.

Hadn't Min said as much to Rinyi? She'd forged the thought as a weapon, but it was strong because at its core was an iron vein of truth.

It was unfair, she thought, that Lu had none of the burden and all of the love. Ridiculous, of course. Min had been *cursed*; what could she expect? She'd been an opportunity for revenge, nothing more. And yet, what Tsai had given her – the power, the secrets – had been the whole of what her life amounted to. However it had been intended, it was all she'd had.

'She was troubled,' Ohn said. Omair. Whoever he was. A prisoner, a shaman, a country healer. How could he be so many different people when she was no longer even one?

'You didn't understand her,' Min said. 'You didn't see what she'd been through.'

And I'm not yours.

That was what Tsai had told those boys, the ones who had held her hands and loved her, or loved each other, all those years past. But it was true now, for Min as well. Tsai was not hers. Not her powers, not her story, not even the residue of her preternatural rage.

All her life Min had been so afraid of nothing. Nothingness. Being nothing or, perhaps worse, being the echo of someone – her sister, her mother, even Butterfly – a simulacrum of something living and meaningful and intentional, possessing a gravity of her own. The missed potential to be someone deserving of love. But now, with the curse torn out of her, she realised for the first time how it truly felt to be nothing. A spent husk, an unworn mask.

Someone else, someone brave, might have called it a kind of freedom, she thought. But she was not brave, and no matter what Yuri said, in the end, she was only a prisoner.

14

The Grand Secretariat

'This isn't a secret anymore!'

Lu's prior impression of Minister Ong had been vague at best; nevertheless, she was fairly certain he was not normally this red in the face. Nor did she remember him ever being quite this loud. His voice echoed through the unremarkable first floor duty office that housed meetings of the Grand Secretariat. The site was tradition – if a somewhat cramped and charmless one.

'We are potentially entering an era of uninhibited abuse of sorcery due to Empress – Princess Min's little display in Kangmun Hall!' Minister Ong ranted on. 'This moon alone there has been a thirty per cent reported increase in demands for banned talismans and spells. *Thirty per cent*! And those are the *reported* figures – imagine the requests that are being filled by less scrupulous shamans. Not to mention those that aren't registered.'

He searched the other faces around the table to confirm they were all suitably appalled by the notion of unregistered shamans. On Lu's right, Yuri was taciturn as ever. Jin, seated immediately to her left, looked puzzled – the idea of restricting sorcery was foreign to him, however she tried to explain it. Across the table, Ministers Ko, Bek, and Qin nodded along with practiced, noncommittal restraint. As for Kommodeur Lamont, his pale eyes had acquired a glassy sheen, though that may have been as much an issue of the language barrier as the subject matter. Shin Mung, at least, looked sympathetic.

As the head of one of the Six Ministries appointed by her father, Ong had been a constant presence in court. But as the Minister of Rites, he had never been the most interesting one, at least in Lu's eyes. Monthly reports about rural animists, or the squabbles between different Mul factions – even when they led to periodic bloody mountaintop monastery brawls – had not been able to compete with the Ministers of War or Justice for her young attention.

'Minister Ong,' she said graciously. 'I assure you we are all as concerned as you are with the breaking of these regulations—'

'With all due respect, your highness, these are not isolated incidents. We are seeing a *cultural* shift. This is a precarious time. Riots and starvation in the streets, flooding in the South, and now bile fever in its wake. Desperate people, all looking for portents and saviours. Small wonder so many seek out contraband magic when their own empress is openly dabbling in it.'

'My sister is no longer empress, I am,' Lu said.

Her sharp tone seemed to deflate him, if only for a moment. 'Of course, Empress. I-I certainly did not mean any disrespect,' he said quickly, his ears reddening.

Then Minister Ko leaned forward. 'And as our new sovereign, how will you punish your sister for her crimes?'

Lu had been anticipating this. That did not make it easier to hear. 'My sister has already been detained,' she told him, producing the mild, firm smile she'd prepared in advance.

'Being sequestered to her royal apartments can hardly be considered imprisonment, especially for someone with her powers!' Ong scoffed, regaining his vigour. 'She is a danger – not just for what she represents, but physically. Who is to say she won't send the whole Immaculate City up in flames, and all of us with it?'

'That will not be an issue,' Lu assured him. 'Her powers have been excised.'

Minister Ong squinted. 'What does this mean, "excised"?'

'It means that Min is no longer a concern of yours.' Lu did not mention Nokhai, and what she had ordered him to do. Ong would not be happy to hear of the number of Gifteds currently in the Immaculate City. Nor would the great many who shared his prejudices.

Beside her, Yuri shifted uncomfortably in his seat. He'd warned her Minister Ong would not let this matter go easily. Perhaps not, but he *would* let it go. She would see to it.

Minister of Justice Ko leaned back, tenting his fingers. 'Even if Princess Minyi is no longer a threat, punishment is not merely a matter of discouraging future misdeeds, but to exact retribution for those who have been wronged.'

Beside him, Minister Bek nodded gravely. 'One of the pages killed during the throne room rampage was my nephew. My brother and his wife's only son. They are inconsolable.'

Lu accepted his words like little dagger points to the

gut, as though she were the one responsible for the boy's death. She had nearly forgotten how much blood was on her sister's hands. It was hard to believe, when she was back here amid the primal familiar comforts of home. When Min looked small and worried in her medicated sleep, so much more like the little sister Lu had thought she'd had. It was easy to forget what they had both become – how much things had changed.

'Not to mention, if the people do not see Princes Minyi punished for her crimes, what then are they to make of the sanctity of the Mul tenants?' Minister Ong pressed, as though they had not heard him the first dozen times.

Shin Mung piped up for the first time. 'It is true. As the sage Lowen said: "If the mightiest will not uphold the weight of the law, how can we expect the meek to shoulder its burden?"'

'I will take that under consideration,' Lu told him, frowning. Shin Mung shrank back in his seat.

'This is a serious matter,' Minister Ong insisted.

'It is.' Lu pressed her hands down on the table in an effort to keep from wrapping them around the man's wiry neck. 'But it is also worth remembering my sister is a child—'

'A child, as my nephew was a child,' interjected Minister Bek, dispelling the memory, at the same time Minister Ong protested: 'Child or not, she was an *empress*—'

No one brought you to this moment but yourself.

'And she never should have been,' Lu countered quickly. 'An empress, that is. That was all due to the machinations of evil men. And now, the error has been corrected. She is Empress no longer.'

'Nevertheless, she still did the things she did—'

'Perhaps exile,' Yuri interjected. Every head at the table turned toward him. Lu felt the vitriol flare in her veins, the unintended fire in her eyes. She whirled to face him. Had he lost his wits?

He leaned in close. 'Your ministers are not wrong. Min must face consequences for her actions. Exile at your mother's family home would not be out of proportion. And she would be safe there—'

'I think we can speak of this later,' she grated out.

'Exile,' mused Minister Ko, and she did not appreciate the way he said it, as though she had not spoken at all.

'*I* will decide my sister's fate.' Lu put enough of the lash in her voice that he flinched. An uneasy quiet settled around the table. 'Let us move on to the matter of the Ellandaise,' she said.

There was a pause, punctuated by the sound of someone clearing his throat.

'*Yes*, Minister Ong?' Lu grated.

'As Minister of Rites, foreign affairs actually fall under my purview as well,' he said, though he looked slightly frightened to admit it.

Lu looked sharply to her right; Yuri shrugged.

'It's ah, true.' Shin Mung coughed apologetically. 'That duty was allocated during your grandfather's reign. The empire had so few foreign relations back in those days, I suppose it didn't warrant its own Ministry.'

Lu resisted the urge to run her hands down her face in frustration, if only because she was wearing a full mask of make-up. 'We will have to reevaluate that,' she told them. 'For now, let us move on to the matter of our alliance with the Ellandaise, and the terms of the agreement reached by me and Kommodeur Lamont. First, in exchange for lending us the service of their ships and their soldiers stationed here to rebuild the parts of the city affected by the fire, we will restart the poppy trade between—'

'The Empire of the First Flame does not trade in poppy tar!' Minister Ong. Of course. He had gone quite red. 'I thought once Princess Min was unseated this matter would be put to rest. I'm horrified to see this is not the case.'

'It is a banned substance.' To her surprise, it was Shin Mung who had spoken. He didn't raise his voice – Lu wasn't sure if he was capable; in the decade he had been her tutor, she'd scarcely heard him speak in anything louder than a pedantic murmur – but there was a slightly frayed edge to it, like a cloth that had begun to unravel. 'Emperor Lu, your own father was the one who—'

In her mind, the impossible pipe that should not exist – could not exist – slipped from between her fingers.

'My father was a good man,' Lu said, perhaps a bit louder than necessary. 'And that decision of his was not without merit. But bans can be overturned provided there is good reason to do so – as is the case now. The Ellandaise have built a new processing station in their southern colonies, just across the Lotus Sea from here, and developed new cultivars of disease-resistant poppy. This has led to a surplus, and a much lower cost than we previously paid—'

'That is not the issue. Use of poppy tar runs counter to the very moral core of the empire,' Minister Ong protested. 'There is a reason it is called "foreign mud". It is a degenerate scourge, attacking both the mind and body. It must be kept out of our cities.' He was looking at her, but he directed his shrill words to the rest of the room.

Lu stiffened. She had reinstated to their previously held positions many of those ministers of her father's who had been stripped of rank and replaced under Min. Perhaps that had been a mistake. These men had watched her grow up, but they did not seem to realise it. All they saw, all they might ever see, was the little girl they had met years before. Yuri was no better, proposing to send Min up to Bei Province without even asking Lu about it first.

She would have to find a way to walk back the issue of her sister's exile. And to communicate her displeasure with each of them later, in private. Dissent was one thing, but this grandstanding was tiresome, and insulting to Lamont, who was both an ally and a guest.

The Kommodeur himself did not appear offended; he brushed a bit of lint from the sleeve of his wool jacket. Perhaps he hadn't understood.

Ong's angle was a familiar one, applying the politics of morals to the smoking of poppy tar, emphasising its foreign origins. It was appealing to those who felt the Ellandaise were given too much power and leeway, and who viewed their culture – or any foreign culture – as a corrupting influence. Such people were not a small part of the court. Lu herself, when only a small child, had argued against allowing the foreigners to set up their own outpost in the Second Ring, had argued that only denizens of the Empire of the First Flame should own its land. Not that anyone had asked her opinion back then.

'Times have changed, Minister Ong,' she declared, straining to keep her tone polite. 'The *world* has changed.'

'Right and wrong do not change,' Ong insisted stubbornly. 'That is what makes them right and wrong.'

'Perhaps,' Kommodeur Lamont interjected, leaning toward Minister Ong, 'I could help put your fears to sleeps.' So he did understand what was being said, then. His voice was a baritone purr that he clearly believed charming. The effect was somewhat ruined by his clumsy grasp of Yueh. 'Tell me what I needs to give to you, in order you feels at ease.'

A stony silence was the only answer they gave him until, finally, Minister Ko leaned forward and cleared his throat. 'I am old enough to recall when we first started purchasing poppy tar from your people. The first year, we imported twenty-five chests, with each chest containing one hundred and forty-five pounds of the stuff. Do you know how many chests we were importing a decade later?'

'Hopefully more than that,' Lamont quipped.

'Nearly ten *thousand* chests. Enough to satisfy the appetites of a million addicts,' Minister Ko seethed. 'Such was the demand for your poison. Such was its nefarious power over our people. It was worse than a plague. At least in a plague, people still wish to live. Those trapped in the thrall of the poppy would happily waste away at the end of a pipe. I do not know how your Ambassador Kartrum managed to receive an audience before Empress Minyi, but it should never have happened.'

'Yes, well, I regrets to inform you Ambassadeur Kartrum has departed his mortal life, so we cannot ask him,' Lamont said with an ease that conveyed little regret at all. Then, leaning back in his chair, he added, 'But in my experiences, there is precious little in this world that silver is not buying.'

'Silver cannot buy dignity,' Ong interjected.

'Enough of this,' Lu snapped. 'This deal is a pledge I made to Kommodeur Lamont, and I intend to keep it.'

Ong's voice made her head throb. And Ko thought he was so clever, emphasising that *he* was old enough to remember the poppy scourge. So was everyone at this table – all except her. Well, unfortunately for him, she was the only person here endowed with a mandate from the heavens to rule.

'A pledge made under duress, in the throes of battle—' Minister Ong began to retort.

She cut him short. 'And one I will honour now that the battle has ended. I am disappointed in you, Minister Ong. You speak so loftily of right and wrong, yet you fail to understand that a promise made is a promise kept. The promise of a sovereign most of all.'

'Of course. But a promise that affects the fate of so many? And made without consulting your advisers ...' He trailed off, his voice straining under the unspoken insistence that *this was not how things were done.*

As though the history of the empire wasn't written by the whims of the men who had sat the throne before her.

'Had you been there with me in exile,' she said coldly, 'I would have been delighted to hear your thoughts on the matter.'

Ong gaped at her. Lamont, conversely, let out a barking

laugh. She was hard pressed to say which she found more irritating.

'Thank you for your presence today, Kommodeur,' she told him. 'We have concluded the item on the agenda that involves you. My handmaidens are waiting just outside the door – one of them will be happy to escort you to the Eastern Gardens for a tour and lunch.'

He seemed a bit annoyed to be shooed out so quickly, but he simply gathered his hat and bowed low to her. 'Empress, you haves honour me today,' he said before exiting.

Lu held in a sigh of relief and instead turned to Yuri. 'What is next on the agenda?'

'Money,' he said flatly. 'We need more of it. Huge swaths of the Second Ring were destroyed in the riots and will need rebuilding. The same goes for all the southern villages affected by the recent flooding and mudslides. And we're receiving reports of epidemic flux as a result of the contaminated water. They're dying like flies.'

'Thank you for that bit of commentary,' Lu said. 'Putting a sword in your hand instead of a brush was a mistake. Clearly you were meant for poetry. What other good news have you for me?'

He frowned at her, but continued reading: 'Kun, Xiawei and Fuyan Provinces continue to report severe grain shortages. Riots have broken out in several villages over claims of price-fixing. And the Governor of Fuyan has disappeared. Some claim he was killed by angry citizens, others say he ran off with his mistress – and a good deal of the province's silver.'

'That's just perfect...' Lu's voice faltered. The names

he'd listed stirred something in her, like hearing a song she had nearly forgotten. And then it came to her: the ledgers hidden in her father's bedroom, along with the pipe that could not exist. 'Which provinces did you say are reporting price-fixing?'

'Kun, Xiawei and Fuyan. Why? Does that mean something to you?' he asked.

She shook her head slowly. 'No. Not to me.' She cleared her throat. 'From my perspective, making a deal with the Ellandaise will bring us the fastest influx of silver. Lamont has offered us favourable terms on a generous loan, and will lend us ships, material, and men to help rebuild the city.'

'And in return, we agree to pay him for the privilege of being poisoned,' sniffed Ong.

'No matter how much silver he loans us, we'll spend it all back a hundredfold buying poppy cake once the public gets a taste and sales begin to rise,' Bek pointed out. 'The foreigner can afford to be generous now, because he knows it will pay off in the future.'

'If we don't solve the issues before us now, we will not have a future,' Lu told him.

'There is another option,' Minister Qin said quietly, his eyes fixed on her. He'd been judiciously quiet until now, his face unreadable. 'We have plenty of wealth. It's simply trapped underground.'

And then Lu realised, he wasn't looking at her, but to her left – at Jin. He went on: 'Empress Lu is to wed Prince Jin – the sole remaining heir to Yunis. Certainly, these newlyweds could work out a place for us to establish new mining colonies in the steppe.'

'No,' Lu and Jin said in unison.

Minister Qin frowned and leaned forward. 'I think this matter must be discussed further. If it is not an option, well, I do not mean any offence, but I do not see what other benefit this marriage arrangement brings the empire.'

'The symbolism is important,' Lu told him firmly. 'We unite the capital and the North as equals. It will legitimise the northern territories in the eyes of those who live there – and perhaps give them some greater say in how they are governed.'

'Oh, and is that something we want?' Minister Ong asked frankly. He looked toward the others. 'More mines sound like a better deal to me.'

'I won't see another mine opened in the North. Not in any borderlands,' Lu insisted.

'It is too volatile in that region,' Jin added. 'It is beyond arrogance to ravage the earth there in that manner – it could be dangerous.'

'We cannot afford to keep expanding in the manner we have been. And we are not in any place to spend that sort of capital, even if we stand to earn it back,' Lu told them.

Yuri's laugh broke the uncomfortable silence that followed. 'How could we stand in the way of such a marriage? Look how compatible they already are.'

Dusk turned the world's edges soft and violet by the time Lu was able to retire. The duty office of the Grand Secretariat was not far from her apartments, but the walk was made long by silence. Once, she would have relaxed in the company of her handmaids, regaling them with impressions of Minister Ong. But there was something hushed and distant about the other girls now – as though they had slipped into some land where Lu could not follow, and returned bearing ghostly scars she could sense, but not see. Joking around them, like this, would have been like laughing at a funeral. She dismissed them at her door.

As soon as they were gone, Lu went for the cabinet beside her father's – her – bed and scooped the ledgers into an unceremonious heap on the floor. She tore open the nearest one and scanned the page. Grain prices for Kun, Xiawei and Fuyan Provinces. Just as she had remembered. The same provinces in crisis now over grain prices. She saw the little columns of numbers now for what they were. Payoffs. She closed her eyes. Price-fixing.

Father, what did you do?

She felt his presence before she heard or saw him. A warmth, the barest hint of a settling shadow falling over her from behind.

She spun and rose, dropping the ledger.

Nokhai.

'You're back,' she blurted. 'I was afraid you'd leave for good.'

He stepped back, as though surprised by how close they were. 'Where would I go?' he asked. 'Everyone I know is here now.'

'How was town?' she asked.

'Burned.' He traced an invisible line on the windowsill. 'But Adé's family is safe.'

'Did your sister return to the palace with you?'

He nodded. 'Like I said: everyone I know.'

'I'm surprised Nasan didn't storm my meeting.'

'Nasan might not respect power, but she understands

how it works. She has nothing to gain from making herself look a fool in front of your Grand Secretariat. And she knows from experience what your soldiers are capable of doing in the name of their emperor.'

We both do. He didn't say it aloud, but she heard it, nevertheless.

She looked at him then – really looked. 'You're different,' she blurted. 'You've changed.'

He looked up. Defensiveness sharpened his dark eyes.

'I don't mean it in a bad way,' she said, and even as the words left her lips, she was uncertain of their truth.

'You're different, too.'

She flinched. She thought of the soldiers at the camp, the young guard in the Ansana precinct. So many lives extinguished by her hand. She hadn't told him – did not need to. 'How so?'

He hesitated, and she saw uncertainty retake him. The questions in his eyes dissolved. 'You have more hair now,' he said at last.

Her lips quirked into a smile, relieved. 'It's fake,' she told him, tapping the hairpiece with the tips of her crimson-lacquered fingernails. The pearls hanging down the sides of her head rattled and swayed in the wake of the gesture.

She pulled the black-lacquered wooden hairpiece up from its position atop the crown of her head. The rows of long, pointed silver teeth that had held it in place, each as long as a man's finger, caught her hair.

'Let me do that.' Nok stepped forward and took it from her hands, tearing it loose. He placed it on the polished surface of the vanity. 'It's heavy.'

'Mmm,' she agreed, rolling her head and shoulders. 'So is this cloak. Would you ...?' She held up her arms.

A delicious red flush rose up the thin skin of his neck. For a moment, she thought she had overstepped, but he slowly extracted her from one sleeve, then the other. She let her arms fall. He held the cloak up uncertainly. She hadn't been exaggerating its weight – double-thick quilted silk spangled with rubies, and trimmed in gilt thread – and he swayed under it.

'How do you even stand in this thing?'

'Just toss it over the stool,' she told him, pointing toward her vanity. He did as she instructed, but slippery with riches, it pooled onto the floor.

'Leave it.'

She made to undo the upsweep of her hair – her real hair – but in doing so tangled up one of her rings. She grunted, more in annoyance than pain, yanking at it again, but then he was there, close, taking her hand to still it.

'You're going to tear out your scalp,' he said, pushing her hand down.

His was warm. Unbidden, her fingers tightened around it. It wasn't quite a squeeze – nothing so intentional. Just an instinctive curl into his touch, like vines reaching for the light.

Her ring was gold, shaped into the face of a tiger, a fiery red stone the size of a dove's egg clenched in its miniature fangs – upon which her hair was also caught. She tilted her head, straining toward the periphery to watch as Nok loosed it with his free hand, gently, a few strands at a time, so as not to hurt her. 'There,' he said when he was done. 'You're free.'

'Am I?' she murmured. 'Thank you.'

'Anything for our emperor.'

She tensed at the jibe – his tone was not exactly disparaging, more just an echo of past reproaches. Their hands were still entwined. She pulled hers away, regretting the loss of his touch as soon as she did. Too late.

'Don't call me that,' she said, wandering over to the vanity while gingerly pulling pins from her hair. She tossed them on the polished surface of the dressing table. She looked up and met his eyes in the mirror's reflection.

'Isn't that what you are?' he countered lightly.

'Not when no one is watching.'

'There is always someone watching in this city.'

'Not here.'

It was true in a literal sense – as far as she knew, at least. The ammas assigned to bedchamber duty had taken up the discreet room beside her own, the thin walls a border in little more than name. And then there were the passages connecting her father's chambers with those of the woman she had called mother for seventeen years. Possibly more that she did not even know about. But there was no one watching her from them right now – unless, of course, there was.

'No one is watching us,' she said again, and she found herself tightening her grasp on him, as though this were some sort of pact, an oath that would make her words true, force him to accept the terms of her lie, her untruths.

But he was not a liar.

'Aren't they?' he said.

This day – and had she been paying closer attention, perhaps her whole life – had shown her that this was a

city of thieves. Avarice and agendas – stacked ignomini-
ously atop one another, like the bricks that built the walls
surrounding its Heart, century after century. A tradition
so ancient it became nothing at all, nothing that could
be seen by the people who practiced it like nature, like
breathing, day in and out.

How, she thought, with an absurd flutter of panic,
could Nokhai survive here?

The copper-flecked humid brown of her eyes met his,
their swallowing blackness ever shrouding something:
doubt, worry, fear. She lowered her gaze, down the broad
ridge of his nose, to his full mouth. His lips were parted,
just slightly. Like they were about to form words. Like
they were a challenge, daring her closer. At the thought,
her hand tingled warmly where it met his. Her skin felt
too taut, too warm, too full, like there was too much
blood rising to the surface.

She knew then that it would never have been like this
with Jin. How could she, when there was nothing there
to imagine with? She'd done her best to believe that kind
of union could be as alive, as reflexive and true as this, but
that was like asking an ox to fly: against its very nature.
A cruelty.

'I thought you were dead,' she said.

'I was,' Nokhai's voice caught on the words. 'Briefly.'

'You're shaking,' she murmured. 'Why? Are you afraid
of me?' she teased, pressing his palm to her mouth.

'Maybe a little.'

'Hmm,' she said, tilting her head. 'How can I make
you feel safe, I wonder?'

She lowered his hand, guiding it down past her neck,

the swell of her breast and her stomach, before pressing it to a rest against her hip.

'Would it help if I held you? Gently, of course – like this?' She wrapped her arms around his waist and drew his body flush up against hers, finally closing the gap between them.

'That's ... nice,' he said, barely above a whisper.

'And if I do this?' She pressed her lips to his.

He let out a shuddering sigh that passed from his mouth into hers. Her fingers clutched at his tunic, grasping along his spine and the small of his back. She felt the hand on her hip tighten its grip.

When they parted, the air between them hummed with shared heat.

'Well, that didn't help at all,' Lu said breathlessly, cocking her head to the side with a lopsided grin. 'You're only shaking more—'

Nokhai drew her against him with both hands and kissed her, drinking her in as though she were water and he were three days dying in the desert. She kissed him back, hard, as though to release him would be to lose him.

Not again – not ever again, she vowed.

This time, neither of them pulled away for a very long while.

15

Divided

Cool early morning sunlight stretched across Nok's face, stirring him. He squinted in the grey-rose glow streaming through the open doors leading out to the tai.

Tai?

A dozen confused thoughts rushed through him all at once before he understood where he was.

Lu's royal apartments in the Immaculate City.

And, he realised groggily, his legs were twisted up rather hopelessly in Lu's royal sheets.

He turned over to kick them loose, and in doing so, saw Lu fast asleep in the bed beside him. For half a moment he thought that perhaps the events of the previous three moons had just been a dream, and that he and the princess were boarding in some flea-infested ramshackle inn, still hopelessly making their way north to Yunis.

Then he saw Lu's bare shoulders peeking from under the tangles of her silken bedding, and the events of the night before came rushing back, along with a blush that seared his neck and ears.

Her coppery eyes opened, gazing back at him.

'Good morning,' she said, with the languorous catlike stretch of someone utterly at ease in her own skin.

Nok chewed his lip – the worried tic of someone, he realised even as he performed it, who had never been. Then, recalling his own nakedness for the first time, he sat bolt upright, yanking the sheets around himself. Unfortunately, in doing so, he pulled them off Lu.

'Oh gods,' he cursed, desperately averting his eyes. They settled on a blanket that had been kicked to the foot of the bed in the night; he quickly swept it over her body.

The room rang with Lu's laughter as Nok felt heat overtake his whole face. He must've been purple. Lu sat up, the blanket falling from her shoulders. 'You weren't so shy last night,' she told him.

'I'm sorry,' he stammered, still refusing to meet her gaze. 'If I did anything … I didn't mean it—'

'Nok,' she said, sliding across the bed, holding the sheets over her shoulders. 'I'm only teasing.' She took his face in her hands, forcing him to look her in the eye. When he brought a hand up tentatively to stroke her hair, she lowered her mouth down upon his.

'This can't happen,' he said, pulling away. 'I mean, we can't do … this … can we?'

'I think we already did,' she said innocently.

He blushed anew and sat up, pulling a bed sheet over his shoulders and head.

'You're modest as a princess,' she said. 'Or, as modest as a princess is meant to be, I suppose. I was never very good at that.'

He ignored her comment. 'You know what I mean. We can't just … Prince Jin … that is, your—'

'Betrothed,' she agreed as she slid off the bed, bare as anything, and strode across the room to her wardrobe. If she could feel his tentative gaze upon her as she plucked a floor-length plum-coloured robe from a clothing rack and swept it over her shoulders, she did not let on.

'So,' he said, studying the coverlet draped in his lap with rapt interest. 'What does ... all this mean?'

'I don't know what it means,' she admitted. 'Does it matter?'

He frowned. 'You're the emperor now. I'm a ... nothing. That will matter to a lot of people.'

'I'm the emperor now,' she agreed, settling on the bed facing him. 'And I – as well as the people who supported me – will write history. A nothing? You're one of the most celebrated heroes of a battle against an insidious army of usurpers. The last Ashina. And the last Pactmaker.'

He flinched.

She bit her lip, realising her error. 'I'm sorry. Has Omair been able to figure out what the problem is?'

He looked away. 'I already know. It's Min. Or, it's her ... curse. Whatever it was that I took out of her ... it's like it's caused a blockage in my energy.' Nok shifted uneasily. 'I can feel it – like a rock, sitting in me. I can *feel* her. Sense her.'

Lu leaned forward in concern. 'You mean you hear her voice? Her thoughts?'

'No ... no. Nothing quite so definite. It's more like, when I search for it, I can feel what it is to be her. When she's alone. Her most private, secret self. When there's no one around to watch – only I *am* watching.'

He shivered, and she stroked his arm.

'Lu, I don't think I should have taken it. Whatever it is. It's like I've broken something. Almost like ... I don't know, forcing the current of a river to flow in reverse. It's unnatural.'

Her lips twisted. 'Min can't be trusted with it, though. You've seen what she's capable of. She could kill us all.'

'I don't know.' He considered. 'Maybe you're right about that. But I don't think I'm meant to have it either.'

Lu considered. 'There has to be some other way, then. What about Omair? Could he take it instead?'

Nok felt a familiar annoyance flare up in him. 'I'm not passing this burden on to Omair. He's old, and he's been locked in a prison cell for moons. Who knows what this would do to him?'

'I only asked because he clearly has more power than meets the eye. I wasn't trying to suggest—'

He stood, yanking the bedclothes up around him like a shroud. 'Just because he doesn't mean much to *you* doesn't mean his life doesn't have meaning.'

'Nokhai,' she protested, standing and taking him by the shoulders. 'That's not what I was saying. I was only trying to think of ways you might fulfil your duties as Pactmaker. To go *home*.'

The surprise of it stilled him.

'Is that what you want?' he asked. 'For me to leave?'

'I don't want to be apart from you ever again,' she said. They both went still with the weight of it. She released his shoulders, looking down. 'But isn't it what *you* want?'

He recalled his father's vision of home, that place of colour and golden light and laughter. That place that had been loved, that had loved its warrior-son Delgar in return. Then he recalled his own.

Could the barren North, with its bleak beauty and its ghosts, be home again? If it ever was in the first place. The thought made him ache, unsettled.

He leaned forward and kissed her instead.

He didn't belong here either. This place, this court of watching, scrutinising eyes, this city of liars. But sinking into Lu's arms, feeling the honeyed heat of her gaze on his skin – that was something he might grow accustomed to. Falling into her felt like falling into a deep, warm sleep. Into something new and familiar, all at once. He might not have a home, but he could give himself this, couldn't he?

'And what if I don't go?' he heard himself murmur. 'If I stayed and kept Min's curse until we figured out a solution?'

Her arms tightened around him, but when she spoke it was with the hushed, disbelieving tone of someone trying not to frighten off a wild bird who had landed in her hands. 'You can do anything you'd like.'

'And what will I be now? Without my caul? Your concubine?'

'Tell me what title you want and I'll make it yours.' She ran the backs of her fingers up and down his exposed arm, making him shiver.

'I don't want a title,' he said, pushing her hand away.

'Ambassador from the Ashina,' she suggested, dropping a kiss upon his shoulder. 'You could establish an affiliation with the Mul priests – we'll call you a Temple Patriarch.'

He shook his head. 'No, I can't. I can't be a part of …

I can't serve the Hu. You know that. I'll stay here with you. I'll be yours, but I can't belong to the empire.'

She frowned. 'And you can live with that? No title?'

'No title.'

And when I marry Jin? Nok could feel the words hovering between them, but she only said: 'We'll have to be discreet.'

'I know better than anyone about discretion,' he told her, forcing a crooked smile. 'Your empire didn't even know I was living in its borders for ten years, remember?'

She ignored the wisecrack and leaned against him, burying her face against his neck. She smelled of unwashed hair and medicinal salve, but he found he did not mind.

'I don't want to hurt you,' she murmured against his skin.

'You won't,' he said firmly, running the tips of his fingers along her back. His callouses snagged on the fine silk of her robe. 'I trust you.'

She pulled back and looked him in the face. There were, he saw in shock, tears in her eyes. She wiped them with the heel of her hand. He took her by the wrist and kissed their wetness away, trailing his tongue along the largest vein that throbbed there under her skin.

'Nokhai,' she murmured. 'There's something I should tell you about, before you hear it elsewhere. I wouldn't want you to think it was true—'

The pocket doors to Lu's bedchamber slid open. The two of them leapt apart.

A girl in a robe the colour of sunrise slipped into the room and closed the doors behind her.

'Prince Jin was here,' she said breathlessly.

Lu's eyes widened in alarm. 'Where is he now?'

'I convinced him to go back to his apartments. Sweet Olive and Syringa went to fetch a tray so he could break his fast – give him something to do. But he's expecting you. I told him you'd come once you were dressed.'

'I should go,' Nok said.

'No – stay,' Lu told him. 'I have to leave, but you should rest.'

As she spoke, the handmaiden gave him an appraising look. There was no surprise in it, but perhaps a trace of amusement. How long had she known he was there? So much for the secrecy Lu insisted they had.

'I'm going,' Nok repeated.

'I'll take you through the service corridor,' said the handmaiden.

Lu nodded. A long pause followed.

Nok cleared his throat. 'Could you perhaps turn around?' he said to the girl. 'No offence. It's just, you're not *my* handmaiden. I don't even know your name.'

Lu started. 'Oh, of course! Nokhai, this is Hyacinth. My nuna. Soon-to-be Head Amma.'

'Nice to meet you, Hyacinth.'

He thought he saw a glimpse of a smile as she turned to face the wall. In a loud, false whisper, she told Lu: 'He's polite, I'll give you that.'

Face hot, Nok collected his things from the floor, dressing as quickly as he could. Hyacinth pushed open the door to the servant's entrance and Nok made to follow. And then he remembered – 'What was it you were going to tell me before?'

Lu glanced to Hyacinth, impatiently holding open the

servant's door. 'It was nothing. Just ... rumours. There's nothing for you to worry about. I promise,' she told him.

Hyacinth ushered him through a series of narrow corridors until he was spat out into a sunny courtyard, still hopping into his boots and belting his tunic. No one was around; good. He slipped around the side of the building – and promptly tripped over an extended foot, barely catching himself before he fell. He stumbled, then whirled around to face his attacker—

'*Nasan?*'

'You slept long enough,' his sister groused. 'I've been waiting here since dawn.'

'Waiting...?'

'It's none of my business whose bed you sleep – or don't sleep – in. But did Lu tell you about that meeting she had with her Great Secretaries—'

'Grand Secretariat.'

'Of course,' she said with an exaggerated, fancy flourish of her hand to show what she thought of that. 'Whatever it's called. I should've been invited.'

Nok sighed. The situation hadn't been ideal, though he wasn't sure it was quite the snub Nasan believed it to be.

'Lu told you herself foreigners rarely if ever attend private meetings—'

'She saw fit to bring that pale man, and Jin. Both foreigners, if I'm not mistaken.'

Nok frowned; there was nothing he could say to that.

'Are you really trying to defend her?' Nasan demanded.

'No!'

'Lu is not who you think she is.'

Perhaps, he thought. But what Nasan saw wasn't the whole of the truth either. Was a person ever really one thing?

Since returning to Yulan City, it increasingly felt to him there were two Lus: the princess-turned-empress – by turns vicious and arrogant and frustratingly, frighteningly inhuman. This was the Lu whose cool, indifferent gaze slid over the servants and gilded furniture that populated her life in court without registering either as the spoils of blood or happenstance.

There was the other Lu, though. The one who called him by his full name, weighting the syllables in such a way that each sounded melodious and important. This was the Lu who was frank, and funny, and who reached for him so insistently, so naturally, it felt like he'd always imagined safety would feel.

But he could not tell Nasan this.

'You should just speak with Lu directly—'

'It doesn't matter anymore,' Nasan said, cutting him short. 'Nok, I'm going home.'

'What?' He stared at her. 'After you've come all this way? There's no reason to give up now. You could arrange a meeting between the two of you, to discuss what your expectations are—'

'I'm not giving up,' she said. 'I've just seen enough. I mean, look around, Nok. Look at this palace, these gardens. You've seen the city, you've *lived* it. You and I, we don't belong here. I'm going home, to our people. And you should come with me.'

'That isn't my home.'

'The hell it's not,' she retorted. 'You belong with your

family. You belong with *me*. Not down here with these city dwellers. Oh, certainly, your princess told us lots of pretty tales of manses and loyalty and the prosperity of the empire. I saw the truth of it, though. We already know their wealth was bought with our blood, but they don't even take care of their *own*! Half of them live in squalor – and that was before the fire.'

'You don't know—'

'Your friend Adé knows,' Nasan countered. 'You've been away, but she told me about the recent food shortages. How the royals eat their way through their stores while children born on the wrong sides of the city walls starve. Did your princess tell you about that?'

'What do you know about Adé?' Nok said sharply. 'You shouldn't bother her with ... leave her out of whatever your plans are. I mean it, Nasan.'

She raised an eyebrow. 'You're awfully defensive. I thought you already had a girlfriend.'

'Lu isn't ...' His reply was reflexive, but he stopped himself, realising he wasn't sure what she was. *Not the point.* 'Adé isn't my girlfriend, either. She's ...' Again, he fell silent. *Like a little sister* made more sense back before he knew he still had one.

Nasan didn't wait for him to finish. 'Well, whatever she is, I haven't been *bothering* her. While you were occupied last night, she and I smuggled food out of this gilded snake pit and brought it to her family and neighbors.'

Nok flinched at that. 'Well, thank you. For helping her.'

Nasan shrugged, looking off to her side with an air of would-be nonchalance. 'I didn't do it for *you*.' But he couldn't help noticing the way her gaze wasn't actually fixed on anything, or the uncharacteristic flush creeping up her neck.

He almost smiled. He'd never seen his sister infatuated with anyone before. But then, they'd been separated before those years of her life even began. Or perhaps it was only that he hadn't paid close enough attention.

'I can't go home – back north with you,' he blurted. 'Once the curse is lifted, I'll give you back your caul. But I can't be your Pactmaker.'

She stepped in, and for a moment he thought she might shake him. Instead, she reached out and took his hands in her own. 'Yes, Nok. You can.'

'I don't even have *my* caul anymore.'

'You said it yourself, it's that curse holding your powers back. Give it back to Min, set it free – find some way to release yourself. Forget these people, Nok! They're not your allies, they're not your friends. Come home, be the leader you were always meant to be.'

'Leader?' He laughed hollowly, pulling his hands out of hers. 'I'm no leader.'

'That's what a Pactmaker is. The start of all things. A creator.'

'Well, I don't want to be all of that.'

'No one who ever *wanted* power was fit for it.' Nasan smiled a little. 'You get it from Ba, you know.'

He looked at her, uncomprehending. 'Get what from him?'

'The tools to be a leader. The disposition to hate it.'

He stared. How could she so misremember things?

'Ba was a born leader,' he said slowly. 'Don't you

remember? Everyone always told us the elders groomed him to be on the council starting when he was little more than eleven years old.'

'Of course.' She shrugged. 'And he loathed every moment of it. Why do you think he was so tense all the time?'

Because I was a failure . . .

'And *don't* say it was because of you being a blight on the family or whatever nonsense apocryphal story you've written about yourself. Ba was hard on you, but you didn't make him the way he was.'

The unfairness of what she was saying! 'That's the way *he* thought of it,' Nok insisted. 'Everything about him – about our family – would've been perfect if it weren't for me.'

Nasan stuck out her lower lip and breathed a noisy huff of air, sending the ever-present rakish hank of hair draped across her forehead flying upward. She was quiet for a moment. Then: 'He ran away once, you know.'

'*Ba?*'

'Yep. When he was all of maybe nineteen, twenty years old. Had enough of things and one morning, the Kith woke up and he was gone. He came back a moon later, new Red Wolf bride in tow. They held the ceremony to induct her into the Kith that night, and that was that. No one ever spoke of it again. Well, almost no one.' She looked at him sidelong. 'Didn't you ever wonder how he met Ma?'

And Nok realised, with some embarrassment, that he hadn't. Perhaps he'd been too young. Perhaps he'd been too preoccupied with his own misery, anthologising the history of his pain, to notice anyone else. 'Who told you this?'

Nasan shrugged. 'One of the other girls – Janu, do you remember her? Probably not. You never really talked to anyone, did you? Well, in this case you made the right choice. Stuck-up little thing. She alluded to Ba running off, so I wrestled her until she told me the whole story.'

'Why didn't you tell me?'

Nasan took a moment to consider it. 'I didn't know that you'd care,' she said at last.

'Why wouldn't I? They were my parents, too.'

She picked at a loose bit of skin on her bottom lip. 'I suppose I thought of it as Ba's secret, and if I shared it with you, it would be a kind of burden. And you seemed like you already had a lot of those. Especially from Ba.'

'Secrets?'

'Burdens.'

'It seems like I still do,' he said.

'Well, this one I can't protect you from.' She smiled sadly. 'Is this really where you want to leave this? Leave us?'

'It seems like I don't have a choice.'

'You always have a choice.'

'So do you,' he pointed out. 'Nasan, talk to Lu. She's not unreasonable—'

Nasan shook her head, though. 'I'll see her before I go. But it doesn't matter. *She* doesn't matter. Can't you feel it? This place, it's like … a sick animal. It eats its own. No one can stop it. There's nothing for me here.'

He met her eyes, the same near-black as his own. Only hers held a ferocity he knew he did not possess. 'I don't want to lose you. Not again, after all this time.'

Nasan clapped him on the shoulder. 'You won't.

There's a few things I need to sort out before I leave. And after I do, I'll come visit, if your Girl King doesn't run me out of her city.'

'She wouldn't do that.'

'Maybe not yet,' she acknowledged. 'But one day.'

Nok narrowed his gaze at the way she said it. 'Nasan, what are you planning?'

'Nothing I haven't already told Lu a hundred times. Autonomy. Freedom. *Real* freedom. A chance for our people to live again.'

'And how do you plan to get it without her help?'

She shrugged and her face split into a wry, clever smile. Nasan and he looked so much alike – always had. But when she smiled like that, he no longer saw himself in her.

'I don't know what I'll do,' she said. 'But whatever it is, I'm not asking for permission. Not from Lu. Not from anyone.'

16

Love

'People will talk,' Hyacinth said as she helped Lu into the tub.

The other nunas had set to work stripping Lu's bed and picking up the clothing she had scattered around the night before, but she could see them throwing surreptitious glances her way. One of them giggled, but when she turned their way the noise stopped before she could discern who it came from.

'People always talk,' Lu said stiffly. 'Whether or not there is something to talk about.'

'Well, you're not exactly depriving them of fodder, are you?'

Lu twisted around in the tub. 'If you have something to say, say it − ow!' She erupted into a yelp as Hyacinth set to scrubbing her back with a hard brush. 'Watch it! I have cuts there, you know.' She glanced ruefully at the other girl. 'And I didn't think I'd be getting such judgement from you.'

Hyacinth's face softened, and she lowered the brush. 'I'm not judging you. I'm just saying that it will take a good deal of care and consideration to keep ... this ... quiet.'

'Well, see, that's why you're my dearest friend,' Lu said lightly. 'No one better than you at keeping things quiet, is there?'

Hyacinth glanced at the other nunas. 'That may be true, but you have other mouths to worry about, too.'

Lu followed her friend's gaze. 'You suspect disloyalty among them?'

Hyacinth's mouth twisted. 'Not disloyalty, exactly. But like I said, people will talk. Nunas love gossip as much as anyone.'

Lu frowned, leaning back in the tub. 'They won't be nunas for much longer. I mean to name you all ammas officially in court by the end of this week. Though now I wonder if perhaps I shouldn't cull some of the looser tongues from the ranks first. Did you have anyone in mind?'

'Exiling them to laundry service will hardly maintain their loyalty,' Hyacinth pointed out, drawing a comb through Lu's wet hair. She'd sidestepped the question.

'I would send them home to their families,' Lu told her.

'And we all know people in sky manses never gossip.'

'Oh, so am I to be held hostage by my own servants now?'

'Only trying to be helpful,' Hyacinth sighed.

'Well, try a little less,' Lu suggested. 'Or at least wait until after my bath.'

Her tone was annoyed, but in truth, she was distracted. Asleep, Nokhai had looked as peaceful as she'd ever seen him. The mask of suspicion and doubt that hardened his face had vanished. Aside from the rise and fall of his chest, and the flutter of his eyelashes against his high cheeks, he'd been utterly still.

Would he come to her chambers again if she invited him? She blushed anew recalling how impossibly soft his sighs had been into the cup of her ear, and how carefully he had run his fingers through her hair. One night with him at her side and it already seemed inconceivable that she could ever fall asleep without him.

It wasn't enough, she thought. And now the warm flood of love was tinged metal and bitter with longing. She wanted to be closer, to feel his dreams, seep under his skin ...

The thought reminded her of something he'd said. How had he described taking Min's curse? Knowing what she was like when she was her most private, secret self?

Lu felt a pang at the memory, and it took her a moment to register it as jealousy. Absurd. Nokhai hadn't meant it like that. But still, that he could have that closeness with Min – a closeness sunk below the flesh, an intimacy of spirit. To know her sister in a way Lu would never know either of them.

If Lu were the one with that kind of access, would she look? Open Nokhai's heart like it was a locked box of rosewood and inlaid mother-of-pearl? She suspected she would.

And would she look into her sister's heart, just as he was trying desperately not to? This time she knew the answer. Knew it like desperation. Her whole life, she'd thought she'd known Min, only to realise she knew nothing at all.

'You know,' Hyacinth said, pulling her back into the present. 'You've begun a trend.'

'What do you mean?

'I heard a rumour the Inner Ring girls are starting to chop off their hair so they can look more like the Girl King.'

'You must be joking.'

'I'm not. Apparently the daughters of prominent families are doing it to demonstrate their loyalty to your reign – and to show how modern they are.'

Lu groaned and buried her face in her hands. 'I admit I've never been one to temper my ambition – but I never wanted *this*.'

'What?' Hyacinth asked incredulously. 'Power? Responsibility?'

'To be a fashion icon.'

Something almost like a smile tilted the corners of the other girl's mouth upward and for a breath Lu saw the face of her old friend, like seeing the barest glimpse of a glorious sunset, before losing it behind a mountain.

Hyacinth took a hank of Lu's hair between her fingers, rubbing the ends together. 'All leaders influence style. The memorable ones, at any rate.' She smirked, and once more Lu saw the mischievous glimmer of the girl she'd thought of as a sister, though her eyes still looked tired. Lined, as though she'd aged a decade in a moon. 'The boy did a fair job. It could do with some touching up, but it's not total butchery. He must be talented.'

'Lu grinned. She could tell it made her look foolish, but she almost didn't mind. 'What do you think of him?'

'Well, I didn't get to speak to him very long, did I?' Hyacinth considered. 'He's quite pretty.'

Lu slid lower into the tub, until the steaming water lapped up at her chin. 'He is, isn't he? Wonderfully pretty.'

Hyacinth tried to quell a smile but failed. 'So ... what was it like? Taking a boy to bed?'

Lu sighed. 'We need to find you a husband.'

'Or just a lover. Like you.'

'Or a lover,' agreed Lu quietly. 'Like me.'

It occurred to Lu then that she ought to be ashamed. Or at least, that people would think she ought to be ashamed. Instead, she felt warm and giddy. Then Jin's face came into her mind – his bright, boyish smile, his trusting eyes – and she felt a stab of guilt.

'Is the bath still hot enough?'

Lu looked up. Hyacinth hadn't mentioned Jin since she'd initially come into the room. What did her friend make of that? Lu taking a lover the same day she'd confirmed her betrothal? There was a time when Lu wouldn't have hesitated to ask. There was a time, she realised with an uneasy jolt, that Hyacinth would have already told her.

Nothing was stopping Lu from asking her about it now. She sat up and opened her mouth, but all that emerged was, 'The bath is fine.'

The nuna nodded, tipping a ladle across Lu's back. The perfumed water sluiced over unseen cuts, making her wince. Hyacinth hung the ladle over the edge of the tub and set to scrubbing Lu's arm with a brush, sloughing off grey peels of dead skin.

Lu watched the girl from the corner of her eye; Hyacinth's brow was furrowed, and beaded with sweat.

She stood to retrieve something from the tray of toiletries, then paused, as though to catch her breath.

'Are you all right—' Lu began to ask, but before she could finish, Hyacinth pitched forward.

Lu was halfway to her feet, water sloshing loudly around her calves and onto the rug beneath when the nuna caught herself, fingers clenched like claws around the edge of the tub, knuckles blanched as old bone.

'Hyacinth—' Lu reached for her, dimly aware of the other nunas in her periphery, frozen at their tasks. Plum Blossom recovered first, rushing forward to help her friend.

'I just need a bit of air,' Hyacinth murmured, waving Plum Blossom back. Lu watched her make her way outside, onto the balcony outside her new apartments. She scarcely registered when Sweet Olive stepped forward to drape her robe over her shoulders.

Lu crossed the room. Hyacinth had left the doors open behind her, and an autumn wind swept in as though to mark her absence. Lu shivered as the cool air pricked at her wet skin.

Outside, Hyacinth stood at the far end of the balcony, leaning against a corner post, pressing a temple to the red-lacquered wood. She'd pulled her hood up against the chill, though Lu could still make out her wan face. As Lu watched, she extracted a ceramic bottle from the breast of her robes with quivering hands. The bottle's stopper was attached to a kind of wand; Hyacinth tipped a few drops of liquid from it onto her tongue. She replaced the stopper, carefully, as though handling something precious, then back into her robes the bottle went. Hyacinth closed her eyes and leaned more heavily against the post, as though she intended to merge into it. A shudder passed through her, and the muscles in her drawn, pinched face finally relaxed.

Lu froze. In her mind's eye, a glint of metal as the pipe tipped from her fingers and fell—

She was striding across the balcony before she even intended it. 'What was that?' Her voice was harsh, hushed. As though speaking it loud enough for the others to hear would make it more real.

Hyacinth's eyelids rose a sliver, as though she couldn't be bothered to open them all the way. 'You know what it is.'

'How – how can you—'

'It's just a tincture. Barely stronger than what the physicians use.' Hyacinth shrugged. 'Would you prefer I smoked tar like some of the others? You're going to open up the trade again anyway, aren't you? That's all anyone's been talking about since yesterday.'

The others . . .

'How long has this been going on?' Lu demanded, part of her taken with the wild urge to shake her friend, to find the bottle hidden in her robes and dash it against the floor. But her body would not obey, stilled with shock. Not just at the sight of the vial, but the realisation of how far her friend had slipped away.

'You have *no* right to judge me,' Hyacinth hissed. 'You don't know what we went through while you were gone. They kept us locked in the dungeons, Lu! For weeks. We didn't know if the next person at the door was coming to give us food or execute us. They threatened it plenty

– they thought we must know where you were, what your plans were. They beat us a few times.' She looked away, her eyes wet. 'Always careful not to leave bruises where they'd be seen. We were still girls from prominent families – though that was something they held over our heads, too. Telling us we'd be joining our fathers and mothers in being boiled alive, or dragged through the streets and torn apart, bit by bit, to make sure we suffered.'

'I didn't . . . ' Lu's nostrils flared in fury. *The dungeons.* Hyacinth had lied to her before. Why? To protect her? When all along it was Lu who should've been doing the protecting. 'Who? Give me names. I'll show them what it is to suffer.'

Hyacinth shook her head. 'It doesn't matter. The people who gave the orders – we'll never know who they were. And if they haven't already fled, they'll capitulate to your rule. Pretend they were loyal all along. And you'll need them, regardless, won't you?'

'I don't care who—'

'It was the poppy tar that saved us,' Hyacinth said. 'The physicians brought us the tears, first, for the pain. They didn't do much. But the kinder of the guards, they would let us smoke from their pipes. And that brought such relief.' She sighed, closing her eyes. She looked, Lu realised with a shock, blissful. As though the memory were so lovely, so freeing, that for a moment, reliving it, she could forget all else.

In Lu's mind, the pipe that could not exist hit the carpet, rolled under her father's bed, disappeared . . .

'Where did they get the poppy tar?' she wondered aloud.

'Gods! Wake up, Lu! They've been smuggling poppy tar into our borders for *years*.'

'Who?'

Hyacinth scoffed. 'Take your pick!' Her eyes glittered with tears and an odd kind of relieved malice. 'The Ellandaise, of course, but it's everywhere. Farmers in the borderlands grow it. The eunuchs live off the stuff more than they do food.'

'But it was *banned*,' Lu said, almost to herself. Her father had had access, clearly, but then, an emperor was never beholden to his laws in the way other men were ...

'Oh, *Lu*.' And now there was contempt in Hyacinth's voice – that voice, so familiar Lu could not even remember hearing it for the first time. This voice that had once belonged to her dearest friend.

'Even you couldn't be so naive,' Hyacinth sighed. 'Do you think it ever really went away? It was here before the Ellandaise. At least now that you're planning to lift the ban, we'll have better quality product.'

Lifting the ban. Lu's mind raced. There was certainly no love for reopening the trade of poppy tar among her ministers. Sentiments would likely be little different among the broader court. But she needed Lamont's coin. She needed this alliance. Didn't she? There were no other options.

Except the one. But she couldn't do that – not when she and Jin had projected such a united front to the Grand Secretariat. Not when she had promised Nasan, and Nokhai, and promised herself.

Hyacinth was looking over the edge of the balcony. 'I thought I could do this, but I can't,' she whispered, the ember of cruelty in her dark eyes at last dying out. With it, went all her life, her verve, and in its place, came exhaustion. 'It's too hard.'

'There must be a way to stop,' Lu said desperately. 'My cousin, Set, he was able to—' And for that moment, she almost regretted Brother's death. He'd found a way to free Set from the grips of this addiction. But perhaps there were others who could help. Omair, she thought. Omair would have knowledge – herbs, spells, talismans. 'We'll find you something to—'

'That's not what I meant,' Hyacinth said, cutting her short. 'I mean, it's too hard being around you. Pretending nothing has changed when I know ...' She could not bring herself to finish the thought, but this time when Lu remembered Wonin's wide, terrified eyes, she knew her friend was seeing them, too. Perhaps imagining worse.

'I understand,' she heard herself say. 'Tell me where you need to go, and I'll send you there.' The words were calm, even. They felt like they'd been spoken by someone else.

Hyacinth nodded, her eyes glittering like moving water. She was staring out into the open air, out into nothing – or perhaps at the distant mountains. This girl, who had been her closest friend, her sister, her confidante – her everything – for so many years. Lu saw now that she was already gone. She'd been gone long before Lu had ever returned.

17

Enthronement

Ahead of Min, three guards strolled side-by-side along the garden path. One was laughing at something, but at the sound of her approach their mirth vanished, and they scattered like hens, each man for himself.

Once, mere weeks ago, she would have enjoyed watching them run. Now, the pointlessness of their fear only reminded her of her impotence.

The cut on her neck, and the deeper one in her side, throbbed. The salves and tinctures Ohn had applied had healed her quickly over the last moon, but she felt the ghost of the wounds with any exertion.

She passed through a brake of dogwoods pruned into dainty contortions and entered a stone courtyard. At its centre stood a pavilion, lacquered in yellow as warm and cheery as forsythias. There were four such buildings, one at each of the corners of these gardens, decorated to represent the seasons. This one, the Bower of a Thousand Springtimes, had always been Min's favourite.

She sat on a stone bench by the entrance. At the peak of summer, there would be flowers in riotous bloom overhead: clambering clematises and heavy, drooping bunches of wisteria, all yellow. But here in autumn, everything had wilted into seed pods and falling leaves – a desiccated stupor Min felt too keenly. All that remained of the summer's beauty were the pale, creamy chrysanthemums clustered around her feet. She toed at them with a slippered foot. She hadn't meant to walk this far; she hadn't even bothered to change out of her dressing gown or put on hard shoes.

Ohn had told her that slow walks in the sunlight would help her grow strong. The court physician had been unimpressed with that advice, suggesting she keep to her bed for at least another moon. She'd ignored the physician, partly out of restlessness, and partly because she did not care for the wary, almost repulsed looks he gave her when he thought she wasn't looking. But perhaps he'd been correct in his assessment. She did not feel she would ever be strong again.

She started when a high-pitched, warbling *mew* leapt out at her from under the bench, followed by another – this one accompanied by a wiry red-orange tomcat who commenced to lacing his way around her ankles. Reflexively, she reached down to stroke his side, and he eagerly arched his back to meet her palm, prancing like a little deer. It startled a laugh from her. The sensation was so unexpected, like a memory long-forgotten, that she nearly burst into tears.

That was how the slipskin boy Nokhai found her: wet-eyed in front of the yellow pavilion, browned wisteria leaves snarled in her unwashed hair, slippers on her feet, and a tomcat prancing cheerily around them.

When their eyes met, he froze. For a moment, she thought he might actually flee.

'W-what are you doing here?' she demanded, torn between embarrassment and suspicion. Had Lu sent him to find her?

'I ... I'm not certain,' he said, and the stricken look that passed across his face bought her trust that, at least in this, he was telling the truth. 'I went for a walk to clear my head and ended up here.'

Her face was puffy from lack of sleep and the threat of crying; she could feel it. Trying to force herself to stop only caused a fresh flush of tears to spring into her eyes. She swiped angrily at them with the sleeve of her robe.

The tomcat trotted over to greet the newcomer.

Traitor, Min thought.

The Ashina boy bent and allowed the cat to sniff his hands. The cat's ears flattened slightly, but in the end, he gave the boy a cautious butt of his head before sauntering back to the bench and crouching by Min's feet.

'Can he smell your ... what is it, your caul?' Min asked.

'Depends on the animal. Even before I had it, it seemed like some of them could. Or maybe they all can, and only some of them care. Cats don't usually seem to care.' The boy shrugged, rising to his feet. 'Is he yours?'

She shook her head. 'I've never had a pet. My mother didn't – doesn't like animals. I think he lives out here.'

'He matches the building.' The boy gestured awkwardly toward the pavilion. 'Yellow.'

Min squinted up at him. He was unassuming enough: wiry and slender and not particularly tall. His face was angled in a manner that made him look perhaps more severe than he really was, but his eyes were large and black and fringed thickly with dark lashes.

'Did she bring you to me?' she blurted.

She didn't say the name. *Tsai.* She didn't have to. He knew who she meant.

'I – I don't know,' he admitted. 'Maybe. I wasn't thinking about where I was going, I just arrived here. I can feel her, sometimes. In me. It's like ... hearing whispers in a crowd as someone passes you by. Only it's not just her voice. Sometimes I see things. Only for a moment, then they're gone. It's like ...'

'Echoes,' Min supplied as he trailed off.

'Yes.' He nodded. 'Is that what you had?'

She closed her eyes. 'No. I had more. Or, I don't know ... Perhaps what I had were the echoes, and yours are only the echoes of those.'

When she opened her eyes, he was studying her, seemingly on the verge of speaking. There was something like regret in his eyes.

A tremendous *pop* resounded through the air like a thunderclap, followed by an inorganic screech. Something shot into the clear, distant sky and exploded into thousands of shimmering, winking stars. The tomcat dashed into the bushes.

Fireworks.

It took her body, seized with terror, a moment longer to understand.

'They must be setting up for tonight,' the Ashina boy said.

'What is tonight?' Min asked.

He looked surprised – then anxious. 'The enthronement

banquet,' he told her. 'The enthronement ceremony itself will start soon ...'

Of course. That was today. She'd lost track of all sense of time in the fog of her healing. Her sister, the emperor, would receive her crown at long last. The crown that had not so long ago weighed heavy and overlarge on Min's head.

'I should go,' the boy said, shifting his feet. 'I told Lu I would be there, and the Heart was already almost full at midmorning.'

It took Min a moment to understand why his comment gave her pause. Then she realised: he'd used her sister's given name – no title.

So, this was the sort of boy her sister liked, then. The thought made her feel oddly embarrassed. Min had not given it much consideration before, in truth. She and her sister were raised with the understanding that these things would be arranged for them, out of their control – though, of course, her sister had turned that on its head when it came to her betrothal to Set. So perhaps Lu had had different expectations all along. There were so many things, Min thought, that they'd never asked one another.

'I think I'd like to attend the enthronement as well,' she said aloud. She stood – much too quickly. She was still weak from her weeks of healing. She swayed, and all went white before her eyes.

The Ashina boy stepped forward to catch her, and she grabbed his arm.

She felt it at the moment of contact. Heat and familiarity churning under his skin – inside his veins. The curse. *Her* curse. It hit her with a force like hunger, like need.

And the curse yearned back. It cried out to her.

The boy gasped. Her eyes locked on his, and all at once she felt what he felt.

A terrible *lifting* beneath the skin, a strain, like too much blood in his veins, struggling to push its way to the surface—

Screams. Flashes of the city. White bone charred grey, dashed to powder against the streets. A ship at dawn, stark and alone on the water. There one moment, the next lost under a curtain of flames. Ash falling like peach blossoms in late spring.

Min flinched in pain – his pain – and released him.

He leapt back from her, and she grabbed the stone bench to keep from falling. She righted herself, turned. The boy was sweating, panting. His golden face had gone grey.

For a long time, neither of them spoke. The orange tomcat emerged from under the bench and meowed inquisitively.

Nokhai shook his head. 'Those things, did you see them as well?'

She nodded. 'Were they your memories?'

'Some. Not all. You ...?'

'Some; not all.'

He hesitated. 'She wants to return to you.'

So give her back, she thought. But was that really what she wanted?

'I ... I know I'm not meant to have it,' he said. 'But I'm starting to think Lu was correct. I don't know that you should, either.'

'That's not your decision to make,' she said.

'Maybe not,' he conceded. 'But I'm making it.'

She could not argue with that. They walked together in silence to the ceremony.

Min had never gotten the chance to commission a new throne, but Lu apparently had: a towering construction of gold-lacquered wood, three times the size of the one Min had burned. It looked less like a chair than a bower, its back rising up nearly to the ceiling – itself repainted, gleaming anew – in a gestural profusion of flames and tendrils of smoke. Behind it towered a five-panelled screen illustrating a delirium of auspicious animals against the backdrop of grey mountains – a clear reference to Yunis that made Min start, and her wounds throb. The screen's centre panel featured a Hu tiger wreathed in flames, looming benevolently over the other beasts.

The room swept down into a collective bow as the new emperor entered through the doors at the rear of Kangmun Hall. Lu walked slowly, deliberately, down the centre of the throne room, before ascending the steps to the throne.

'Rise,' she directed.

They did.

Her sister sat beneath the painted tiger overlooking the throne. Her posture was erect, yet somehow, she seemed well at ease, as though she had practiced this many times. Perhaps she had. She wore a man's robes, nearly identical to the ones their father had worn to court: cut broad to give her the appearance of strength and size, the heavy layers of scarlet and crimson silks threaded with gilt to catch the light.

Min looked sidelong at the Ashina boy. He was looking around the crowded throne room anxiously. Searching for someone? The two of them were far off to the side of the room with their backs to the wall, but Min could feel people staring. Some at him, perhaps, but most at her. She was haggard and thin these days, and she must have looked more than a bit mad in her soiled dressing gown and slippers.

She ignored them; these cowards wouldn't say a word to a witch and a slipskin.

Her sister's enthronement was not so different from Min's. The same droning, solemn speeches and readings from the Analecta. The blessings from the Mul monks. The bowing and scraping, and the presentation of weapons and gifts. A ceremonial golden collar was clasped around her sister's long throat. Its edges flared out ostentatiously at the shoulders, almost giving the impression she had wings. And the beaded golden circlet that had once graced Min's brow now sat upon Lu's.

Once the ceremony was complete, Lu stood to speak. Min had not been offered that opportunity.

'So begins a new day in the empire,' her sister's voice boomed. 'One that brings with it both hope, and loss.'

Min examined the faces of those gathered as her sister described the hardships faced by the residents of the Second Ring, the tragedy of those lost to the fire, and the imperative to rebuild. Most looked bored. Some nodded thoughtfully along to her sister's blandishments.

Sycophants, Min thought. Perhaps it was only exhaustion making her ill-tempered, though. She felt a wave of nausea, chased by dizziness. She had exerted herself too much, for too long; she needed to sit. She needed her next dose of poppy tears.

'. . . in this time of great turmoil, great change, we must look to a more harmonious, prosperous and, above all, peaceful tomorrow. Sadly, that peace does not come without a cost.'

There was a hitch in her sister's voice. Min looked up sharply. Her sister was looking into the crowd, at someone seated toward the centre of the hall, amid the ranked families.

Min followed her gaze and found Minister Cui and his wife. Lady Cui was clutching the hand of the girl beside her, gently stroking the backs of her shaking fingers. As though to escape Lu's eyes, the girl turned her head to the side.

Only then did Min recognise her. It was the Cui's daughter, Hyacinth.

Min had always envied Lu and Hyacinth – perhaps in near-equal measure. If it wasn't enough that they were ever finishing each other's thoughts and dissolving into an exclusive, estranging laughter, they even had the temerity to look alike. A stranger seeing the two of them might have guessed they were the sisters: lean, athletic, and sun-kissed.

But this Hyacinth was a fragile, birdlike creature. Her lank hair was pulled into an elegant upsweep that almost seemed a mockery of the wan, grey face below it. And, Min realised belatedly, something else was strange: she was clad in pale jade silk, cut high above the waist, in the old Hana style. Aside from nightclothes, she had never seen Hyacinth wear anything but the sunrise-coloured robes of a nuna.

'Peace ... always comes at a cost,' Lu repeated from the throne. She was still looking in Hyacinth's direction, but the other girl's head remained turned away from her. 'In order to have peace, we must have order. And there is no order without justice.'

The Ashina boy shifted at Min's side.

'Some have attempted to take advantage of the turmoil that has afflicted our empire these past moons. They have betrayed this throne, and all who serve it. A society is only as strong as its whole. Even the slightest rot must immediately be dug out and eliminated.'

It was not difficult to decipher of whom her sister spoke: the officials and courtiers who had leapt to serve Set, and then Min, in exchange for rank and title and land. But her sister was also speaking, at the core of it, about Min herself.

Lu paused, slowly drawing her gaze from one end of the throne room to the other. For a moment, her eyes rested on Nokhai – and then on Min. Min met her sister's gaze, saw the ripple of surprise in them. Lu hadn't expected her to be there. Then her sister was gazing back out at some unfixed horizon, once more addressing the crowd.

'Yet, justice must come hand-in-hand with mercy. I would have my reign begin with grace, not with executions. Too much blood has been shed already. Instead, I hereby exile to the Xin Basin in Bei Province: Minister Gao and his family – the Lady Gao, and three sons, Gao Munir, Gao Pakho, and Gao Kai. Minister Chen and his family—'

And so Min's short reign ended and her sister's began. Those who had gambled and won would reap the rewards: sky manses left empty by the exiled; wealth and status for generations to come – until perhaps one day they too made the misstep of supporting the wrong side.

'Minister Cui,' Lu said, and the quaver in her voice broke through Min's thoughts. 'Minister Cui,' her sister repeated. 'And family. His wife, Lady Cui, and his daughter, Inka.'

At the utterance of the name – her given name, Min realised – the girl who had been Hyacinth looked up at Lu. But her sister's gaze had gone vague and wide, focused on nothing, no one. She stayed that way as she read off the rest of her list.

Once finished, she went on. 'With that resolved, I would like to address a happier subject: that of our allies. I mentioned the imperative to rebuild the parts of the city that fell to the fires. These new alliances I have made will assist in seeing that completed. They will also bring us all great prosperity in the days and years to come—'

Lu's eyes slid toward the front row of the crowd. Someone seated there was stirring. He was not difficult to recognise with his stiff woollen jacket, misshapen hat and lazy leer.

'Kommodeur Lamont,' her sister announced. Then she paused, waiting for him to sit again. When he did not, she cleared her throat and moved on.

Beside Min, the Ashina boy uttered a derisive sound under his breath.

'Prince Jin,' Lu said, gesturing this time to the other side of the centre aisle from Lamont. 'Silver Star of the

Yunian Triarch. We have agreed to unite our people.'

The Yunian man stood. Min recognised him instantly in his green tunic, sword hanging from the working of leather straps around his middle. He lifted a hand to wave to the crowd, and Min flinched as her mind's eye replaced him with an echo, the slim grey form of his priestess sister, Vrea. Min saw too the ball of light and heat that had left her own hands and slammed into Vrea's chest, stilling her ancient heart.

Jin bowed toward Lu before returning to his seat.

'Yunis was long little but a site of myth and legend for the young people of Yulan City. For too long. War and turmoil closed it off from the rest of the world,' Lu said, leaving out that it had been their family, their empire that brought war to the steppe. 'But today, Yunis enters the fold of our empire through friendship, and the promise of marriage. Marriage, and prosperity.'

Across the hall, Lamont was still standing, confusion cutting a deep furrow in his broad forehead. Lu did not give him so much as a glance. Instead, again her searching eyes settled on Hyacinth. Inka. Whoever she was now.

'Given our new sovereignty in the North, delivered by this inviolable alliance, I am pleased to announce we will be expanding our mining ventures into the steppe.'

For a moment, Min was certain she had misunderstood. Growing up, Lu had espoused many ideas about how best to govern. In truth, Min hadn't listened very closely, but this much she remembered: that the North should be left to the Northerners, that the war decimating the slipskins had been wrong, and that whatever lay beneath the dry earth of the steppe did not belong to the empire.

She *must* have misunderstood. The fever, the missed dose of poppy tears, were addling her mind. Then she noticed the Ashina boy beside her, his face a rapidly paling rictus of horror and distress. And, she recognised, a feeling she had come to know all too well: betrayal.

A murmur of confusion surged through the crowd. This was not the expected course of things. The ministers seated toward the front of the room were turning to whisper amongst themselves. Min almost laughed, then. Her sister could not stop causing trouble, not even for herself.

There was a loud shout from the front of the room. Min craned her neck and saw Lamont's reddened face as he gestured violently up at her sister. He was shouting, but Min could not hear his words at that distance.

Lu gazed coolly at the foreign man. Then she looked out at the crowd, straightening her back just the much more, as though mustering a last reserve of regality.

'That is all,' she said.

Lamont's companion, Missar Anglimn, reached out and placed a would-be calming hand on the bigger man's arm, but Lamont threw it off and stormed down the centre aisle, out of the hall. Anglimn followed, bowing his head apologetically at anyone with whom he made eye contact. No one moved to stop them.

'What do you suppose that was about?' Min murmured to the Ashina boy. But when she looked up, he was gone.

18

Aftermath

'What the hell was that?' Yuri thundered. The ante-chamber behind the throne room was packed with advisers waiting to speak with her, but his voice rang out loud enough to stop Lu midstride.

She felt the unnatural urge to flee. She, who had never fled anything less than an arrow aimed at her heart. Perhaps it was the ceremonial robes she wore, their heavy layers pinning her down, making her feel like prey ready for the taking.

She ignored Yuri, calling out to the room instead: 'Can someone remove this damned collar? I feel like a yoked ox. Where is Hya—' The name was like a reflex on her tongue, a force of habit. 'Where are my ammas? Someone find Syringa,' she snapped.

'Empress Lu!'

She turned to find Ministers Ko and Ong coming toward her, fighting the tide of the crowd.

'A brave show,' Minister Ong said, reaching her first. 'You've made the moral choice. As soon as I heard your words, I knew the heavens were truly speaking through you—'

'And how not?' Minister Ko admonished him. 'She is the true empress, after all. This we already knew.'

'Of course, of course,' Ong said quickly. 'Nevertheless, a highly auspicious start to your reign — may it last for a hundred years.' He waved to someone across the throng. 'Ah, Minister Shum! A moment—'

They bowed low to her before wading their way back into the crowd.

'"The moral choice." You must be very proud of yourself.' Yuri's voice came from over her shoulder, all sharpened steel.

She turned to him, attempting to fold her arms across her chest, but the collar prohibited that. She put her hands to her hips and found the collar impeded that gesture as well, banging against her shoulders. She dropped her hands in annoyance. 'Those are the clowns *you* helped me reinstate to my Grand Secretariat. Shouldn't you be pleased that they are?' she groused. 'This is what everyone wanted in the first place.'

'Yes, well,' Yuri said mildly. 'They did not see the sort of weapons the Ellandaise have, did they?'

Lu recalled Ambassadeur Kartrum, gone up in a blue streak of flame, leaving nothing but a greasy puddle and charred boots to remember him by. And he'd been Lamont's superior. She did not like to think what the Kommodeur might do to someone who meant less to him.

Perhaps she would find out now. Across the room, the doors opened to admit Lamont, led by Missar Anglimn. The latter was clearly trying to placate the former, a nervous, mollifying hand fluttering at the larger man's elbow.

'Girl King!' Lamont snarled, locking eyes on her. This time, his ridiculous accent did nothing to undermine the menace in his voice.

Lu's hand went for her hip – only to remember that the sword currently hanging there was ceremonial. Bronze, plated with inscribed gilt, and a sharkskin-wrapped handle. Not properly weighted, and likely too dull to cut through much more than a rice cake.

Behind her, Yuri cleared his throat. That gave her some comfort, at least. He too was clad in an embroidered thicket of ceremonial garb, but he was never without a true weapon.

The Kommodeur bore down on her like an angry hound. 'You betrays us! After all promises you make about poppy trades.'

He was a tall, broad man, and clearly no stranger to using his size to intimidate others. She did not move, though, even when the toe of his black boot scuffed up against the brass-plated tip of her own.

'I have not revoked my promise – yet,' she reminded him coolly. 'But yes, given new information, I decided against unveiling our trade agreement today.'

'New information?' Missar Anglimn repeated, trying to subtly wedge the Kommodeur back using a narrow shoulder. A ground squirrel would have had as much luck pushing a bull elk.

'I was not fully informed about the detrimental effects of poppy tar on the body. Nor the true extent of its addictive nature,' Lu told him, surprised by the weight of accusation in her voice, and the vitriol.

'Play nicely,' Yuri murmured. 'You're not blameless here.'

Any temperance he might have coaxed from Lu though, was dashed out by the chill memory of Hyacinth's mother, stroking the backs of her daughter's frail, quivering hands. Even so, Lu softened her voice when she added, 'I must consider what is best for my people. But I believe there is still a chance to mend this friendship, Kommodeur.'

'Yes!' exclaimed Missar Anglimn eagerly. 'You see, it's just as I told you, Lamont. We can resolve this. Let us arrange a meeting. I can more thoroughly explain the positive economic outcomes of the poppy trade—'

'To my understanding, poppy tar is not your only export,' Lu interrupted with more than a twinge of annoyance. 'Or am I mistaken in that?'

'You sees, Anglimn! You sees? She mean us betrayal.' Lamont spat the word at her.

'And you mean to sell me and my people *poison*,' she hurled back.

'Please!' Missar Anglimn slid between the two of them, hands raised. 'Please! We can still salvage this—'

'You are foolish little girl!' Lamont said, smacking Anglimn's hand away from his chest.

Blood rushed to her face. 'And *you're* never getting your deal,' Lu snarled, no longer minding Yuri's tempering caution, no longer thinking at all. 'I suggest you spend the long journey home thinking of an explanation for Ambassadeur Kartrum's untimely demise to tell your king.'

Lamont's face had gone a shade of red nearly identical

to that of Lu's robes. He made to close the gap between them—

Yuri swept out from behind her, the movement elegant and economical as only a warrior of his stature could execute. His expression was bland and friendly though, his hand resting lightly upon the hilt at his waist. Lu slid a hand down to the ceremonial sword on her hip. A trinket, yes, but the foreigner likely wouldn't know the difference, would he?

Besides, she thought. *A dull blade hurts more.*

Lamont's gaze wavered back and forth between them. Then, seeming to think better of it, he barked out a harsh laugh before stalking away, toward the door.

'This country, so barbaric,' he called back. 'Come, Anglimn. We returns next week, when inevitably there is new child ruler to contends with.'

Anglimn, ever the pallid inverse of his friend, had blanched at Lu's words. 'Emperor Lu, you can't mean to reestablish your cousin's banishment of foreigners?' he asked in a hush. 'I will talk to Lamont – bring him back to the table, as it were, so we might discuss how to repair this ... momentary disharmony.'

Lu glared at Lamont's retreating back, but tried to smile at the bloodless man standing before her, reminding herself they were not the same person. 'We will speak again, soon,' she assured him. And then, perhaps with a bit too much force, 'I am not my cousin.'

Anglimn hesitated, but perhaps finding no other argument to add, nodded and hurried after the Kommodeur.

'I will follow them,' Yuri said, stepping after the slight foreigner. 'To make sure they do indeed leave.'

Lu nodded gratefully. 'Go. At a distance – no need to offend them further.'

The room had stilled to watch her confrontation with Lamont, but now the gathered ministers and courtiers began to filter out, bowing deeply before her as they did. Toward the rear of the thinning crowd, she saw Omair. And beside him, Nokhai.

The boy's dark gaze locked on hers, then immediately flashed away. It was enough, though. His face remained cagey, closed-off, but she could sense the withdrawal in his eyes, as vividly as if he'd placed a warm hand on her bare skin, then suddenly removed it. She moved toward him—

'Empress.' She felt a tentative touch at her elbow. She whirled in annoyance, expecting Anglimn – and found Jin.

'Oh, it's you,' she sighed, but her relief was cut short when she saw the concern he fixed on her.

'Empress,' he repeated, and Lu found herself hoping his stiffness was only a reflection of his desire to appear formal before the milling courtiers. 'Your speech—'

'The mines,' she said quickly. 'Yes, Jin, I know. I should have consulted with you before – we will speak privately—'

It was unwise, but she could not help it. She glanced back to Nokhai, entangled in a heated exchange with Omair. Jin followed her gaze, just in time for both of them to see the Ashina boy stalk out of the room without a backward glance.

Lu looked back to Jin, but his eyes remained locked on where Nokhai had been standing. When he did turn to meet her gaze, a deep furrow had appeared, cleaving his brow, though he said nothing.

'We will speak later,' she told him again, reaching out to brush his hand with her fingertips. 'I promise.'

He pulled his hand away from her. Gentle enough that it may have been an unconscious gesture.

'If that is what you wish,' he said curtly.

And then he too, was gone.

Lu closed her eyes, and when she reopened them, found Yuri had returned.

'Is Lamont gone?' she asked tiredly.

But he did not answer her question, merely seized her by the arm and pulled her out of the room and down the corridor.

'Shin, what is—'

He shook his head sharply, once, and she saw his mouth had gone into a straight, flat line, the way it did during her lessons, when he felt she was making easy errors. The result, he was fond of gritting out, of apathy and arrogance – the two worst traits a person could possess.

He led her down a narrow maid's passage, empty and far from the scattering crowds, walking so quickly that when he finally stopped short, she stumbled, caught off balance by her heavy ceremonial robes – gods, she needed to remove this absurd collar – and her back slammed up against the wall.

'What do you think you're doing?' she demanded.

'The more pressing question is what *you're* doing,' he shot back.

'I don't know what you—'

'I saw you just now. I saw you, looking at that Ashina boy. And I saw Jin, looking at *you,* looking at the Ashina boy. How long has this been going on?'

Lu stopped. 'You can't ... how did you ...' A charge of chagrin ran through her before she could catch herself. She scowled at him, then drew herself up to her full height. She was no cringing child. And in any case, what did she have to be ashamed of? She was an emperor now. She shook her head. 'He's not just some boy. He has a name.'

Yuri snorted in a manner unbecoming a man of his station. 'I, of all people, know *exactly* what he is, and you can't afford to have him here. You may wear the trappings of an emperor' – he gave the collar about her neck a sharp rap; it dinged hollowly and she flinched – 'but half those ministers would happily tear them off you given the chance. You need more friends in this court, and keeping a slipskin as consort is not the way to make them. Nor is parading your dalliances in front of the prince you just promised to marry.'

'Whether men pledge their loyalty to me or not has nothing to do with Nokhai!' she snapped. 'And don't *call* him that. I never thought you a bigot.'

Yuri jabbed a finger at her. 'No matter what I call him, that's what he is in the eyes of everyone who was seated in Kangmun Hall today. His presence further detracts from your credibility, and you know it.'

'I'm not sending him away.'

'Then give him a title, a position, and learn some discretion. Give them a reason for his presence. At least show you know what the *semblance* of propriety looks like.'

She stiffened. 'He doesn't want a title.'

'Then what he wants and what you need are at odds.'

'I can't make him take one.'

'You can make him do anything you like – you're the emperor now. Even if you lack the judgement of one.'

'Judgement?' she retorted. 'You speak to me of the judgement of emperors when my own father – the very fact of my birth—'

'Don't!' Yuri's voice was harsher than she'd expected. He jerked his head around to make certain they were alone. 'Never – never speak of that aloud. Not ever.'

She flared at his scolding tone. How could he both demand she act the part of the emperor, while also treating her like she was still the child he'd taught how to hold a sword?

'Give the boy a title,' he told her. 'Put the rumours to rest, if nothing else.'

'He sees it as becoming part of the empire, and he *hates* the empire, Yuri. You saw firsthand what they – what we did to his family, his people.' She could not bring herself to mention what she had just done in committing to increasing the number of mines in the North. Exactly what she had promised him she would not do.

'Find a way. Or find a way to get rid of him.'

'And if I don't?'

'Then you are a fool.'

The word landed like a slap. Nearly half her life, Yuri had been her teacher, and ever a stern one at that. But though his praise was faint and far between, his criticisms at times cutting, he had never stooped to cruelty. Never resorted to insults.

'And I suppose *you* have all the answers I need?' Contempt turned her voice ragged, harsh. Ugly. But she could not stop. 'You, who purports to be my shin, my most *stalwart* and trusted adviser?'

His brow creased in confusion. 'I have always been steadfast in my loyalty to you.'

'That's quite a claim,' she snapped, 'when you also appeared steadfast enough to my cousin that he entrusted you with my assassination.'

He stared at her, and for the first time in her life, she saw she had surprised him. She had also surprised herself. The memory of him grabbing her in the forest – that moment when she believed he could kill her – came back to her then with shocking force, twisting her gut. So much had happened immediately afterward that she hadn't realised how angry she'd been that he had let her believe, even for an instant, that he might betray her. She hadn't realised either, that the idea, the physical sensation of it, had planted a seed in her. An uncertainty that betrayal might come from any quarter – even from Yuri.

'You can't think ... Lu, I saved you then. I was the one who told you to run—'

She should have felt shame. So why did the brittleness, the hurt in his voice only make her angrier? She surged on: 'And where were you when Set came to Yunis? You didn't think I could have used your help then?'

'Your cousin was already suspicious of me after the botched assassination in the wood. He instructed I stay behind—'

'You must have seen what Min had become. You should have stopped that! Or – or followed them somehow. Found me.' She was being unreasonable, the logic of her admonishments fracturing around her.

'I considered it,' he told her. 'Truly, I did. But ulti-mately, I thought it best to remain in the capital, rally forces to your claim. Keep your name alive.'

'And allowing the city to fall into chaos and starvation? Was that part of your plan?' she demanded. 'What of the riots and the fire? Two hundred people *died*, Yuri! Hundreds more are without shelter, and now I must break the oldest promise I ever made to myself to find the silver to pay for all of it.'

That wasn't his fault. Of course it wasn't. But her father wasn't here, and so someone had to take his share of the blame.

'You don't have to move forward with the mines. You could go back to the Ellandaise,' Yuri said. 'They want their poppy trade more than Lamont needs his pride.'

Two paths before her, both ending in misery for tens of thousands. And she had to choose one. Choose the labour camps, the reek of them, Roensuk's raw, red ankles. Nokhai's haunted eyes, Nasan's feral mistrust of the world. Or, her father's rapidly narrowing face, the way he seemed to fade over the years. Hyacinth's gaunt throat rising up out of her oversized robes. Addiction spreading like sickness through her court, into the Outer Ring and beyond.

There are no moral choices to be made here, she told herself. As if that might absolve her.

'I can't,' she said. 'I've seen what their poppy tar can do. It's too dangerous. I won't do it.' There was a wheedling in her voice. A child's plea for something Yuri could not give her.

He did not try. 'If that's your decision, choose it with

your whole heart. Commit to making those mines the most productive this empire has seen. And ensure that the Ellandaise will not be an enemy you need to worry about.'

She nodded. And then she asked: 'Did you know about my father?' The words tumbled out unbidden, but tumbled out nevertheless. Perhaps she did not want to let either of them – Yuri, or Daagmun – get away with their secrets.

His eyes widened in surprise, and that was all the confirmation she needed.

'Which came first, the wasting disease, or the poppy tar?' she asked. 'Or were they one and the same?'

He answered her forthrightness with his own. 'I don't know. Smoking poppy tar was fashionable when we were young, but it was a weaker creature back then, cut with tobacco. We all did it on occasion. But by the time your father was your father, and growing ill ... well, he and I weren't friends. Perhaps we never truly had been.'

She frowned. 'Because of my mother?'

'Your mother, and much else besides.'

This time she hesitated before she asked, 'Did you love her?'

There was a weighty pause. 'At the exclusion of all else,' he said at last. And then he shook his head. 'I was young. We all were.'

There was so much more she wanted to ask, but something in his reticence made the words swell in her throat, stick there, too much, too big, too barbed with hidden aches she was reluctant to discover. She saw her father's pipe again, its cold weight balanced on her fingers. She shivered.

Fear. What she felt was fear.

She, who had killed, who had plunged into combat and emerged victorious, was frightened by this: the promise that the two men who had held up the weight of her world since she could recall might have done something fallible. Something that might make her loathe them both.

Perhaps that was the trouble with knowing someone, loving someone, too long. All the years of their bond had been built upon this faulty axis: the unseeing adoration of a child. But she saw their faults now, cracks in dry earth, sprawling out further and further, until they were here, beneath her very own feet.

According to legend, the enthronement banquet for Kangmun, Lu's great-great-grandsire and the first Hu emperor, ran for eight drunken days and nights, requiring the slaughter of every grown pig in the imperial stockyards, and drawing singers and acrobats from every province. Three men were killed in a massive brawl, and another two were said to have danced themselves to death.

Lu's banquet ended shortly after sundown. There would be whispers of what an inauspicious start to her reign the near-solemn evening had been, but she was far too grateful for the respite to care.

She found Nokhai waiting in her gardens, seated on a stone bench under her bedroom window, but he wasn't alone.

'Quite the stirring speech this afternoon, Emperor,' Nasan said, rising to her feet. Her brother did not look up. 'I suppose congratulations are in order. Now that you've been properly "enthroned".'

Lu turned to her ammas, ignoring the jolt of sorrow she felt every time she found Syringa at her side, rather than Hyacinth. 'Leave us.'

They bowed as they left to file into her apartments. She watched them go; seeing their familiar faces shrouded in persimmon-orange rather than the saffron-yellow she had grown so accustomed to over the years was more jarring than she would've expected.

'I never meant for it to come to this, with the mines,' she said to Nasan. 'I owe you an explanation—'

The other girl laughed, flat and humourless. 'Not at all. If anything, I think I might be the only person who *doesn't* need your explanations. The benefit of never having expected any better in the first place.'

'Nasan—'

'I had the foresight, you see, to know you'd never treat me like an equal.'

'Then why are you here?' Lu demanded, and discovered there was a kind of pleasure in irritation. It felt so much more comfortable than guilt.

Nasan shrugged, irreverent as ever. 'What causes anyone to make poor decisions? Fear, desperation. Weakness. I pushed this alliance because I thought I needed it. But now I've seen what you have to offer me. I've seen your city, this ... this diseased, swollen heart of your empire. And I realised that I don't need it. I don't need *you*.'

Lu bristled, but the girl had a point. Even the prisoners they had freed from the labour camp had seen it, hadn't they? When they chose to forge into the unknown north, rather than return to Yulan City, where many of them had been born.

'My people already have everything we need. Maybe I just needed to see this place in order to prove it,' Nasan went on. 'Now it's time for me to return home. And I know that this time? When you come for us, to put us in your camps, or press us into working your new mines, or just to steal our land? We'll be ready.'

'Is that a threat?' Lu asked incredulously. 'What, you've gathered your observations, and your Pactmaker, and you're ready to dismantle the largest empire this world has known?'

'She doesn't have "her" Pactmaker,' Nokhai interjected sharply. He stood and glared between the two of them. 'I'm not going.'

A cold cascade of unexpected relief flooded from Lu's gut down to her knees.

'I ... I'm glad to hear it—'

'I'm not staying for you.' The frost in his voice cut her short. 'Omair thinks there may be a way to expel Min's curse. Bind it in something to keep it safe. He wants to serve you for the heavens only know what reason, and I'll stay with him – for him – until we find a way.'

'And after that?' Lu asked.

'After, he'll return home,' Nasan supplied.

Nokhai turned sharply toward his sister and frowned.

'Is that what you want, Nokhai?' Lu asked, and she hated how thin and young her voice sounded.

He met her gaze with his black, burning eyes. 'Why? When have you ever cared what *I* wanted?'

Nasan whistled, and he whirled on her. 'The same goes for you! You only ever think about how to get your caul back, get your land back. Well, that land you love so much up there? It's not my home anymore. I'll give you back your caul as soon as I can, but that's it. I can't go back there with you.'

'It's not about *me*. You have a duty to all—' Nasan protested.

'I won't do it. Before you came back into my life, things were bearable. And that's all I want. For things to be bearable again.'

He was already walking away when he spoke again. 'Omair and I are going to bind this curse, and once that's done, so am I. I'm going, and you won't find me again. Either of you.'

They watched him go.

'He's full of shit and he knows it,' Nasan retorted. 'What he calls bearable? Sounds a lot like defeat to me. Despair.'

Lu said nothing.

But the Ashina girl fixed her penetrating stare on Lu as though hearing her thoughts. Nasan had been split from her Gift when she had lost her home, but she had the memory of the wolf in her blood, the rapt, undeterrable stare of a predator.

'Let him go,' Nasan said, and Lu was surprised to hear a plea in her voice. 'He doesn't belong here. *We* don't belong here. We Ashina ... we're not meant to leave our land. Being down here, it'll kill him. Maybe not right away, but it'll get him slow. He needs to come home.'

'You mean *you* need *him*,' Lu countered hotly. If she felt a twinge of guilt at Nasan's suggestion she was keeping Nokhai away from his home, well, that did not change the fact that Nasan had her own agenda. 'He's not just a brother to you, is he? He's a weapon.'

'Our Gift is not a *weapon*. Leave it to a Southerner to think that.'

'I'm not a Southerner, I'm Hu. My people had the Gift not three generations back,' Lu pointed out. 'We conquered the South with our tiger cauls. Subjugated an entire empire. What do you call that if not a weapon?'

Nasan scoffed. 'Three generations! How much can be lost, forgotten, in a *single* generation? By a single soul winking out? The things we all lost when our elders were...' She drew a sharp breath and shook her head. 'If you truly knew how cauling felt – what that deep connection felt like – you would see how disgusting it is to call it a weapon. But that would require you to have the capacity to feel more than bloodlust.'

'I swear to you, the mines – none of it will be as it was when we were children,' Lu said fiercely. 'I am going to work with Jin to make certain they're established in such a way that does not affect the balance of the mountains. Stay and meet with us – your people can prosper from this, too. There's enough land for all of us.'

'And none of it belongs to you,' Nasan snarled.

'You have to be *realistic*,' Lu snapped back. 'I don't want to hurt anyone, but we must move forward with the mines. What can I give you – some sign of good faith – to make you believe me?'

'My brother,' was the reply. 'Release Nok. Tell him whatever's between you is over so he can give me – give all of us – back our cauls, and come home.'

'It's the curse that has your cauls hostage. And you

heard him yourself, he's not staying for me. Whatever we had ... it's already over.'

Nasan looked at her. 'If you believe that, you're stupider than even I thought.' She began strolling in the direction her brother had gone.

'When will you go?' Lu asked.

Nasan stopped, turned back to her. 'I'll be gone by morning. Don't worry. Or, should I say, don't try to stop me?'

A breeze stirred then, and the garden seemed to shiver and contract around them, like all the world was a great cavernous chest, drawing in breath. The wind tousled the hanging branches of the silver trees overhead, loosing a scintillating flurry of small, pale leaves. They fell about Lu and Nasan, lighting softly upon their shoulders and in the loose tangles of the Ashina girl's hair.

Like snow, Lu thought.

Then: *No. Like ash.*

She'd never given these trees much thought before, but then, botany hadn't been a priority in her studies. Min had enjoyed it. One of the few subjects at which she'd excelled over Lu.

Lu plucked a leaf from her shoulder. At the brush of her fingers, it seemed to issue a gasp of perfume like a sleeping child issues a sigh. The aroma was sweet and musky, but beneath that Lu detected something almost sickly.

Her stomach turned and a nameless dread suddenly filled her. She felt light-headed, unreal.

'The next time I see you,' Nasan said. 'I don't know that either of us will be very happy about it.'

Part Two

19

Dens

The ink went onto Nok's bare skin cold: a long, single stroke down his spine, three cutting horizontally over the left side of his ribcage.

It did not take long for the burning to start.

He bit back the groan of pain as another line seared across his shoulder blades. His teeth gnashed down on his bottom lip until he tasted iron. Still, a whimper managed to emerge.

Instantly, the brush was gone from his back. He hated how good the absence felt. Like shade in the desert.

'Does it hurt?' Omair demanded. 'I told you to tell me if it started to hurt.'

'Keep going,' Nok gritted out. Pain meant the curse in his blood was rankled, and that meant that the talisman was starting to work.

'Under no circumstances,' the old man said, already wiping the ink from Nok's back. 'Does that feel better?'

Nok leaned forward, panting. The pain dissipated so quickly it was easy to believe he'd imagined it in the first place. Already, annoyance was taking its place. They'd been at this for moons, to no avail. He patted around until he found his tunic and pulled it back on. 'You should have kept going. I could've handled it.'

'I already told you, this sort of spell is far outside my usual area of practice. I'd prefer not to risk your life, and I should think you'd feel the same.' Omair wiped his hands on his robes before moving to close the decrepit tome he'd been copying the talisman's script from. 'Damn,' he muttered, noticing a drip of ink on the page. 'Librarian Fu will not be pleased with me. This was from his private collection.'

'Well, you don't have to give it back right away. We can try again.'

'Not like this, we won't,' Omair told him firmly. 'We'll find a way to ... dispel her that doesn't hurt you.'

'I don't know that we will.' Nok did not miss the euphemism Omair had chosen. *Dispel.* Neither of them liked to dwell on the fact that what they truly intended was to *kill* the thing inside him. Perhaps that wasn't so wrong – the curse that coursed through his blood was more like a disease than anything truly living. No one ever apologised for ridding someone of a fever, let alone apologised to the fever.

But then, a fever did not have memories or a name of its own. Did not force him to relive snatches of someone else's anger and sorrow and giddiness and pain.

He held in a shudder and stood. 'If you don't want to try anything else today, I should go,' he told Omair, striding toward the door of the palace apartments he shared with the apothecarist. 'Nasan is in town.'

'Bring her by here,' Omair suggested. 'I'd like to get

to know her better. Yuri's coming by for lunch, so I'm cooking extra anyway.

Nok's mouth twitched. Yuri came by for lunch nearly every day. And dinner. And was often still there to break his fast the next morning. Omair hadn't broached the subject with him yet, but he'd seen enough furtive glances and unthinking, instinctual touches between the two older men to know why. And while he still wasn't sure how well he himself trusted Yuri, he was happy for them. One day he'd have to tell Omair as much. But maybe not today.

'Nasan won't come,' he said instead. 'She's afraid the emperor will have her arrested. Or something.'

'And did you tell her the empress is currently out of the city?'

Nok shrugged. He didn't want to think about Lu – nor where she'd gone. 'I doubt that would matter to Nasan. She's grown a bit paranoid of late. Anyway, she's busy doing more recruiting around the Outer Ring for her little army. Harder to convince landed ministers and sky manse owners to join a rebellion than it is blacksmiths and orphans.'

'Recruiting again? Wasn't she just here?'

'Not since Second Moon. I remember it was snowing.'

'Has it been that long already?' Omair marvelled. 'The older you get, the more slippery time becomes. You'll see.'

Nok was pulling on his boots. 'Who's old?' he teased.

'Flatterer,' Omair scoffed. 'Well, go on, then. And take that sack of wolfberries on the table there with you as a gift. Oh, and don't forget your identification pendant – I left it hanging by the door.'

Nok pulled the pendant off its hook. All residents of the Immaculate City were given one – a uniquely carved stick of jade on a slim gold chain. His, much to his chagrin, featured the glowering head of a wolf. Most people wore them outside their clothes as a sign of status; Nok kept his tucked under his dun-coloured tunic.

'You really should just keep it on,' Omair told him. 'One day you're going to forget it and not be able to return.'

Nok sighed. *Maybe that would be for the best.*

Scrap-Patch Row rang with the banging of hammers and the thuds of journeymen traversing wooden scaffolds. Clay and paint and freshly split timber scented the air. Rebuilding had begun early in Third Moon as winter passed into spring and was now well underway.

As Nok neared Adé's family home, he stopped at a familiar intersection and stared. Long ago, before he and Omair had left the city for Ansana, he used to sometimes purchase eggs from an old, near-blind woman and her grandson at this corner. They raised the chickens on their roof; occasionally, after a hen had aged out of its egg-laying years, or a rooster grew too troublesome, they would also sell cups of rich, hot stock.

The rickety boards-and-spit structure they'd called home had burned along with the rest of the street and was being steadily replaced with a looming two-storey wooden frame. Far more elegant – and expensive – than anything else historically found in Scrap-Patch Row. In fact, all the new construction looked like it would better fit the finer areas of the Second Ring.

Someone shouted from above and Nok whirled, narrowly missing being struck in the head with a bucket of filthy water being dragged up at the end of a rope.

He hurried on, deeper into the Row's rambling arcade. The streets were full of workers hauling away piles of scorched debris and ash, but it was also clear that untouched, surviving homes were being torn down as well – presumably to be replaced with the new sort of buildings he had just seen.

The old woman and her grandson would not be back to the site of their old home. Nor the birds that had once roosted upon their roof. That building would never be inhabited by anyone who had to sell eggs for a living. The city was changing.

And where are they getting all the silver to pay for it? he thought scornfully. But, of course, he knew the answer to that.

The first of the new northern mines was not yet opened, but the gossip around the Immaculate City was that prospects were very promising. Clearly, that imminent fortune had been factored into the rebuilding costs, people said. It was unsettling, the way they spoke of the North down here. Poor and rich alike. As though it were a thing to be used up, wrung dry. Entirely devoid of life, or people.

He was so consumed by the thought that he nearly collided with a man emerging from a building to his left.

'I'm sorry—' he began, then recoiled when the man grabbed his arm. It took a moment to register this rickety old stranger was not attacking him, merely falling. Nok caught him by the elbows and helped him up. Looking him in the face now, he was surprised to realise the man was not old at all, only skeletal, cheekbones stretching high and starved through greyish papery skin.

Nok smelled it then: that telltale cloying, pungent smoke with the faintest suggestion of fish oil, emanating from the darkened doorway where the man had emerged. The windows of the shopfront were hung with dark crimson fabric: a hardly subtle code signalling its purpose.

Behind the man, through the open door, Nok glimpsed a darkened room crowded with men and women lying upon ratty, rumpled sofas, some with long pipes at their lips, others asleep, or merely gazing into nothing with glazed, rapturous eyes.

A poppy den.

There had been rumours of their numbers increasing – a result of the Ellandaise flooding the illegal market – last time Nok had ventured into the Outer Ring to see his sister, but there hadn't been so many he could stumble upon one by mistake—

'Thank you,' the man slurred, blinking and cringing in the sunlight. Then his slitted eyes landed on Nok, and widened.

'It's you,' he whispered in wonder.

Nok released his bony elbows, perplexed. 'I'm sorry, have we – ?'

'Ai, Yong!' someone shouted from within the poppy den. 'Mind the rules and close the door behind you, you fool! You're letting in the light.'

'It's him,' the man Yong shouted back, apparently

insensible to their complaints. 'Look, Yin! The Blue Wolf of Heaven!'

Nok had to resist the conflicting urges to close his eyes in annoyance, and to flee. Neither of which would resolve this.

He'd mourned Nasan as dead for all those years, but he thought he might just kill her now.

'No, no,' he said aloud. 'I'm afraid you're mistaken. I'm not—'

'It *is* him!' slurred a woman – presumably Yin – from within the den, sliding gracelessly from her couch onto the dirty floor. 'We saw his sister speaking on the street this morning,' she told the others excitedly. 'He looks just like her. She told us if we go north to join her militia, he'll make us a magic coat that'll turn us into any animal we like ...'

'Well, I'm certain she didn't quite say it like that,' Nok told her. 'But nevertheless, I'm not who you think I am.'

'I want to go,' Yong said, and now it was he who held Nok by the elbows, his long, bony hands surprisingly strong. 'Your sister told me she wouldn't take addicts, but I'm no addict, I swear it. I just use it to relax now and then. Please, I lost my home and my wife, two sons, in the fire. There's nothing here for me, now. Take me with you, Blue Wolf—'

'Let him go,' drawled a second man's voice from inside the den. His was deep and languid in contrast to Yong's high, sweaty frenzy. 'You don't want to join any militia, and you certainly don't want to join whatever death cult this charlatan is leading. He'll only get you into trouble with the imperials. They don't like when you worship these types – a man can't serve two emperors.'

'It's true,' someone else called from within the shadows. 'These frauds crawl their way out of the rubble any time there's a disaster, Yong. Follow him and he'll empty your pockets and leave you for dead along the side of Kangmun Boulevard, if he doesn't get you arrested.'

'He won't!' Yong squinted at Nok with pink, rheumy eyes, shaking his arms. Omair's sack of wolfberries fell from his hands onto the street. 'You wouldn't do that, would you?'

'I'm not—' Nok tried again, but before he could finish, a metal decanter flew out of the poppy den and hit him in the leg. It was a cheap, lightweight thing and did not particularly hurt, but he yelped in surprise.

'Get out of here before you get us all arrested, slipskin!' someone shouted. Nokhai decided this was not the time to point out that he was actually the only person here not partaking in a banned substance.

Another object flew toward him. This one fell short and skittered across the floor under Yin's sofa. Things were getting ugly, and very quickly. Instinct urged him to caul – but of course, he couldn't.

This time it was a porcelain gaiwan that narrowly missed his head. Startled, Yong released his arms. Nok seized the opportunity. He ran.

'White Wolf of Chicanery!' someone shouted after him.

And then, Yong's voice again: 'It's *Blue* Wolf, stupid.'

★

322

When Nok arrived at the Mak house, he found Nasan and Adé seated on the floor sharing a bowl of halved loquats.

'Here,' Nasan said by way of a greeting. She tossed a fruit his way; he fumbled but caught it. 'You look well.' Then she paused to actually take him in. 'A little testy. As usual.'

He ignored her. 'Good afternoon, Adé. It's nice to see *you*,' he said.

Adé smiled warmly, standing to embrace him. 'Nok. It's been too long.'

'She gets a hug and I don't even get a "hello"?' Nasan demanded.

'How's this for "hello": I saw one of your followers,' he groused at Nasan, throwing the loquat back to her with more force than necessary. 'Delightful fellow. He stumbled into me as he came out of a poppy den. I had to run four blocks before I lost him. So, thanks for that.'

Nasan was grinning, clearly pleased with herself. 'Not my follower, brother. *Yours*.'

He glowered at her in frustration. 'I don't want anything to do with it. I mean it, Nasan. Play this game of a building a militia at your own peril, but leave me out of it.'

'I'm afraid I can't do that, dear brother,' she sighed with exaggerated mournfulness. 'You're the Pactmaker. You're the one with the Gifts to Give.'

'Not right now I'm not.' He sighed. 'Truly. I had a gift for you from Omair, and your mad followers made me drop it back there.'

'They're not *mad*.' Nasan sat up, all mirth fading from her face. 'Why shouldn't they want to escape this wretched place and their wretched lives? To belong to something bigger than themselves? I think it's mad you're not interested in getting your power back so you can help them. Clinging to a curse to hide from your destiny – who does that?'

It was unsettling, how quickly she could from change his jocular, mischievous little sister to – whatever this was. A creature cunning and unknown and perhaps, he feared, unknowable, to him.

'I'm not clinging to anything,' he snapped. 'You don't know what I've been through trying to rid myself of this thing.'

'And when you do, you'll come back home?'

'And help you build your rebel militia?'

'Help me build the *Common Kith*.' This was what she'd been calling her vision. An amalgamation of surviving Kiths and new converts. A new nation.

'I don't even know if I *can* Gift all these new recruits you're getting!' he said. 'There's complex ties to the land involved. Migration patterns—'

'You contain a hundred beast gods in your body. I think you can figure something out.'

Nok looked at Adé as though for help. She just shrugged, resuming her seat beside Nasan, sitting close enough that their legs bumped up against one another. His sister absently dropped her hand on the other girl's thigh.

Well, speaking of new things. He felt a pang of something imprecise. Not so much regret for what he hadn't done, hadn't said, but perhaps a kind of sorrow for what might have been if he *had* done and said those things. It wasn't quite jealousy, but then, it wasn't entirely *not* jealousy, either.

He had always told himself he thought of Adé as a sister. But he had a sister, and what he felt for Adé, he had to reconcile now, was not what he felt for Nasan.

Although mostly what he felt for Nasan right now was irritation.

As though hearing him, his sister spoke again: 'People are desperate, Nok. I don't know how much you hear in the capital, but last summer's drought, followed by all the winter rains, caused landslides throughout the Northern villages. They're devastated up there. You can bet they're not going to see the money from that new mine. A lot of the people looking to follow you now are probably refugees.'

'You think I don't know that? We heard about the landslides,' he said, regretting the defensive tone of his voice even as the words left his tongue. Nasan didn't mention it, but the *we* hung between them, all edges, prickly as a shard of glass.

'Does she know I'm here?' Nasan asked. There was no need to ask who *she* was.

'I have no idea,' he said coolly. 'Anyway, haven't you heard? She's up north with Jin, visiting the site of the new mine.'

'I heard,' his sister confirmed. 'I was careful not to cross paths with her retinue.'

'Well, there you have it.'

'I also heard that she's due back any day now,' Nasan went on. 'And I thought perhaps you might have gotten news directly from her, before she left.'

'Hard to do that when I haven't spoken to her in weeks.'

It would've been longer, had Lu not visited Omair under the pretence of needing medical help the previous moon. It was surprisingly easy to avoid encountering the emperor in the snake pit of the Immaculate City. She was frequently occupied, and travelled with a retinue of doting ammas and eunuchs, and a flock of favour-seeking ministers as noisy and obvious as sparrows.

'Well, if you see her when she returns—'

'I won't.'

'Tell her—'

Nok glared. 'I *won't* see her, and I won't be telling her anything.'

'Nasan, let it go,' Adé said, gently nudging his sister with her shoulder. Then she fixed her with a sweet, winning smile. 'All this arguing is going to ruin my appetite, and you know how grouchy I can be when I haven't eaten. Let's have lunch. We'll all be better-tempered afterward.'

Nasan gave Nok a look that suggested this conversation would pick right back up when they'd finished eating, but she let Adé take her by the arm.

'Why do we have to eat in such a fancy part of town?' Nasan grumbled as they made their way toward the garment district.

'It's hardly *fancy*, it's a noodle shop. The girls and I go here after work,' Adé scoffed. 'Anyway, it's my treat. I can afford at least that much these days.' The Blue Peony had been spared in the fire, but several of the other shopgirls had not been so lucky: their homes were gone, and they'd been forced to relocate. Adé's hours had been increased significantly as a result.

'You shouldn't have to,' Nasan said. 'We could go somewhere cheaper.'

'Oh, hush. We can get that grey porridge you're so fond of any time,' Adé teased. 'This is a special occasion. How often do you see your brother?'

Not as often, Nok was suddenly beginning to realise, as Nasan came into the city. The casual intimacy between her and Adé already should have told him as much. This was not a relationship built on two visits.

He supposed he shouldn't be surprised – clearly, his sister doubted how estranged from Lu he truly was, and there was much about her recruiting activities she was keeping quiet as a result. Still, it stung. Did she really think that just because he refused to play the part she wanted him to that he would betray her? Was it so impossible to believe, at the very least, that he could be impartial in all this? And she had even convinced Adé – *his* dearest friend – to join her in this deception.

As they passed the Blue Peony, Adé paused to make a rude gesture at the sign. 'That's for the Ox,' she told them. Her boss. Nok wondered if his sister knew – but judging by her smirk and the kiss she placed on the shell of Adé's ear, it seemed she did.

They were in the doorway of the noodle shop when Nok noticed it again. That smell. Pungent, sweet, fish-tinged smoke. Looking around for its source, he saw the two-storey apartment building beside the noodle shop had crimson cloth hanging in each of its windows, top and bottom.

Adé followed his gaze. 'Oh,' she nodded. 'They turned that place into a poppy den a moon or so ago.'

'And no one's reported it?' he asked incredulously. It was one thing to stumble across a den in the ramshackle maze of Scrap-Patch Row; quite another to see one so brazenly erected on a main shopping street.

'They're too afraid,' Adé said. 'The Ox was complaining it would hurt the reputation of the neighbourhood, but word is, the Ellandaise own it in conjunction with one of the local gangs – they use them as enforcement.'

All of that – Lu's broken promises, the labour and infrastructure required to erect the new mines – and at the end of the day, the Ellandaise had gone ahead and done whatever they wanted. It couldn't last, he thought. It would only be a matter of time before Lu put a stop to them.

As though in rebuttal to his thoughts, the door to the poppy den opened and a group of pink men staggered out, hissing at the sudden daylight. They were followed by a well-appointed Hana woman, clearly sober – and rankled.

'Don't come back unless you can find the coin!' she shouted after them in annoyance. The proprietress, Nok supposed. He could see through the open doorway behind her that this establishment was considerably different from the dank hovel he'd stumbled across earlier. Here, the floors were well-swept and covered with thick rugs and heaps of plush pillows. The smokers were attended to by young women dressed in crimson robes helping them pack their pipes, and bearing fresh matches on small, bronze trays.

The general arrangement was the same, though: narrow couches lining the walls, nearly all of them occupied by a languid smoker, or someone drifting off into an indolent euphoria. One such occupant turned over in her half-sleep, and the loose hanks of black hair that had been covering her eyes fell back to reveal a familiar face.

'*Hyacinth*?' Nok said.

The proprietress turned to him, then – after a sceptical, appraising look – frowned. 'Paying customers only,' she told him. 'This isn't a charity.'

'No,' he told her, taking a step forward. 'You misunderstand. That's my friend in there—'

The woman quickly yanked down a heavy curtain that hung just inside the door – perhaps to keep the telltale smoke trapped within, and the sunlight away from sensitive, sleepy eyes. 'And you can join your friend after you pay.'

'Nok?' Adé asked. 'What's going on?'

'There's a girl in there who isn't supposed to be,' he said. Then, lowering his voice, 'It's Lu's former handmaiden.'

Nasan shrugged. 'If she's not her handmaiden anymore, what does it matter?'

'She was exiled with her family six moons ago. They're supposed to be in Bei Province ... I don't know what she's doing here.'

Adé pushed the thick curtain aside, ignoring the proprietress's indignant '*excuse* me.' She frowned. 'Nok, she doesn't look very well. You're telling me this girl was an imperial handmaiden? She doesn't look like she's eaten in moons.'

The proprietress yanked the curtain back down, blocking Adé's view further with her body.

Adé rolled her eyes and fished a fistful of coins from her pouch. 'Here. Now, can we enter?'

Without waiting for a response, the three of them filed past her, pushing the curtain aside.

'Let one of the attendants know if you need anything,' the woman sniffed, closing the front door behind them. Then she disappeared into a back room, behind another thick curtain.

The den felt smaller on the inside. Perhaps an effect of the dimness, or the clouds of eerie, blue-tinged smoke that hung sullen and heavy in the air, illuminated by the flickering glow of poppy pipes. They could still hear the wagon wheels and chatter of the street outside, but the sounds were muted by thick crimson curtains. Inside, the smokers were silent, save for the uneven snores of one old man toward the rear. It felt as though the rest of the world were suddenly very far away.

Nok made his way to Hyacinth's side. She must have heard his approach; her eyes opened. They held no surprise, and he assumed then that she didn't recognise him. But all at once she fixed him with a bland, oddly content smile. 'Why, it's the pretty boy who cuts hair so well.'

He frowned in confusion. 'No, it's Nokhai. I'm Lu's ...' He glanced up at Nasan. 'I'm Lu's friend,' he said firmly.

The girl's face dropped. 'Lu doesn't know I'm here. You won't tell her, will you?'

'I don't think Lu would...' he stopped, realising he didn't really know what Lu would or wouldn't these days. 'Listen, Hyacinth—'

'Hyacinth,' she repeated slowly. 'That name doesn't belong to me anymore. I lost it, you see. I'm only Inka, now. Inka of Family Cui. And not really even that ...'

'Nok, let me talk to her for a moment,' Adé murmured. She waved down at the girl. 'Hello. Inka, is it? I'm Adé. May I check your pulse?'

Unexpected tears rose in the girl's eyes. 'You're so lovely,' she murmured, holding her wrists to Adé, as though in supplication. 'Lovely and kind.'

Adé smiled down at her sympathetically, but her face quickly turned grave as she touched the girl's pulse points. 'Nok, she needs to see a physician now.'

'All right,' Nasan said, springing forward to loop one of Hyacinth's arms around her neck. 'Up you go, then,' she said, hoisting the girl into her arms like she was light as straw. 'Which way to the nearest physician?'

'No,' Nok said. 'She's not seeing some Outer Ring quack. We'll bring her to Omair.'

Nasan laughed, moving to hand the girl off to him. 'Then you can carry her,' she said. 'I'm not setting foot in the Immaculate City again.'

'Fine,' he snapped.

'Neither of you is going to make it anywhere alone carrying her, let alone back to the Immaculate City, I don't care how light she is,' Adé pointed out in annoyance. 'Nok's right, Nasan. Omair is the best option. If you won't, I'll help Nok get her back to the palace.'

Their arguing drew the proprietress from the back room and she peered suspiciously around the curtain.

'What are you doing with my customer?' she demanded.

'This girl is ill,' Adé replied sharply, hands on her hips. 'How long has she been in here?'

The woman sniffed. 'You're a nosy little thing, aren't you?'

'If by "nosy" you mean I care when someone's being murdered in front of my eyes, then yes, certainly!'

'Customers stay for as long as their silver is good,' the proprietress said. 'I have no responsibility to them beyond collecting their coin.'

'This girl is a day away from starving to death. You would allow that in your establishment?' Adé snapped.

'Allowed it?' Nasan retorted. 'She would've encouraged it, then picked her pockets afterward.' Her arms tightened around Hyacinth as she spoke, possessively, as though she were a parcel the woman was trying to steal.

'Put her back,' the proprietress said. 'Or I'll have to call on the *enforcers*.'

The way she said the word gave it an obvious, implied weight. Nok remembered nervously what Adé had told him about the den being owned jointly by the Ellandaise and local gangs.

'We need to go now,' he murmured to Nasan.

She nodded tersely. 'Understood.'

'Move aside,' he told the proprietress.

She fixed her contemptuous stare on him. 'Or what?'

For a moment, he desperately wished he still had his caul. A wolf suddenly appearing in her poppy den might be good for this woman. And then he remembered, he did have a wolf. A smaller one – but possibly more effective for the situation.

He pulled the identification pendant out from within

his tunic.

'Do you know what this is?' he asked.

The sudden pallor in her face told him she did.

'Step aside,' he said.

And like a magic trick, she obeyed.

Nasan swept past her, Hyacinth slumped dreamily in her arms. Adé and Nok followed.

'We'd better hurry back to your palace, then,' said his sister.

20

Hunger

Lu could not resist pulling back the curtain in the window of her palanquin as they passed under the shadow of the Immaculate City's Northgate. High above, sky manses spangled the centuries-old wall. She let the curtain drop and sighed with relief. The city air felt dense and humid, stinking of refuse and too many people packed into close quarters. But it was the smell of home, and a welcome contrast to the dust-suffused aridity of the new mining colony she and Jin had spent the last week touring.

She glanced at him, sitting stiffly across from her as though his seat were a bare plank, rather than a richly cushioned bench. His sword was laid across his lap, a soldier's constant companion. He was never what she would describe as talkative, but he'd been especially quiet during their travels. It wasn't difficult to imagine why.

'The new mines won't interfere with anyone still living up there,' she told him for what was easily the hundredth time.

He blinked, seemingly stirring from a stupor.

'No,' he said. 'Certainly.'

She smiled encouragingly. Patiently. 'You weren't re-assured by the tour.'

Jin shook his head. 'No – that is, yes. It was ... fine. Perhaps just jarring to return up there.'

Of course. They hadn't gone so far north as the Ruvai foothills, where Yunis had once stood – and also not-stood, suspended by magic in the immaterial Inbetween of this world and the next. But it was still as close as Jin had been in moons to the site of his brother and sister's deaths. The loss of everything he had ever known ... known for more years than she had been alive. It was easy to forget he was at once both an ancient thing, reborn countless times, and a sheltered, callow boy who had never left his tightly-knit cloistered home. She could not really understand either, but she ought to try harder. He was soon to be her consort, after all.

'It's only one mine,' she reminded him.

He looked to the window, but did not lift the curtain. Still, his gaze was faraway, as though he were looking to some private horizon she could not see. 'One mine. For now.'

She felt a prickle of annoyance. They had chosen the location of this new mine together, had they not? Agonised over it for weeks, had the area thoroughly scouted for signs of life. Even had a contingency of Hana Mul monks observe the area for signs of feral magic. Admittedly, their conclusions had been vague, but in the end they'd blessed the land in the name of the Empire of the First Flame, and at the time that had seemed enough for Jin.

'It's a good location,' she said. 'We chose well.'

He turned back and blinked at her again. 'You can't

know that,' he told her. 'I can't know it, either.' And she saw he looked puzzled, as though he could not understand why she would say a thing she didn't mean. For all his otherworldly peculiarities, truly the oddest thing about him was his lack of guile.

The litter slowed to a stop.

'Only Vrea could have known that,' he said softly. He didn't finish the thought, but Lu heard it anyway. *And she's dead.*

The doors opened, and afternoon light flooded the cramped interior of the palanquin, catching on the gilded walls. Lu peered out and saw the stone-paved plaza in front of her apartments. They were home. Or, at least, she was.

She allowed Jin to disembark first. He gave a perfunctory, athletic stretch before strapping his sword back around himself.

'I am tired after that journey,' he told her. 'I'll retire to my apartments, now. Will I see you for dinner?'

Before she could answer though, a breathless Lotus emerged from Lu's apartments and hurried over.

'Emperor,' the amma said with a low bow. 'You received an urgent message this morning.'

Lu frowned. 'It was common knowledge I was away, and I've only just returned. Can this wait until I've at least had a change of clothes and a meal?'

Lotus hesitated, her eyes flicking toward Jin, then back again. 'The message is from Master Nokhai. He and Master Omair requested I speak to you as soon as you returned—'

All she could think was how dire it must be, whatever it was, for him to reach out to her.

'I'll go now.' Lu pulled off the travelling cloak she wore to protect her robes from the dust and dirt of the road and tossed it into Lotus's arms. 'Go help Syringa and Oleander unload my things.'

She turned to Jin. 'I'll see you tonight.'

He was still for long enough that she felt a surge of agitation; did he not see she was in a hurry? But of course, he did. That was the problem. At last though, he nodded before turning away.

The creature sleeping on a bedroll on the floor of Omair's parlour looked almost familiar. It was a girl, Lu decided. Skinny. No, beyond skinny: skeletal. Grey and moaning, her brittle hair soaked with sweat – wet enough that Lu could've grabbed a hank of it and wrung it out. The girl was draped thickly in blankets, their edges tucked in around her, and for a moment it struck Lu as cruel. It was a spring afternoon, unseasonably, and she was clearly *hot*—

'The empress is here,' Adé whispered. 'She's come, Hyacinth.'

The girl's eyes shot open, overbright with fever. And now Lu could not deny who she was, not any longer. Her friend's body might have been laid before her, a brittle echo of what it once had been, but there was no denying her eyes – shining now with pain and fever rather than mischief, but shining familiar all the same.

Her dry lips split open, and she whispered, 'Lu. It's really you? You're really here this time ...'

It took all Lu's will not to recoil. Not to flee from the room. But she was a warrior born and bred, and she had not spent years training her body into perfect discipline for it to betray her now. She relaxed her posture, forced herself down onto her knees, arranged her face into a smile.

'Hyacinth,' she murmured, reaching out a hand, then withdrew it. The girl's skin looked so papery, she feared even the lightest touch might cause it to tear. They stared at one another, and Lu felt a thrill of terror, realising she would have to speak, not knowing what to say—

'You look awful,' Hyacinth rasped.

The laugh that tore out of Lu was genuine, if only for a moment.

'Have you been letting Oleander at your hair? I always told you that girl can't plait for shit.'

Lu touched the upsweep of her hair. 'Is it that bad? I've been up north, travelling. No mirrors.'

'Should've taken the boy with you,' Hyacinth told her, turning her head toward where Nokhai stood at the edge of the room. He was far enough away to convey respectful distance, but close enough to hear, though he pretended not to.

'I don't know if his skills extend much beyond cutting,' Lu told her.

'Oh, I imagine they do,' Hyacinth said innocently, and she emitted a weak laugh when Lu's face reddened. It quickly tapered into a high whine though, catching in her throat as she began to cough. It wracked her frail form, leaving her gasping, the tendons in her neck straining with the effort to suck in a breath.

Lu stumbled back. 'Help her,' she stammered. 'Do something!'

'Here,' Omair said, stepping forward with a ceramic flask. 'Give her some of this.'

Lu reached for it, her hands were shaking too badly, worsening with each of Hyacinth's hoarse coughs.

'I've got it,' Adé said, taking the flask from Omair's hands and bending to the girl's side. 'Easy,' she cooed, gently smoothing back the girl's filthy hair. When she finally stopped coughing, Adé poured the contents of the flask between her parched lips, a sip at a time.

Lu did not realise she had been scooting further and further away until her back hit the wall. She flinched in surprise, then stood, shaking her head to clear it of the horror she'd just seen.

'What is that?' she asked Omair, gesturing toward the flask in Adé's skilled hands.

'A poppy tincture,' he told her.

'*Poppy*?' she repeated angrily. 'You're giving her more of that poison?'

'Only a mild tincture. She needs a consistent amount to prevent sickness. Abrupt discontinuation would kill her. This state she's in is the result of moons of starvation and secondary illness taking its toll. In truth, the poppy might be the only thing that's been keeping her alive.'

'And when did she arrive here?' Lu demanded.

'She didn't,' Omair told her. 'Nok found her in a poppy den in the Second Ring two days ago. He and the girls brought her to me.'

Lu nodded, choking down the guilt of not having returned sooner. If she'd known, they could have ridden through the night rather than stopping to rest. She and Jin might have skipped transferring to the litter outside the

Outer Ring wall, and instead ridden straight through to the palace – a risk to the public and her own safety given how crowded the city was, but one she would've gladly taken.

'So, what do we do for her?' she pressed. 'What is the treatment? How long until she recovers?'

Omair hesitated. 'I've been administering sugar water and oil, but the motility of her throat muscles is quite poor. Her pulse troubles me as well. Her heart is not working properly, nor her liver, It's worth considering—'

'And what can we do to improve that?'

'There is little ...' He paused, then sighed heavily. 'Emperor. My greater concern is she seems quite uninterested in improving. In my experience, this means that the body is dying, and the spirit has accepted it. Or, the spirit is ready to die, and is simply waiting for the body to cease fighting.'

She stared at him, disbelieving. 'You're a healer, are you not? Heal her. I command it.' Her voice was rising. In her periphery, she saw the others turn sharply toward her – all but Hyacinth, who just let out a low moan. Nokhai fetched a bowl of water from the sideboard and dabbed at Hyacinth's forehead with a damp cloth. There was something shocking in his gentleness, when all she had seen from him in moons was anger and distance.

Omair hesitated, drawing Lu further away from the group. 'Emperor, please, hear what I'm trying to tell you. It is too late.'

Too late? Was her friend not still breathing? Speaking?

'That's unacceptable,' Lu told him. 'Where are the court physicians? Why haven't you sent for them?'

'She begged us not to – she feared that they would have her imprisoned, or insist on sending her back to her parents' home. She became quite agitated; I thought it best to keep her calm.'

'You seem to think a lot of things while accomplishing very little.' Lu pushed past him to return to Hyacinth, kneeling at her friend's side.

The girl was gazing up at the ceiling, eyes hooded and calm. The tincture appeared to have done what it was intended to do.

'Lu?' she murmured, her voice swimming drunkenly.

'I'm here.' She drew in closer, and Hyacinth's vague, dreamy gaze settled lightly over her, unfocused as fog.

'It's really you this time? I have to be certain.' Her friend's face clouded with doubt, a hint of fear. A quaking hand emerged from within her blanket, and she reached out to rest it on Lu's knee.

'It's me,' Lu assured her, covering the bony hand with her own, biting back the revulsion, the terror that the other girl's clammy skin aroused in her. She had killed before; was she going to be frightened by a little sickness?

'I came back,' her friend whispered, 'because I had to tell you something.' Her face changed then, and Lu watched as the confusion, the haze of the poppy tincture was chased away by the clarity of shame. 'My father. The other exiles you sent up to Bei Province. They're plotting something. Your mother's family is involved, too.'

I have no mother, Lu thought.

'Plotting what?'

Hyacinth shook her head. 'I don't know. They ... they kept me locked up most of the time once we moved.

341

They cut off my access to poppy tar so abruptly ... I think some of the servants thought I was possessed. Gone mad.' She looked away. 'In a way, I had. It's terrible. It feels just ... terrible. I'd never been more afraid in my whole life. I thought I would die. Even now, when I'm actually ... but it felt worse, then, somehow.'

You're not going to die. But the words would not even deign to form on her lips.

Hyacinth went on: 'Maybe this is all a lie. The poppy, it makes you a liar. Or... perhaps that isn't it. Perhaps it makes the world a lie to you. Inverts everything. In any case, I said I came south to tell you about my father. That is what I told myself when I forced one of my chambermaids to trade clothes with me and locked her in my room. That is what I told myself when I broke into his office, stole all those strings of coin. But in my heart, perhaps I always knew I'd end up mired in some poppy den in the Ring. Maybe that's all I really wanted.'

Her dark eyes were still directed upward, not looking at Lu – not quite looking at anything. A shine had returned to them. This time it was not only the fever, but a fresh flush of tears.

'It doesn't matter,' Lu told her. 'What's important is you're here now. And I'm going to see to it that you receive the best care. I'm going to make you better.'

Hyacinth turned her head back toward her. 'Oh, Lu,' she sighed. 'I know you're not that stupid.'

Her lips cracked, splitting red as she essayed a smile that Lu could not return.

'It's not so bad,' she croaked. 'The tincture ... it takes away the pain. And I'm so happy you're here, now.

Truly. I saw you so many times, but they were all just dreams ...'

Lu shifted, but Hyacinth's hand came off her knee to grasp hers, holding her in place.

'I need you to promise me something. I know I should've come to you sooner, but maybe you could see it in yourself to do this much for me.'

'I ...' Lu's voice caught in her throat. 'Anything,' she said. 'Anything at all.'

'Have my body sent back north to my parents' home. My father is a traitor, I know, and in truth, I don't know if he'll even want me, not after what I've done—'

But Lu was already shaking her head, already pulling her hand away from her friend, rising on one knee to ... what, exactly?

'You're not going to die. How can you even think I would let you—'

'Oh, Lu,' Hyacinth sighed again. 'My brave, stupid, beautiful Lu. Come, sit. Sit back down and be with me.'

And Lu, who could not even bring herself to weep, because to weep would be to acknowledge there was something to weep for, did as she was asked.

'They had Wonin's remains sent there to be buried on the family's new plot of land,' Hyacinth went on. 'I ... want to be with him. I just want to be with my brother. Could you do that for me?'

'I will,' Lu whispered. 'Of course I will.' Hyacinth would not say it, but Lu knew the truth. She owed it to the both of them, Inka and Wonin of Family Cui.

The dying was slow. It plodded on, cruel and sullen and stubborn, as the shadows in Omair's parlour lengthened.

Yuri arrived as the sun went down. Lu looked up when he entered the room, but he went to Omair. The two of them spoke in hushed tones and Lu watched as her sword instructor rubbed the other man's shoulder with surprising, uncharacteristic tenderness.

Lu did not know what to do with herself. There was nothing for her to do. No bloodshed beyond the bright red cracks at the corners of Hyacinth's once-full lips. No obvious pain, as Omair and Adé took turns tipping sips of poppy tears into her gaping mouth. Somehow though, the quiet made it all the worse.

Lu felt a presence at her side, and she looked up to see Nokhai offering her a ceramic cup of water. She accepted it, taking a sip, then realised how thirsty she had been and drained its contents. The water immediately came back up; she barely made it to the basin in time.

In the end, Hyacinth slipped away like falling asleep. Perhaps it had been the poppy tears that did the last of it. Omair had given her more and more to stop her trembling as the hour drew late and she became more agitated. A kindness. For all of them.

Lu forced herself to watch their ministrations, and their handling of the corpse. This was Hyacinth, she reminded herself. Not just any limp, cooling body. This one had belonged to the skilful, mischievous child she'd watched ace the companion tests to become her nuna some ten years prior. The girl with whom she'd learned to tell bawdy jokes, who shared her bed, drew her baths, rolled her eyes and told her the truth about herself when no one else dared.

All of that gone, now.

And Lu knew who was to blame.

21

Temptation

The bell around the orange cat's collar pealed as he chased the string Min dragged back and forth across the garden path. The cat pounced, nabbing the end of her robes instead; she let out a laugh, stooping from her seat on the stone bench to pick the creature up. He struggled in her hands, trying to scrabble back down to his 'prey', but gave up when she drew him onto her lap, rubbing him under the chin. She smiled as he began to emit throaty, hedonistic purrs.

A shadow fell over them, dark and sullen in the dying light of early evening. At first she thought it the swaying of the elm tree overhead, but all at once the cat went from pliant to stiff under her hands.

'Minyi.'

She looked up sharply. Her mother stood at the far end of the bench.

The cat sprang out of her lap, wending his way into the hostas clumped under the bench. Min had to resist the urge to follow him.

'Mother,' she said instead. At long last she stood and bowed her head – a force of habit too compelling to resist.

Rinyi sat, and gestured for Min to do the same. She remained standing.

'What brings you out here?' Min asked.

'A mother shouldn't want see her own child?' Rinyi smiled. In this light she looked tired, drawn. Perhaps a bit older than Min's memory of her, still beautiful. 'You haven't been by to see me, so I suppose it's up to me to find you.'

Min stiffened at the involuntary guilt that seized her gut. She hadn't seen her mother since that day, moons ago, when Brother had drugged her and attempted to steal her curse. The day she had lost her throne, and Lu had returned to Yulan City a victor.

It wasn't that she hadn't thought of her. It was difficult not to; Rinyi sent messages at least once a week requesting her presence. But what would Min have had to say to her? They hadn't ever been the sort of family that could sit down for tea and make cheery small talk. And Min was no longer the sort of daughter willing to tolerate being berated and belittled in filial silence. From Rinyi's regular missives, it had been clear Min's mother was safe, and despite what they'd discussed all those moons ago, in no hurry to leave the capital. That had been enough.

Her mother gestured ruefully down the garden path to where two bored-looking soldiers stood. 'Your sister is less trusting of me than you were. I have escorts everywhere I go now.'

'You did try to kill her,' Min said stiffly.

'Don't be dramatic,' her mother sighed.

'I'm not,' she snapped. And she wasn't, truly; her mother was far too well-bred a lady to dirty her hands directly, but she had been complicit in Set's plans. More than complicit: helpful, providing knowledge and insight. Encouragement and opportunity.

Her own daughter, Min thought for the thousandth time. And no matter what the truth of Lu's parentage was, it was, to some degree, true. Would always be so. Hadn't she watched Lu grow from a mewling, helpless infant? She might never have had any real love or even fondness for her, but she had allowed Min to. That could not be taken away: Lu was Min's sister, and Min was Rinyi's daughter. They would always be kin of a kind.

Lured out by the silence, the cat emerged from beneath the bench and set to rubbing against Min's leg. Her mother's eyes narrowed, focusing on the cat's fur against the silk of her robes. Min followed her gaze, then looked back boldly, as though daring her to say something.

'Why do you have that thing?' Rinyi said.

'He's a *cat*,' Min told her coldly. And then, unable to resist, she added, 'He lives with me in my apartments. Do you like his collar? I had Tea Rose make it from some old robes—'

Her mother sighed, turning away as though that would make the cat disappear.

'Min,' she said. 'Be serious. I came here because there is something important I must discuss with you.' She touched the bench, directly beside herself. 'Come, sit.'

Min did not sit. Instead, she bent and scratched gently behind the cat's ears, eliciting a rumbling purr.

If it was important enough, her mother could move. To her surprise, Rinyi did, resettling on the end of the bench closer to her her.

The cat, clearly as startled as Min, once more disappeared into the greenery.

'You should get a dog instead,' her mother said, watching it go. 'More loyal.'

Rinyi had always been repulsed by dogs. Even the small, snowy-coated ones court ladies trained to dance and pander for treats. Min was debating how best to point this out when her mother spoke again.

'Your sister is about to lose her throne.'

Min looked up sharply.

Her mother was watching her with shrewd, careful eyes. She went on when she saw she had Min's attention.

'There is a coalition of forces coming to usurp her. She has managed to make quite a few enemies in her short time as emperor. No surprise, given her disposition.'

A coalition? It was true, Lu's early reign had been wrought with challenges: a city half in ashes, a shortage of silver to pay for its repair, allies with conflicting demands. But much of that could just as easily be laid at the feet of their father, or Set – or Min herself.

That was something she would rather not consider.

'You should tell Lu about this, not me.'

'I'm telling *you*, because you alone have the opportunity to fix things.' Her mother moved aside on the bench. 'Here, sit back down so we can speak properly.'

Min hesitated.

'*Please*, Min.'

She sat. 'Who is in this ... this rebellion?' she demanded. 'And how did you hear about it?'

'I was approached by a coalition of Hana loyalists – men

348

who supported your cause. Men who your sister carelessly exiled.'

Min frowned. There was something cagey in the way her mother was phrasing things.

'You're leaving something out.'

'These men, they've partnered with the Ellandaise—'

There it was, Min thought, resisting the urge to scream. Resisting the urge to shake her. 'We need to bring this information to Lu. Those men, Lamont, Anglimn, they are dangerous – and untrustworthy. Lu will—'

'They want *you.*'

'For what?' Min scoffed. 'To be what Lu wouldn't? Their puppet?'

'To be the leader this empire needs!'

'So, their puppet,' she repeated.

'Not a puppet,' her mother insisted. 'And I told you, this is a coalition effort. The Hana men in exile are the true leaders here – the Ellandaise are merely providing soldiers and support—'

'Mercenaries and coin, you mean.'

'What does that matter?' Rinyi hissed, suddenly all flashing teeth and vicious reason. 'Don't be a child, Min. This is happening, these men are coming to tear your sister from power, and you have a chance to—'

'What?' Min demanded. 'Help them do it? Earn a paper title out of the deal?'

'No. You have the chance to save this city, this empire. To bring back peace and stability.'

'How? By fomenting a rebellion? A war? If you want *that* sort of peace and stability, tell Lu what these men are planning and she'll give them all that they can stand.'

'Your sister will never back down—'

'No, I don't imagine she will.'

'But nor does she have the military strength to handle what the Ellandaise have prepared for her. I've heard it directly from Hana men I trust, Minyi. They have something dreadful. Some weapon that could obliterate the palace, the Immaculate City – the whole of Yulan City, even.'

Min looked away. Could that be true? Even if it was, it did not mean they would use it – or that they would even have the opportunity to do so.

'We'll make certain the foreigners don't achieve too much power – the Hana men in exile are smart, experienced. They would conduct a careful, precise takeover,' Rinyi insisted. 'But I worry what the Ellandaise will do if they are loosed on the city in all-out war. And that will be the path your sister chooses – you know it, too.'

Min frowned, wanting to doubt, but unable to shake free of the truth in her mother's voice. Or perhaps it wasn't truth that she heard and trusted. It was fear. Her mother was frequently irritated, excitable, petty. But she was rarely truly afraid.

'I'm telling Lu,' Min said, standing. 'There must be something she can do to stop them – catch them unawares before they strike.' But she could hear the plea in it, the tremor, the lack of conviction that was still – ever – her instinctive state where her mother was concerned.

There has to be another way, she told herself.

'Lu will find a way to keep us safe—'

'I don't know that she can,' Rinyi mused, and it was almost mournful. 'But ...' She paused thoughtfully. 'There may be a way *you* can.'

'What do you mean?'

'I heard what your sister did. How she had that slipskin lackey of hers take your ... powers.' Even now Rinyi could not say the word without a curl of distaste on her curved, painted lips.

'My curse.' It seemed important, Min thought, to call it what it was. It was hers – hers in a hungry, feral way that her heart called out for before sleep, in the hours of her dreaming. But she hadn't chosen it, had been burdened with it through no fault of her own, and that was part of it as well.

'Fine. Your curse,' her mother acknowledged. 'Call it what you like; they took it from you. If this agreement with the coalition were to come to pass, you could have it back.'

You mean I could force them to return it to me.

And even if she did not intend it – even if she hated herself in the moment, and certainly in the moments that followed – she could not deny that her heart leapt at the suggestion.

She pushed it down, but her mother had clearly already seen the spark of want in her eyes. Doubt – and a hint of fear – rose in her own. Remembering, perhaps, that day in Min's apartments, now so long ago, when her daughter had become something that was no longer hers.

'What do they need me to do?' Min asked carefully.

'I will pass word along to the exiles that you are interested in partnering with them.'

'And the Ellandaise? How do we ensure that they won't double-cross us?'

'They need us. They cannot win our throne without a ruler to sit upon it. Your claim is our leverage.'

Min shook her head. 'That's precisely it. They need *a* ruler. Not me, not you. What leverage is that?'

'So, then, what do you suggest?'

'We need real power. I need *my* power,' she said, standing. 'It is high time I collected it.'

22

Cure

The parlour was empty when Nok returned from helping Omair and Yuri with the arrangements for Hyacinth's body, but the pocket doors that led to his bedroom were open. He hesitated for a long moment before he went through them – following a trail that had clearly been left for him.

His bedroom was cool, night air wafting in through the open doors leading out to his tai, lifting the long silken curtains and threatening to gutter the flame of the lone oil lamp someone had lit on his dresser.

He found Lu standing outside; she turned to him when he cleared his throat. Night had fallen in earnest while he was away. In the black sky, a waxing moon rose silver-white and pendulous. Lu looked back out over the railing of the tai, onto the stone pathway below, lit yellow with oil lamps that dotted the route.

'Is it done?' Lu asked.

'It's done,' he confirmed. Hyacinth's body would be transported back to Bei Province and her family.

'I'm sorry I couldn't do it myself.' She shook her head. 'It would've drawn too much attention if I'd been there, and the fewer people know Hyacinth was back in the palace, the better.'

'We were discreet,' he assured her.

She looked up at last, and he saw the sheen of tears in her eyes glinting in the moonlight. Exhaustion, too. 'Thank you.'

'Yuri did most of the work.'

That seemed to vex her, the way his self-deprecation often did, but then she smiled a little. 'You're still here, in the Immaculate City, so I take it you and Omair haven't found a solution to your problem, yet.'

'No,' he agreed. 'Not yet.'

'And as soon as you do — you're gone?'

He nodded.

'Back to Nasan and your people?'

'Does it make a difference to you?' he asked. Perhaps because he did not have a better answer to her question. The gods knew he had asked it of himself enough times.

She shrugged, but turned to face him, arms akimbo. 'Some of my advisers are growing concerned about your sister's activities up north. There are reports of a militia, hundreds strong, running drills in the forests. Teaching old forms of martial arts.'

'There's no law against exercising, is there?'

'There are laws against treason. And your sister isn't helping her case by brazenly recruiting people to her cause on the streets of the Outer Ring.'

'Is Nasan going to be arrested?'

'Why do you ask? So you can go warn her?' Lu seemed genuinely curious.

'She's my sister,' he said simply.

She turned away. 'We have different relationships with our sisters. I'm not sure what that word means anymore.' She sounded more sad than bitter.

He sighed. 'Just tell me how much trouble she's in.'

'None, for now,' Lu said. 'So long as she manages not to piss off the city guard. My advisers scarcely know her name – just that she's a ... nuisance, of sorts.'

'And you?'

'Oh, I've known she's a nuisance for some time,' Lu said lightly. When he didn't smile, she sighed. 'As far as I'm concerned, I'd rather address this with diplomacy. But I think your sister knows that.'

'I'm not sure she does,' Nok mused. 'I think it would be hard for her – or any of her people – to treat with you. You lost them when you chose to build that mine.'

She looked sharply at him, and he could see his words echoing through her.

You lost them. And me.

Was the cost worth it?

Standing this close – when had they moved together? Had it been just one of them, or was it the unconscious, hapless shifting of boats cajoled by the tide? – he could feel the warmth of her. Or perhaps he just imagined he could. It was surprisingly, exquisitely painful. He ought to leave – only this was his bedroom, Omair's apartments.

'If you wanted, you could give Min back her curse,' Lu told him, the words spilling from her. 'You're free to do that, you know.'

He hesitated. He'd thought of it – he couldn't deny it. 'It's too dangerous,' he told her.

'I don't know about that,' she said, though her voice

was doubtful in spite of herself. 'Min has changed. I think. Or, at any rate, she seems more docile.'

Nok shook his head. 'I don't know …' He did not know how to explain to Lu what he'd felt, what he'd seen in the garden the day of her enthronement. 'If she's changed, it's because the curse was removed. To give it back now … I don't know what that would do to her.'

'And Omair?' Lu asked. 'I know you said before that you couldn't put him at risk like that, and I understand—'

'It wouldn't just put him at risk,' he told her. 'Min used it to her own ends, but at its core, this thing is a curse. It shouldn't be given to anyone with an aptitude for it. It shouldn't be *used*. Its nature, its purpose, is to corrupt. And it will do that, whether it makes them mad with power, like your sister. Or just … weak. Like me.'

She was silent for a long moment. Then, slowly, curiously, 'What if you gave it to someone with no aptitude? Someone who couldn't use it, whether they wanted to or not.'

He shook his head. 'Honestly, I imagine it would kill them …' And then, seeing the look on her face, he broke off. 'Wait. You can't be thinking … no, Lu, have you lost your mind? This spirit, it's malignant—'

'She's my mother.' The words rang in the still of the night, and he heard in them a terrible vulnerability, gilded by her usual defiance. For the first time, he realised the power this truth held over her. It didn't matter to him – that was, its repercussions on her claim, her parentage, her pedigree. It likely mattered least to him, of all the people in her life. And yet, even in front of him, she had scarcely ever addressed it. It had taken him a long time – perhaps up until that moment – to understand the sorts of things that Lu feared.

'It's not really her,' he told her gently. 'It's more like an echo of her – who she was. An isolated, concentrated part. Cruel and violent. Think of how complex a person is – all those contradictions and different faces bound up together. That's not what this is. It's ... it's hard to explain.'

'So, show me,' she said. 'Let me see it for myself.'

There was a recklessness in her right now, beyond what was normally there. Perhaps it was the loss of Hyacinth. Lu, he had come to recognise, did not stomach grief well. And like anything Lu didn't care to feel, she would try to transmute it into action. Any action. But Nok forced himself to bite back the refusal that rose in his throat. Saying 'no' to Lu only ever seemed to harden her resolve.

He'd have to show her the danger, instead.

He recalled how Tsai had made herself known when Min had touched his arm. The curse longed for Min because it had been placed upon her, and in that manner, it belonged to her. But it had been born out of Tsai's desire for revenge – her rage at Min's mother, and the world that had denied her her own daughter. Perhaps in that way, she also belonged to Lu. Enough, at least, for him to give her a taste of what the curse felt like.

How though, to initiate it? It had been instantaneous with Min – a simple fact of nature, like shards of mineral coalescing toward a lodestone. He and Lu had touched with far more intensity and frequency than Min's accidental grab of his arm, but none of that had impelled Tsai to make herself known – which, he couldn't help but think now, he was grateful for. If this curse and Lu did have a bond, it was not quite of the same nature, and he would have to initiate it differently ...

'Can I touch you?' he asked. She blinked at him in surprise. 'No, I meant ... I just want to try something,' he explained quickly. Her face arranged itself out of an expression of – what had that been? Amusement? Hope? – and into one of cool unconcern.

'Touch away,' she told him, holding her hands out to him.

'No, not there ... here.' He gestured toward her forehead, just over the bridge of her nose, between her eyes. Where the Our Mother had touched him. She had used the point to send him into himself, his reverie, but it had also given her access to his pulses, his meridians. Perhaps it would allow him to access the incorporeal parts of Lu as well.

'Oh.' She lowered her hands. 'Go ahead, then.'

The tips of his fingers hovered over her, hesitant. He could feel the heat, the nearness of her. 'You might feel me ... it may be a little invasive—'

'Nokhai,' she said, cutting him short. 'Just do what you're going to do.'

He nodded, licking his lips. He pressed his fingers to her forehead.

For a moment: nothing. And then he *pushed*, the way he had felt the Our Mother push her energy into his, and his eyes – his mind – opened into a brilliant, unseen world.

Lu was, in a word, golden. Her energy flowed in eddying streams of molten sunlight. The Our Mother had discovered an archipelago of blockages in his meridians; Lu's surged with the ferocity of overfull rivers, through her limbs, and the palatial expanse of her wide-open heart. It was almost too much. Distantly, he felt his hand shaking and had to force it steady, urge himself onward, deeper.

He sensed something solid at the centre of all that energy, like a boulder seated at the churning base of a waterfall. He reached for it with his mind, isolating it from its surroundings.

It came forward, glowing, hovering before him. He could see it clearly now: it had the look of a kind of seed, oblong and gleaming, like an acorn. Like the rest of her, it too was golden. The moment he touched it, he was inundated with a cascade of images, sensations. Ringing laughter and the clash of steel. A ship cutting through dark water, suddenly transformed into a wall of flame. And now, walking through all that fire, unscathed, perhaps even fortified, a massive copper-eyed tiger. The old beast god of the Hu. Was it an echo, or a remnant? If he wanted, could he Give her this caul, so long-ago forsaken by her people?—

Before he could wonder further though, he felt a sudden *pull* in himself. As though something were being dredged up out of him, dragged to the surface. A surge of warmth came over him, effervescent and overwhelming, pouring from the crown of his head and pooling down to his feet. A deep, inexhaustible fondness – tinged with a longing so vast it made him ache physically in sympathy with it.

'Is that her?' Lu murmured. 'I can feel her.'

And Nok himself felt, rather than heard Lu's voice, like a tremor in the air. Felt, rather than heard her wonder, and her own longing, matched only by her mother's.

'It's her,' he confirmed.

'Let me take her for you,' Lu told him. 'Give her to me.' And it wasn't quite an order so much as a truth. The sun rose in the east, stone was denser than wood, and this echo, this residue, this curse – was it only that, after all? Immutable and malign? He no longer knew – belonged with her.

He called it forth from his blood, his own energetic pathways, felt its hundred thousand fragments rise and coalesce. Then he released them.

He saw the moment they transitioned from being his, to being hers. What had been grey and rankled as a swarm of gnats transmuted into shattered starlight suspended in amber. The golden glow of it dusted over the golden glow of her energy landscape.

Nok blinked.

He was back on the tai outside his bedroom. Lu stood before him, her eyes still closed, his fingers still raised to her forehead. Perhaps she felt his gaze; her glinting, burnished eyes opened and gazed into his own.

'Are you all right?' he asked, lowering his hand to touch her shoulder. Then he remembered himself and let it drop to his side like a stone.

'I'm fine,' she breathed, her own hand reaching to touch the place on her forehead where his fingertips had been, then moving to her chest, just over her heart. 'I feel ...' She hesitated, searching for the words.

'Powerful?' he asked with some trepidation. It occurred

to him suddenly that he didn't actually know the full extent of Lu's natural aptitude for magic. Her mother had been a powerful shamaness. Perhaps they had been rash in assuming no part of that had been passed down to her.

'It does make me feel a kind of strength,' she conceded, but then shook her head. 'But it's not power. It's quieter than that. More like ... certainty.'

He thought of the undying font of warmth, the fondness he'd felt emanating from Tsai. The undercurrent of ferocity it held. Certainty was a good description of that, he thought.

'How do *you* feel?' Lu asked.

It took a moment for him to understand what she was asking. Of course.

They'd lifted the curse.

He'd been so preoccupied with confirming that Lu was safe that he'd forgotten the whole purpose of their experiment.

'I feel ...' He considered the question. Then he cocked his head and laughed. 'Like waking up that first morning after a long fever has broken.'

'And your caul?' she enjoined eagerly.

For the first time in so many moons, he could feel them again, thrumming just under his skin. There his wolf, all loping strides and clever economy, and the shrewd, cautious pit adder, and the golden eagle with its vast readiness for the open sky.

The wolf was the instinctive choice – the most familiar, most readily at hand. But it wasn't quite right for this location ...

Nok breathed deep, the night air cool and bracing. All

at once, the pattern of feathers fell over him like a shadow, streaking his ochre skin with veins of white and grey. He closed his eyes, and when he opened them again, the world of the night was suddenly lucid as midday.

He leapt from the railing of the tai, making a delicious, swooping pass through the courtyard, plummeting so close to the path below that he felt the brush of the pavers at the tips of the owl's wings. From above, he could hear Lu gasp and call out to him in admonishment. He almost laughed. As though she wouldn't do the same – or riskier – if she had this power, this freedom.

With two beats of his wings, he was riding an upsurge of air that lofted him higher than the red-tiled rooftops of the palace, above the swaying reach of the trees. Looking down, he could see Lu leaning over the railing of his tai, waving up at him. She was grinning now, and her joy for him was so genuine, so unfettered, he could not help but feel his own heart swell.

He did not even mean to angle the arc of his flight back toward her – and yet, suddenly, there he was, back on his tai, slipping from the caul. It had been some time. He stumbled forward as his weight and centre of gravity shifted. She caught him around the shoulders. His hands went instinctively to her wrists, bracing himself.

'Careful,' she said. But her grin was fading, perhaps as she remembered now why this touch was unusual, why each of them had to choose when and how to extricate their hands from the other.

Nok had always preferred the brutal mercy of a quick, clean cut. He pulled away first.

'It worked, then,' she said, voice choked with false cheer.

'It did,' he agreed, but already the worry was setting back in. 'Listen, Lu. The curse doesn't seem to have affected you so far, but you should be careful—'

'I'm fine,' she said stubbornly. 'And you're free now. Go, be with your sister. You could give her her caul now. Not just her – all her people. Your people.'

He could do that. He ought to: this Gift wasn't just for him. So why did he feel such reservations? Lu had accused his sister of wanting him for a weapon. Nasan had denied it. And Nok knew that if asked, he would defend her aloud. Lu could not understand what the caul meant to them. But he suspected she wasn't as wrong as his sister would like to think.

He studied Lu a long moment. 'Is this meant to be your remuneration? For the mines?' he asked. 'Because it doesn't work that way. You don't get to give me something and absolve yourself—'

'Of course not. I'm glad to do this for you. I know I can never undo ...' She shook her head, looking away. 'You told me before that I don't know the cost of anything. I think I know now.'

He felt faintly embarrassed. 'I've said a lot of things to you that I didn't really mean.'

'I don't think so. I don't think you're capable.'

He looked up and found her bold, dark eyes fixed on him. No good could come from being this close to her. And yet, he was so loath to move away.

There was a knock at the open pocket doors leading out to the balcony.

The two of them leapt apart. Syringa stood in the doorway, her form backlit by the oil lamp, her face nearly eclipsed by shadow under the shade of the covered tai.

'My apologies, Emperor. The doors to Master Nokhai's chambers were open,' she said with a curtsy.

'No, of course,' Lu said hastily. 'What brings you here?'

'Two matters: Prince Jin was waiting in your apartments for much of the evening,' she said hesitantly. 'He said you had arranged to meet him for dinner.'

Lu closed her eyes in consternation. 'I completely forgot. I will send for him tomorrow, to apologise. Would you draft a message to send to him?'

Syringa curtsied again. 'Of course.'

'And the second matter?' Lu asked.

'That is why I came to find you,' Syringa explained hesitantly. 'She was very persistent.'

'She?'

Syringa glided aside, and another figure emerged from the dim bedroom. Nok took her for another amma at first, until she stepped out fully onto the tai, out of its shadows.

'Min?' Lu asked in surprise.

Moonlight sluiced over the girl's round face, tinging her pale eyes with an eerie blue cast. 'I have something to tell you,' she said.

23

Cache

Sunrise swept over the harbour, golden and unnoticed. The imperial soldiers swept in with it, a wave of blue and green uniforms, and were most certainly noticed, if the sleepy-eyed residents peering out from behind papered windows and yawning in their doorways were any indication. The soldiers paid them no mind, their task lay elsewhere: over a dozen Ellandaise ships in port were to be simultaneously searched from bow to stern and down to their bilges.

Lu paced the deck of *The Banga*, studying its captain. He'd been yanked from his quarters and wore only a nightshirt. He had the look of a Lamont that had been left out too long in the elements: a slighter, washed-out reiteration of the real thing. But he was still a robust man of some presence, even barefoot, with his hands bound, and held as he was between two of the larger of her personal guards – carefully chosen for this task because of their size. She saw him wince at the ring and clink of her brass-plated boots as she drew herself up to her full height before him. She was no taller than his bearded chin, but his light eyes flitted toward the sword at her waist and seemed to grow fainter still with fear.

She gave a nod and her guards released him. He stumbled forward, but stabilised before he fell to his knees.

She smiled pleasantly. 'Captain Musprat, is it?' She went on without letting him respond. 'This is your ship?' *The Banga*. Named for another empire to the South; another site of Ellandaise plunder. Was there a lavish boat floating in some Bangalese harbour called *The First Flame*?

'A very fine vessel,' she said, the words tightening her throat. 'I'm not surprised to hear it is the one Anglimn and Lamont favour when they need to travel by sea.'

'You will not finds them here,' the captain told her haughtily. His Yueh was unpractised, and he over-enunciated in such a way that it bordered on mockery to Lu's ears. Still, she was faintly amused to find his grammar was significantly better than Lamont's. 'They have gone. Long times ago.'

She raised an eyebrow in mock surprise. 'Left the comfort of Yulan City? And where to?'

'No wheres you shall find them.' The man considered, all innocence. 'Back to Elland, perhaps.'

Lu hadn't thought Min lying when she'd come to her the night before, telling tales of their mother Rinyi and covert dealings with the Ellandaise. She was starting to wonder, now, whether her sister's information wasn't confused.

Outwardly, she gave a sunny smile. 'Curious. It was my understanding the Kommodeur did not intend to return to Elland until he had something worthwhile to present to your king.'

The captain seemed unimpressed; he shrugged. 'The Eastern Flame Import Company is essential part of Ellandaise economy. Who is true king, I wonders? One who wears crown, or one who has silver to buy it?'

'I do not know how things are done in your part of the world,' Lu told him. 'But here in the Empire of the First Flame, a crown is merely a symbol of a ruler's gods-given mandate. And one cannot purchase the grace of the gods.'

There was a rush of boots coming up from the hold of the ship. Jin emerged at the top of the stairs, breathless. 'They're not here—'

'I tell you already,' jeered the captain. 'The Kommodeur and Directeur Anglimn left city *days* ago. You never will finds them. Certainly not heres, on my ship.'

'Oh, of course. And why wouldn't I have simply taken your word on that?' Lu retorted, quelling the urge to give the man a good shake.

'They're not here,' Jin repeated, wiping at the sheen of sweat on his upper lip with the back of his hand. He shook his head. 'But there's something you need to see.'

Min's information, as it turned out, had not been confused. In all, their search of the foreign ships resulted in the seizure of 1,200 tonnes of poppy tar. Lu surveyed it, Yuri, Jin, and Omair silent and exhausted at her back. It looked harmless enough, stacked there on the sandy shore at the mouth of the Milk River: an outsized and out-of-place foothill of debris, crates and chests, some splintered to reveal a suggestion of the tightly bound contents within. All awash in the mournful golden glow of the day's end.

Another day, Lu thought, that Hyacinth would never see. Hyacinth, and how many others like her?

She glanced behind her. A long, stone retaining wall separated the narrow beach from a pathway leading back toward the city. Already, dozens of her citizens were gathered there to gawk. What would they whisper about this tonight? That the empire was overrun, plagued by this foreign pestilence, like a tiger infested with fleas? That she, the first woman emperor, had destroyed nearly overnight the civilization it had taken her ancestors centuries to cultivate? Or, some sour part of her thought, would they just resent her for destroying their supply of poppy tar and oblivion?

When they had discovered the first batch of contraband in the belly of *The Banga*, Lu's men had unloaded it onto the docks. They searched two more ships before it became clear the total amount to be confiscated would not fit. Lu had ordered they move the pile a half mile downstream, where the river fed out into the sea.

'I want it burned,' she said. Her voice was low and steady, but anyone who knew her would hear the knife's edge in it.

'We need to think about this,' Yuri cautioned her. Of course it was he who spoke. He was perhaps the only person present who both knew her well enough to hear the danger in her words, and believe he was exempt from it.

'No,' she said slowly, the reality of the situation dragging at her words, weighing down her limbs, seeping sludgelike through her gut like nausea. A shift in her understanding of all things so great that the world was slowed, was spun out of orbit, tilted and jolted on its axis.

These men, these Ellandaise, who did they think they were? Drifting into her kingdom, her empire – *the* empire – on their painted boats, from their pallid, beggarly little backwater island. Her great-grandfather had been the first to accept trade with them, years before she was born. They'd spread their wares at his feet: whirring mechanisms that sang songs to tell the hour of the sun in the sky, glinting bits of gold and ivory, stolen from other lands. The picked-over magpie's plunder of a country with nothing of its own to share.

Emperor Kangmun had waved it off; the pink men had nothing he needed. Nothing he even wanted. But *they* wanted plenty: tea and sparkstone and silk and spice and more tea, still. And so he had deigned to take their silver, taels and taels of it, while giving them little thought otherwise – as little thought as a tiger gives a sparrow flitting overhead from tree to tree.

A mistake, Lu saw. Too late. For no man, no matter how small, no matter how mean or stupid or slight, ever thought himself the sparrow.

'No more warnings. No more appeasement. These men do not understand the kindness, the charity, of a "yes". They only see it as a gateway, a bridge, to the next "yes", and the next, until they have eaten all our stores, stolen our children, and are asleep in our beds.'

Yuri shook his head. 'We should convene the Grand Secretariat to discuss the best course of action—'

'You mean to talk the matter to death,' she said scornfully. 'What is there to discuss? It is illegal contraband. It should be destroyed.'

'The Ellandaise may see that as an act of war,' Jin said, his voice troubled.

'The poppy tar belongs to the Eastern Flame Import Company, not to the Crown of Elland,' she countered.

But would these foreigners make this distinction? Captain Musprat's words on the deck of *The Banga* came back to her. *Who is true king, I wonder? One who wears crown, or one who has silver to buy it?*

'I want it burned,' she repeated. 'Right here, on the shore, for everyone to see.'

'Burning the stuff would not be safe,' Omair said. 'The smoke will drift back toward the city – sicken many. And likely intoxicate even more.'

She frowned and turned to him. 'What do you suggest?'

He considered. 'I am not an expert. But perhaps it could be poured into pits here on the shore, then neutralised with something – lime or salt, for example – and flushed out to sea.'

'How long would that take?'

He shook his head. 'With this much tar? Weeks, I would imagine. Maybe a moon or longer.'

'Fine,' she said curtly. 'I leave you in charge of this. But save the crates. Especially anything with an Ellandaise logo or inscription. I want those piled back into a heap here and burned. Do it during the day, so it's visible.'

As she turned to head back toward the city, her eyes fell upon the gawkers lining the retaining wall. She frowned. 'And have a manned fence placed around the beach. Anyone caught stealing so much as a handful of the stuff should be executed on sight.'

★

Lu found her sitting room full when she and Jin returned to her apartments. The doors leading out to her tai were open, and Adé and Nasan stood outside, looking down over the balustrade, the Ashina girl's arm draped loosely around Adé's waist. Nokhai sat rigidly on an overstuffed sofa, picking at his fingernails. Upon Lu's entry, he quickly stood and made as though to approach her. But as Jin entered through the doors behind her, his face contorted with unease – and, she thought, perhaps more than a touch of guilt – before closing off entirely. He did not sit back down, but neither did he greet her.

Movement at the far end of the room drew her eye away from him. It was only then that Lu noticed the final person present. Min stood hugging the wall, looking as faint and uncertain as a shadow that might disappear at any moment with the changing of the light.

'You're back.' Nasan's voice drew Lu's attention away.

'And you're still here,' Lu countered.

'I'm still here,' Nasan agreed, making her way into the room. All the casual tenderness she'd exhibited toward Adé had vanished so completely Lu wondered if she'd imagined it. 'It's of interest to me whether or not your empire is about to start a war.'

Lu looked sharply toward Nokhai, but he shook his head.

'Don't blame my brother,' Nasan said. 'Half the city was woken by your soldiers marching down to the harbour before dawn. The word is out all over that you're living on borrowed time, burning poppy tar and beheading addicts on the beach.'

'I haven't beheaded anyone,' Lu retorted in annoyance.

The rumours came as no surprise; she'd intended for the city folk to see a show of strength against the foreign scourge when she led her soldiers down to the harbour. It was troubling though, that the fantasies they spun featured her attacking her own people – and the most vulnerable among them at that. She recalled then, Hyacinth's sweating, sunken face ...

'The people should realise I'm protecting them,' she said aloud. 'Sensible folk will understand that.'

'I don't know that they will.' To Lu's surprise, it was Adé, not Nasan, who spoke. The Second Ring girl seemed surprised herself; a flush reddened her ears. But she continued: 'Banning poppy tar never made it disappear. Jailing addicts neither. People may see it as merely another cruelty.'

Again, Lu saw Hyacinth, laid out on her deathbed, more bone and ash than girl. 'The Ellandaise have been allowed to carry on as they please for too long, and they must be dealt with before the epidemic worsens,' she said sharply.

'Don't speak to her in that tone,' Nasan snapped, stepping forward. The movement was all instinct, without any real threat behind it, but all at once, Jin was there, sliding between the two of them.

'You should mind *your* tone when addressing your emperor,' he told the Ashina girl coolly.

'Perhaps she should not question my intentions toward my people!' Lu shot back, stepping around Jin to address Nasan head-on.

'I wasn't questioning anyone!' Adé exclaimed. 'And I *am* one of your people.'

'She's no emperor of *mine*,' Nasan hurled at the same time.

'Nasan,' Nokhai interjected, at last striding over. 'You said you just wanted to stay long enough to ask Lu whether war had been declared.' He turned and looked at Lu, black eyes meeting her own. 'So, has it?'

She shook her head. 'No. We never found Anglimn, nor Lamont. Several of the ships' captains told us they'd returned home to Elland, but I highly doubt that.'

'You searched the Anglimns' home in the foreign sector?' Adé asked.

Lu was surprised by the hesitation in her voice, but then remembered her engagement to Anglimn's son. Of course the girl would be concerned – though whether or not she would be concerned enough for treason was another matter. It might be worth keeping an eye on her. For now, though, Lu nodded. 'The house was empty. We weren't even able to find their servants.'

'So, that's that, then,' Nokhai told his sister. 'Satisfied?'

Nasan was still looking at Lu, though. 'And what do you intend to do when you do find them?'

'What concern is it of yours?' Lu demanded. 'You've made it abundantly clear you don't belong to this empire.'

'Estrangement doesn't preclude proximity. Wouldn't you care if your closest neighbour chose to set her house on fire?' Nasan countered.

'It's not a matter of choice. They have broken our laws. They must pay the consequences,' Lu told her.

'They may think otherwise.'

'No doubt. But they will have to reckon with the truth of our power.'

Nasan frowned, clearly sceptical. 'I've seen the kind of ships the Ellandaise have. Their weapons. And it's well enough known that all that wealth they trampled the world acquiring goes straight into developing more of them. Are you so certain you have the military and naval might needed to fight them in the coming moons? *Years*, even?'

These were questions Lu had asked herself – without satisfactory answers. Questions that she might have weighed more judiciously had the memory of Hyacinth's final pained, rasping breaths not been seared into her; their uneven cadence a rhythm to her dreams during the precious few hours of sleep she had had since. But she did not need Nasan to know that.

'That is the business of my Grand Secretariat,' she told the girl sharply. No need to tell Nasan the Grand Secretariat would likely be less than pleased by her actions that morning. 'It is no concern of rebel interlopers.'

'And yet, this rebel *interloper* remains concerned. What do you think will happen to the surrounding territories if the Ellandaise conquer your empire? Do you think they'll reach the borders and respectfully stop there? Have you ever considered those of us on the fringes at all?'

The unfairness of it left Lu fumbling for a response. Before she could speak, though, Adé placed a mollifying hand on the Ashina girl's bare forearm, where the sleeve of her tunic had been rolled back. 'Nasan,' she cautioned. 'This kind of fighting amongst ourselves is pointless. None of us want to see this come to war—'

'Are you certain of that?' Nasan countered. 'Because it seems to me the empress – emperor – here is ready to burn everything she has for a bit of petty vengeance.'

'It's a matter of order,' Jin interposed. 'There is nothing petty about it.'

'What else would you call it when you insist, out of pride, on fighting an opponent who has you outmatched?' demanded Nasan.

'*Justice!*' Lu said, shaking with it. Because in the end, that was all she had: the certainty of her righteousness. The belief that not another person should die the way Hyacinth had.

'Do we know beyond a doubt that the Ellandaise would outmatch the empire in battle?' Adé asked, breaking the silence that followed. 'What of the sparkstone your cousin developed? Lamont said there was a cache of it some-where in the palace.'

Lu shook her head. 'I had Set's apartments searched. Lamont must have misunderstood.'

'But it could be elsewhere,' Nasan pointed out.

Lu thought of Ambassadeur Kartrum, his body barely recognisable under its shroud of blue flame. Something like hope was beginning to unfurl inside her. Lu felt Jin shift beside her. She turned to him and was surprised to see a nascent fear chilling his warm brown eyes.

He was frowning, a troubled furrow between his eyes that she was growing ever more familiar with. It made him look far older than he was, and for a brief moment she thought perhaps that strange affliction, his occasional inability to maintain an age, a place in time, had followed him from Yunis. But, no, that bit of magic had disappeared with the rest of the hidden city.

'You don't think it's a good idea,' Lu prompted him.

'It's dangerous. A weapon like that won't follow the

laws of nature – you can't predict it, can't control it. Its very essence is of another world. It wasn't meant to exist in this one. It wasn't meant to exist at all.'

'But it does exist,' Lu countered. 'And better we have it than the Ellandaise.'

'You *don't* have it, though,' Nasan pointed out, cutting short any response Jin might have had.

'The palace is only so large, and it *is* my home. If Set hid it here, I'll find it,' Lu told her.

'So, where should we begin?' Nasan asked.

Lu gave her a long look. What game was the Ashina girl playing at? Lu wasn't in any position to be chasing off potential allies, but then, Nasan was no longer merely running with a pack of wayward, well-armed youths. She was the rebel leader of an insurrectionist militia. And Lu herself was no longer a desperate exile; she was the embodiment of the empire Nasan so dearly hated.

'How many ways do I have to state that your fate is my concern as well?' Nasan said, exasperated, clearly reading Lu's thoughts on her face.

'Fine,' Lu snapped. 'The first place we should check is Brother's old apartments.'

'Not there.'

The group cut their eyes towards Min, still hovering uncertainly at the perimeter of the room, as though she hadn't yet made up her mind whether or not to run for the doors. Lu had nearly forgotten she was there.

Her sister flinched, as though feeling their collective attention like a physical blow. Lu was struck with a sense of unexpected recognition. It was like seeing a ghost of the Min Lu had grown up alongside. The Min she was no longer certain had ever really existed.

'Go on,' Lu told her.

Min hesitated but continued. 'Set would never have trusted Brother with something so powerful. The secret, yes, only because he would have needed him to formulate the weapon. But he would've known better than to leave anything of tangible value with the monk. Set lent Brother power by favouring him – a tethered kind of power. He was careful not to give him anything he could run off with and use on his own.'

This last part she said with a grave knowing, a darkness that made her seem much older. And just like that, the ghost of the girl her sister had once been disappeared like a patch of sunlight eclipsed by shadow.

'Where do you think we should look, then?' Lu asked.

'There was only one person he would have really trusted: My – our – mother,' Min said. 'Set spent all the time he wasn't with Brother with her. And Mother loved him like a son. She would guard his secrets with her life. If we want to find the weapon, we need to ask her.'

'You told us that your mother was in an alliance with the Ellandaise, though,' Nokhai said, ever the voice of tempered reason. 'If that's the case, the Dust of Annihilation is as good as theirs, isn't it?'

'Not necessarily. Mother chose to ally with the Ellandaise because she saw them as her only option. But desperation doesn't buy trust. She'll take what she can get from them, but knowing her, she would save any leverage she could for the future, when she might need it.' Min shrugged. 'Above all, she would want to keep herself and me – that is, me and my sister – safe.'

It was a protective gesture – Min would not reveal the truth of Lu's parentage to Nasan and the others. But Lu thought she also sensed a sort of deeper kindness in the words. Rinyi had not been much of a mother – certainly not the one Lu would have chosen for herself – but she had been something she shared with Min, no matter how differently they'd been treated, and nothing could alter that.

'Rinyi's apartments, then,' Lu said aloud, already moving toward the door. 'Now.'

Jin slid into step beside her, hand moving comfortingly toward his sword belt. His was ever a reliable presence, and one, Lu thought with a shade of guilt, whose constancy she hoped one day to earn. If she ever could, after all she'd done.

Like a spectre of that thought, Nokhai fell in on her other side. Nasan followed, flanked by Adé.

Lu stopped and turned back, realising one person was missing.

'Min?'

Her sister's pale, nervous eyes met Lu's own. 'You think I should come?'

Lu smiled. All reflex – cocky and easy. The sort of response she'd learned as a child to soothe her fretful little sister.

'Of course you have to come. Do you think Mother would spill her secrets to any of us?'

They moved forward as a group of six. As Lu reached for the inset handle of the pocket door, though, it slid open.

She looked up in surprise, but it was only Syringa. Lu had a moment to register familiarity, and then, unexpectedly, an acute sense of displacement when she saw terror in the amma's wide eyes. Another moment, another pang of bewilderment, and Syringa was stumbling into the room, falling to hands and knees, shoved from behind by—

'Lamont!'

Lu recognised the voice instantly. Familiar, and yet deeply out of place.

Missar Anglimn.

Too late, too late.

The Kommodeur's bulky frame filled the doorway. One hand was still extended from pushing Syringa. The other was raised level with his chest, holding a gun pointed directly at Lu's head.

The memory of burnt hair and wool came first, chased by the stench of flesh seared like meat. Then followed the vision: Ambassadeur Kartrum, lit like kindling. Lamont's dispassionate gaze as he watched his countryman scream and burn.

For perhaps the first time in her life, Lu froze.

Jin did not. He was a soldier born. He had no use for confusion, for hesitation. He strode forward and raised his sword.

Lamont raised his gun. Slightly higher now than when he had aimed it at Lu.

Blood and life and urgency surged back into her limbs. 'Jin, *no!*'

There was a bang like something heavy collapsing, like a crack across the face, and then Jin was falling to the floor. An ordinary bullet, but it worked well enough.

Jin went down hard on one knee. As Lamont advanced, he slashed his sword in a wide, wild arc.

He missed. Lamont levelled his gun between Jin's warm brown eyes and did not.

The Silver Star of Yunis pitched forward limply, without further ceremony, his skull striking the floor with a sickening crack, a soldier to the end.

24

War

Min stared at Kommodeur Lamont's gun as it expelled a sleepy plume of blue-white smoke, then down at the body splayed at her feet.

Jin.

The name rang in her head, oddly hollow. Meaningless. Those limp limbs like dropped sticks, that paling flesh, had been the last surviving member of the Yunian Triarch not a moment earlier. Now they would be nothing but rot. From beneath him spread a pool of dark blood. All that red had been his life, and it had spilled out of him so easily.

'Min!'

She looked up. Her mother stood in the doorway beside Missar Anglimn, flanked by four uniformed Ellandaise soldiers.

Before Min could decide how to respond, there was a sound like a growl from beside her. She looked up and saw Lu flying forward, stooping to grab Jin's fallen sword from the floor. Her sister hacked gracelessly at the Kommodeur, who let off another shot from his pistol.

She was all rage, he all startled reflex. Both sword and bullet went wide.

But the Kommodeur was recovering, levelling the gun once more at her sister. Min watched helplessly as it happened, her body gone oddly cold, unable to move. Lu saw it, too. She raised Jin's sword again – too slow, too late. And, Min realised with exquisite despair, outmatched. The gun drew faster, fleeter, and with greater range. A weapon of convenience rather than one of skill. Terribly, lethally modern ...

All at once, a blur of silvery grey erupted from the floor and latched itself to the Kommodeur's raised arm. The blur became a writhing mass of clenched white teeth and fur and rigid muscle.

Impossible, Min first thought. And then, realising what it meant for Nokhai to have regained his ability to caul:

He's killed her.

Tsai was gone. But there was no time to feel bereft, or even confused. The wolf gave a snarling tug with its great head, then dropped back to the ground. Min did not understand at first. Then she saw the pink-streaked foam lathering its jaws, and the gun – and Lamont's hand – clenched between its teeth.

Lamont screeched, a terrible, otherworldly sound. Min saw a flash of bone, whipping ribbons of sinew, an arc of blood.

Missar Anglimn yelped, shoving past Rinyi. 'Lamont!' he shrieked, stopping short as the spray from the other man's arm caught him across the face. He went white as thick ice and slumped down to his knees, retching.

The wolf flung both hand and gun away, drawing back its mouth into an eerily human expression of distaste.

Nasan! Somehow, Min heard Nokhai's voice in her ears. *Get out of here.*

'You – your caul!' his sister exclaimed, her voice equal parts accusation and shock.

No time, the Ashina boy said sharply. *Take Adé and go.*

But it was too late; the Ellandaise guards moved as one into the room. Min saw in horror that they were armed with long, sinister-looking rifles. She retreated in alarm, but this time, her sister did not hesitate. Lu lunged forward with Jin's sword, impaling the first man through a gap in the side of his armour before he had his weapon lifted. He screamed and fell, the rifle clattering from his grip.

'Those are ranged weapons!' Lu told the others, spinning and striking a second guard. She caught him in the thigh with a blow that rattled harmlessly off his chain mail, but it was enough to unbalance him. 'Force them to stay close! They'll have difficulty getting a shot off without hitting one another!'

Nasan rushed in and gave him a punishing kick to the small of his back, sending him sprawling to the floor. At the same time, Nokhai leapt atop one of the remaining two guards. There was a flash of teeth; the man yelped, then fell silent.

The final guard moved in toward Lu. Unlike the others, he left his rifle holstered, and instead drew a small silver pistol, similar to Lamont's, from his belt. He went down on one knee, bracing his arm against his thigh, and aimed.

In that moment, Min came alive. With someone else's fluidity, someone else's nerve, she seized a heavy bronze

mirror hanging by the door, raised it overhead, and
brought it down with a mighty crash on the man's head
just as he pulled the trigger. He stumbled and fell forward,
the helmet rolling off his head, revealing a shoulder-length
crop of straw-coloured hair beneath. His shot went wide,
shattering a window on the far wall.

Min screamed and dropped the mirror at the sound
of the gun discharging. She hadn't struck him very hard;
he recovered and drew himself back onto his knees, his
armour weighing him down. He whirled around, drawing his lip back in fury as his eyes fell on her. In the fallen
mirror, she could see what he must have seen: her own
petrified face, wan and sunken and terribly young. A little
girl who had got lucky with one furtive blow, but whose
luck had now run out. He raised the pistol toward her—

'No! Not her, not my girl!'

Min looked up, and so too, did the foreigner.

It was her mother, rushing into the room, as though to
throw her body between the two of them.

In that moment, a hand seized the foreign soldier by a
hank of yellow hair, jerking his head back. A thin silver
blade drew a red line across his throat. The cut was thin
and stark at first, then blood suddenly gushed all at once,
like water from a bucket.

Lu released his hair and the man's head fell forward,
limp and heavy, onto his chest. He slumped to the floor,
and like Jin only moments before, the life poured out of
him until he went still.

Rinyi followed suit, her legs giving out in what Min
assumed must have been relief. She looked up at Lu. Min
didn't know what she expected to see in her mother's grey

eyes – gratitude? Awe? – but she found them as stony and spare as they always were when gazing upon her sister.

Nasan, Nok's voice resounded in their heads once again. *Take Adé and go.*

'I'm not leaving you—'

Now! I have my caul. I'll find you again, I promise. Go. Find Omair and get off the palace grounds.

The Ashina girl's mouth flattened, but she jerked her head in a nod and seized Adé by the wrist, and then the two of them were running out the door.

The room had gone eerily still in the wake of so much bloodshed; the only sounds were the heaving, uneven breaths – slowing now – of the first soldier Lu had run through, and the keening groans of Lamont, lying wretched and curled on the floor.

In this relative quiet, it was not difficult to hear the click of a pistol being cocked.

Min turned. The pistol was aimed squarely at her face. It was Lamont's weapon – now held in the shaking hand of Missar Anglimn.

'N-none of you move,' the thin man quavered. Sweat beaded on his upper lip and plastered his limp hair against his forehead.

'Min!' Her mother's cry was anguished, fear flooding her voice once again.

Move, Min's instinct told her. The uncertainty of his grip, the rattle of the weapon – he could no more hit her while she was in motion than he could shoot a mayfly out of the air. And yet, Min stared at the muzzle, down the small black hole through which her death at any moment might appear, and found she could not move.

'Anglimn.' It was Lu who spoke. She strode forward slowly, like approaching a skittish animal.

The gun dipped precipitously, but he jerked it back up. 'Don't come any closer!' he shrieked. 'I'll do it, I swear it, I'll shoot the girl—'

Lu stopped, holding up her hands. There was a beat of silence, broken only by Lamont's fevered moans. The last surviving soldier had fallen silent.

'Point the pistol at me, Anglimn,' her sister told him. 'I'm the danger, here.'

His eyes tracked uncertainly from Lu to Min, then back again. Min could see the calculation, the doubt in them. He'd seen her set the throne room ablaze with nothing more than her hands and her fury. And while he must have known she no longer had her powers, it would be a difficult image to shake. On the other hand, only moments ago he'd watched Lu cut down several of, no doubt, his best hired swords.

Her sister took a cautious step forward.

The rattling gun lurched toward Lu, and off Min. Yet Min tried and found she could not swallow the heart-sized lump in her throat.

'Back away! Not a step closer!' Anglimn brayed.

'This is a bad situation for us both, Anglimn. But we can make it better,' Lu said. 'It's not too late.'

And then, as though a refutation from the heavens, Min heard it: the sound of a thousand boots marching smartly through the courtyard outside. Soldiers.

Anglimn heard them as well. 'Are you trying to bargain with me, Girl King?' he scoffed. 'You have no leverage here. No allies, no mercy left. Your own people have betrayed you!'

'Those I already exiled for treason, perhaps. I am aware,' Lu said calmly, though there was a knife's edge in her voice. Anger – and fear. Min felt the prickle of it herself, like icy water moving through her shoulder blades, in the marrow of her arms. A banging sound came from down the hall. Shouts, followed by the blunted, fist-like explosions of gunfire from behind closed doors.

'You s-should not have moved against us this morning,' Anglimn told her, voice still quavering, pistol still pointed at her head. 'There was no need for war, but you've forced our hand. Can you not hear that sound? We have your palace surrounded, and my hired army draws close, cinching you in here like jewels in a silk pouch ...'

Lu, Nokhai's voice was low and urgent in their ears. *I could kill him for you now, before the others arrive.*

Anglimn had heard it as well. His eyes widened, and he shifted the gun from Lu to Nokhai, then – seeing Lu's hands tighten around Jin's sword – back again. There was a fresh fear in him; he looked scarcely equipped to shoot either one of them, but he must have realised that even if he did manage to get a bullet into Nokhai's wolf, that might not be enough to stop it.

'No,' her sister told the Ashina boy. 'Nokhai, you need to leave now. Go after Nasan and Adé. Find Yuri and Omair.'

Not a chance.

'They'll need your help getting out of here. And I need you, too. You're no use to me dead.'

I won't die, then.

'These men, they need me alive. They see no use in you. *Please*. Go.'

The creature watched her with wary eyes, and Min was struck again by how human they looked. He huffed, stamping heavily on the floor.

Anglimn looked between the two of them uncertainly. 'No one is going anywhere,' he told them. 'I forbid—'

The marching of boots struck the hallway outside Lu's apartments, and just as the first of the soldiers filled the doorway, the wolf barrelled forward. Anglimn screamed and discharged the pistol just as the creature's immense paws slammed into his chest, knocking him flat onto his back. The gun flew upward, firing a second shot into the ceiling. Nokhai used Anglimn's chest to launch himself into another leap – and suddenly, the blue-grey coat stiffened into russet and blonde feathers. The wolf's body shrank away like dissipating fog, and an eagle emerged in its wake, soaring for the window Lamont's earlier bullet had shattered.

'Get behind me, Min.'

Min looked up to see her sister sweeping in between her and the foreign soldiers flooding the room. Behind them, she saw Magistrate Cui and several of his household guards.

'Cui,' barked Anglimn. 'Lamont's been injured. Find us a physician immediately.'

The man surveyed the room, the pools of blood growing tacky and dark on the wooden floor. He paled and rushed back out, chased by his men.

The foreigners closed in on them. Lu raised Jin's sword, and instantly some dozen rifles were trained on her.

'Wait!' Rinyi rushed forward, pushing her way between Lu and Min. 'Let Minyi go. She hasn't done anything. I told her about the alliance, and she agreed to your terms. Let her fulfil her end of the bargain, and you'll have an empress who will grant you the trade deals you desire.'

'Is that true?' Anglimn demanded. He turned back to Min, though this time he did not raise his pistol.

Min looked toward the guards blocking the doorway, then back at Anglimn's wan, sweating face. She looked to her mother, nearly as pale, standing over her. It was perverse, to see a parent looking so desperate.

And she looked past her mother, at Lu. Lu, with her hands still clutching a dead man's sword, her face freckled with a spray of someone else's blood. Two women, each willing in her own way to die for Min.

She searched her sister's expression for – what exactly? Apprehension that Min would betray her? Anger at the belief that she already had? But she saw neither of those things. Instead, Lu looked back at her, beseeching. Expectant. One sister to another. Equals – partners, co-conspirators. A unit apart from and unassailable by mothers, by lovers, by death and fear.

When she spoke, her voice was raspy and taut, as though her throat had been clutching it too hard. But it was loud enough for Anglimn to hear. 'I'm no empress. Certainly not yours.'

'Chains,' he said coldly. 'I want both girls in chains.' Then, as though remembering who he was speaking to, he barked another order in Saxil.

His hired army moved in around them. Lu raised her

sword, but Anglimn was finished with her. 'Drop it, or my men will shoot your little sister.'

The sword fell from Lu's hands.

'No, *no*! Min!' her mother was screaming. A soldier moved in and pulled her away as though she were light as a bird.

Someone grabbed Min, yanking her upright and toward the door. She felt a lance of fear, and then a sharp tug on her arm, warmth in the palm of her hand. She looked up and saw Lu's fingers clenched white at the knuckles, entwined with her own, refusing to let go.

25

Kith

Dusk was falling upon the Immaculate City, and with it, bedlam. Ellandaise mercenaries and turncoat imperial soldiers flooded the courtyards in droves, splintering doors and dragging out screaming ministers and petrified servants alike. Nok watched it all unfold from above, soaring in his eagle caul, using its sharp gaze to search for Nasan and Adé. Far off, he could see that the gates to the city had been sealed. Several courtiers clustered around each, pounding to be released, but to no avail.

Nok cursed silently. The city was locked down. There was no chance that his sister and Adé had made it out before the gates shut – they had to be hiding somewhere on the palace grounds. He swooped back in the direction he'd come; best to start searching near Lu's apartments and spread out from there.

But it was swiftly growing too dark for the eagle to see. He needed a different form. He perched upon the upturned eaves of a nearby roof, allowing the golden brown and russet of his feathers to shift into ash greys, stony whites. The eagle's golden eyes rolled back and were replaced with those of the owl, and the world rushed back into brilliant focus.

Shouts reached the owl's ears, also significantly stronger than the eagle's had been. Nok recognised one of the voices, though he couldn't quite place it ...

'Unhand me, you foreign pigs!'

Casting the owl's gaze downward, Nok watched two Ellandaise mercenaries haul a man out of his home. He recognised him now: Minister Ong, from Lu's Grand Secretariat.

Ong looked somewhat diminished from his usual station, dressed in a silk nightshirt and soft linen pants. His family and servants trailed behind, filling the doorway. A woman – his wife? – clutched at the frame and cried out as the hired soldiers threw him to his knees.

It must have hurt; Ong's face spasmed in pain. But haughtiness quickly won out. 'Can you even speak Yueh? Do you have any idea who I am?' he demanded, making to stand. One of the soldiers frowned dispassionately. He sent a lazy kick to Ong's shoulder, knocking the minister back down.

Another scream from his wife, and then the whole family was rushing out to surround him. His wife threw herself over him, pleading for the guards to leave them be. Ong's servants and his three young daughters formed an uncertain half-ring around them, watching with wide eyes.

Ong pushed his wife off of him. 'Stop – stop, none of that,' he chided. 'Take the girls and get back into the house—'

'What have we here?' said another voice sharply. Another imperial minister pushed his way into the fray.

Nok recognised him from Lu's enthronement cere-mony. Minister Cui. Hyacinth's father.

'*Cui*?' Ong squinted up at him in apprehension. 'What are you doing back in the capital?'

'Exile did not suit me.' Cui looked a harder man now than the last time Nok had seen him. Had he learned the fate of his daughter, his firstborn and final remaining child? Nok wondered. Lu had sent word that Hyacinth's body was en route, but was it possible Cui had already left home before that letter arrived?

Cui turned to the Ellandaise soldier. 'He's one of them. Part of the Grand Secretariat,' he said shortly, jerking his head toward Ong.

The foreigner stared back, uncomprehending.

'For heaven's ...' Cui muttered. He repeated in loud, exaggeratedly slow Yueh, 'He's one of them. A *target*.'

Nok did not understand right away, but the foreign soldier did – apparently, he did in fact speak some Yueh. The man grunted, strode forward, and drew the sword from his belt. Without ceremony he raised it, and in two heavy blows, cleaved Ong's head from his body.

The head rolled, heavy as a dropped cabbage. His body collapsed, painting the courtyard in wild, red streaks.

Shrieks filled the air – from Ong's family, and too, from the servants gathered around them. One of the daughters, a girl no older than Nok, broke and ran. Two of the servants followed suit.

The same Ellandaise guard threw his bloody sword back into its scabbard, cursing, and unsheathed a pistol. He hesitated, waving the gun between the three fleeing girls.

'That one, you idiot!' snarled Cui, pointing at the daughter's swiftly retreating form. 'Who cares about the servants!'

The Ellandaise man recovered and fired a single bullet into her back. She pitched forward, hitting the ground with such force it sent several of her teeth skittering between the paving stones.

Nokhai had seen enough. He lifted off from the roof and rose into the darkening sky.

Nasan! Adé! He called out to them at last, too panicked now for stealth. His sister wouldn't be able to answer, but perhaps she could signal—

A crossbow bolt flew past him, so close he felt it breathe through the tips of his left wing. He took a sharp turn away from it, all instinct, then swooped back in a wide arc to catch a glimpse of his attacker.

Far below, an Ellandaise soldier cursed and cranked his crossbow in preparation for another shot. Beside him, a foreigner in cream-coloured Hana robes stabbed his finger upward, at Nok.

Anglimn.

The foreigner couldn't have known for certain the owl was him, but then, Nok supposed the creature was rather conspicuous.

With two, three heavy beats of his wings, Nok thrust himself higher into the sky, circling around an elm, putting the tree between himself and the crossbow. Certain that he was out of range for the weapon, and out of sight for human eyes, he made eastward.

His intuition served him well. Four figures slunk behind the building that housed Omair's apartments, hugging the far side away from the clash, so heavily fringed with fir shrubs that they would be difficult to spot from the ground. Not a problem for the owl; Nok noticed them by the swaying tops of the bushes they disturbed in their wake.

Nasan! Adé!

The four of them froze. Nasan pulled out her knife and cast about wildly, until she registered that the sound came from within her own head. Adé understood first; she reached forward to touch Yuri's sleeve reassuringly – he was the only one who had not yet experienced Nok in caul.

Look up, Nok told them, swooping in low. Omair's face was already turned to the sky, searching. He swept downward, alighting in one of the fir trees sheltering them, causing the flimsy branches to sway under his weight. *Keep heading east*, he told them. *There's a garden they haven't reached yet. There are four pavilions, one in each corner of the garden. Go into the yellow one.*

They followed him as he hopped overhead from tree to tree to the eaves of nearby outbuildings. They moved in relative quiet, though the sound of their every footfall resounded impossibly loud in the owl's sensitive ears. It must have only been moments later that they arrived at the Bower of a Thousand Springtimes, though it felt like hours.

The others filed inside, casting nervous glances over their shoulders. Nok swept in after them, alighting on the floor just an arm's length from his sister. Behind him, Yuri and Omair pulled the door shut, entombing them in darkness. A waning moon cast its pale silvery glow into the room through a series of narrow vents close to the ceiling, giving them just enough light to make out the contours of each other's faces.

Nok released his caul as he landed, the warmth of the owl's plumage sweeping away so suddenly that the mild bite of the spring night pricked at his bare arms. 'They've taken the central courtyard,' he told them. Then, turning toward Yuri, 'They're taking out members of the Grand Secretariat. They executed Ong in front of every—'

Two strong hands planted themselves on his shoulders and pushed hard. He stumbled back, barely catching himself before he fell.

'*Nasan*,' he exclaimed. 'What—'

'Nasan!' Adé chided at the same time.

But his sister would not be chastened. 'How long have you had it? How long?' she demanded, surging toward him again.

'What? My caul?'

'Yes, your *caul*! When were you planning on telling me? Or, *were* you planning to?'

'Of course I was,' he insisted. And it was true. Or, at least, he hadn't intended not to tell her. 'I only got it back last night,' he said. 'There wasn't time—'

'Don't you *dare*,' she snarled. 'If you had the time to breathe in front of me, you had the time to tell me about this.'

'How did you do it?' Omair asked.

Nok turned toward him, grateful for the distraction. 'Lu,' he said. 'She took it. Or, rather, I gave it to her.'

'But, how … ?' Confusion flickered across Omair's face, but only for a moment. Unlike Nasan and Adé, he knew the truth of Lu's birth. 'Of course,' he murmured. 'Tsai wouldn't hurt *her*, would she?'

'Lu?' Nasan repeated, looking between the two of them. 'Are you serious? You gave that kind of power to *her*?'

'She can't use it,' he said quickly. 'She doesn't have the aptitude.'

'If it was a targeted curse,' Omair broke in, 'it wouldn't affect everyone in the same way.'

'Still, it seems like a bit of a risk doesn't it? Giving her a weapon like that?' Adé said. 'And couldn't it be dangerous to her, too? Wasn't that the whole problem with giving it to Omair to possess?'

'Yes, my thoughts precisely,' Nasan agreed.

'I ...' Nok grasped for an explanation that wouldn't break Lu's confidence. He was a terrible liar – hadn't Lu herself said he was incapable? – and his sister had a nose for lies like a hound's for blood.

'It's obvious, isn't it?' Yuri said brusquely from the deep shadows by the door. Nok had nearly forgotten about him. 'Min and Lu. They're sisters.'

Nok breathed a sigh of relief. At least someone here knew how to lie.

Omair nodded quickly. 'Of course. The curse likely feels the familial connection between the two girls.'

Nasan frowned, perhaps finding the explanation a bit thin for her liking.

'I can give you back your caul.' The words leapt from Nok before he had a chance to think them through.

It worked; all thought of Lu slipped visibly from his sister's mind. Her eyes went wide, then hard.

'You mean that?'

And he found, to his relief, that he did. It had never been a question of *if*, not truly. Only a matter of *when*. Perhaps a part of him hadn't wanted to give it to her because doing so meant she would take it and go. That she would be free to start her new life, with her new family, her Common Kith. And that it would be the end of their story.

'I'm ready now,' he told her.

She licked her lips, her eagerness vying against a wariness he wished he didn't inspire in her. 'Now?' she asked.

'Yes. I'll try. If you want me to.'

'Do it.'

Uncertain where to begin, he started as he had with Lu: reaching out a hand and placing the tips of two fingers at the centre of her forehead. And when he closed his eyes, a different sight opened within himself, and he *saw*.

Where Lu had been golden, Nasan was the glinting silver-white edge of a blade catching the light. Her energy flowed in wide, rapid rivers, all calculated precision. As far as he could see, she shone with a cold, acute gleam to counter Lu's molten effusion.

And at the heart of it, at the heart of *her*, he found the kernel of her being. Steely and sealed against the world. Within it, though, he sensed the thing she had lost, the thing he now sought. He could feel its restless energy, pacing, a wild thing caged for a decade and longer. It had never left her. No one could have ever taken it from her, so integral was it to her essence. As Nasan lived, so did the wolf. What had been severed was only her ability to draw it out into the world.

He reached out for the creature, felt it feel him. Felt it

398

feel the call of the beast god within him – and watched it emerge, awoken to its full power once more. It slunk toward him, liquid and impossibly strong. He had time to reflect that there was a kind of danger without enmity in its movements, just before the creature coiled down on its haunches – and sprang forward toward him.

Nok fell backward, his fingers breaking their contact with Nasan. All at once he was back in his body, sprawling onto the floor, a tremendous weight pressing him down. His eyes flew open, and he found himself face-to-face with his wolf.

No, not his. *Nasan's.*

She recovered before he did, letting the caul slip off her, natural and elegant as if she'd only lost it for a day rather than since she was a small child.

'You did it!' she hissed excitedly, grabbing his hands to yank him off the floor. He'd scarcely stumbled back to his feet before she was flinging her arms around him, pulling him close. He winced. Over Nasan's shoulder, Adé met his eyes with warmth and something like awe. Beside her, Omair glowed with a kind of pride.

It was too much; Nok averted his gaze.

'I knew you could do it!' Nasan enthused, holding him by the shoulders. 'This changes everything. Do you understand? We can build a Common Kith—'

He stepped back without intending to. 'Nasan,' he said sharply. His sister was so single-minded; he should've known. No matter what he promised her, she would only want more – want back the whole world she had lost. That *they* had lost. 'I said I'd give you back your caul, not that I'd help you build your militia.'

Her face darkened. 'It's not just a militia, Nok. Don't you see? We can get it all back.'

'Get what back?' he demanded. 'Ma? Ba? Idri? They're all gone – blood and bones under the sand. Dust.'

'What about our dignity?' she retorted. 'Sovereignty!'

All just pretty words without the people who gave them meaning. But there was no convincing his sister of that. She trusted in the idea of her tomorrow with the zeal of a prophet.

'It doesn't matter anyway,' he told her shortly. 'We don't even know that I can Give the Gift to just anyone. Half your "Common Kith" aren't even from the North originally – who's to say it'll work with them?'

A pause lingered, and Nok felt certain that was the end of it.

Then Adé stepped forward. 'You could try it on me,' she said.

He stared. 'You?' he blurted. 'But you – how can you … Wait, are you going north with her?'

Adé looked toward Nasan, then back at him. 'We've discussed it,' she said. 'One day. When the time is right.'

'But Adé,' he said. 'What of your family? The twins?'

She smiled sadly. 'They're thinking of leaving as well. You haven't been back to the Outer Ring since the fires, Nok. Things are bad. Half of Scrap-Patch Row is gone, and the people who lived there have either disappeared, moved out of the city, or are sleeping on the streets.'

He thought of the fine new buildings erected all along the streets that had once housed the ramshackle shanties he'd known so well. He'd seen the truth then; it just hadn't occurred to him that Adé and the Maks would be among those being displaced.

'Adé, you've never been up north,' he said. 'It's barren land up there. Harsh and remote and miserable. It might seem romantic now—'

'I'm not a fool, Nok. I've thought this through,' she countered sharply. 'And however you see me, I'm not your little sister. I don't need you to tell me how the world works. I know; I've seen it for myself. There's no place left here for people like me. My mother, the twins. In Yulan City, you're either rich or you're dead.'

'So, you're joining this Common Kith, then? That's your solution?'

'I don't know that life has solutions,' she said, her smile faintly sad. 'But it's my choice. So will you help me?'

Had it been anyone else, he would have refused. But this was Adé.

'I don't know if it'll work,' he said cautiously. 'Growing up, they told us Pacts were made on the basis of pledging stewardship to the lands connected with a specific beast god.'

'That can't be all, though,' Nasan leapt in. 'That's what we were told, and yet look at us, you and me. You were able to give me back my caul, Nok. After our tie to the land was severed. You said it yourself – we'll never get that exact life back. But I have my wolf again. That has to mean something.'

'But you had your caul before,' he said. 'It was still in you after all this time, only dormant. It's another thing entirely to forge a new Gift.'

Wasn't it?

'You're a Pactmaker,' his sister argued. 'That's *your* Gift.'

'What's the harm in trying?' Adé said.

He sighed in defeat, raising a hand toward her like an offer. She smiled, stepping forward to meet his touch.

If Lu was ostentatious gold and Nasan was the cold edge of steel, Adé was like the rosy glow of sunrise: ethereal and warm and hopeful.

He found the seed at the centre of her being, just as he had done with his sister – and hesitated. With Lu and Nasan, he'd had something to focus on, something to grasp for. In Lu's case, it had been the curse churning through his own bloodstream. With his sister, he had seen the wolf within her.

For Adé, he had to recreate a ritual for which he had no instruction, scarcely even any mythology. Growing up, a Pactmaker had been spoken of only in the abstract. So ancient a concept it was like the birth of the sun. What words could be used to describe a thing that had happened before the birth of language?

Help me, he thought to no one, perhaps to himself. *Show me what I'm meant to do here.*

Before him, as if in answer, his vision flickered. One moment, he was standing amid Adé's essence, and the next, he was on the shore of Yunis, shrouded in fog. He saw their shapes again, mere shadow emerging from the damp white, and then receding once again. All but one, which stepped through the thin veil between there and here. Nok's vision flickered once more, and the rocky shore disappeared, but the creature did not.

He recognised it immediately. It had been the first to

approach him all those many moons ago, back when he had fallen from the sky and somehow lived.

A spotted deer with delicate cloven hooves and silvery horns. It stopped and raised its head toward him, liquid limpid eyes of honey-brown regarding him with tranquil solemnity. And then, gracefully, it bowed, lowering its racked head in deference. Not knowing what else to do, he repeated the gesture in kind—

And found himself back in the dark pavilion, surrounded by Nasan and Omair and Yuri. He blinked, realising his hand was still raised, though he and Adé were no longer touching. He lowered his hand, and all at once felt his body slacken with it. His knees gave out, and suddenly his sister was under him, lifting him by the underarms.

'What happened?' Omair asked, studying his face in concern. 'Are you all right? Over here, there's a bench – sit, sit.'

At the same time, Nasan demanded, 'Did it work?'

'I—' Nok shook his head, feeling strength rushing back into his limbs. He turned to Adé. 'How do you feel about deer?'

Adé's eyes widened.

Nasan looked up sharply, licking her lips. Funny, he thought. It wasn't hard now to see the wolf had been within her all along.

'Try it, love,' she said to Adé.

'I don't know where to begin.'

'Think of it as a reflex,' he suggested. 'Something that comes naturally, like falling asleep, or—'

'Find the strength of it in you. You'll sense it, like a thread of iron in your core,' his sister interrupted. She'd had access to her caul for all of a handful of minutes, but already she knew better than him. Nok suppressed the urge to roll his eyes. This had been a long time coming for Nasan, and it had always meant more to her than it did to him.

It took a few tries, but in the end, Adé disappeared before their eyes, replaced by the tawny pelt and silvery antlers of a snow deer in its summer colouring.

Gods. Adé's voice was a hushed whisper in their ears. *Is this really me?*

Nasan turned to Nok, a wide grin splitting her face. 'This changes everything,' she said.

He did not return the smile. Adé's deer lurched uncertainly, and away slipped the caul of fur and horns, leaving her sitting on the pavilion floor, once more a human girl.

'It's too bad she wasn't chosen by something with wings,' Yuri pointed out. 'A deer and a wolf together are not going to have any easier a time walking out of the palace gates than the two of you would as yourselves.'

'A deer and two wolves,' countered Nasan. 'We're not going anywhere without Nok.'

'You'll have to. I'm going back for Lu,' Nok told her.

'To do what, exactly? Face two armies on your own?' she asked incredulously.

'I don't know yet,' he said stubbornly. 'But I promised I'd help her.'

'This is the best chance we have, Nok. We need to leave now. With you,' Nasan interjected, putting herself between Yuri and Nok.

'Oh, certainly,' he snapped, with more resentment than he had realised he felt, up until that moment. 'It wouldn't do to leave behind your most valuable asset.'

'"Asset?"'

The hurt on her face was startling. He so rarely saw unmitigated feeling from his sister, with the possible exception of—

'You're my brother, you idiot.'

Anger, he finished. There it was.

'Either way,' he said. 'If you want me to come, you'd best help me find Lu and free her. Because I'm not leaving until I do.'

'If that's the case,' she snapped, 'what's your plan? I've got recruits, but they're all in the Outer Ring. Meaning we'd have to leave the Immaculate City. Which you could do – only they have no reason to trust your word, because you've done nothing to familiarise yourself with them, or earn their trust, this entire time.'

Nok squeezed his eyes shut and scrubbed his hands over his face. Over and over in his mind, the Ellandaise soldier brought down his blade, parting Ong's head from his shoulders with a deft, practised blow.

That one, you idiot! Minister Cui screamed, pointing at Ong's daughter. The Ellandaise pistol fired, and she dropped like a stone in water. *Who cares about the servants—*

Nok's eyes flew open.

'We don't need to leave the city,' he said. 'Everything – and everyone – we need is already here.'

26

Kin

It was cold and tomb-dark in the cell. The sort of dark that was hard to come by in the world of the living: no flicker of oil lamps, no white sliver of moon. Only the displacing vacancy of perpetual night. Lu found herself uncertain at times whether her eyes were open or closed – it made no difference, either way.

She had her other senses, though. She could hear the intermittent drip of the water that clung to the dank walls. Smell the mildew thriving, thick in its wake. And she could still touch, hold Min to her, stroking her fingers slowly through her little sister's hair, letting the tips of her blunt fingernails scratch lightly at her scalp. It was something she'd watched Rinyi do for Min a hundred years ago, back when her sister was yet little, and laid sick in bed with a fever, chasing sleep and crying in discomfort instead.

Lu didn't know why that action had stayed with her all these years – why she'd studied it closely enough to repeat it. Tenderness was one of the few things in which she had never been a quick study. And, she supposed, it wasn't one of Rinyi's stronger qualities, either. Perhaps that had been what made it memorable. Meaningful.

'What does it feel like, for you?' Min murmured.

She did not know what her sister meant. Neither of them had spoken in quite a while. It felt like hours, though Lu suspected that was just an effect of the darkness, flattening time, forcing her to contend with the interminable length of every moment with nothing but the beating of her own heart to distract her.

'What does what feel like?' she asked.

'The curse,' Min said.

My mother.

'It doesn't feel like much at all,' she admitted. 'When Nokhai gave her – it – to me, I felt something. Or at least, I thought I did. But not since. I guess it's because I don't have the aptitude to use it.'

It was hard not to perceive it as a kind of failure. Silly, but she wasn't accustomed to lacking in talent much. And after all these many years of accepting that she would never possess a mother's love, to realise that she did, that she could – to feel so little of it even as it coursed through her veins, was disappointing.

Min sighed, the faintest puff of sadness in the dark. And Lu was surprised to hear a chord of longing in the sound.

Though perhaps she shouldn't be so surprised. This bit of magic had hung over Min, ravaged her body, made her sick with rage. But it had also made her extraordinary, and powerful. Lu could not begrudge her that feeling. And in fact ...

'What if you tried to take her back?' Lu asked.

'What?' Min jerked upright, pulling out of her arms.

The cold rushed in to replace her sister's absent limbs, and Lu felt suddenly bereft.

'I said—'

'I heard what you said,' Min told her sharply. 'It ... It's not a good idea, Lu.'

'Just for a little while. You could use it – the power it gives you – to get us out of here. And afterward, I could take it back, or rather, you could return it to—'

'I wouldn't.' Min's voice was taut and thin, cutting as a potter's wire through clay. She drew a shaky breath. 'I just know I wouldn't. It's taken me moons to get to this place, Lu. To feel I can breathe without it. To go more than a few moments without thinking of it. You don't know what you're offering me.'

'I didn't realise. You don't have to—'

'I know it's stupid.' Her voice broke over the word. 'It's only, I've reached a place where things feel tolerable. I know I – *we* – might die if I don't try to do something ... It's only, I feel I might die if I *do*. Not just die. I feel, no, I *know* something terrible will happen. And I don't want to die like that. Not with that sort of rage in me.'

'You don't have to explain yourself,' Lu said firmly.

She could hear Min breathing in the dark, quick and rabbity. 'Don't I?' Her voice was small.

'Not to me.'

Lu fumbled forward in the dark until she found her sister's cold hand. Her own was hot; she squeezed them together until they reached something close to equilibrium.

★

They came on the morning of the third day.

Lu could not recall when she'd fallen asleep, but at some point she must have, slipping out of one darkness and into another. Now, the dank cell flooded with the weak yellow glow of a jailer's lantern, stinging her eyes as though it were the bright sun of midday.

'Get up.'

A heavy boot toed at the bottom of her slippered foot. She squinted up at Lamont's face, swimming above her. Behind him, Anglimn, never far off, shouldered his way past the jailer, who hung the lantern on a hook by the door and bowed his way back out into the corridor.

'What's happening?' Min asked blearily.

Lu shook her head, helping her to her feet. 'Stand behind me,' she muttered, placing herself between her sister and the men.

The Kommodeur gave them an ostensibly satisfied smirk, but Lu could sense the effort behind it, and the pain. Her eyes fell to his arm – or rather, what was left of it. Nok had torn the hand clean off at the wrist. Someone had treated the open end, bandaged it, and placed it in a sling, tucking the wound close to his body. The wrappings looked fresh and clean. Lamont saw her looking. He shifted, and the wounded arm moved out of her line of sight. The forced smirk had fallen from his face; she donned one of her own.

The Ellandaise had her at a steep disadvantage, but it was an uneasy one. She'd pushed their hand raiding their ships when she had – they'd been forced to move more quickly than they had planned. What weaknesses had that left them with?

'I trusts you had a restful night,' Lamont rumbled.

She raised her chin, drawing herself to her full height. 'I imagine yours was less so. There are many in my court who will oppose whatever you have planned.'

A muscle in his jaw ticked. 'There were somes, though not as manys as you might wish. And they were eliminated. Quickly.'

'Were they. I wonder.' Cold constricted her veins, but she kept her face placid, stony. *Yuri*. Surely he had managed to escape; he was nothing if not a survivor.

She did not dare to press Lamont for names, though — to do so risked revealing who she held nearest to her, or exposing those who might be hiding among his ilk, waiting for her to reemerge.

'Enough of this,' Anglimn said brusquely. 'Lamont, tell her what we want, and let us be done with it. This place smells like a sewer.'

The Kommodeur shrugged. 'Very well.' He turned back to Lu. 'Tomorrow, there is big ceremony down at your harbour. You will be sign a treaty that concedes control of Yulan City to us. You will be, as they say, our—' He glanced again at Anglimn. 'What is the word?'

'Puppet.'

Lu laughed with a boldness she did not feel — did not know if she were capable of ever feeling again. 'I'd sooner die.' The words, at least, rang true.

'That can be arranges,' the Kommodeur said sharply. 'But first, we will kill your little sister and make you watch.'

It took all her restraint not to attack him with her bare hands and fingernails. 'Is that so?' she said with as much calm as she could muster.

'What the Kommodeur means,' Anglimn interjected, 'is you should know that you are not irreplaceable. Neither of you. Should some tragedy befall you, we can always exchange you with your mother. We'd prefer to have you as a figurehead – you're far more popular with both the court and the city folk than either Rinyi or Min, and it gives the people the illusion of stability if your reign continues – but know we can very well move forward without you.'

Lu's nostrils flared as she breathed out again. 'Is that all? I would prefer to be alone, if so. Your company has worn a bit thin of late.'

Lamont frowned at her defiant tone. 'We comes here to move you to kinder accommodations, but I thinks for that comment alone, we leave you here until time of signing tomorrow. We shall have great public ceremony on deck of our new warship – *The Ryvan*. It arrives in your harbour last night, much to awe of your city folk. In centre of city.'

For all to see. So there can be no doubt as to the treaty's legitimacy, Lu thought with a sinking heart.

The Kommodeur turned heel and left the room. Anglimn turned to her once last time before following.

'Just do as you're told,' he murmured. 'It will go easier for you.'

Lu raised an eyebrow in exaggerated surprise. 'And what about me has given you the impression I prefer things easy?'

She managed to maintain her bravado until the door closed behind Anglimn and they heard the locks rattle back into place. As soon as the silence returned, though, she deflated.

It had been a very long time since she had wept like this, and the first time she could recall doing it in front of another person. It was the sort of crying that was less the fall of tears than the violent heaves of a body purging itself of poison. She wept for Hyacinth and her sardonic smile, gone forever. For sweet, trusting Jin, who had fallen for some mistaken ideal of her that did not exist. For herself, and the swiftly vanishing future she had imagined.

She crammed white-knuckled fists against her mouth to muffle the sound, not wanting it to carry down the corridor and reach Anglimn and Lamont.

They'd left the jailer's lantern behind, and in its paltry glow she could see Min's shocked face.

'Lu,' her sister murmured, reaching out a tentative hand. 'You're *crying*.'

'Of course I'm crying!' she snapped. Or, tried to. It was difficult to maintain any bite around the sobs still wracking her body.

'I didn't think ...' Min must have seen on Lu's face the amalgamation of hurt and irritation that shivered through her; she fell silent.

'What?' Lu said. She wiped the tears away with the heel of her palm, as though that might somehow mash them back into her body, but fresh ones only welled up to take their place. 'You thought I don't cry?'

'I suppose I didn't really believe you got scared,' her sister said. And then she added, 'It sounds pretty foolish now, when I say that aloud.'

'Of course I get scared,' she said, laughter burbling up

through her wet sobs. 'But I'm not crying because I'm scared. I'm crying because I'm *angry*.'

She supposed being angry didn't mean she wasn't also afraid, but she didn't want to mention that. Min had a tendency to feed off the worry of others. Her sister continued to watch her in the dim light. There was a wariness on her face that Lu recognised – like that of a struck hound who kept coming back for more because it did not know where else to go. But there was something new dawning there as well.

Hesitantly, Min reached out and, using the sleeve of her robe, wiped the tears beading along Lu's jawline. When their eyes met, she smiled, almost a bit regretfully, as though apologising for seeing Lu in this state. Or perhaps, apologising for never seeing her in this state before now.

That's not your fault, Lu wanted to tell her. Instead, she said, 'Maybe I'm a little scared.'

A startled laugh escaped her sister. And then all at once, both of them were laughing, the sound ricocheting off the cold, dank walls of the cell. It did not last long – neither of them had the energy or the humour left for it. Lu sighed, looking around the confines of the room. It was bigger than she'd originally thought – and somewhat less bleak than it had felt in the dark. The rushes beneath their feet were relatively fresh, and a pair of narrow benches lined one of the far walls.

'What're we going to do?' Min asked, her voice faint, as though the laughter had taken all but the last of that as well.

Before Lu could answer, the locks on the outside of their cell door began to jangle once more. Both girls stepped away from it apprehensively. For a vainglorious moment, Lu looked to the jailer's lantern and briefly imagined herself slipping it from its peg by the door and smashing it over Lamont's head as he reemerged into the room—

But as the door opened, four very different figures entered, escorted by the jailer from earlier, and draped head to toe in yellow batik robes.

Nunas?

Their hoods were up and their heads bowed in deference. The two girls in the lead held neatly folded stacks of silk in their proffered hands; Lu recognised her own scarlet outer robes embroidered at the shoulders with cranes, and the matching fringed gauze vest.

'They've been sent to help ready you for the signing of the treaty tomorrow,' the jailer told them.

His eyes cut to the lamp hanging beside the door, but before he could reach for it, Lu called out, 'We'll need that to dress, don't you think? Your new foreign masters would not be pleased if we appeared tomorrow looking dishevelled.'

The man frowned, but left the lamp behind when he departed.

The nunas had already begun busying themselves with finding a place to lay Lu and Min's clothing that avoided the damp or the muck clinging to the cell walls and floor. Two of them had lowered their hoods – Lu recognised Butterfly and Snowdrop immediately.

'Where are the rest of you?' Lu asked them.

'They locked us in Min's apartments,' Butterfly said.

'Just as they did when you ran – that is, back when you were exiled by Set,' Snowdrop supplied helpfully.

'Well, that was a temporary situation, much like this,' Lu told her as brightly as she could manage. Then she turned to the remaining two nunas. 'And who else have you brought with you?'

The taller of the two lowered her hood.

'*Nasan*?'

The Ashina girl grinned back at her. 'What do you think? Does yellow suit my colouring?'

'Not in the slightest,' Lu said, slipping into the insult as comfortably as if were an old pair of boots. 'How on earth ...' She gestured wordlessly as the last of the nunas pulled back her hood to reveal a nervous, heart-shaped face – also familiar.

'Adé!'

'I've never seen you so surprised,' Nasan said, inappropriately smug given the circumstances – but then, Lu thought, she could hardly be surprised by *that*.

'It's a bit disorienting,' Lu admitted. 'I've never been happy to see you before.'

'Well, you can thank Nok for it later,' the Ashina girl told her, her satisfaction quickly giving way to pragmatism.

Lu felt her heart leap, in a rather unpragmatic fashion. 'Nokhai found you, then – he's safe?'

'He's with Omair and Yuri. Safe as he could possibly get for now.'

So, Omair and Yuri were alive and well, too.

'Are you here to get us out?' Min asked eagerly.

'And how exactly would we do that, little princess?' Nasan asked. 'The door's locked, and we're on the wrong side of it.'

On instinct, Min recoiled at the carelessly sharp words, but Lu saw her sister steady herself, instead of fully shrinking back.

'Well, what are you doing here, then?' Min asked, a bit hotly.

Lu frowned at Nasan, folding her arms over her chest. The truth of the situation was beginning to sink in. 'Now there's six of us trapped here, instead of just two. I hope you have some weapons or tools under those robes.'

'Not quite,' Nasan said. 'If you want a weapon, the Yunian sparkstone is still our best option. You just need to get us to where you think it's hidden. Adé and I disguised as handmaidens are going to have a much easier time smuggling it out of the palace than you will.'

'If you think I'm just going to hand it over to you so you can do gods know what with it while I'm still a prisoner—'

Nasan shook her head. 'Once we're out, we can use it against the Ellandaise—'

'And I'm just supposed to trust you'll come back for us,' Lu concluded. She and Nasan fell silent, glaring at one another. 'We don't even know if that secret cache of sparkstone exists, let alone how to get to it,' Lu went on stubbornly. 'Or do you have some brilliant plan for that as well?'

'You said it yourself, the palace is *your* home—'

'So, the answer is "no," then.'

Min's eyes had been tracking between Lu and Nasan as they argued back and forth. Now, she spoke for the first time.

'I think *I* might have an idea,' she ventured timidly.

27

Grown

'You need to stop this, Lu,' Min insisted, looking nervously between her sister and the door. So far, the door remained shut, no jangle of the lock, no footfalls outside. The guards would not be far off though. '*Please*. If they see—'

'They won't see,' Lu countered loudly from across the cell, where she was at work, hunched down over one of the benches lining the wall. Min could not see exactly what she was doing, but her sister had insisted she could fashion a weapon out of its component pieces. And whatever it was, their jailers would not be pleased.

'Just calm down and stay quiet,' Lu added. The remark was thrown over her shoulder; she did not even bother to look at Min as she said it.

'Calm down?' Min demanded. She could hear how shrill she sounded, but could not stop. 'You're going to get us *killed*!'

'Keep your voice down!'

Footfalls emerged from the corridor, the pace unhurried. A guard making his routine rounds, most likely.

'I'm not dying for your vanity,' Min said, louder this time.

'Min, shut up and stop being such a *child*.'

That was it. Min whirled toward to the door and banged on the dense wood with both fists.

'Help!' she cried. 'It's my sister! She's trying to escape!'

An animal cry of rage tore out of Lu. With terrifying speed, she was across the room, strong arms wrapped around Min's waist, hauling her back.

The door banged open and a guard rushed in. Min caught the blur of his face as they both went tumbling to the cold floor, landing amid the rushes. A Hana mercenary; a traitor.

'*Help!*'

'What is going – you! Stop that!' The guard made to pull Lu up, then seemed to think better of it and ducked back out into the corridor. 'Ay! I need assistance over here!'

Two more men rushed in as Lu pinned Min to the floor. One of them helped the first latch onto Lu. 'Don't just stand there, go get help!' He cursed as one of Lu's gyrating arms caught him in the throat. 'And wake that foreigner up as well. These are his damned prisoners.'

'Get *off* me!' Lu screamed, still flailing.

'She's crazy!' Min sobbed as the third guard pulled her to her feet. 'Thank the gods you came when you did. She was going to kill me—'

'I still might,' Lu growled, lunging toward her with a ferocity it took both men holding her to contain.

Min whimpered and ducked behind the remaining guard.

'What's the problem here?'

Anglimn appeared in the doorway, flanked by a trio of Ellandaise soldiers, his face greyish and crumpled with sleep. He'd thrown on a robe, but Min could see the white edges of a nightgown underneath. He must have been quartered nearby to arrive so quickly – the Ellandaise seemed to have turned the palace into their own while Min and Lu were imprisoned.

He surveyed the scene before him grimly: Lu, hair dishevelled, white teeth flashing as she strained against the grip of two guards. Four nunas cringing in a far corner, faces hidden beneath their hoods, heavy and drooping like wet flowers. And Min herself, shrinking behind the guard who had been forced to pick her off the floor. A creature so meek and hapless she could not even be called cowardly, as that might suggest she had the potential to be anything else.

'Watch out! My sister, she's been trying to make a weapon from that bench over against the wall!' Min yelped.

'Traitor! You little worm!' Lu growled, making another leap toward her.

Realising she had no face left to lose, Min gave in and burst into tears.

Anglimn winced at the sound.

'Crying, as always,' Lu scoffed.

'I want to see my mother,' Min managed to choke out at Missar Anglimn between sobs, grabbing his arm with the desperation of a drowning thing. 'I d-demand to be taken to her.'

'It's a bit late for that. We gave you that opportunity, and you turned it down,' snapped Anglimn.

'I was wrong. I should've listened before. My sister – she's gone mad. She's going to kill me!' Min whined. Then, when his face remained impassive, 'My mother wouldn't be very pleased if her favourite daughter were killed on your watch. You wouldn't want to lose her loyalty, would you?'

That seemed to gain the foreigner's attention. He huffed, looking between the two girls: Min pleading and wide-eyed, Lu wild and seething. The three, four days they had been locked away had worn at them, left them raw as exposed bone. That must have been by design, but Min could see the doubt creeping into the edges of Anglimn's thoughts – and the irritation that chased it. He'd intended for the isolation to wear them down, make them brittle and quick to break, but not at the expense of his own comfort.

'Fine,' he said brusquely, turning to the guards. 'Escort her to the empress dowager's apartments.'

'Thank you!' Min sagged with relief, grasping Anglimn's sleeve in her hands for balance.

'Don't thank me yet,' Anglimn said, shaking himself loose. 'I'm in no way granting you the same deal you were offered originally. You'll stay with your mother until the signing of the treaty. We'll decide afterward what to do with you.'

He made to go, and the guards guided Min toward the door to follow behind.

'Wait!' She paused before the four nunas cowering in the corner. 'May I take my handmaidens with me? To help me dress for the ceremony tomorrow.'

Anglimn did not even bother to turn. 'Take them if you like. Just do not trouble me again.'

The nunas fell into step behind her. As the lot of them passed Lu, she sneered at Min.

'It's repulsive you ever sat upon my throne. Don't believe for a moment that you ever belonged there.'

She drew back and spat into the rushes at Min's slippered feet. In spite of herself, Min flinched away. But when she looked up again, Lu winked.

Min did not dare risk returning the gesture. But there was no need, she thought, as the guards shuffled her out the door; all was going according to plan.

'You should have followed our plan!' Rinyi chided, dipping a cloth into her glazed washing bowl and wringing it out. She used it to scrub at Min's face. Min twitched; the water was colder than she'd expected.

Like Anglimn, her mother had clearly just been roused from sleep. Min was startled to see burgeoning lines in the thin skin around her eyes and mouth – were those new, or had she just overlooked them before? Perhaps they had been hidden beneath her mother's rouges and powders, layered carefully as armour.

'What were you thinking, following your sister like that?' her mother went on.

What would she think if she knew the truth of it? That Min hadn't followed Lu into anything at all – she'd made a choice to reveal the Ellandaise plot. Had been equal partners in the decisions that had led her here, to this point. The thought of telling her quickened Min's pulse.

Whether out of excitement or fear though, she couldn't say.

Her gaze anxiously cut to where her ammas – no, nunas, she reminded herself; they had been demoted when she'd lost her crown – stood against the wall by the apartment vestibule. Butterfly and Snowdrop would be accustomed to Rinyi coddling Min in this way. Still, her face reddened in embarrassment. Not that any of them were paying attention; the figures that must have been Nasan and Adé looked half poised to slink back into the vestibule, out of sight.

'How could they keep you in that dungeon?' Her mother grimaced with what looked like real pain. She did not wait for a response, though. 'How frail you are! I could die just looking at you.'

'I'm fine,' Min mumbled, but Rinyi was yanking at the sleeves of Min's robes, pulling up the ties to inspect the ends, dirty and matted from being stepped on in the dark and dragged through the rushes. She made a sound of disapproval.

'You—' Her mother waved toward the closest of the nunas. When she did not respond right away, Min realised it was not a true nuna at all, but either Adé or Nasan. Based on the girl's height, she would wager Nasan. Her mother frowned, waving again. 'You, there! Wake up.'

Just do what she says, Min thought frantically. *It's not that difficult.*

Although, given what she knew of Nasan, maybe it *was* that difficult.

'Yes, Dowager Empress,' Butterfly said, swiftly stepping forward as though she had been the one addressed.

It worked. Rinyi's eyes slid to her without hesitation – one servant was as good as another. 'Go to Min's apartments and fetch her a change of clothing. The peach-coloured robes embroidered with camellias should do nicely.'

'Yes, Dowager Empress,' Butterfly said. Snowdrop fell into step beside her.

'I don't have those robes anymore,' Min realised, as the two girls crossed toward the door.

'Whyever not?' her mother demanded. 'I had them made for you not two years—'

'I destroyed all the clothes you had made for me once I was enthroned,' Min told her.

The edge in her voice brought a flicker of fear to her mother's eyes. Rinyi's hands fell away from her, and she threw the damp cloth down on the table beside the basin. She strode over to her vanity and began sorting through the items strewn across its surface, shovelling hairpins and baubles into its drawers with a good deal more force and noise than seemed necessary.

Min ignored her. 'Bring me something dark,' she told Butterfly and Snowdrop. 'The cobalt robes with silver stitching should do nicely.'

Taking advantage of her mother's preoccupation, Min circled over to Adé and Nasan, who were still hovering by the vestibule. Their posture was all wrong, the former shy and sheepish, the latter tense, stance too wide, like a stable hand – someone prepared to lift something heavy, rather than dress a lady. The faster they executed this part of the plan the better.

'Why don't you two fetch us a tea service? My mother

seems weary. And I've had a long morning.' She turned to Rinyi. 'That is, if you think that would be allowed.'

Rinyi sniffed, not looking up from the manufactured task of sorting her trinket. 'I don't see why not. Unlike your sister, I am not a prisoner here.'

Min thought it best not to question the fact that her mother viewed this as a point of pride.

Instead, she returned her attention to Nasan and Adé, ushering them into the vestibule where her mother couldn't overhear. 'Are you two still willing to split up? Nasan, you—'

'Gather reinforcements and meet at the harbour, got it. I know a few places where I might be able to find reliable recruits.'

Min nodded. 'And Adé? You remember the directions I gave you to the physician's office?'

The other girl nodded, but when she peered out from beneath her hood, her dark eyes were anxious. 'I'd feel better if I knew what sort of sedatives he kept on hand. And you're certain you don't know anything about how he organises his supplies?'

Min shook her head grimly. The physician had always come to her, not the other way around. And often enough, modesty demanded he attend to her through the buffer of a gauzy curtain. The only time this had not been the case was when he'd come to treat the wounds Brother inflicted on her, and she'd been in no state to observe the arrangement of his kit.

'You'll do fine,' she told Adé. 'Omair said you had years of training with him.' She did not actually know how relevant that work had been, but at this point what the girl needed more than knowledge was confidence.

'We'll be back soon,' Nasan promised.

'You really rid yourself of all your clothes?' her mother asked when Min slunk back into the main room of the apartment.

'They were clothes made for a little girl,' Min said. That had been what she told herself at the time. That seemed so long ago now – was that who she had been, someone who could be so satisfied over that incremental bit of meaningless rebellion?

'Well, that was foolish of you,' Rinyi huffed, but despite the reproach conveyed by her words, her voice was carefully mild.

'I suppose you're right. There was no need to destroy them,' Min murmured. She didn't feel chastened by the thought, though. Did not feel as though she'd lost something in admitting as much.

Her mother regarded her cagily, an oddly girlish uncertainty softening the stone grey of her eyes. The expression felt, Min thought, uncannily familiar – though she'd never seen it before. It was one she herself had made so many times.

Rinyi's lips parted as though to speak, but before she could, the front doors slid open. Butterfly and Snowdrop had returned, Min's cobalt robes draped carefully over Butterfly's arm.

Her mother's face shifted, like the sight of the nunas had suddenly reminded her of who she was supposed to be. 'The sun will be up soon enough,' she told the handmaidens. 'Hurry and dress her.'

Snowdrop began stripping Min of her soiled things as Butterfly laid out the fresh pieces. Rinyi retreated, perching on the hard edge of her bed. Min expected her to supervise as usual, but she gazed out the window instead. She felt acutely the absence of her mother's attention, much to her own irritation.

Adé returned, her face creased with worry. 'I couldn't get in,' she whispered. 'The physician's office was locked.'

Sweat beaded along Min's hairline. Was all lost?

Stupid. She had a mission here, and she'd wasted enough time already out of fear, just as she always did. Perhaps that was the core of the problem. Her insistence on doing what she had never done – getting what she wanted from her mother – by doing what she always did: avoiding, hiding, stepping apologetically around the point.

'It must be lonely,' Min blurted.

Rinyi looked up sharply. 'What must?'

Min licked her lips. She had such precious little practice being open, especially with Rinyi. The closest she had come had been *that day*, all those moons ago. But loneliness – that was a truth about her mother. And it was a truth Min knew herself.

'Being locked away by yourself. For all these moons,' she said.

Her mother's face hardened, eyes shooting between Min's nunas. Butterfly met Min's eyes and raised an eyebrow. Adé froze. Snowdrop's skittish gaze darted to the floor.

Min nodded at them. 'Go wait in the hall for now. I'll call you when I'm finished.'

When they'd gone, she removed the last of her soiled robes, then pulled one of her mother's dressing robes.

'It was unkind of Lu to lock you away,' she continued. 'Even with what she knew... She shouldn't have done that.'

Her mother's chin lifted. 'That girl was born trouble.'

'But you were lonely even before then, weren't you?' Min murmured. 'I didn't know any better because you'd been like that since I was born – longer, perhaps.'

Rinyi was watching her like she'd never quite seen her before.

'I only noticed once Set came back to court, as an adult,' Min said. 'It must have been like having a piece of your home here. Someone who also didn't belong amid all the Hu. All those people who believed in the lie of Lu's parentage. It must have felt like they were forcing you to be her mother. But not him.'

Her cousin had never been particularly warm, or kind. But he'd been canny enough to see in a base sort of way what people needed – or thought they did. Min had found that out firsthand. Rinyi would have been too smart by half to fall for that, but she might have allowed herself the indulgence of pretending now and then.

'He knew about Lu and Tsai, so he knew you. Was that the way of it?' Min murmured. 'And he was the only one. The only one on your side. You would have done anything he asked.'

When she looked up, there were tears in Rinyi's eyes. Then her mother blinked, and they were gone, as though they had never been there at all.

'Whatever you think you know—'

'You have the sparkstone, don't you?' Min asked. The room was growing lighter with the break of dawn.

Rinyi's jaw tightened. 'I don't know what you're talking about.'

'Did he tell you what it was? Or did he just ask you to hide it?' she pressed.

'It's none of your concern—'

'It is entirely my concern. Mother, we need that sparkstone.'

Rinyi's eyes narrowed. '*We*?'

But Min would not be cowed, not now, when she was so close. 'Yes, *we*. Lu and I have a plan to use the sparkstone—'

'Against the *Ellandaise*? A plan? And with Lu. Have you lost your mind? Do you not see the situation we – our family, our empire – is currently in? How am I to keep you safe if you won't—'

'It's not your duty to protect me anymore,' Min interrupted.

'Of course it is. You're a child. You *need* me.'

But the way she said it, Min could sense her sudden uncertainty in this, the core of their relationship. As though she had looked for something familiar and found it was no longer where she'd left it.

'The Ellandaise can't be trusted,' Min said. 'You know this, or you wouldn't have kept the sparkstone hidden from them.'

'What makes you think they don't know about it?'

'Because you still have it.'

Rinyi went silent at that.

'It's no accident I'm here,' Min told her. 'Lu and I have

428

a plan to disrupt the signing of the treaty tomorrow. But we need that sparkstone.'

'I'm afraid you'll need to think up a new plan, then. It shouldn't be too difficult – clearly you're both too clever for your own good.'

'Mother,' Min said softly. Rinyi's anger, she saw now, germinated from fear. Just as it always had. 'You've spent my whole life protecting me. And you succeeded. I'm grown – I have what I need. You've done right by me. So now, allow me to do the same for you.'

Her mother regarded her for a long, silent moment. Then: 'Come,' she said. And strode to the far side of the sitting room. Min followed and watched as she hunched down beside a settee and tossed up a corner of the rug. The exposed floor looked unremarkable, just a stretch of glazed tiles. But then her mother pulled the pin from her hair, loosing her enviable black locks in long cascades around her drawn, determined face. Using the point of the pin, she lifted the edge of a single tile and pried it from its setting.

Nestled in the space left by its absence was a stack of ageing papers tied with a thong, a folded silk blanket, and a fistful of rings and bracelets – modest, enamelled fare mostly, and rather dated. Nothing so precious it warranted hiding. At least, not as far as Min could tell.

Her mother held up the cloth Min had taken for a folded blanket. She saw now that it was a richly embroidered cloak, gathered at the collar with a series of silver links and an intricately carved amethyst clasp.

'Pretty, isn't it?' her mother said, admiring the cloth in the morning light. It was spangled with tiny panels, each depicting a different type of flower. 'In Bei Province, it's an old custom for girls to sew betrothal cloaks for themselves before they marry. It's believed the more beautiful the cloak, the happier the marriage will be. Of course, I never had much a knack for embroidery, so my mother had this one commissioned for me. Perhaps that was where my bad luck originated.'

She let it fall; Min watched the silk pool on the floor. 'Hold these,' her mother instructed, heaping the cheap jewellery into Min's lap, followed by the bundled papers.

Min's eye was drawn to a familiar block of spidery blood-red ink emblazoned on one of the pages. Her father's stamp. She glanced up quickly; her mother was bent over the recess in the floor, immersed in her task. Min unfolded the bottom half of the paper to reveal the end of a letter:

> — And again, please do not concern yourself with the short duration of our courtship, nor the matter of your prior betrothal to Hwangmun. Neither of these factors could dampen my enthusiasm for our marriage. I mourn the loss of my late brothers, of course, yet I can think of no greater consolation than knowing you and I will honour their memory together, as man and wife.
>
> With the deepest fondness,
> Daagmun

Had she not seen for herself the blunt, childish strokes of his penmanship forming the words, Min would not have believed her father capable of writing them. It was hard to say which was more unlikely: their tenderness, or their eloquence.

She hastily refolded the paper, but when she looked up, her mother was watching her.

Min reddened, but before she could apologise, Rinyi said, 'He made lovely promises, didn't he?' Her mouth tightened into a smile that was both acidic and wistful. 'His letters filled my head with all sorts of ideas of what my life would be like in the capital. Of course, once I arrived here, I realised your father had all the passion and wit of a stone, and that those letters had been written by his tutors, then painstakingly copied in his own hand. I suppose I should have been flattered I warranted such deception. But perhaps I'll tell you about that another time. For now, this is what you want.'

In her hands, she held a bundle the size of a brick, wrapped in plain white silk. Min reached for it, and for a moment she thought her mother was going to pull it back. But the panic and doubt on her face smoothed away, and she handed it over.

'Careful,' she cautioned. 'Set told me it was volatile. Even the smallest amount could kill either one of us.'

Min gazed down at the unremarkable parcel in her hands. It was surprisingly dense and heavy, and perhaps it was only her imagination, but she felt an ambient warmth coming from it. It felt almost alive.

'What will you do with it, then?' Rinyi asked.

Min hesitated. She had imagined herself walking out to the harbour with the sparkstone tucked under her robes. But the Ellandaise would likely search her and Lu before-hand, wouldn't they?

Her eyes fell to her mother's betrothal cloak, still pooled on the floor.

'You said you weren't much for embroidery. How about just basic stitching?'

28

Treaty

Lu winced, feeling every bump and jostle of the palanquin ferrying her to the harbour. She hadn't slept more than an hour in her dank cell before the guards returned to escort her to her apartments where several of Min's nunas had been conscripted into dressing her. They'd done the best they could – Lu's things had been heavily looted in the chaos of the Ellandaise attack and there were scarcely any hairpins or jewellery left to pair with her robes – but she had still emerged into the pale morning light looking every bit a prisoner.

They had put Min and Lu into separate litters, and Anglimn rode with her sister in the second. The nunas would walk alongside them. Across the cramped box of Lu's palanquin, the Kommodeur stared intently at her. She looked back, deliberately resting her gaze on his short arm, in the place where his hand had been. Last time she had seen him, he'd worn it in a sling. That was gone now, and the bandage was covered by the sleeve of his stiff formal jacket. Someone had pinned the end closed, neat as a parcel. When Lamont dropped the arm down to his side – he did so now, tucking it against the folds of his coat, just above an enormous belt heavy with weapons he could no longer wield – it was scarcely noticeable at all. If one did not know what to look for.

'It must hurt,' Lu said lightly, allowing the sparest smile. When he did not answer, she went on. Like worrying a scab. 'Today's treaty signing is an exercise in pageantry, isn't it? One of your leaders being so grievously injured does not agree with the image of strength you wish to convey. I imagine you will have frequent trouble with this going forward.'

'We not need for pageants. We have true strengths. And you, only weakness,' Lamont told her. Under the neat trim of his moustache, a pale, false smile appeared to match her own.

'Weakness,' she repeated evenly. 'Is that what I'm meant to feel right now?'

To her surprise, he laughed. But the sound was wrong – hollow and harsh. A weapon rather than a reflex.

He leaned forward, eyes tracing the contours of her face, the whole of her form, in a way that left her feeling swallowed whole and spat up again. His posture foisted desire at her, but in the feverish wells of his eyes, she recognised revulsion. A hunger and a hatred that were inextricable from one another.

'I wish you could sees how exquisite you are,' he told her. 'I travels the world over and never see anything like you. How many times I have written home to Elland about the Girl King of the Hanaman? Just as many time as I fails to describe your magnificence. And these strange eyes of yours . . .'

He raised his remaining hand and stroked a finger across her cheekbone, following the contour of her eye.

It took all of Lu's will not to smack him away. Instead, she turned her head, slipping free from his touch.

'Kommodeur,' she said evenly, 'I may be your prisoner—'

'Not prisoner. Think yourself my ... guest.'

'Whatever I may be to you, I am still a Hu Emperor. I will always be a Hu Emperor. And I do not know what etiquette you practice back in the land you call home, but here in the Empire of the First Flame, commoners do not *touch* the emperor.'

Perhaps she had spoken too quickly for him to follow her Yueh. For a long moment he did not react. Then the large man's pale, glassy eyes flashed in anger and his mouth tightened into a short, whitening line. For half a breath, Lu thought he might strike her, here in the tight confines of the covered litter.

'The bitch queen mistakes my meaning,' he said. 'Where I comes from, men do not take up with leavings of dog. Nor *wolves*.'

Lu stiffened, returning his triumphant gaze with forced cold contempt. She could not let herself lose control. Soon enough, she would have all the revenge she could stomach. But not now.

Mercifully, the litter came to a stop. She smelled brackish air, rotting fish innards under a hot sun. They had arrived.

Bright early morning light assailed them as they emerged from the cocoon of the palanquin. Lu squinted, and when her eyes adjusted, she saw the ship. It rose from the lapping water like a wall before her: an Ellandaise-style junk, all dark wood and brass trim. Big enough that, from this close, it seemed to block the estuary where the Milk River met the bay, and the stone jetty and open ocean beyond that.

Turning back in the direction they had come, she could see the harbour path snaking alongside the river. Eventually, the path would join back into Kangmun Boulevard, which ran unbroken, save for the gates between the Rings, from here to the Immaculate City. At her back stood a retaining wall that stabilised the steep drop between the city's edge and the harbour. The wall was interrupted periodically by large, arching footbridges that allowed quick passage between the docks below and the city above. The city that would soon be hers again, if she and Min were successful.

Min and Missar Anglimn were already waiting at the foot of the ship's gangplank. Her sister was wearing an ostentatious cloak Lu had never seen before. Its embroidery was shot through with seed pearls and clasped at the throat with a carved chunk of amethyst the size of a child's fist. No doubt something Rinyi had foisted on her.

'Go on then,' Lamont said brusquely, giving her a shove at the small of her back.

She stumbled, shooting him a poisonous glare, but made her way over to the ship. Min looked up at her approach, her face carefully neutral.

She ought to look more afraid, Lu thought. She fixed her own expression into a scowl. Min seemed to understand; she made a show of flinching.

Lu was startled to find the docks crowded. And not just

with sailors. She saw farriers in their heavy leather aprons, and shopkeepers, and tanners with their arms stained up to the elbows with dye. Some were clustered with their families, trailed by small children. Ordinary city folk.

Had they all come to gawk at her? And could Nasan's people really be in their midst?

'Pink scum!' someone jeered from the thick of the crowd. Lu looked up sharply as something flew through the air and smacked onto the stone path by Anglimn's feet, glistening wetly. She recognised it more on smell than sight. A long-expired octopus, no doubt pulled from the bait stores of one of the fishing boats clustered along the harbour.

Anglimn recoiled.

'Take your foreign mud and go home!' Another voice, this time coming from one of the footbridges overhead. It was followed by a shower of rotting vegetables, small stones, and worse. Lu ducked. The Ellandaise guards surrounding them hoisted their weapons uneasily, but Anglimn waved them down.

'No shooting!' he said sharply. Then he lowered his voice so the gathered crowd could not overhear. 'Idiots! Look how many of they there are. You shoot one, the rest will fall upon us like swarm of hornets.'

'Or flee like the lowing beasts they are,' Lamont seethed, clearly still entertaining the thought of picking off one or two.

'We should have conducted this signing in the palace Heart as I suggested, without all the rabble,' Anglimn told him.

'We needs these rabble,' Lamont countered. 'They will

sees for themselves how their Girl King concedes power to us. It is legitimise our treaty. They are our witness.'

Anglimn frowned, casting an anxious glance back at the hostile crowds as he turned toward the gangplank. 'Let us get this over with quickly, then.'

Lu made to follow him aboard, flanked by Min and the ammas.

'No servants,' Lamont said sharply, speaking more to Anglimn than her. 'We not wants to remind people these two have power over anyone – even little girls in yellow robes.'

'They are meant to escort us at all times. An empress, even a princess, does not attend formal occasions without them. It will look strange,' Lu objected, doing her best to keep the panic from edging into her voice.

Lamont reached down to his belt and extracted a pistol from its holster. He pointed it at the head of the nuna closest to him. The girl looked up at the weapon, her hood slipping back over her plaited black hair. It was Snowdrop. Her round, startled face bloodless, disbelieving.

Lu stared. The Kommodeur had lost his gun hand to Nokhai's wolf, and he held this pistol with the other.

Lamont followed her gaze, pressing out a thin smile as though reading her mind. 'It is perfectly capable of pulling a trigger. At this distance, I can hardly miss, yes?' he told her. 'Now, these girls is going back to palace. Or we leaves them here on ground. You understands?'

Snowdrop made a sound like something small being stepped on.

'Go on,' Lu told the girls, keeping her voice as even as

possible. Butterfly grabbed Snowdrop's hand and yanked her into their fold, glancing back. Lu met her dark eyes as they peered out from under her hood.

Lamont reholstered his gun, then touched his hand to Lu's shoulder as though to guide her forward. The gesture must have looked gentle enough to the gathered crowd, but she felt the malice in it. 'Do not thinks to cross us, Girl King. You will sign the treaty, and makes no trouble.'

He took his hand away from her and rested it on the butt of his gun.

'No trouble,' she agreed.

29

Bridge

The footbridges were already packed full when Nok managed to squeeze his way onto one. He wasn't able to get far – the densest of the throng had congregated at the centre of the arch, which granted the best vantage point from which to watch the Ellandaise ship. But as it turned out, he did not need to.

'Nok!'

He turned toward the sound of his sister's voice. She waved at him as he made his way toward her.

She was packed in as tightly as anyone else, flanked by a group of recruits that regarded him with anything from mild hostility to curiosity to—

'The Blue Wolf of Heaven!'

It took Nok a moment to place the man grinning at him as though they were old friends. Then the thin sheen of sweat on his forehead and the telltale blown black pupils reminded him.

'The poppy den! You were there,' he blurted. And then, with some annoyance, 'You *chased* me.'

The man had the grace at least to look sheepish. 'I was excited.'

'You could've got me killed!'

Nasan interjected. 'And I'm sure Yong is very sorry.'

Nok looked at her. 'You did hear him say I met him in a poppy den, right? I thought you weren't taking addicts.'

'I gave it some thought and decided it was a rather backward position on my part,' Nasan told him. And then she shrugged. 'Besides, we need all the help we can get right now, no?'

'I'm ready to defend my city with you, my new family. My new Kith,' Yong said eagerly.

Nok frowned. His sister was right about needing all the help they could get – there couldn't have been more than a dozen or so recruits following her. 'This is everyone?'

'There are others—' his sister started.

'They've arrived!' someone shouted, and impossibly, the press seemed to grow denser still as those already on the bridge were shoved forward by new onlookers. Nok closed his eyes as he was jostled, having the distinct sense that if he lost his footing now, he might simply be carried forward by the pressure of the bodies closed in around him.

Beside Nok, Yong trembled with excitement. 'Nasan promised we will receive our cauls as soon as this is over,' he said.

Nok sighed. 'Did she, now?'

'I'd like a creature with wings,' Yong told him. 'I've always wanted to fly.'

'That's not really how it works. You don't—'

But he forgot what he was saying as a line of palanquins arrived and came to a rest just before *The Ryvan*. Anglimn and Min rose from the first, along with Min's ammas.

Lamont emerged from the one behind it – followed by Lu. She was far enough away that he could scarcely make out the contours of her face, but he knew her well enough to see the exhaustion in her posture, the prickling straight-backed wariness with which she tracked Lamont's movements as he herded her and Min toward the ship's gangplank.

Min looked scarcely better, though that was largely due to the way she cowered and shrank away from both Lamont and her sister.

'Min better have the sparkstone, or we're all screwed,' Nasan muttered from his side, clearly sceptical. 'Do you think she's capable? We've got a lot of lives hinging on her.'

Nok thought of the shrinking, shiftless creature he had first seen as a child, and of the rage-stoked conflagration who had nearly killed him in the Inbetween. Then he thought of the tired, thoughtful girl petting a cat in the garden, the morning of Lu's enthronement. The cord of steel that he had perceived running through her.

'People can change,' he said.

His sister looked sidelong at him. 'Not in my experience.'

30

Treaty

Lu watched from the main cabin as *The Ryvan* cast off. They did not have far to go – only to the centre of the Milk River, where they would be visible from both banks. Nevertheless, the dock was lined with dozens of uniformed foreign guards bearing rifles, flanked by several rows of imperial soldiers keeping the excited crowd at bay. She wondered what the crowd might have done if they'd broken through. Torn Lamont apart, perhaps. But what of her? Was she still theirs, or would they have turned on her, too, for her part – her weakness, her failure – in all this?

The crowd began to thin as *The Ryvan* drifted further out onto the water. They had seen the rifles, watched Lamont and Anglimn disappear into the ship. Their window for action had closed, if it had ever existed at all.

Fanfare without substance. The Ellandaise had won, and they would do what they would do. Either way, the poppy tar would flood the city even more than it already had – regardless of whether she signed their bit of paper or not.

'You may as well sit,' Lamont told her. He filled the

entrance of the cabin, leaning his good shoulder against the doorframe. She looked away, but she could feel his eyes upon her, as though his gaze had a weight. 'You're not going anywhere. Even your sister knows that.'

He nodded toward Min, seated at an ornate table. Anglimn sat adjacent, elbows propped on the tabletop, face hidden in his hands. Min's were folded in her lap, and she looked smaller than she truly was under the gaudy weight of the cloak draped over her shoulders. When Lu looked at her, Min's eyes darted up to meet hers, mouse-quick. There was something else there besides nerves, though. A desperation that went beyond the terms of their current situation.

Her sister was trying to tell her something.

What, exactly, could have been any number of things. Where the sparkstone was, to begin with. How they might ignite it — surely if her sister had managed to acquire the sparkstone, she wouldn't have forgotten a bit of flint to set it ablaze. And — crucially — how they might escape afterward.

Feigning a posture of defeat, Lu slumped into a chair across the table from Min.

'Doesn't that feels better?' Lamont said with false cheer. 'I go above now. I thinks you can manage watching two girls, Anglimn?'

Anglimn started, as though being pulled awake from an unexpected sleep. He nodded belatedly. 'Of course.'

Lu studied him as Lamont departed. She and Min could not talk openly in front of him, but she found she had questions she wanted to ask him as well.

'Missar Anglimn. You lived here for years,' she said slowly. 'You brought your wife here. You raised your son here. How can you just stand by and watch that oaf tear this country apart?'

Anglimn slowly turned to look at her. The way the cold morning light hit his features left his skin looking like tallow. Had he always been so thin? She likely didn't look much better. The past few moons of strain and sorrow had left her hollow-cheeked and pallid. But she was still a creature with a purpose. She still had something left to do, something to kill for; he did not.

'You won't win me over, Girl King,' he told her.

She knew that. His loyalty was to his own people – his own interests. Just as it always had been. But she was curious. 'There must have been some part of you that thought of this place as home.'

He looked away, silent for so long she was ready to give up. But then he spoke: 'I was fascinated with your kind. Ever since I was a little boy. I devoured every written account in our city's library, every tall tale a sailor ever told. No one understood my fixation. They all told me you were barbarians – decadent, backward. Ruled by heathen despots. In school we were taught about the first of our explorers who made contact here. Do you know the story? Not the one involving your great-grandfather Kangmun. Much earlier. Our men sailed into port with the purpose of bringing our gold, our trade, our faith. Your emperor snubbed them—'

Lu knew the story; anyone with a basic education did. 'That was merely a Hana king, not an emperor. He was not Hu.'

'He snubbed them,' Missar Anglimn went on, as though she'd never spoken. Perhaps he saw no difference. Not between the Hana and Hu, and not between her speaking and her silence. 'Your emperor feared the unknown,' he told her.

'He wasn't an emperor.' Lu looked across the table in surprise; it was her sister who had spoken this time.

Anglimn continued. 'So, this exploratory Ellandaise party, they returned to their vessel, only to find they had been moored in place by low tide. And then, do you know what your people did?'

Not my people, she thought. *My mother's* – But no, they weren't even that, were they? She had no mother. Not truly. Tsai had only been the ghost of one, and Rinyi, less than that ...

'They set fire to the ship,' she heard herself say, rote as reciting a history lesson. But the words awoke something in her. *Fire.* That which had given the Hana life, and that which they had used to fight darkness and death. A simple weapon, but poetic. And poetry held power; Kangmun had understood this when he merged the Hu tiger of his banners with the First Flame of the conquered Hana, forging the two into one. Into whatever Lu – and her sister – were now.

Anglimn began to speak again, but this time, Lu cut him off. 'As your men emerged from below deck to escape the smoke, our archers filled them with arrows from shore. Many Ellandaise were burned alive. Those who swam to shore were bludgeoned to death.'

Anglimn watched her, grey and brittle as unglazed porcelain. 'Such savagery,' he said. 'Sitting upon such immense wealth. Such possibility. All for the taking.'

He said it so easily she thought perhaps she'd misheard him. But no, not this man with his carefully cultivated manners, his flawless, studied Yueh. His bloodless precision.

'Once, I thought it more than that,' he continued. 'Lamont—' He waved a dismissive hand at the other man's name. 'Lamont sees this land as nothing more than an opportunity. A frontier to be conquered. It could be anywhere, to him. He's fixated on *you* – but you could be any woman, so long as she was foreign. New. But I saw this place for what it was, and more fool me, I found it beguiling. Your language, your dress, the backward ways you stumbled into beauty, art. I always thought of the wealth I acquired from my business as merely the means by which I could continue living here. The means by which my son could live here – *be* from here in a way I could not.'

Lu met his pink-rimmed eyes, gazed into the shivering pale blue of his irises. She'd always sensed intelligence in them, curiosity. A keen anxiety to dissect and consume the world. Now, those same eyes were tepid wells of despair. They saw nothing; perhaps they never had.

The man lowered his gaze first. 'It turns out, wealth is all there is – and all there ever was,' he told her bitterly. 'So, I will take what I can, and leave the rest to rot.'

She stared at him, but he fell silent and did not speak again.

There were so many ancient things in this world. Ancient things with ancient weight. This world was so much older than money, than nations, than men. It was not her fault Anglimn, with his coins and his charts and his poisoned grief, could not comprehend that.

But soon enough, she would help him see. She only needed one chance.

Abovedeck came the sound of the crew stirring and setting to work. Slowly, the ship drew to a stop. Out the window, Lu could see the wide breadth of the river, embraced by its twin banks. On the north side, the rambling stands and shops, the tumbledown runoff of Scrap-Patch Row. And to the south, the high, elegant walls of the compounds of wealthy foreigners like Anglimn.

Lamont reappeared in the doorway. 'It's time,' he told them, his pale eyes bright and eager.

Anglimn moved to join him, muttering about particulars, and in that moment Min spoke: 'The cloak,' she whispered as she stood.

'Not your finest look,' Lu said, with a lightness she did not feel.

'No. *It's* sewn into the lining of the cloak.'

Lu resisted the urge to turn and face her. Instead, she gestured for her sister to go first, ahead of her. Min began moving slowly, deliberately toward the doorway where Anglimn and Lamont waited. As she did so, Lu murmured, 'We'll do it abovedeck, when we're meant to sign. Drop and ignite it—'

'The deck is filled with soldiers,' Min pointed out. 'We'll be shot full of holes before they even know what we're up to, and *poof*! There goes the sparkstone. And me along with it—'

'What are you two whispering about?'

The Kommodeur sauntered forward, and the weapons on his belt shifted and rang with the off-kilter rhythm of his steps. Lu glanced down at them. His remaining hand was resting on the butt of his gun – poor odds she would be able to wrestle it away from him. But the sword that hung uselessly from the other side, below his shortened arm, was a possibility. Unlike the gun, it might be ceremonial, but then, it might not. At any rate, a ceremonial blade still had an edge.

And, she reminded herself. *A dull blade hurts more.*

He was too far away, though. She needed to draw him closer.

Without a second thought, she whipped forward and grabbed Min around the throat. Her sister let out a shriek of surprise that she did not have to fake.

'You think once you're rid of me you'll sit on the throne again?' Lu growled, giving Min a hard shake. In the process, her hand slipped and dislodged the amethyst clip of her cloak, sending it cascading to the floor.

Min's eyes widened in surprise – and relief.

'For heaven's sake—' Lamont growled, lunging forward to pull them apart.

Lu dropped her hold on Min and in one smooth arc, yanked the sword free from Lamont's belt. It was of a foreign make, weighted heavier than she was used to, but even the wild hack she leveraged at his face was enough to force him back.

'Anglimn!' Lamont shouted, but the other man was no fighter; he thought for too long and reacted too little. He stood rigid, confused, and in doing so gave Min the time to seize one of the chairs from around the table and slam it into his back. It wasn't a hard hit, but hard enough. He stumbled forward, allowing her to strike him again, more precisely this time.

Lamont went for his gun and fumbled, his remaining hand too slow. Lu saw a chance and took it, drawing back with the clunky blade and jabbing him. The dense weave of his coat caught much of her momentum, but the point sliced through and sank into the soft meat of his belly. She pulled hard to extract it, and in its wake a dark pool rapidly appeared.

It took the Kommodeur by such surprise his face hardly changed expression at all. The gun slipped from his hand and he stumbled back, reaching to brace himself with the hand that was no longer there. Instead, the bandaged end of his arm slammed into the wall behind him and he let out a throaty cry.

Lu ran forward and kicked the gun away from him. It skittered wildly across the smooth, new floor of the cabin and hit the adjacent wall. They both watched it go, then looked at one another. Lu made for the weapon; Lamont fled out the door and up the stairs.

Lu cursed. 'Min! Grab the gun!' she shouted.

Anglimn recovered, and hearing her words, cast about wildly until he saw the weapon lying on the floor, not two paces away. He scrambled for it on hands and knees, just as her sister reached out for it—

Lu leapt over and slammed a foot down on the merchant's back. The breath burst out of him, and he rolled, landing on his back, belly up like a dying roach. She rested the tip of her purloined sword at the base of this throat, where the skin was thinnest.

'T-think about what you're doing,' he squeaked out, hands raised before him in supplication. 'If you kill me, you have no way of getting off this ship. A dozen of my men would cut you down before you even tried. But if you had leverage – say, if you took me as a hostage—'

'I have leverage,' Lu told him, as Min approached from behind her, holding both Lamont's gun and the weaponized cloak. Lu reached out her hand and felt the cold, dangerous weight of the pistol-like weapon nestle against her palm. 'I have this – and the cache of sparkstone Set left in the Immaculate City. And with it, I can obliterate this entire ship, and everyone on it.'

Anglimn looked up at her with fear-glazed eyes. For a moment, neither of them spoke, the air filled with the sound of their panting. He licked his lips.

'You should have gone home while you had the chance,' Lu said, and was surprised by the twinge of genuine pity she felt. 'That's what you wanted, wasn't it? After your son died? But you stayed. It is strange, how we sometimes do things simply because they are expected of us. Or perhaps because we expect them of ourselves. It's sad, though. It will take your spirit a long time to find its way back. The stretch of sea from here to Elland is so vast, as I understand.'

'My spirit ... ?' A flicker of life returned to his face, and some part of her words seemed to connect. Or perhaps it was not her words, but the look in her eyes. She could not see it, of course, but she could feel it. Terrible and white-hot as the heart of a fire.

She plunged the sword down.

31

Blessing

Min chased her sister up the stairs, in pursuit of Lamont. They found him on the quarterdeck of *The Ryvan* — standing beside a podium that no doubt held his precious treaty. He was flanked by some dozen foreign soldiers, rifles raised and levelled at their heads. On either bank of the river, Min could see gathering crowds of city folk. They shouted at the ship, though she could not make out their words.

'It's over,' Lamont seethed, and this time he had no air of impudent nonchalance, no smirk. He was upright, but hunched to the side, his hand pressed against the growing dark spot on his coat, where Lu had stabbed him with his own blade. 'You moves, speaks — breathes in a way I don't likes — and these men shoot you full of holes.'

'It's all right, Min,' Lu said loudly. 'They won't do it. The sparkstone might kill us, but it'll take this whole ship up — and them with it.' Her voice was robust with what sounded like her usual bravado. But Min had grown up hearing it, and she could tell the difference between the real thing, and the imitation her sister put forth now.

'Fair assessment, but these mens aren't armed with sparkstone,' Lamont sneered. 'Just ordinary bullets. Still, ordinary bullet? Enoughs to kill a man – or girl. Two girls, even.'

'Do it, and we all die.'

Unlike Lu, Min's voice trembled, and there was nothing she could do to stop it. She held her mother's cloak aloft, taking care to spread it out before both her and Lu. 'They might not have Yunian sparkstone, but *I* do. This fabric is lined with my late husband's cache of the stuff – you heard him speak of it, did you not? One shot – one wrong move – and we'll all be burnt to hell.' She wasn't sure if that was true, but she felt the fear of it nevertheless. Maybe they would feel it, too.

'You lies,' Lamont said, eyes narrowing. Min noticed however, that he didn't move toward her.

'She's not lying,' Lu replied stonily. 'But if you're so certain she is, why don't you try it and see what happens?'

Min looked sharply at her sister. Lu lifted her arm from behind the cloak, and with it, Lamont's gun. The one loaded with his remaining supply of Dust of Annihilation.

Lamont stared at her, uncertain. For a moment his pain seemed forgotten and he attempted to step toward her. Lu cocked the gun. 'Don't think I won't do it,' she told him. 'I've already killed your friend Anglimn, and frankly, I liked him a little better than I like you.'

The Kommodeur stopped short and winced, clutching his side. He did not seem particularly upset by the news of Anglimn's death. 'Think of what your sister just say! If you shoots, perhaps we dies, but also, you dies. Entire ship goes up in flame.'

He took another step forward. 'You gives the gun to me.'

'Stop right there,' Lu warned.

He did not stop.

Her sister discharged the gun. She wasn't much of a shot; it went wide and struck several paces off from where Lamont stood. A miss, but far from harmless. Instantly, an icy blue plume of fire taller than a man blossomed up in its wake.

The odour was eerie – there was the reek of burning varnish, and the wood beneath, but beneath it Min smelled something cold and clean and brutal, like smelling stone, or the first bite of a frigid winter day, the sort that stung tears to her eyes. It made her think of the mountains of Yunis.

'What are you waiting for?' Lamont shrieked as the soldiers fled from the crater formed by Lu's stray bullet. 'Kill her! Kill them both!'

But Lu was already grabbing Min by the hand, throwing the cloak over both their backs.

'Aim for their heads!' Lamont hollered. 'Don't hit the cloak!'

Lu led them past the main mast, toward the boat's prow. One, two shots followed them, but no more, the risk of hitting the cloak apparently too great. They were passing the foremast when another shot rang out. Min felt someone give her a great push – or at least, they must have, because all at once she was falling. She landed on her hands and knees, slipping out from under the cloak as Lu kept running, oblivious to what had happened.

What *had* happened? Min felt a strange heat in her arm, small at first, then spreading, almost like a blush.

She'd been shot.

'Min!' Lu stopped, made to turn back, but another bullet whizzed by, forcing her behind a stack of crates. Min watched as her sister tore open the lining of the cloak, using her hands, then her teeth. Finally, with shaking hands, she withdrew one of the packets of powder Min and her mother had patched into the lining.

'We should jump,' Min panted. The shock of being shot was beginning to wear off, and in its place, a burning pain. Not good. She was at best a poor swimmer, and the idea of dropping down the full height of *The Ryvan* into the murky, brackish deep of the Milk River with a wounded arm sounded as close to certain death as she'd ever been. But they'd reached the absolute fore of the ship, short of crawling onto the spar that stabbed out from its hull. It was either that, jump, or turn back to Lamont and the crackling blue fire engulfing the quarterdeck behind them. Min imagined it consuming, with cold implacability, the captain's cabin below. Anglimn's body, left sprawled on the floor.

Another shot rang out. It struck one of the crates Lu was hidden behind, embedding itself in the wood with a thud.

'Lu,' Min said, staggering to her feet. 'It's either the river, or surrender. Or we both die.'

Her sister's full mouth had become a thin, grim line. She had scooped powder into the narrow barrel of the pistol and was using a small stick folded into its underside with a hinge to pack it in. 'You're not going to die.'

And then Lamont was there, standing not ten paces away. He had his own weapon; he'd taken up one of the long rifles carried by his men. With some difficulty, he balanced it on the end of his maimed arm and levelled it at Min.

'You comes out *immediately*, or I shoots your sister,' Lamont bellowed at Lu. His voice drew closer, and Min could hear the heavy, unsteady stomp of his gait. How deeply had Lu stabbed him? Perhaps, Min thought with the desperate optimism of the cornered and dying, he might drop dead before he reached them. It wouldn't save them – the soldiers at his back would see to that – but it might at least be satisfying.

'There is nowhere left to goes,' Lamont continued. 'My mens, they lower the lifeboats. We take you back to shore – this, it not have to go badly.'

Lu loaded another lead ball into the gun, cocked the hammer, and stood. She came out slowly, from behind the stack of crates, pointing the gun at the Kommodeur with one hand, and holding aloft the flint with the other.

He nodded in acknowledgement of the situation. 'You puts down the gun, and we makes bargain, here. Man to man, if you wills. Anglimn, you say he is gone, so I speaks for the Eastern Flame's interests now.'

Lu did not respond.

'Hurry now,' Lamont urged. 'You, protected by that cloak, but not your sister. I only needs one of you. Drops the weapon, or I shoot her.'

The pain in Min's arm was finally beginning to register in full – searing. Blood dripped from it, painting the hang of her robes, and splatting wetly onto the deck. For a moment, there was only that sound, and the furious crackle of the steadily approaching fire.

The gun shivered in Lu's grip. And then she crouched down and set it on the ground.

'You, now. Kicks it here,' Lamont said.

She did as she was told.

Min hurried over to her as Lamont picked it off the ground, sagging in obvious relief. 'It's over,' he told them. 'Get in lifeboat. We redraws the treaty and haves you sign it in your palace Heart.'

Behind him, the fire drew closer, moving unnaturally fast, eating through the ship like it were made of straw. Already one of the lifeboats had caught, and then men who had been preparing it abandoned it to the flames. As they ran to the other side of the ship, Min could see the sweat pouring down their red, panicked faces. One of them leapt from the gunwale, apparently preferring to contend with the Milk's temperamental currents.

'Lu,' Min implored. 'Let's go. It's over.'

But her sister shook her head. 'It'll never stop,' she murmured to herself, and Min was puzzled to see tears in her eyes. 'If we leave them with anything, they'll only want more, and more, until they take it all.'

What do you mean? Min wanted to ask, but the words died in her throat, fell to dust, and she choked on them. Her body sensed the answer before her mind – or perhaps it was only that her mind refused to accept the knowledge of what was about to happen.

Lamont seemed then, to sense it, too. Both of them a little too late.

Lu swept the cloak over Min, grabbed her by the arm, and ran toward the edge of the ship. It wasn't far.

This is it, Min told herself as the edge came closer. She couldn't swim much, but her sister could. That might be enough. Lu wouldn't leave her.

And then Lu leaned forward and kissed her on the forehead. The gesture sent ice radiating through Min's veins. Something was wrong. Her sister could be loving, in her own loud, forceful way. But she was never tender.

This kiss was, though. Tender, and oddly warm. Searing beneath the skin, almost like the bullet had. Close to familiar, like something she'd felt in a dream, keenly, then forgotten until now—

Another shove. This time a real one, not a bullet. And Min was falling backward, plummeting through the air. Alone.

Below, the churning murky water rose up to meet her. And when she looked up – that one last moment, oddly still, impossibly quiet, suspended timeless in her mind as though in amber – Lu was turning away.

She wouldn't leave me, Min thought again.

But her sister was already gone.

32

Ignite

Lu could only hope the fall wouldn't kill Min. Her sister had never been much of a swimmer, but better the water than what was to come.

'What do you thinks you're doing?' Lamont demanded, looking incredulously between her and the edge of the ship where Min had disappeared. He strode forward, wincing every time he put weight on the side where she'd stabbed him. 'Girl King—'

He should not have called me that.

Lu's fist caught him directly in the stab wound. She plunged it in and twisted. She'd have preferred to go for his throat, but he was too tall. No matter; he crumpled like a dried leaf. Something metal on the deck near his feet caught the sun. A sword. Ellandaise make. Dead weight abandoned by a fleeing mercenary, half fallen out of its sheath. Lu seized it, then hefted it in both hands.

'Your blades are rather inelegant,' she told him. 'A bit too heavy for my tastes. But I think I'm getting used to them.'

Astonishment splashed across Lamont's broad face. It dissolved, and was replaced by an unspeakable anger. His was the rage of envy, of wanting and not possessing. A rage born of weakness, of cruelty.

And hers?

She could feel the blood thrumming through every pinprick-slim capillary in her fingertips, each ecstatic beat of her fine, strong heart. The movement of air seemed a silver song ringing across her skin.

There was no turning back now. If he left this ship alive, he would not rest until her city, her empire, was in ashes.

How strange. She was good as dead, and she had never felt more alive, as though her body were burning hot and fast through the unfelt sensations of her next forty, fifty, sixty years. Years she would never know, compressed into these final moments like a diamond. It nearly made her swoon, the weight of all that time she had already lost.

She recovered, planted herself firmly on two feet. Wretched with grief, but still upright. She was more than human now: a terrible machine burning through blood and sorrow and spirit, all that potential life become kinetic. It must have shown somehow; Lamont flinched away from her as though from a sudden flash of light. As though from an ancient and terrible god.

'Thinks about this! – *Thinks*,' he protested. 'We both mights gain from a deal. We still has the treaty—'

'Treaties are paper,' Lu told him imperiously. 'And paper burns.'

She lifted her sword.

He fired.

In one stark moment, she saw it all: the neat, symmetrical lines of the cannons along the edge of the deck, the alarming red trickle of blood that ran down from Lamont's hairline, the impossible blue of the river below. And far off, she thought she glimpsed something on the horizon. A bird – an eagle – soaring high upon the wind.

It made her think of Nokhai, that distant point of darkness in the wide, white unknown above. It made her smile.

The bullet struck. She felt it burrow deep, and begin to burn. Her clothing went up in flames – spreading from her chest, down, down ...

She ran. And then her arms were around Lamont – not in an embrace, but as a predator seizes its prey. She was all claws and sinew and teeth. He raised an arm before his eyes, as though that might save him.

It did not.

The fire covered her, and then it became her. As inextricable as bone, or a soul.

This is what I was born for. Someone else's words, someone else's voice. One she'd never heard before, at least not that she could remember. She knew it though, the way she'd known her own heartbeat. Something primal and first.

Like a mother's love. She hadn't meant to think it – it came to her like a ray of sunlight cutting through water.

She didn't think anymore after that.

There was a sound bigger than the sky, then there was terrible pain, and then there was only the red of the flames.

33
Wings

Fly.

Nok hurtled through open air, headfirst. The salty wind hit him full in the face, making his eyes water. He closed them reflexively. A warmth flew down upon him, enveloping his whole body. He blinked, seeing the world now through the eyes of a raptor. Where there had been grasping fingers, long, elegant feathers rode the sky.

The boat was easy to find – the sole solitary vessel, anchored in the centre of the river. Half a boat now, really, its rear end burnt to char, a few splintered remains bobbing morosely in its wake.

Lu! he thought, hoping, praying she was close enough to hear him. He dove down, closer, so close he could see the sparse moustache hairs on the upper lip of a soldier who happened to look up. The black felt of Lamont's absurd hat. And there she was, on the deck. A crown of black hair, plaited simply, and a heavy, embroidered cloak thrown haphazardly over her shoulders. Not her usual ceremonial attire—

Lu, he called out again.

No answer came, of course. But something else did.

462

A flash of light – and then a sound so loud it threw him through the air like a sparrow batted by a cat. He was falling. His wings! He ordered them to move, to take him higher, but they did not obey.

He saw red, then white, then a murky nothing as the river swallowed him whole.

34
Inferno

The inferno broke bright as a new star, splitting the clear sky. Below, the churning barrier of the Milk River deadened the sound, diluted its violent oranges and reds, turned them abstract and meaningless as spilled ink.

For a moment, Min could almost pretend it wasn't real. That this fire had no heat, no devastation. That her sister hadn't been its spark, kindling, its flint.

There's nothing left to bury, she thought. Her robes were soaked through, the weight of them dragging her down into the depths.

There's nothing left.

The breath rushed out of her, and brackish river water rushed in.

It was not a choice when she stopped fighting, but it came with a kind of relief. She'd been so tired, for so long. Lu had been the stronger of the two of them, and she'd stopped fighting. Had chosen the surrender of death over staying with Min.

Rage flooded her. It was fitting in a way. Her last moments of consciousness, and she would spend them angry at her sister.

Something plunged into the water beside her. She took it for a bit of detritus blown from the ship, but then it moved. Her dying mind recognised two enormous wings thrashing gracelessly, churning the water full of sediment and spume. And then the wings were gone, and a boy was swimming toward her.

Nokhai caught her under the arms and tried to pull her up with him, but like a stone she sank them both deeper into the silty dark. He released her.

Good.

But he was there again, this time tugging off her sodden robes, the dual leaden weights of her pot-bottom shoes, the sculpted ebony headdress from her hair. These things drifted down, disappeared, while buoyed in his arms, she rose.

She broke the surface sputtering and coughing. Her eyes were stung shut with salt; the first thing she registered was not sight, but rather, how loud it was to be alive. She could hear the smoulder and crackle of the burning *Ryvan* above her, broken bits of ship knocking together on the surface of the river, Nok's rapid panting as he laboured to keep them afloat.

They were moving. She blinked rapidly, and tears flooded her eyes, flushing out river water. She could see now: a passing orange haze that became a flotilla of tiny fires, bits of flotsam from the explosion. Nokhai's wiry arm cutting through the cloudy water, the other looped around her.

Let me go, she wanted to say. Meant to say.

A scream pierced the air; she looked up in its direction. City folk poured onto the beach, breaching its fences, to meet the Ellandaise soldiers swimming their way to safety.

The first of them made it to shore and emerged from the water wearing only grey trousers and white under-shirt, having had the sense to remove his heavy uniform. The city locals that met him did not seem concerned he was unarmed and choking up gouts of cloudy river water. They fell upon him with sticks and makeshift cudgels, and their own bare hands.

Min cringed as the first blow visibly cracked open his head, grateful they were too far off for her to hear more than the crowd's shriek of triumph.

A shadow darkened the sky, and when she looked up, she saw they had floated under a bridge. Nok hauled them up onto one of its pile footings, jutting above the surface of the water like a tiny stone island.

She rolled from her back onto her knees and promptly emptied her stomach, gagging on acid and frothy brown water, and the little her mother had been able to cajole her into eating that morning.

Mother, she thought. And she was struck with fear, not knowing Rinyi's fate, and the lonely realisation that she was now the only family Min had left.

'Min.' Nokhai took her by the shoulders, frantic. 'Where's Lu? I couldn't ... I'm going to go back and look for her—'

She whirled on him, and she could feel it on her face: a grief so strong it bordered on ferocity. A hunger bigger than starving. She saw the knowledge descend on him like a vulture.

He was shaking his head before she could speak. 'No,' he said. 'There has to be – I'll find her. I'll go back. I-I have a porpoise caul. I can search the water. I'll go back and I'll find her—'

There's nothing left, Min thought again. And this time the anguish of it bloomed inside her, filling her chest. As though sharing it with him had made it real.

'That's not – she can't be gone,' he told her. 'Not Lu. It's not possible.'

And she understood what he meant. How could someone like her sister ever deign to die?

'I'm going back for her,' he repeated.

Don't. There was nothing of Lu that remained for him to find. Nothing either of them would want to see. His insistence to hope almost felt like cruelty, like masochism. But her voice stuck in her throat, dry and barbed, and then, a moment later, he was gone, and she was alone with her unspoken words.

She lay back on the bridge footing, the cold of the stone biting into her wet skin, through her cotton underclothes.

More screams came from far off. She allowed her head to loll to the side, too exhausted to turn properly, and watched dispassionately as more foreign men swam their way to shore, only to be torn apart by the city folk waiting on the beach. A few of them, seeing the fate that met their compatriots, retreated into the water, or attempted to paddle their way along the river's retaining wall, searching for another outlet. Some were pulled under by the current and the weight of their own armour. Others managed to cling to bits of detritus drifting by, like rats in a flood.

It was too much to bear. Min closed her eyes. This was the world as she had always suspected it: hard and ugly and chaotic. Once, she had wondered if she was mistaken. But it had been Lu — ever the monolith of optimism in her mind, ever the dominant counter to her own glum smallness — who suggested that possibility to her, simply by living. And now she was gone.

Min lay still, hearing the indifferent river rushing beneath her, and the men dying on shore. Fresh tears flooded her eyes and she opened them, blinking rapidly against the sting. She could see nothing but brightness — a writhing light that she had first seen the morning of her sister's betrothal ceremony, a thousand years ago.

She felt it then: the point on her forehead that Lu had kissed, right before she'd pushed Min into the river, saving her life. Breaking her heart. The skin there throbbed, as though she were feeling it all again for the first time.

And spreading out from it, beneath the skin, seeping into her blood, Min felt a familiar searing heat.

'Lu?' she whispered.

Tsai.

But, how? Min sat up when it hit her. *The kiss.*

Her sister was gone, but the power that had come into being to avenge her, to protect her, Lu had left that behind. Had given it to Min.

Perhaps that was why it felt different this time. It — Tsai, the power, the curse, whatever it was — felt no softer, no kinder, but no longer haplessly, wretchedly cruel, either. It felt — and Min felt — new. To call herself *cursed* no longer seemed right. So what did that make her, now?

Min found she did not know.

35

Before

There is too much blood.

Tsai knows. She has seen this before. Back in Yunis, they would make her attend births. She was a shamaness, an unclean creature, and it was her lot in life to handle the unclean products of the body. She hadn't understood when they'd first explained it. She'd only just arrived at the temple, a child novice of no more than seven years. How could an unclean thing make something clean? It didn't make sense. She told the head shamaness as much and was rewarded with a slap across the face so hard it split her lip. She'd understood after that. Not the logic, perhaps, but her place within it.

Most births were unremarkable. Some were long, and some short, but there were always the same peaks and valleys of pain. The lowing and the eerie mantras that tore from the mothers like reluctant, primal magic. There was vomit, and shit, and always blood. Different kinds of blood: brown and thick, blood slippery with mucus, and blood that was bright, keening red. And sometimes there was too much. Great black-red gouts, when the afterbirth would not come, or only came in tatters, and that was when she knew the woman was going to die.

She has seen so much dying. Almost as much dying as birth. When the empire stormed the gates of Yunis, she had watched them slaughter the elder shamanesses. The way they fell one by one under the sword, their screaming no different than braying goats at slaughter. She had watched until she had stopped feeling, until the cries were indistinct, lost in the chaos of that day.

But that does not make the dying any easier, any less terrifying. No more than it had done for the birth. Too late, she understands that both the birthing and the dying are a business of the body. The mind may understand, it may repeat certain comforting truths about itself, but it cannot birth on its own, and it cannot die on its own. The body can. It does not need the mind. And it carries its own infinite and animal well of fear.

There is a cry, and she looks down at the baby in her arms. Though she has attended countless births, she has never had much contact with children. Her own body is rapidly cooling, her legs rattling with the bone-deep chill and the aftershocks of her long labouring, but the baby is surprisingly warm. Its skin is taut and wet and plump to the touch, like a creature pulled from the sea. It writhes in her arms, looses another throaty wail.

It has no idea, Tsai thinks, of the pain and terror and lies that have gone into its creation. The bodies left in its wake.

It mouths at one of her breasts, unaware that the creature attached to the breast will soon be cold and gone. And unaware that without her, it too will die.

The notion brings the surprising sting of tears to her eyes. Tsai makes to wipe them away, but her arm is so weak all she manages is a feeble swat toward her face. She is not sad, exactly. It is hard to muster what could reasonably be called sorrow for this mewling creature. She spent the last nine moons pretending it did not exist, hiding the swell of her belly under loose robes and winter cloaks, despite the late summer humidity. But there is a frustrating futility in it, that she would labour this long, this furiously, and have it all come to nothing.

She closes her eyes, and when she opens them again, the room is dark and the sun has gone down. How long has she been there? She does not know when the baby was born. The baby ...

Her body starts in panic, and the motion stirs the child. Relief floods her as it cries out and begins to root angrily at her chest.

'Tsai.'

A face hovers above her, pallid as a full moon set in the black of a starless night. For a moment, she thinks she must be dreaming, or dead. But why would her mind conjure *him* of all people?

Her eyes follow Ohn dully as he crouches down on the floor beside her. He has an oil lamp in hand, that is what has lit him in that ghostly glow.

'Tsai,' he repeats. 'Can you hear me?' He leans forward, bracing himself on the straw-stuffed mat beneath her. But he pulls it away almost instantly, rocking back on his heels. When he raises it to the lamplight, they both see the palm is crimson with blood. He curses, softly, and the reverence, the horror in his voice tells her he too knows she will die here.

'Does Daagmun know you're here?' she rasps.

'In a run-down inn in Scrap-Patch Row? No, not yet.' He shakes his head. 'He sent me to find you. I've been looking for you for moons. I'm supposed to take you and the child back—'

She laughs. Or, her body tries to. A scraping groan escapes from between her dry lips.

'We both know that won't happen.'

'Why did you run away?' Ohn demands, and there is both irritation and fear in his voice. Once it might have been fear of her, but now it is only the fear of the callow looking death in the face.

'Why?' she repeats. What reason should she give, she wonders: the illegitimate child of the newly enthroned emperor swelling her body – a child that, if they knew of her, a great many in the court would make certain was never born? The treason she committed? The forbidden magics she harnessed to murder the crown prince and foment the fall of the empire? Or the friends whose trust and energy she stole in order to do so? There is no shortage of things to run from in her life.

But Ohn does not wait for an answer. 'Daagmun – he's going mad not knowing where you went,' he tells her.

She closes her heavy eyes, just for a moment. It feels wonderful. Almost delicious. *That idiot boy*, she thinks.

'What of his new wife?' she asks. 'I saw her retinue enter the Immaculate City. She was very beautiful.' A legitimate bride, who would birth him legitimate heirs.

'He hasn't noticed what she looks like, I can tell you

that much. He can't focus, can't rule, can't pay any mind to her – all because he's consumed with worry for *you*.'

How naive must someone their age be to confuse one afternoon of rutting for love? How lonely? Her eyes sting again, but this time there are no tears. Her body has lost too much water to spare those now.

'Take the baby if you want it,' she tells Ohn. Her voice shakes. It makes her sound scared. She wants to tell him she's not, that it is only the chill replacing the blood leaving her body, but she doesn't have enough left in her to muster that. 'Maybe Daagmun can find a place for it. As a washerwoman, or one of those fancy lady's maids with the yellow hoods, or ...'

A shamaness. That is what her child would've been in Yunis. Another glorified servant touting the title of neophyte. Unbearable. But then, so too is the thought of her child serving the empire's royal household.

Ohn peers closer, watching the resistant kick of the baby's legs. 'She's strong.' Then, studying her small face, 'She looks a bit like Daagmun's older brother. Hwangmun.'

Fitting, Tsai thinks. She took Hwangmun out of this world with the spell she'd tricked Ohn and Yuri into making with her, and now she has given her life bringing his likeness back into it. Blood for blood.

Fitting too, that Daagmun would be too weak to produce a child with his own face. That his daughter would default to looking like his older, best beloved brother. That even in this, he would fall back into the shadows, while Hwangmun shone for all to see.

'What do you want to call her?' Ohn asks.

Tsai shakes her head. 'I'm no poet. All I ever learned to speak were curses. Tell her father to name her.'

'Yuri will want to know about her,' Ohn muses, almost to himself.

'Where is Yuri?' She is surprised in a way, that it is not he who tracked her down here, in this dank, cramped hole of an inn. But then, he is lazy and feckless. A high-born boy like that enjoys the fantasy of a dalliance with someone like Tsai, but loses interest quick enough.

'He's been sent north,' Ohn says tightly. 'To serve on the front lines of the Northern expansion.'

For a moment, she does not understand. And then, all at once, she does.

'They're going to have their war anyway,' she rasps. She has been so stupid. As stupid and naive as she thought Yuri, or Ohn, or even Daagmun. Did she really think killing two princes would be enough to bring the bloated beast of the empire to its knees?

'It's already begun. It had begun before we even... All the magistrates that would've helped Hwangmun have his war have simply launched it without him. Daagmun is no true emperor – you know that. Even if he had the courage and wits to protest, he has no leverage,' Ohn says, and his voice is equal parts fury and sulk and terror. All of it adds up to an accusation. What would things look like now, if she had just done the spell they'd asked her for in the first place? The spell to keep Yuri out of the fighting, and safe in the capital. The spell they had asked for because Ohn saw Yuri's future: dying on a battlefield.

It's not too late for Yuri, she wants to tell Ohn. *Dreams are not prophecy, and prophecy is not etched in stone.* But she's never been good at giving comfort, and he knows better now than anyone, not to believe anything that leaves her lips.

'He's forgiven you,' Ohn tells her, and he sounds incredulous even now. 'Yuri, I mean. He wanted to help find you. Tried to get out of his assignment, just for you. He kept saying *we* were to blame. That we shouldn't have asked you for anything in the first place.'

She feels a pain. Different from the seizing pains of birth, and different from the shivering cold of death. A corrosive ache in her gut. Guilt.

It is quickly chased by despair, and then, more comfortably, rage.

She had always thought that there might be some peace in dying. She's imagined it ever since she was a little child, curled up in her cramped shared bed in the neophyte dormitory. The release of not having to try anymore. But the empire has stolen even that from her, and now, all she feels is anger. It's not *fair*; she killed Hwangmun and his brother, and it still wasn't enough. She hardened herself against the possibility of friendship, and freedom, and love, and Ohn and Yuri and even Daagmun still found gaps in her armour.

The baby is heavy in her weakening arms. She looks down – it is less a concerted motion than her neck slumping, losing control. The baby, her daughter, gazes back with black, pitiless eyes. Uncomfortably familiar. That much, at least, she has inherited from Tsai.

And – there is one more thing.

Tsai reaches out with her mind, searching, probing until she finds it. It courses through her daughter's blood,

saturates her muscles, but it emanates from something like
a stone, a kernel, that sits just inside her skull, between
the eyes. She can see it, then, clear as day. The thing from
which the pain and filth and pressure of her gift – her
curse – flows.

She wrenches it free. Her daughter howls in pain and
she nearly laughs with relief.

It ends with me, she thinks. She cannot give her daughter a mother or a father, nor a station worth having – not
even a name. But she will not doom her to walk this earth
possessed of magic.

And almost unbidden, she thinks of Daagmun. The
family he will surely have, to perpetuate the empire and
all its grasping and taking and ceaseless wars. She knows
then, what she must do.

It takes the last of her lifeblood. She feels it rush out of
her with the effort of the task, black and thick and hot.
And then, she *splits* herself.

A part of her cleaves away, shedding the rest like a
snake sloughing old skin. What remains, this separated,
pared-down part of her, binds itself to the kernel of her
gift, the curse she extracted from her child, and departs.
It floats like a spore on the wind, through the neglected,
muddy roads of Scrap-Patch Row, past fruit sellers and
cobblers and beggars waving bowls in the street and a
farrier's forge. Like light passing through glass, it moves
through the walls of the Second Ring, and again through
those encircling the Immaculate City.

And there it floats, subtle and mortal as a plague,
through an open window in Daagmun's pretty new wife's
apartments. The young woman is reclining in bed, and

Tsai is surprised to see the drying tracks of tears under her eyes, incongruous with the haughty pout of her lips, the proud lift of her chin. Great gouts of loneliness pour off her like cold grey smoke.

Her belly is empty; no child yet. But the sliver of Tsai that remains settles in her womb nevertheless, still clutching the seed of her gift. And once in place, it begins to consume, to corrupt, to spread. Making its home in each of the empress's eggs, like the grub of a gall wasp working its way into a chestnut.

Back in Scrap-Patch Row, the rest of Tsai — the body, and whatever else is left without her rage, her loathing — is still lying on the stained bed. It smiles faintly, gazing upward, looking at nothing.

The end of one life, and the beginning of two.

36

First Flame

At the centre of the palace Heart, under its stone pavilion, the First Flame crackled and seethed, just as it had done for a thousand years. According to legend, the first people, the first Hana – Min's ancestors – had fumbled in darkness, forced to eat nothing but green plants and raw scavenged meat, until they had pledged themselves to the gods here. In return, they had received this gift: a single torch – a drop of the sun – to deliver them from the darkness, the cold, the predation of beasts roaming unseen in the night. This fire from which all other fires – and thus, all civilisation – had emerged. The Hana had kept it alive, feeding it with branches of oak and hickory, sheltering it from rain; this blessing, this constant in a fickle, changeable world.

Min stared into its writhing red depths now, waiting. She did not have to do much of that these days – when an empress called, most people tended to come quickly.

Empress. Once again. The court had been split over her reclaiming the throne. It had helped that many of the gentry and city folk alike had rallied around after the immolation of *The Ryvan* on the Milk River. Most seemed certain that it had been Min who had killed the foreign devils and saved the city from their tyranny by using her sorcery. Overnight, she had become something of a folk hero. Her powers were no longer alien, but belonging to all. Tales were now being spun of how the Ellandaise guns and boats and swaggering might had fallen in the face of something old and original to this land and its people. Such was her popularity that even the Mul monks no longer dared to speak against her. Hand-painted banners bearing her name, surrounded by talismans of luck and protection, hung from the footbridges in the harbour. There were flags, too, for her sister, though these were marked with messages for a soul's safe passage to the heavens.

The Hana kings of old, had meditated here in front of the First Flame. The Mul's faithful had their rites, writing out prayers on slips of paper that they would then burn in its flames as an act of consecration. Kangmun had converted to the Mul tradition after his conquest of the Hana as as a perfunctory means of appealing to his new subjects, but it had been his son Kaalmun who had the convert's zeal – his religious fervour in part driving the war he waged against Yunis. He'd died before Min was born, but supposedly he had done devotions here daily.

Did the First Flame really come from the sun? Was it really a gift from the heavens? Min had asked Lu when they were small.

It doesn't matter if it's true, her sister had told her with an assurance well beyond her years. *What matters is people believe it.*

Had Lu thought of that on her own, or was it something one of her shins had said? Min wished she still had the chance to ask. About that, and so much else.

Min's immediate family had never been particularly religious. Her father had not had the piety of his father before him – a change great enough that the Mul monks had fretted about the security of their favour when he ascended the throne. Her mother could recite her prayers as well as any literate Hana woman of her breeding, but she took no comfort in them.

And as for Min, the closest she had felt to the divine had been through the conduit of a curse.

'I hope I haven't kept you waiting.'

She turned. Nasan stood between Min and the monolith of Kangmun Hall. Sunrise, sliding up over the walls of the Heart, cast a golden glow over the building's broad red face, and the Ashina girl as well. She'd approached from behind, rather than through the front gate, as expected. Min had no idea how she'd gotten in.

A troubling omen, if one were inclined to read into such things. Min wasn't certain if she herself was the omen-believing sort of person, but she kept her face neutral in case Nasan was.

'My guards are waiting at the front gate to admit you,' she said. *My guards are nearby*, the words implied.

'Yes, well. I tend to be a bit wary around soldiers,' the Ashina girl said evenly. She glanced around. 'No hand-maidens?' she asked, as though Min might shake out her robes and send them scattering to the pavers.

'You said you wished to speak with me alone. I told you I would honour the request. So here I am,' Min replied.

'Good,' Nasan said approvingly. Min was starting to understand why Lu was always annoyed with her. 'I need to know what your intentions are for the North.'

'We've agreed to cede back sovereignty to the groups already living there.'

'And the areas that are currently uninhabited? Those you still intend to mine?' Nasan prodded.

'The empire has its debts. A flourishing copper mine would certainly help matters,' Min admitted. 'But we do not intend to extend the borders further than they are now.'

'I and my people plan to return home. How do we know the land we reclaim won't be taken from us all over again the next time you have want for coin? We need to know if we can trust you to remain peaceful.'

'I could say the same of you,' Min replied, but she kept her tone pleasant. 'I hear you're still recruiting in the Second Ring for your little militia.'

'I don't think you'd call it "little" if you saw it,' Nasan said, with just the slightest flare of irritation.

Min nodded slightly, neither in acknowledgement nor dismissal. 'Is that so. I expect it isn't quite as big as the imperial army. Nor – and if I'm wrong about this, correct me – do you have a navy.'

'Maybe not,' Nasan said. 'But I do have some of that Yunian sparkstone.'

Min felt the bite of an unpleasant surprise, cold and cutting. It must have shown; Nasan's face relaxed into an expression of catlike satisfaction, if only briefly.

'You didn't think I'd help you smuggle it out of your mother's apartments and not ask Adé to take a bit for me as well, did you? I confess, she wasn't thrilled about what she called "stealing", but we agreed to consider it a kind of tax.'

'What do you plan to do with it?' Min asked.

'That depends on *you*,' Nasan replied. 'My people want autonomy. We're willing to do what we have to in order to secure it.'

Min nodded slowly. 'I see. So, we honour whatever borders you choose for your territory up north, or, what? We wake up tomorrow with Yulan City in flames?'

'Maybe. Or maybe we'll be charitable and wait to commandeer that hypothetical copper mine you've been going on about.' Nasan's mouth flattened into a grim line. 'We want our land. There are lives — thousands of them — on the line. I'll do what I have to do. I'm their leader.'

'I'm familiar with the concept,' Min said. 'An empress must think of what is best for *her* people as well.'

'Trust me when I say this is in their best interests.'

'Trust you,' Min mused. 'And if I give you what you're asking for now, what happens in one moon, six moons, two years down the line, when you return asking for more?'

Nasan's teeth flashed as she essayed something like a grin, though it looked more like she was biting back frustration. 'I'm not asking for more than we're owed. I come to you now in good faith—'

'You've come levelling threats,' Min interrupted.

Nasan's hands went to the bony ridges of her hips. She released a noisy breath, blowing the hank of coarse dark hair that ever hung in her eyes. 'Your sister made me a lot of promises she didn't keep. And there was nothing I could do to hold her to them. I won't make that mistake again.'

'I'm not my sister,' Min said.

'No,' Nasan agreed. 'I understood Lu. I don't know you at all.'

'Is that good or bad?'

The Ashina girl ran a hand through her short, ruffled hair. 'I'm not sure yet,' she admitted. 'Truth be told, Lu wasn't all bad. I even think some part of her wanted to keep her promises. But it's a rotten thing, your throne. Sit on it, touch it, and you've got the rot now, too. Lu wasn't at all dumb, but she was arrogant. She thought she could control the title, control the empire. But that isn't how it works.'

Min considered her a moment. Then she looked back into the dangerous red flicker of the First Flame.

'I always found it strange,' Nasan said, 'that the Hana chose fire as their symbol.'

'Fire is powerful. It gives heat, light. Life,' Min said, and felt vaguely that she must be reciting something she'd learned as a child.

'But your foundational myth is one of humanity seeking order. Civilisation bending nature to its will,' Nasan continued. 'Fire bends to no one. You can contain it under this nice pavilion and give it a fancy little title, but reach out to touch it, and you'll still burn.'

The heat of the fire prickled at Min's face. Her blood felt overwarm, too close to the skin. It felt like the crackle of power. The last time she'd felt this had been on the deck of *The Ryvan*, as her sister pressed her lips to her forehead.

Would she ever again be able to see a fire and not think of Lu?

'Keep your sparkstone,' she told Nasan. 'But I don't want you in my city. I'll lend you whatever carriages and elk you need to transport you and your people north, but no more recruiting from here.'

'And Lu's mine?'

'The mine will be closed,' she agreed. This was something she had already discussed with her Grant Secretariat. The borders of the empire were too broad. No wealth generated by that mine could pay for the infrastructure or works necessary to support it. But let Nasan take this as another victory.

She was drawn again toward the fire. The thrum under her skin was almost painful, almost intoxicating. Hovering at the brink. Was it something she could control this time? Lu must have believed that, or she never would have returned it to her. This curse, this blessing.

She reached forward, into the fire.

'Don't – !' Nasan leapt to grab her hand, but she must have seen something on Min's face that stopped her: the marvel, the euphoria, of discovering something utterly new.

Min extracted her hand, and cupped in it was a fistful of flames.

A drop of the sun, she thought. Then she slipped the flames back into their source – that source of all things.

Nasan watched her. 'Is that meant to be a threat?' she asked.

'No,' Min said immediately. And she was pleased to find it was true.

Footsteps echoed through the Heart. Butterfly approached.

'Empress,' the amma said apologetically. 'You asked me to come find you when it was time to dress.'

Min nodded, then turned back to Nasan. 'Your land is your land. I will announce it today, in court, if you care to attend. My Grant Secretariat will help us draw up a treaty.'

Nasan nodded. 'I'll meet with you a afterward regarding the treaty, but I don't think I'll be attending court. I confess I tire of being around so many nobles.'

Min smiled. 'You seem to have grown at least a little fond of my sister.'

'Dead people are easy to love. They can't disappoint you anymore.'

Min considered her for a moment. 'Why do I feel that you and I will meet again one day?'

'Because I think you're likely right.'

'I suspect too, that it will be under somewhat less happy circumstances.'

Nasan was not the sort to rely on a polite lie, nor did she flinch or lower those bold black eyes of hers. 'I think so, too,' she said evenly.

'I hope when that day comes, you'll find it in yourself to be merciful,' Min said.

'And you, as well.'

'May we never give one another cause to forget our mercy.' She extended her hand to the Ashina girl. Nasan took it; her hand was colder than Min would have supposed.

Min smiled wryly. It felt unpractised, a new shape for the muscles of her mouth to take, but somehow familiar. It was a face Lu might have made.

'Have a safe journey north,' she told Nasan.

'Oh, you don't mean that,' said the other girl.

'I do,' Min said firmly.

Nasan released her hand. The sudden absence of the cold was a blessing.

'I'll see myself out,' she said, with an exaggerated curtsy. This time, Min noted, she used the front gate.

It was an odd feeling, to sit upon the throne again. Lu was gone now, but the chair and its dais, that which had been her design and her destiny, remained. It felt, Min thought, too large for her.

'We bring to session the court of Empress Minyi, daughter of the late Daagmun, granddaughter of the late Kaalmun . . .' the court crier announced.

The room itself felt bigger than Min recalled as well, as did the murmuring crowd of courtiers. She could see Omair seated in the front row. Off to the side of the dais, Yuri, now the head of her guard, stood with a hand resting on the hilt of his sword. Arrayed around the throne were Min's ammas. She tried to take reassurance in their familiar faces.

Something brushed against the hang of her robes. A bell tinkled. She looked down and found the orange cat gazing back up at her through golden eyes. She bit back a laugh as he leapt into her lap, circled once, then curled into a hot bundle on her knees. She stroked his head.

'Before the court begins its scheduled business, may I request the empress's audience?'

Min looked up in surprise at the unexpected voice. Her mother stood before the dais.

Rinyi came forward, fully restored from her year spent as a half-prisoner. There were no tears in her robes, and her face was once more made seamless with powder. Crimson lacquered her lips. Min felt oddly reassured by it.

There was the barest hint of movement off to the side of dais. Yuri. Moving closer, the better to address any potential danger.

On her lap, the orange cat wriggled. Min looked down and realised she was gripping him by the scruff. She let go, expecting him to flee, but instead he resettled and began to purr.

'Speak,' she told her mother. The word emerged a dry whisper, so she cleared her throat and tried it again. 'Speak.'

'I've come to ask your permission to leave Yulan City.'

Ask your permission. Word's she never would have expected to hear from Rinyi.

'It has been many years since I last saw my family in Bei Province,' her mother continued. 'If the empress allows it, I would request leave to visit. My own mother is quite old, and I would like to be there for her before her body returns to the earth.'

And then, Min understood. Her mother was asking to leave in a manner that would save face. But it also gave Min the power, in front of all, to grant her this kindness. To release Rinyi from this haunted court to which she no longer belonged.

'Granted,' she said. Then, 'Are you certain this is what you want?'

'It is what we – what I need,' Rinyi told her.

Min tried to clear the swell in her throat, but failed. 'Will you return one day?' she asked, and it was only by a miracle her voice did not crack, did not thin to that of a frightened child.

'If I'm needed. But right now, I am not.'

Her mother smiled up at her, and Min had the sense she had already left in a way. That she had already made this choice in her heart when she'd given Min her cloak, unpacked the precious cache of jewellery and letters she'd buried the sparkstone under. Those trinkets of her lost youth, those tokens of her resentment.

'Very well,' Min said, clearing her throat and sitting up straighter. 'Go safely.'

Her mother retreated down the centre aisle of the courtroom, followed by Amma Doha and two other handmaids.

The crowd watched them go, then turned back to Min, every eye weighing heavy upon her. They did not love her yet. Min still did not, would never have Lu's offhand charisma. But she'd learned how to live without it. She gazed back at them and for once, felt no lack in herself. She'd been a sister, a widow, a destroyer of worlds. Now she was an empress, and a woman grown. More alone than she had ever been before, but unafraid.

'Let us begin.'

37

Return

A wolf alone was an unnatural creature. A useless hunter
– doomed to waste away as it scavenged carrion, picked
off rats, dug grubs from the earth for the paltry remainder
of its days. The pack, the Kith, the family: that was the
source of all survival. That was what the boy who had been
called Nokhai was taught. Like much of what his father,
his elders, had told him, though, it had little bearing on his
lived life. The first night alone in the northwood, he had
caught himself a hare. Large, if a bit rangy. He'd crushed
its bones in his jaws, swallowed down the pulpy mash of
marrow and muscle, and been well enough satisfied.

The other beasts of the forest seemed to sense his wrongness. He wondered if they could smell the remnants of the
boy on him, the way certain livestock and domesticated
animals used to be able to detect the wolf in him, long
before he'd even received his caul. Small prey scattered
from him out of fear, but even the furtive red foxes and
wild dogs gave him a wider berth than necessary.

Nok himself avoided the wolf packs – easy to detect
from the stink of the urine that marked the borders of
their territory. One night though, he did pass another lone

wolf. This one an elderly female, coat a bit thin, walking with a slight hitch. She did not stop, perhaps fearing he would attack her. He gave her a wide berth. As she slunk by, she gave him a wary, searching look. As though he were something she didn't quite understand.

It did not bother him; he'd never had much success blending in as a boy, either.

He could not say how many days he passed in this manner. Time did not matter to the beast, and living did not matter to the boy. They slept through the height of the day and rose to hunt at dusk, allowing the night to envelope them in the unreality of darkness.

It was Nasan who found him – or rather, her wolf. He should have known. They were of the same pack, and like called out to like. He'd ignored his caul's impulse to mark the perimeters of his own territory, but she must have smelled him anyway. Perhaps he'd stayed in one place too long.

He'd curled up to sleep in a shaft of sunlight in a clearing, and when he awoke a short time later, the sunlight had moved, and someone was there. He turned and saw her standing at the edge of the clearing.

It's time, she told him.

He'd stood, squared off with her for a time, wondering whether, if he ran, she might believe him just another wolf. He turned, thinking to lope off through the brush at the far end of the clearing, when a deer emerged. It was the wrong sort for this forest – any forest, really. This creature belonged to the grasslands, to the prairie, to the steppe.

'*Adé.*'

And then there was a girl emerging out of the dissipating

haze that had been the deer. Its tall ears and delicate horns were the last part to fade, and for a moment the illusion of them hung over Adé's hair, like a vague, silvery crown.

'Nok,' she said. 'We've been worried.'

'*Worried you'd lost your Pactmaker, you mean,*' he said. His tone was so nasty even he thought he might have meant it.

'Yes.'

He turned back to the opposite end of the clearing and saw Nasan too, had slipped from her caul. 'Yes, that's right,' she told him, striding forward. 'I was worried I'd lost my Pactmaker. *And* my brother. Although I don't know why I would care about him, since he's clearly an idiot.'

'*I'm not your brother anymore. I'm not anyone at all,*' he said angrily, and then made to stride past her. To plunge back into the deep of the wood, and the sanctuary of rote, animal survival.

'Oh, for the love of—' His sister was swiftly changing back, letting the dense blue coat of her caul sweep over her. Before he could register what was happening, she took one, two bounds, and leapt upon him, great white teeth sinking into the loose folds of his scruff.

'*Get off!*' The boy shouted; the wolf yelped. And then they were heaped in a tangle, Nok's caul mouthing at Nasan's. He caught a leg in his jaws. He bit down – not as hard as he could have – and tasted the splash of blood in his mouth.

'*What are you going to do?*' she demanded. They tumbled and she pinned him against the matted grass beneath them. '*Live like an animal forever?*'

'*I don't know!*' he told her stubbornly. '*Maybe. If it means I don't have to feel like this.*'

The weight lifted from him as she stood, caul melting away once more. Adé had come to stand behind her, but she crouched next to Nok now.

He looked up at her through the wolf's eyes, and the tenderness with which she gazed back made him grateful that animals could not weep.

'I'm so sorry, Nok,' she murmured. 'It hurts, doesn't it? I know it hurts.'

'*How would you—*' And then, remembering Carmine, he stopped short. '*Gods,*' he said. '*I'm sorry. I should've – I'm sorry.*'

But Adé just smiled faintly. She understood. 'We came to find you because we wanted to show you something, Nok. Will you come see?'

Nok allowed his caul to melt away as they stepped out from the dark of the Northwood. For a moment, he did not understand what he was looking at. A line of carriages – a caravan, emerging out of Yulan City, and stretching down the slate-paved road leading north. The same road he and Lu had followed on their journey to Yunis. Had that only been a year prior? How could he feel so much older?

'What is all this?' he asked.

'A gift,' Nasan said. 'From Empress Minyi. Transportation and supplies to move our Kith home.'

'And the land?' he heard himself ask doubtfully.

'It's ours. It's all ours now, brother. All we have to do is go.'

He stared at the caravan. At the dozens of city folk seated atop its wagons, or leading livestock, or simply trailing along beside it on foot. Young folk of age with him, and families with babies. Barefooted children leading still smaller children – orphans, most like.

'So, this is the Common Kith,' he murmured.

'The start of it,' his sister agreed.

'You did it.'

'We all did it. Change is always collective.' She smiled proudly, though. 'Come with us – we need you. And you need this, too. You don't have to be alone, Nok.'

He hadn't been. Not always. There had been brief windows of respite. Ma, with her warm arms, smelling of vinegar and clove. Nasan, sometimes, when she wasn't getting them into trouble – and sometimes when she was. Adé, making him laugh as they sorted herbs in Omair's cosy tree up on the hill. Vrea, with her uncanny, amused eyes. Jiwa. The Our Mother.

And there had been Lu. She'd been so alive, brimming with golden energy. Colours were brighter when she wore them, food was sweeter when she shared it.

And impossibly, she was gone. While he, grey and sullen and exhausted, remained.

Nasan was watching him. 'Each of those people have the potential within them, don't they? To take up a caul.'

They did. He closed his eyes and felt the thrum of it – all that excitement, surging and struggling within. All that possibility – another word, he realised, for hope.

When he opened his eyes again, Adé stood before him, one hand clasped in Nasan's. The other was held out toward him, offering a new start. One he'd never imagined or asked for, but that hovered before him now, resplendent and real.

He took Adé's hand. The three of them stepped forward, out of the shadow of the wood and into the light. The whole of the future sprawled out unknown and unwritten before them.

It wouldn't be home. Not the way it had been. But he would go anyway.

They had a world to make.